Ambient Light
A Novel

Kate Stout

AMBIENT LIGHT: A NOVEL
Published by Saltcoats Press
First Edition
Concord & Nantucket, MA

Copyright ©2023 by Kate Stout. All rights reserved.

No part of this book may be reproduced in any form or by any mechanical means, including information storage and retrieval systems without permission in writing from the publisher/author, except by a reviewer who may quote passages in a review.

All images, logos, quotes, and trademarks included in this book are subject to use according to trademark and copyright laws of the United States of America.

ISBN: 979-8-9887411-0-7 (Paperback)
ISBN: 979-8-9887411-1-4 (Hardcover)
FICTION / Literary

Cover design by Vicki Johnson, copyright owned by Kate Stout.
Interior design by Victoria Wolf, wolfdesignandmarketing.com, copyright owned by Kate Stout.
Author headshot by Beverly Hall Photography.

This is a work of fiction. Names, characters, businesses, places, events and incidents are either the products of the author's imagination or used in a fictitious manner. Any resemblance to actual persons, living or dead, or actual events is purely coincidental.

QUANTITY PURCHASES: Schools, companies, professional groups, clubs, and other organizations may qualify for special terms when ordering quantities of this title. For information, email saltcoatspress@gmail.com.

All rights reserved by Kate Stout and Saltcoats Press.
Printed in the United States of America.

SALTCOATS PRESS
Concord · Nantucket

For

Bob Barnett
dream believer

and

Pete Funkhouser
MOTL

*The end of all our exploring
will be to arrive where we started
And know the place for the first time.*
—T. S. Eliot, "Little Gidding"

*Truly great souls do not pay homage to a barren cult of the self;
Instead they awaken in others a sense of their own majesty ...*
—Robert Musil, *The Man Without Qualities*

Contents

Chapter One   The End   1
Six voices from in and around the present

Chapter Two   The Middle   95
Six voices from in and around the late 20th century

Chapter Three   The Beginning   191
Six voices from in and around the 1960s

The End

It is a time of ambient light. Above the city, the moon burns through the earthly illumination like a jellyfish forms an eerie cloud beneath the sea's surface. Streetlights whitewash the sky; sleepless apartment dwellers, who burn the midnight oil; factories belching their carbon refuse from chimneys into fiery spurts like dragon breathe; ovals of sports arenas; automobiles restlessly scouring the city streets for an open bar, a party, a pickup or a hookup. Afraid of the dark, humanity switches on lights from one end of the earth to the other. The dark is forbidding, kept at bay by this kiss of illumination, for the dark signifies the unknown—the depths of the Amazon, the frigid poles, the mighty Pacific Ocean with its wide wide expanses of nothingness. Even the Atlantic is dotted with tiny ship lights winking into the night, like a connect-the-dots game of self-preservation. After all, where there is light, there is man, and where there is man there is help. From the international space station, floating men look down on an earth outlined in light.

Behind the curtain of ambient light, unseen, the Milky Way wraps the earth in its mantle of galaxies, solar systems, constellations and mere stars. Behind this curtain of ambient light, unseen comets and meteors fling themselves like painters' brush strokes onto the canvas of the night sky, not chunks of ice and rock, but stunning messengers of the gods, inspiring fear and awe. Meteor showers, occurring annually, go unseen, except from country roads or the deck of a sailing ship somewhere between Henderson and Pitcairn Islands.

What goes on above us in a world of ambient light is humanity's connections to, and place within, the universe. And without that sense of place, we are wanderers along the only pathways we know, the one's man has built to take us from A to B but not to the stars and back.

Adeline

In the end, I was the first to leave and the last to know.

No idea why this thought is coming to mind at this particular moment, sitting here in my bay window looking out at the lake. Perhaps because I just learned of Grady's death and that news instantly propels me back to Sebastian's living room, where we all grew up together. Grady was, so far as I know, the last remaining member of the pack except me. Tony may still be alive. But we lost track of him years ago. He seemed to go up in smoke. Mary Clay, she was dead a couple of days before her body was found under a shroud of cherry petals, so fitting when I think about it, always with her hands in flower beds and all. Hard to believe she's been gone almost four years now. Jude though, just last March. Breck died of a terrible fate. The first of us to go. No, the second. Sebastian led the way into that dark night. Too soon. Too young. Not gently.

I don't know which is worse, the feeling of being orphaned after your parents die—doesn't matter how old you are either—or the sure knowledge that the last of your kindred spirits is gone. Grady's wife Beth called this afternoon to tell me. A couple of months after his accident. She said it took her awhile to reach out to strangers. Strangers? Grady and I? What a thought. Still I'm glad she finally did, because it explains why I never heard from him that day and because I did not have to say anything about that to Beth. Who knows if Grady told her we were reconnecting after all those years, thanks to social media. And if he hadn't told her, far be it for me to add to her grief, even one little ancient scintilla. She told me I was on a list of To Be Notified that Grady left behind. Then she dropped the bomb.

—Do you want Sebastian's old guitar? He gave it to Grady years ago and I don't know what else to do with it.

—Yes.

That's all I could get out. A yes. It was as if the Ark of the Covenant had just come my way.

Thinking back now, that list of Grady's was a good idea. Not that I have one or would especially need one now. The important people to me are all gone. My children being the obvious exceptions.

My children. Well. They have my best interests at heart. Or so they tell me. So frequently it makes me suspicious.

As when the Covid shoe dropped. Back in May 2020, when my kids, both of them independently, could see the plague taking New York by storm, they bolted. Packed up their respective cars and their dogs and headed for the coast of Maine. To the summer house I bought when the kids were little. I mortgaged my life away to buy it. I looked at it then, as I do to this very day, as a lifering tossed to me by my dead husband. The sea. Where our love began and ended. I desperately needed/need proximity to it.

Elise mother-napped me, right outside my apartment building. Said she wouldn't allow me to stay behind in New York City with hospital tents popping up all over Central Park and refrigerator trucks serving as temporary morgues outside every hospital. I was, she so coldly reminded me, in the very high-risk category.

Adeline

—Mom, it's dangerous in the City for you now. For us now. Come on. We're all going to Maine till this blows over. You could die!

I will die, you nitwit. But, I conceded only to myself of course, she was right. Still, it does not have to be from Covid.

We all thought it was for a matter of weeks or maybe a couple of months, so why not get paid to have a long and leisurely summer vacation? The men could work remotely; the grandsons go to school remotely. I could read remotely and even Zoom with my docs if need be. For all that, Covid dragged on. And on. And on. Soon the house filled with testosterone—four of my five grandsons moved in too. Elise's boys, twins themselves, had been sent home from college because of Covid, only "home" was an apartment in the City locked up with the water and electricity turned off.

The older one (by minutes) used the lame excuse of primogeniture to annex the attic because, up there, he had a shot at real privacy, albeit sleeping on an ancient horsehair mattress, and he could also pirate the bandwidth of some unsuspecting neighbor. His brother had to settle for a proper bedroom, where he set up a couple of sawhorses and a sheet of plywood to call a desk. Then two of Michael Junior's three boys came up the driveway weighed down by enormous backpacks like sherpas. One from another university that had thrown out its student body and the other back from Vail. Covid shut down the slopes even before spring snow was gone and there was no going to Block Island for his summer job waiting tables. The restaurant didn't even reopen after its winter hiatus. Michael's third is backpacking around Europe. Or was, until Covid forced him to hole up in Amsterdam and live off charity checks from Dad.

It's amusing to stand back and watch three generations of a family, who never spend more than a holiday in each other's company try to negotiate a settlement in cramped, now very cramped, quarters. With everyone wanting the kitchen, everyone finicky about what he or she will eat—vegan this one, omnivore another; smoothies with kale and protein powder or just fruit; the smell of bacon repugnant to the vegan; the vats of ice cream horrifying to the dieters. There are constant rumblings of insurrection, of moving back into the city or going back to schools and reclaiming their old lives. But the truth is, they have a negotiated detente. My son and daughter-in-law have the two-bedroom apartment over the garage, usually reserved for summer help, and the large family room for living space to call their own. Elise and her husband have the rest of the house, the formal dining room, the living room, two bedrooms. Not the master, though. That's my domain. Both have come to enjoy working out of the old house, laced as it is with childhood memories and an uncommonly pleasant workspace. In New York, you just can't walk into town for a lobster roll fresh off the boat, everyone duly masked and six feet apart; or take walks on the beach to discuss over Bluetooth the next takeover or buy out or sell out, or whatever those two do in the financial world. While the boys carve out their own paths, silent about their comings and goings, selectively deaf thanks to earbuds and somehow going to class while simultaneously hiking Acadia or kayaking offshore.

But even the best peace treaties are subject to collapse. Weeks slipped into months and months into a change of the season. September. What now? Schools were still remote. Business dealings were too. But the days were growing shorter and cooler while tempers grew shorter along with them. I was uniformly ignored when I tried to talk about a summer house is a summer house is a summer house, a la Gertrude Stein. In other words, even the three woodburning stoves would not be enough to take the chill off come October and beyond.

That's when I got a little squirrelly. After all, the only thing really ailing me is a couple of herniated discs. When I think I'd be months out

Adeline

from surgery by now, but for the pandemic, I sometimes feel gypped. I've been scheduled and rescheduled for back surgery and canceled out now twice. It's possible I could wait for my surgery till the cows come home, and still there are no guarantees a bed would open up for me, especially since I am now three hundred miles away from New York Hospital. My kids fought me at first, when I said I was going to move out. But they were fighting about everything by then. It had been in no one's game plan to make a semipermanent arrangement out of life en famille.

When I found this little cottage online and took Michael and Elise out to look at it with the realtor in tow, I thought Elise would have a conniption fit. Michael, thank god, was more sanguine about it. Maybe because having me out opened up a bedroom for his attic-bound boy. Whatever. To assuage Elise, I had to promise to wear an alert lanyard. Instead of rolling my eyes and giving her more fodder for a fight, I smiled my best granny smile and agreed—then, the moment the lease was signed, I tossed out the batteries. The lanyard I wear. As a token.

Life is calmer now, more agreeable for everyone. Every morning the sun's first blush signals the new day right outside my bay window. I'm glad my kids eventually agreed to this nice lakefront cottage. Here, where I can live on one floor, have a study with a fireplace for my books and my attempted musings, a pile of cushions on the bay window bench, where I linger over the morning paper, the lake right outside my door. Outside, a little gravel path meanders drunkenly to the lakeshore bank, with steps down to a dock.

If I need my kids or the boys, they are not so far away, only about six miles from here to the summer house as the raven flies. Having the young men nearby is downright handy. Mowing my lawn comes to mind, as does shoveling snow, lots of snow. If, that is, those families can last out the winter in that underheated, under-insulated summer house.

Companionship is of no interest to any of us. I do not bake cookies. I've never had their handprints on my fridge. Their poetry, well, that's another thing. That I cherish, every effort. Otherwise, we waste no time with familial niceties. Pre-pandemic Christmas, Thanksgiving, the Fourth of July were ample doses of them all for me. Not like ipecac. No. A dose like speed or LSD. Perks me right up. So up, I get complaints from my heart, it goes all fluttery with all the excitement. Or maybe that's acid indigestion. Surely, we eat ourselves into catatonia at those events. No. I prefer my solitude, my lake, my walks, my books.

Funny. I wasn't brought up anywhere near a body of water, except for one very forbidding river, filthy, heavily trafficked with enormous lumbering barges teeming with the mother lode of coal. But ever since I was in my mid-twenties in the 70's and my newly minted PhD in English Lit turned out to be as useful as a deadbolt without a key, when I found I had no teaching prospects and a student debt with no visible ceiling, I went a little berserk, I guess. I signed up for a scuba diving course, determined to see the world, if not the inside of a college seminar.

For some people it's the mountains, for others the desert. I like to think of it as the sea finding me. Truth is, I blame it all on Lloyd Bridges and the show *Sea Hunt*. Oh, how I wanted to *be* him, and swim with the fishes, even the scary ones. I was thirteen when I took my first dive class, in the heavily chlorinated waters of a YMCA pool. I was hooked but there was no way my parents were going to support that interest in any real way. The desire, though, didn't go away, it just went underground. Until it could go underwater again. So, yeah, a little berserk. I did my first check out dive in a cold, dark quarry. Not the optimum locale but it got the job done. I got my Open Water certificate, then my Advanced Open Water, before I'd even set eyes on the Caribbean. Step by underwater step, I worked my way up to Dive Master. Once I had that under my belt,

Adeline

I could chart my own course, anywhere in the world. As a dive master, people paid me to work in the Caribbean—too good to be true, right?—on one island after another, at one resort after another. My first gig was in the British Virgin Islands. But then there were Turks and Barbados and Anguilla. Once I'd saved up enough money and accumulated enough irresistible experience, I could get a job on liveaboards anywhere in the world. First on my wish list was the Great Barrier Reef, there where I would meet Michael. He and I stuck out that gig until the fish began to vanish and the reef to bleach—long, long before it was reported anywhere. We saw climate change firsthand, before Al Gore. Then it was whale shark hunting off Honduras, followed by a stint in Borneo, where the mud diving is outstanding. Loads of black coral and seahorses. After a couple of seasons there, we signed on with a dive operation in the northern Red Sea, out of Sharm El Sheikh. Untouched by storms, the coral flourishes there. Or it did, then.

Finally, I was tired of damp clothes and sticky hair. I'd seen the best seas in the world from the best perspective, underwater, and was fed up with not having any decent books to read. Junk, that's all divers travel with. The mantra on liveaboards is dive, eat, sleep, dive. Five dives a day. It's enough to make Agatha Christie an uphill climb. Mostly, I longed to spend time in a library again, to dive into an obscure poet and emerge refreshed. To hang up my fins and hang up my diplomas. It wasn't easy to convince Michael, who had no Plan B. He was a dive master first and only.

A massive life change was not so easy to engineer from my floating office, at the end of my bunk in a port where I might get an unsteady signal at best. Eventually I landed an assistant professorship at Hamline College in Minnesota. From sun to ice. Michael's condition to follow me into ski country was one last junket, one last liveaboard gig. In Indonesia, out of Flores. Our beat-up old freighter snaked in and around all the little uninhabited islands between Flores and Komodo National Park, dropping us divers into pristine waters. Bursting with coral, the water sometimes dark with mantas, the currents challenging. It was one of those that got Michael. But not before we got married on the Komodo beach, dragon tracks all over the place, my hair laced with frangipani, Michael naked to the waist and holding a nautilus shell he found on the beach. My wedding ring woven out of Michael's own black-brown hair. By him. His wedding present to me. I wear it still. Our skipper did the honors, and all was well until the second to last day of that dive trip. It is not something I like to revisit, even this many years later.

 I didn't last long at Hamline College, but it got me started on my academic career well enough. I needed to put that PhD to work. I needed to earn a living because I arrived, unbeknownst to me, seven or eight weeks pregnant with twins. Michael's parting gift. For the two years I was at Hamline, Michael's mother lived with us as live-in childcare for Michael Junior and Elise, children Michael would never see and a father they would never know. When I moved east to another small college in the Boston area, she returned to her home in Arizona. I was glad-sorry. The kids were in a good daycare by then and I at least had some privacy back. But I missed coming home to a cooked meal and my babies happy.

Over all that time and distance, literal and psychic, I lost touch with most of the pack. Mary Clay's letter telling me of Sebastian's AIDS diagnosis took weeks to reach me, bouncing as it did from one old dive operation to another. So the news about Sebastian, about whom I hadn't given much thought, except to think of him whenever San Francisco or gay pride flashed up on my radar screen, was beyond sobering. We were in our late-thirties. Life just taking off. But not for Sebastian. Nor for Michael.

Adeline

A crime. A crime against both those vital men.

All that comes back to me learning now of Grady's passing. I move away from the window and into the library to set a fire for the evening. Get it going nicely, before I head down to the dock. Grady at least was granted a longer life, had lived, as Zorba put it, the full catastrophe—wife, children, everything. And was happy, prosperous, as I understand it. I wish we'd had that FaceTime call. I would have liked to set eyes on the older version of himself. Fine wine or old fruit? See if I could still see the boy in the old man, that toothy grin and the flamboyant head of curly black hair. One holds dear that first flame. They are memory markers of a time not just long gone but time-touched, glistening gold. Of a carefree time. Or at least of a time when our cares, by grown-up standards paled. Innocence versus experience. Blake.

Yes. Grady. He was my first real boyfriend. There was Breck and certainly Sebastian. But they were pack members. Friends first. We—Jude, Mary Clay and I—all experimented on those two. But Grady was the one who wanted me, for me. Back when we were babies. Good god, I remember when my old friend Mary Clay and I were about fifteen and I knew, the way you just *know*, that Grady was going to kiss me that night. My first kiss. Only I didn't know how to kiss a boy, so Mary Clay's older sister taught me how.

—Open your lips just a little. Now press them on your forearm. Move your head gently back and forth. Good. Now, stick out your tongue—

—Stick out my tongue? I remember saying, horrified, sitting up and pursing my previously loose lips.

—Not like a little kid sticks out his tongue. Just let your tongue come between your lips. Now kiss your arm again. Relax. Make your lips soft. Then touch your arm with your tongue.

—What if my tongue goes in his mouth?

—That's the point, silly. That turns a kiss into a French kiss.

— A French kiss? That's disgusting.

—Noooo. No, it is not. You just wait. Trust me now. Lips soft, tongue ready. Now kiss your arm again. Good. Good. Now you've got it. When Grady kisses you, do to him what you just did to your arm.

Let me just close these old eyes and remember that afternoon.

So began my sexual initiation, an initiation I could not wait to get started. Fifteen seemed so old not to have a boyfriend, not to have been kissed or made out or anything. That's another thing I was determined not to do: die a virgin. And, somehow, dying a virgin seemed not just a likely scenario but the worst possible fate, ever. If I didn't fire up my jets, pronto. But I was scared too. Completely inculcated with the specter of pregnancy and my parents' disownment.

Not that I lost my virginity to Grady or Breck or anyone in the pack. The yank toward that goal did not come my way until my senior year in high school, when I was truly convinced that a virgin death awaited me, old as I was, and that's why I was the first to leave. Sex. Sex with an older guy, though not that much older it seems to me in hindsight. My orthodontist in fact. He'd have his fingers in my mouth in the afternoon and up me when we rendezvoused in the evenings. If I was seventeen at the time, he was closing in on thirty. The same age as my oldest sister, which made the age difference not seem like such a big deal. Almost all of us had been to him for braces, so they knew him, just not about our affair. Which, also in hindsight, would have grossed them out. Grosses me out now to think back on it. Especially the married part, and the back seat of the car part. But kids are idiots, especially ones that are hot to trot. I was desperate to get on with my life and being condemned to virginity was worse than the nunnery, where at least you made a choice.

Adeline

I'm pretty sure Mary Clay, so then of course Jude, suspected. But I lied. I simply slipped away from the pack like a caterpillar emerging from its chrysalis, in my case more moth than butterfly. I didn't stop going over to Sebastian's house. Not altogether. But it was much less frequent and never on weekend nights, when the pack always used to hang out, because I'd be getting laid in the backseat of the doc's car those Fridays and Saturdays, from November till I went away to college nine months later, leaving all my friends wondering why? Where was I? Now, when I hung out with the pack, it was laden with awkward silences, uncomfortable for everyone. I wasn't about to explain myself. Answer questions. Identify the mystery man. They all knew I was keeping something, something very important, from them, which was against all our rules. It took splitting up for college to end the unspoken inquisition. That is, for all of them except Tony and Jude.

Jude, she thought she was Juilliard bound. But she messed up the audition and was rejected. Tony turned a summer high school job at the Red Cross into a pitiful excuse for a career. The rest of us signed on to four-year programs. I got into Bard, amazing myself, not just because I was accepted but because they thought my poetry showed "promise." Sebastian went to State to avoid the draft and Breck to DePauw for the same reason. Grady went to Oberlin, bent on a career in music. Mary Clay went to Colorado State to ski and find a husband, because that was the expectation for all us girls back then. Ironically, not one of us fell into that trap, at least not directly.

Drop mercury and that would be us in September 1967, scattered all over. Not that we all stayed put where we landed. It was the 60's and our generation was on the move. Doesn't matter. Some of us got higher education. Some of us didn't. We all got educated in social responsibility, from the March on Washington to Vietnam, from conscientious

Ambient Light

objecting to sit-ins on campus and town squares. I know that if Sebastian were alive today, he'd have been a white fist raised for Black Lives Matter. After all, he was the kid who wanted to be Black. He had an activist's soul. He would have been there. Had he lived. If only he had. Which is why, after all, he worked on Harvey Milk's campaign to become a city supervisor in San Francisco and why he was an organizer for Act Up out there too.

I wonder, though. I wonder. If Sebastian had lived? But what's the point in even going there? He died young. Still, there was something about him. Something hard to nail down. Even now, all these years later. He was the bright illumination in our dark teenaged years. That much is sure. But I don't think he ever understood how he, he alone, held us in such thrall. Had he lived? What was he as an adult? A house painter, a health food store clerk, a weekend DJ, a lifelong protester. Just a man going through the days he was given. It was as if that light had gone out. Did he outgrow it like a childhood allergy? Or did he become conscious of it as he matured, and purposefully snuffed it out? Was he fearless? Or reckless? Choice, it's all about choice. Whether to wait for the light to turn or dodge the traffic in hopes of making it to the other side faster. Covid, I think, is not so different from AIDS. It's that risk/benefit thing. Each of us, whether Sebastian and AIDS or me, hiding out here in the woods from Covid, we, each, all of us, must choose. Risk is what we step into when the benefit lures us on. He was unafraid, and it killed him. I am afraid, and live.

Ah, the day is fading, and I want to see the sunset from down on the dock. There, I have a clear shot west. Should be a good one this evening, too. There's a bank of cumulous clouds low near the horizon. Sebastian can come with me, since he is occupying my thoughts, thanks to Grady's death and the tumbleweed of memories that brought on.

Adeline

I hang up my nostalgia and put on my winter coat. All my life I've dreamed of this place, like writers and painters dream of retreats, where they can focus entirely on their art. For me, it is all books and memories, those are my touchstones. All I need. I thought when I retired, I'd finally get around to the Great American Novel but by then I knew that all the lovely words had already been written, and I chose to savor those and keep mine to grocery lists.

Twisting a scarf around my neck and grabbing my walking stick—vanity forbids the cane everyone from my daughter to my doctor tells me I should use—I tug the door shut behind me. No need to lock up. Here, in these woods, on this lake, there is no fear, except maybe of an angry goose in springtime defending its gosling armada. The path down to the dock is graveled but covered over, this time of year, in pine straw. I take my time, breathing in the air. I catch the scent of snow coming, yes. It will be an early winter, I guess. The path meanders toward the water as if it were drawn by a drunken contractor. Probably was.

My son has added a handrail down the steps to the dock and screwed a garden chair permanently in place. No slipping out from underneath me if my landing is not direct; no blowing into the lake and disappearing if a wind comes up. What I love about my kids is that, no matter their reservations on the issue, no matter their anxieties for me, they let me be. They respect me. My daughter says she'll come out here one day and find my body decaying in my bed. My son disagrees. He says he will come out here one day and find me face-planted—his term—in the woods or on the lakebed just beyond the dock. However it happens, it will be on my own terms. After all, I don't want them messing things up and denying me my reckoning. I will not put the battery back. Not that I'm sitting around twiddling my thumbs waiting for the Grim Reaper's sickle to drop. No, though I'm sure that's what it must look like I'm doing. Why must retirement be perceived as having one foot in the grave? Back when the Social Security Administration set the retirement age at sixty-five, they knew the average male life expectancy was only sixty-eight years. Short payouts, they figured. But now? Retire at sixty-five or, as I did, thanks to the pandemic, at seventy, I could still have an entirely new career ahead of me. Not that I want another one. Still, I probably have twenty years left. Or at least fifteen. Surely ten. The life of the mind, that's my gig now. But the life of the mind, well, it can look to the busybodies of the world a whole lot like thumb twiddling. But those busybodies would be, well, dead wrong. Ha! I mean, why cut out before the big event? The pursuit of experience has propelled me through my entire life to date. Why stop now? I want to see what happens. I want to look Death in the eye and wink, not blink.

Carefully, I one-step down the wooden risers and step over to the dock. Carefully because with this tricky back of mine, I am not immune to the fear of falling, not by a long shot. Hand on railing, and then scuff scuff across the dock. Each rocking step causes a zinger to shoot down my back, so I lower myself with care into this rickety but anchored chair. We are made for each other. My butt imprint in the webbing proclaims it so.

A loon cry echoes across the lake, too far away for me to see the bird. Though I long to. It's polka-dotted feathers always remind me of the whale sharks I once dove with off Honduras and may account for my leaning toward spotted things in general, from lady bugs to summer dresses. The loon, so solitary, so self-assured is my avatar. He cries again. Closer now. But the burnish that the setting sun throws across the water erases him from view. Now my eye is naturally drawn to the cloud bank where magenta and burnt orange and pink tinges battle for superiority against the deep blue coming of night, and the sun sinks among them rearranging the colors with new and every-changing flourishes, a celestial

Adeline

artist gone mad. Until that big old star is gone and only the pink tendrils remain to recollect the passing of the day.

Before it is too dark, before there is only the porch light to guide me, I start back up the stairs, as cautiously as I came down. Maybe more so, because the end of the day is the worst time for my back—Atlas after a long day of bearing up the world. At the top of the steps, I pause to taste the night air and look up again. The stars are just beginning to come out. Pale Orion peeps over the line of the horizon. Another reason I love this place is that there are still stars to see. Not the Milky Way's white streak across the sky that I recall from my childhood, a brush stroke of white glitter on black velvet. Back in my diving days, you could still see the Milky Way from the sundeck of the dive boat anchored miles off the coast of Indonesia, like an old friend wearing a white sequined cape. Nowadays? Well, I wonder. The disappearance of the night sky seems like such a metaphor for our times. We have so built up this planet that the universe, once so visible in all its majesty and mystery, is almost completely obliterated. Only the most tenacious stars break through. In the cities, that is. Out here, well—

Ah, but philosophizing makes me tired. And sad.

The door sticks.

—Open, damn you.

Apparently dependent on my command, it opens with a little jerk that makes me totter backward. The porch railing catches me, thank heaven. Is this the door's revenge? Oh, Adie, you are anthropomorphizing a door! Maybe it's time for a dog. Someone—only not a someone—to talk to. There I go doing it again. This makes me break out grinning, working muscles in my cheeks that have not had sufficient exercise in who knows how long.

I hang up my coat. Place my stick in the corner by the door. Decide on tea, bed and a good book. Where would I be? Out here in this primeval forest? On this planet, were it not for the comfort of books? You would think, Adie, that after thirty-three years of teaching twentieth century literature, you would have had enough of books. Enough of words. But no. Never. This is something your mother did to you.

—Look it up, she would say whenever I asked her the meaning of a word. So maddening, when I knew, *knew*, she knew and was withholding. Until, by the time I was eight or ten, I would march around with an unabridged dictionary tucked under my wing. Risking even the inevitable bullying at school because if a word came up that fascinated me by sound—juxtaposition, say, or macabre—or tickled my curiosity when a teacher used it, I would not have to wait to find its meaning. Today, there is the internet to rob a child of that great pleasure turning page after page, running a finger down column after column, until—voila! Word found! Such a loss, such a pity.

The tea steeps its rooibos—red bush—earthy aroma over my mug, and I head into my bedroom, putting the tea on my bedside table and, sitting on its edge to take my clothes off, a task once so fluid and instantaneous. Bending to wrestle off my boots, my back twinges in pain. I curse my pants' legs that must be coaxed to the floor. My socks? Welcome on this cold night, and a good thing too, because it is hard for me to reach and roll them away off my toes. I tug one arm, then the other free of my sweater, so I can loop it over my head, pain radiating up into my shoulder, and toss it onto the chair not five feet away. I work my fingers over the buttons of my blouse, peel it off and toss it, too, onto the chair. From under my pillow I retrieve my ancient flannel nightie, get it over my head, shoulders still complaining, and I am ready for bed. I still must haul myself off this bed, brush my teeth, pee for the first of probably four times this night, and finally finally pull back the covers and lie back, groaning with fatigue and relief and the pure pleasure of being supine

Adeline

at last. Is there anything more blissful than being under the covers on a cool night? I can hear my back sighing.

For several long minutes I let my body settle, listen for and hear a barred owl that lives in the ancient stand of trees behind my cottage. He often tucks me in, and when he doesn't, when there is silence from the woods, I worry that misfortune has befallen him, that nature has taken its course. Then I give myself a stern reprimand, for I want no one worrying about me. Death, when it comes, for any of us creatures, is simply the next phase of a universal continuum. An eagle has come for the owl and will feed his chicks. I, one of these days in the not too distant future, will feed the insects that feed the birds that pollinate the flowers, so that fields and fields of them may grow to delight the living. I will live on in flowers. That is both remarkable and beautiful and is hands down better than an invitation through the pearly gates.

Ah, philosophizing again! So, I turn to my night table and take down two books. The novel I am reading and a collection of Shakespeare's sonnets. I must have fiction every day. It's like dope. Always transporting. Tonight, it is Toni Morrison. Who died just a few years back and with whom I once shared a panel discussion on the role of the disenfranchised woman in modern literature, she on Hagar and I on Diane di Parma. So it is *Song of Solomon* once again that will sing me to sleep. That and my bedtime balm, one of Shakespeare's sonnets. I want to be sent off to dream on the wings of the most beautiful language to flow from any pen. I finish my tea before I savor tonight's choice. It is Sonnet 64, When I have seen by Time's fell hand defac'd. I linger on its final couplet:

> *This thought is as a death, which cannot choose*
> *But weep to have that which it fears to lose.*

Closing my eyes, I think about what I fear to lose. Time's fell hand. Which, oddly, brings me back to thoughts of Grady. Gone now. As are they all. Mary Clay. Jude. Breck. Tony, I suspect. And Sebastian. I think about him often with my head upon the pillow, darkness and a Tramadol offering a sleeping draught. He had a smile that always made me think of "The Wife of Bath's Tale," that is, once I'd read Chaucer in an AP English class senior year. Like Sebastian, she had a gap in her front teeth, which was a sign of Venus and lust. Who knew that at the time? But it appears Chaucer was spot on about that gap, and its meaning, even for Sebastian. Because, man-o-man, that boy exuded something powerful, without ever knowing it, a siren call to us all. Back then, I had no gay-dar. There was a whole lexicon of words that were simply not in our vocabulary. Addict. Alcoholic. Bipolar disorder. Autism. Homosexuality. Lesbian. Gay. Gay was my mother's word for lighthearted, carefree.

—A perfectly delightful word ruined, she opined once. Even though gay meaning homosexual dates to the nineteenth century.

Lying here in the dark, the furnace rumbling to life beneath me, I can see the young Sebastian perfectly. In a pose so common, so winsome, we, or maybe just I, never suspected. Head lazing to one side, a slight twist to his upper body, arms spread like wings, enormous grin and a voice he could, and often did, pitch high. If I saw a boy in that pose today, I would know in an instant. But I didn't. Not then. Indeed, I was the last to know, and the only one of the pack Sebastian did not tell personally. I've wondered about that all these years. Why didn't he? Why couldn't he tell me himself?

I can rationalize. Yes, I was out of the country for most of my twenties. Yes, I fell away from the pack, abandoned them really, when I got caught up in a relationship that needed to be kept undercover—ha, ha, my punny self again. Still. He could have written.

Adeline

I sip the last of my cooled tea. He could have reached out. He told everyone else face to face. Just not me. Maybe he feared I'd be the critical one, the one who would see him as a pervert. Little did he know, given what I'd been up to during our senior year. Eventually, Mary Clay told me. I admit I was shocked. Because I had a virgin sensibility about the world then. A painful thing to acknowledge, even this far along. But also because I, like the others, had loved him for so long, for so many years. The fact that he might have feared my reaction shreds my heart. But this is not the thought I wish to be my last before sleep. I want to remember him for what he was to us, a rogue planet and us mere moons, helplessly, haplessly, happily caught up in his force field, a force field so powerful that when he jettisoned off from us to go to California, leaving us to zing out into our own splinter universes, his hold on us, me at least, held fast. Crazily a part of me is still, always will be in Sebastian's orbit. Now. Then too. It was that boy who gave me a political conscience, made me a music lover, made writing poetry a manly art and not just one for lonely spinsters, brought me along, coaxed me into the wider broader world with purpose. He seeded ideas in my heart like children. The job of parents presumably but also of prophets. But, in the end, he was just a boy.

If only I'd learned the truth from him.

I stack my books and my memories neatly on the bedside table.

And so to dream.

John Breckinridge

All I hear is the hospital machinery around me. It is background noise to me now. I have a window. It looks out on a parking lot and beyond that a stand of trees. There are no leaves. So I'm told. I cannot turn my head. It is winter. That I remember. Some month. I don't know. I've lost track. Couldn't tell you the day either. I could tell you the time, because there is a clock straight in front of me. Only I can't because I am unable to speak. That clock is counting me down. The hours minutes seconds until I am dead. I hope the batteries will die first. That way, I will win this one.

I am in a private room now. It's a mixed blessing. Any company, even a groaning, snoring, wheezing, crying one may be better than these four walls bearing down on me. I don't know. Is it better, more reassuring to have another human being breathing in the next bed?

Sometimes I have visitors. My daughter comes every Thursday. She sits with me, reads me the newspaper, charges my phone so I can listen to music, feeds me—apple sauce, Jell-o, ice cream. All my nutrients come down a tube and into my stomach through a hole they cut there. Kind of handy, really. No messy dishes to clean up, no Feed the Father Like a Baby his adult Pablum for her. And of course, all the initials come into my room, all unannounced—MD, RN, PA, PN, ANP, GNP—along with gaggles of interns who crowd around the bottom of my bed and stare at me, as if I were a rock they could will to move. Their favorite activity, directed by the ever-vigilant doc, is sticking my legs up and down with a safety pin. The doc hands the safety pin around and they all take turns. It's a game. They know I can't feel anything down there, so what's the big deal? The big deal is that I can see what they are doing. I can see them jab it in, sometimes drawing blood. I can see them. To them, I am a rubber doll they're poking. Or a voodoo doll. For all they care. For all I can feel. It is surreal, not feeling anything at all. I try to turn off my head, stare at the clock, count the seconds, or take myself to one of my favorite places — hiking at Yosemite at dawn and stopping at the waterfall of fire or hoisting the sail on a bare boat cruise in the Caribbean. This is my technique for falling asleep but it is only working to distract me now. It's hard to shut my mind off at these times because I want to hear what the doc says. In case he says something that might be hopeful. But those days are gone, as near as I can tell. At my bedside, to the wide-eyed interns he explains that I have a variant of "locked-in syndrome."

—The patient's cognitive function is perfect. He can see and hear. Can't you, Breck?

I blink, twice.

—He can blink his eyes, as you can see, but he has no lateral control. The one anomaly here is that this patient can swallow. But only very soft food or fluids in very small amounts.

—Is this Guillain-Barre? One smart-ass intern, looking to impress, asks. There's one in every crowd. Believe me. No, stupido, I answer in my thoughts.

—No. Hemorrhagic stroke, massive.

—How long ago? This one is a beautiful young girl with a swishy ponytail. But no breasts. I am a breasts man.

John Breckinridge

—Four weeks. Problem for Breck here is that it happened when he was alone and it was a couple of days before his daughter found him. There is scan evidence that he may have experienced a stroke progression. You know what that means? Anyone?

—It got worse? Some dummkopf intern asks. Notice, it's a question.

—We think an ischemic brain event may have progressed into a hemorrhagic one, featuring bi-hemispheric bleeds.

There are palpable gasps. I would gasp too if this news were news. But it's not. I hear the same litany every time a group of interns comes through. At least their visit is a twenty-minute diversion in my day. Because what else is there? Yes, the clock, and its metronomic death chant and the television. Which the morning nurse used to turn on every day promptly at 6:30a.m. when she came in to bathe me, without even bothering to ask me if I want it on because to her I am just a corpse-in-the-making. That TV went non-stop from morning till lights out every day for God knows how long because while I have a clock, I do not have a calendar. What would I need one of those for? It would imply both time passing and time promising. And there's none of that for me. Then one Thursday my daughter Rae asks me how I could stand the afternoon soaps. It was a rhetorical question for a minute, then she saw the look in my eyes.

—Oh, God. Oh, Pop.

She finds a way to unplug the TV and puts up a big note that says, DO NOT TURN ON WITHOUT PATIENT PERMISSION. Inside, I was laughing at that one. My permission? Two blinks yes, one blink no. But who's asking? No one. Except Rae. Sometimes, when she can get away in the evening, she will sit with me and we will watch NOVA on PBS or Saturday Night Live. To pass the time. To keep me company. For laughs. Rae says I can laugh with my eyes. But I'm not sure about that. Nice thought though. Best is her fragrance. I can remember when she was a baby, being carried away by the smell of baby oil and talc. Set my heart rocketing around the room. Now, I guess, what I pick up is her shampoo. It is lovely and feminine and makes me wish I could just set my nose down on her shoulder and breathe it in forever. She will stay an hour or so, until I begin to fade, and then kiss my grizzly cheek goodnight.

After she's gone home and after the last round of visits from the nursing staff, the ghosts come. They are a panoply of old faces. My ex-wife. The staff at the restaurant I managed for forty years. My poker buddies. Rae when she was a tot. Rae when she was an acne-riddled, self-conscious, esteemless thirteen-year-old. Rae as a fully blossomed rose, silky-haired, clear-skinned, reaching for the sky, thorns tucked in. Rae on her graduation day. God I was proud. When my ex comes, which for both our sake's is rare, we hash out the same old saga. Why, when I knocked her up, did we bother getting married? How could she leave her daughter behind? Because, she always says, you are the lover, Breck, of women and children. But you are her mother. And back and forth we go.

Sometimes my old track coach from high school stops by to give me a pep talk, or my own dead dad stands at the end of my bed, alternately looking at me and the clock. Funnily, never my mom. Or it might be Sebastian and the old crowd, Mary Clay, Tony, Adie and Jude, stopping by. When the ghosts, any of them, are here with me, they bring with them, the old days, those times, those occasions when we were together, that have solidified in my memory like totems. Some, like my dad and my ex, come bearing unfinished business.

Mostly, thank god, it is Rae and Sebastian. With the other ghosts making cameo appearances only when summoned by some shock of memory. Probably because they are the two people my mind gravitates to unconsciously. I'm not sure why Sebastian, although I understand why Rae comes. Because I hold the image of the just-left Rae in my mind's eye. The phantom Rae, the after light of her.

This night, the nurse has left my door ajar, so the ghosts don't come but voices from the nurses' station do. It's just across from my room. They're talking about me. Luckily—or unluckily—my hearing is acute.

—He was supposed to be transferred to Good Shepherd Nursing Home last week.

—I know, I know. We just can't keep him here much longer.

—People are saying it's a pandemic. It's all over the news. And nursing homes—

—A novel coronavirus. From China? Remember SARS?

—And Ebola—

—Yes, yes. Have you seen what's going on downstairs? The hospital is being outfitted for an alien attack. Have you seen? All available floors are now designated Covid only. If it gets worse, they'll take over this floor too.

—Oh my God. How did it get here?

—Just mark my words, all of you, we're going to have to make some tough decisions. They're going to need all us nurses down there. It's just a matter of time.

—Maybe that's why the medical director is coming up here tomorrow to speak to us? Did you see that post?

—But we have patients here on this floor. What do we do with them? Throw them out on the street?

—I know, I know. And no matter how bad it gets, there will still be strokes and heart attacks—

—And car crashes and kids falling out of trees—

—What will become of—of him?

Ambient Light

I can feel all twelve eyes swing in my direction. Luckily, I cannot swing my eyes toward them. Cannot confront them in their fear or give away mine.

—I think they're discussing sending him home with his daughter, you know with visiting nurses and others.

Oh, no. I think. Not to Rae's. I panic, and in this inert body that feels like barbed wire behind my eyeballs.

—We just can't keep him here—

Someone shuts my door. The talk becomes a mumble, but I can still make out their anxiety. This disease that seems to be eating its way across America is not real to me. Just a news segment, one dressed up, as the newscasters do, when they want to heighten attention to their show, with Breaking News banners. I know I've overstayed my welcome here. I know that. Hospitals, these days, it's in and out. People get their hips replaced and walk out the next day. One of my poker buddies fell on the ice, broke his hip and didn't miss our weekly game. And I've been here a month, if they're to be believed. I haven't thought about the next step. Didn't think there would be one. Thought I'd be carried out of this room stiff. It's bad enough, being here. But being here, I guess—well, I guess until now, I've always thought that meant there was some hope. Nobody has mentioned a nursing home to me.

What, Breck, did you really think you were going to walk out of here? Be miraculously cured? Get a free pass? I panic myself into a stupor, nearly sleep. My eyes, lids as heavy as lead, want to shut it all out. Just as my eyes close to the sliver of light coming under my door and the anxious voices beyond, there he is, Sebastian sitting in Rae's chair, smoking a Camel, blowing smoke rings over my head.

—Remember, Breck? Remember when we collected all those dead Christmas trees and took them to the nursing home near your old apartment building?

I do. I am smiling now, in my mind's eye.

—Remember after Christmas we went around my neighborhood with my mom's car, and Adie's parent's station wagon, and Jude's mother's Rambler? Remember that?

The ghost of Sebastian is reliving this ancient prank and amusing himself, bent over double in the chair, slapping his thigh, choking on the smoke he'd swallowed because he's laughing so hard.

—Remember we collected all the trees left out on the curb for trash pick-up, stuffed them in all the cars.

—Gawd, we must have had fifty trees.

I want to add, if I could add, Yeah, some still had tinsel and a couple ornaments that people couldn't see to take off. Instead, I play the movie in my head, with Sebastian as narrator. And I laugh along with him, in my head. It's the irony of ironies that here he is, a ghost, and here I am, a vegetable, and we're both laughing our guts up.

—Remember? We drove up to the front door, late. What, maybe two in the morning? And dragged all those trees onto the Home's porch. Stuffed 'em all up there, so that nobody was going in or out of that door. And you—

I rang the bell. One, two, three times. And we took off like bandits, pulled the cars around the corner and parked where they couldn't be seen, and then all of us, you, me, Jude, Adie, Mary Clay and Tony sauntered up the sidewalk to watch the hullabaloo unfold.

Remember, Breck, old friend?

I do. I do. I am walking with an arm thrown around Adie, watching the police arrive, their red lights spinning around and over the spread of dead trees. Trees up to the porch roof.

—Two in the morning, one cop says, turning his flashlight on us. Kinda late for you kids to be out walking the streets, ain't it? You kids didn't have anything to do with this, didja?

Ambient Light

—What exactly is the problem, officer? We're just on our way home, sir, Sebastian says, pouring on the respect for the authorities. Party at a friend's house, ya know? Nice night for a walk, sir—

—Cold night, the officer says, pointing his flashlight in Sebastian's face. Then mine. Then Tony's.

—Didn't have the bus fare, officer, and didn't want to wake somebody up to come and get us. We're fine, really, officer. Thanks for your concern.

Sebastian leads us away on up the sidewalk and around the corner, cool as a cucumber.

My eyes are closed now, remembering.

Sebastian drifts away, laughing, laughing though fading. I stand outside myself, the old teenaged me, and see my grinning self under the streetlight while all hell breaks loose at the Home across the street. If this is a dream, I'll take it.

The door creaks open, and it awakens me. The light in the hallway is dimmed to nighttime illumination. It does not sting my eyes the way the fluorescent overheads do. The staff is reduced to bare minimum. The door creaks closed.

—Pop?

Oh, it is the ghost of Rae. I close my eyes not to miss her. She's come to hold my hand through the night, to rub ice sponges over my parched lips, to sing me a lullaby. I smile in my head at the memory. Rae a baby, an infant, late at night, when she would howl and keep us both up, me pacing with her in my arms, not able to sooth her. Until I put her in the car seat and drove for miles, in circles, just to get her to go down, me singing "Swing Low" until she purred herself to sleep. Now she is doing that for me. Whatever happened to baby Rae? Blink and she's a competent woman, a lawyer. Blink. Whoa. Should've found another word.

—Pop. Wake up. It's me. Rae. I'm taking you out of this place.

Next thing I know, one of the night nurses and an EMT roll a gurney into my room. I blink. Blink. BLINK. BLINK. No. No. No. I don't understand. I trust Rae, of course, I do, but I'm afraid now. Why at night? Where is she taking me?

She sits beside me in the back of the ambulance. A little runner light illuminates the inside. She can see my fear, terror now.

—Pop. Look. Everything's going to be OK. Pop, just hang on, and try try to understand. We're transferring you to a hospice.

BLINK

—Just listen. The nursing homes are petri dishes for this virus that's killing everybody. I won't have you go there. So I found this hospice—

BLINK

I pause, then again, to add emphasis to my no,

BLINK

—You'll like it, Pop—

BLINK

—It's not what you think, Pop. It's a special place I found about an hour from here. Deep in the woods. The loveliest of settings. It used to be a school for unwed mothers but now it's just a home for, well—

I think, for lost causes.

—for adults needing acute care. It's more like a home, Pop, only twenty-four residents.

BLINK

Please, Pop. You can't stay in the hospital any longer and I didn't want you to be there anyway. All the hospitals in the country are becoming war zones now. If you had stayed, you might have gotten sick and died.

Blink blink

—You want that? You want to die?

Blink blink

—Oh, Pop.

I can see tears causing the whites of her eyes to glisten. A wave of guilt washes over me.

—Well, I don't. I don't want you to die. You can still beat this.

I close my eyes and wish for the ghost of Rae. The road beneath us sings up to me. The air now is country air, not hospital antiseptic ventilation recycled. I take a deep breath. Why is life so contrary? The moment I am resigned to death, prefer it to hospice and what that most certainly implies, the air is so sweet here, wherever we're going. The driver has his window cracked to keep the windshield from fogging up, I guess. Balsam and rain and humusy earth flood my senses. Wherever I am, wherever Rae is taking me, it is God's country.

When I open my eyes, Rae smiles and tells me I've been asleep for hours, almost missed a whole day, she says. Cheekily, I want to ask her, And what exactly did I miss? I see I'm already hooked up to fluids and my feeding tube has been reconnected. My bed faces a window. Outside, nothing but white pines wagging their lollypop heads in the wind. Rain streaks down the glass. I relax a little. This is better, I think, than the hospital. Thank you, Rae, I want to say and smell her hair and kiss her cheek. I want to know how she found this place. I want to know is this really a hospice? Or what? Instead—

Blink blink

—You like it? Oh, Pop, I'm so glad! It's pretty far for me to drive, so I won't see you as much, but the staff here will help us Face Time, and we can do that every day if you like. Best of all though, Pop, there's someone here who knows you. Recognized your name when I registered you. Went to high school with you.

Blink

John Breckinridge

—Yes, it's true. She said she'd stop in this evening after work before she heads home. Her name is Brenda something. Doesn't that ring a bell?

Blink

But I am lying. I think, it could not be *that* Brenda.

I do not recognize the matronly woman who walks into my room sometime later. She is square, in the way middle aged women become. Her hair is dyed blonde because I can see the white streak along her part. And she is smiling, like I'm some long-lost friend. Maybe I am.

—Why John Breckinridge Taylor, you are a sight for sore eyes.

BLINK

She giggles, blushes.

—Honey, I didn't mean it that way. Your daughter, Rae, is it? She told me you can communicate with your eyes. Yes and no, she said, but I'll bet we can improve on that in a matter of days. If you want to. I don't blame you for not recognizing me. I'm not the slim long-haired blonde cheerleader I used to be when I dated your friend Sebastian.

Blink blink

—So you do remember?

Blink blink

So, she *is* that Brenda. The doe-eyed bimbo who was crazy about Sebastian when we were seniors in high school. She seems whole enough, so I want to ask what she's doing here. I want to ask so much.

—Do you mind if I sit down and reminisce a little with you, Breck?

Blink

What am I supposed to say? She's going to do it, one way or the other.

—I know something you'll remember! Remember that egg fight?

I do. I surely do.

Blink blink

I think of my dad. Unwillingly. My father never really spoke to me after that, after I borrowed his car that night. There are moments in life when a Detour sign pops up in front of you, and things are never the same again. My dad's reaction to getting his car back all messed up—his word was damaged—was one of those times. I don't know how I would have survived his disappointment, his anger, his brutal silent treatment, if it hadn't been for the pack, my one true family, thinking back.

—I had a date with Sebastian that night. Oh, I can tell you now, I thought that boy would never ever ask me out. I think I had a crush on him since the third grade. Even if that night was way too wild for my taste.

She giggles kind of apologetically and gazes off into space, remembering I guess, loving Sebastian all over again and in spite of him dragging her into that melee. Of course I remember Sebastian dating her, sort of. For about two months, maybe three. I remember, too, what Adie said.

—That girl tricked him into asking her out. Had tickets to a Wilson Pickett concert. He'd have sold his soul to go, and he did. Sell his soul.

That's what Adie said. I didn't think anything of it, except that Adie was jealous. Every girl I ever saw, who saw him, wanted to be with Sebastian. For Adie or Mary Clay or Jude to be jealous was just a natural way of being.

Then Brenda is talking again, all about Sebastian. What I've never understood is why all conversations lead to Sebastian, like all those roads to Rome. You can't be in the room five minutes with someone who knew him before it's Sebastian this Sebastian that. I'm hardly listening to her, dozing off, but then something snags me like a fighting fish. She's going on about having been married, three darling children, but it didn't last long, seven years—

—Seven-year itch, I guess, and she is smiling but looking down in her lap like it pains her. You know, Breck, I'd have married Sebastian.

Right out of high school. Or whenever. If he'd have had me. He really was the love of my life.

I force myself not to blink one way or the other. Just stare straight ahead. This is real, if not surprising news. She and Sebastian went out, maybe six times. Always doubled. He never touched her as far as I know. Adie told me once the only thing she'd ever seen him do was hold her hand. I wonder if Brenda knows. I wonder if she figured out why. And if she did, why she carried a torch for a gay guy all these years.

—Oh, I see you're drifting off. I'm sure it's been an exhausting day for you, Breck. I'll stop in tomorrow and make sure you have everything you need. Maybe I, or one of the aides, can help you expand your vocabulary—she winks at me with this little joke. We have a system to teach—oh, never mind. It's good to see you, Breck. It's good to see someone from the old days. When we were so young, so open.

She pats the side of my bed and I hear her leave the room, closing the door softly behind her.

And I want to scream, DID YOU KNOW HE WAS GAY?

Instead, I blink once, to myself.

Why did he have that kind of sway with girls, anyway, I ponder, as I have pondered millions of times before, and close my eyes. Next thing I know, Sebastian is lying beside me. We are at Grady's swim club, sharing a beach towel on the grassy fringe, both of us wet and wasted from playing in the water for too long. He lights up; I light up. I reach for my glasses.

—Thanks for doubling last night, with Brenda and me.

I shrug.

—I broke up with her. She's nice and all. But—

I don't ask about the but. In some ways, I'm glad. We're all a lot happier when there's no outside romances going on. And when it's

Sebastian, it throws us all out of sync. How can we hang at his house if he's got a girl in there? We're best, happiest, the seven of us, when no one from the outside complicates things.

—Why don't you come with me? he says.

—Where are you going?

—You'll see. I'll show you the way. Come on, Breck.

It is so real. I open my eyes to darkness and the rain tapping on the window. He's gone. The phantom Sebastian has left me. And hasn't. I swear I can smell the faintest hint of chlorine. I swear I can still feel him. And wherever he's headed, I want to go too.

Blink blink

Jude

Oh, cold, cold darkness bringing me down! From my nose to my toes to my frigid fieldstone heart. Come on, won't you, light the candles and warm this poor heart of mine? There they sit, six little sentinels, six tea candles, one for every year we were together. Because, deny it as you will, we *were* together. Renegade teenagers. Simpatico to our cores. Our voices, one. Our thoughts, telepathic. We could have made it, you know, you and me. Could have played Woodstock or anyplace, we were that good. If only. If only, what, Jude? If only what? It didn't happen. Not even after you chased him to the West Coast. Why did it all seem so possible, even you said so, at fifteen? At seventeen? When did your heart change? When did your head shut me out?

Six candles. How many times have I replaced them over the years of missing you? Half a century's worth? I light each of them, whenever I feel this longing, whenever I remember how wordlessly you left me. I'm tired, tired of one-night stands, playing my guitar or waking up with a stranger. And I'm old now. Burned out. I have become the little old witch of fairytales. I see it in the mirror. If/when I take a hard look. Right down to skin tags on my neck and waist length hair streaked with kinky grey. Men only look at me with pity now. Once, they paid my bills, now no one does, not even me. Why does it shock me when I remember you are dead? Who gave you that permission? Not I, Sebastian. Not I. You made your bed of roses, more thorn than petal, and it angers me. That you could sing so close to heaven, bring me to my knees, with a bluesy Piedmont kind of feeling, and let it all slip through your fingers. Through mine. You didn't care. How could you not have cared? You flaunted your Adonis face in mine and traded that perfect pitch—for what?

What did Michelangelo say? The greater danger for most of us lies not in setting our aim too high and falling short; but in setting our aim too low and achieving our mark.

At least I believed in us. Believed in me. I've always believed in myself. Sad, sad, sad. Look where it got me? You get the last laugh, Sebastian. Are you laughing at me from six feet under? Look at me now? Where are the gold records on these peeling wallpaper walls?

You achieved your mark. Ironic, isn't it?

I was the one among us destined for fame. Why did it elude me? Why did it leave me a broken panhandler and a nobody? If you hadn't bowed out, run away to California, together we could have struck gold.

I have not paid rent on this place since last March, when Trump kindly put the brakes on landlord collections. Almost a year now. I thank the pandemic for that. Perfect, I thought at the time. Why in God's name should anyone be required to pay rent on a dump like this, when you can bake alive in the Tennessee summers because, of course, there is no A/C; and bake again all winter with heat you can't control. And the cockroaches run relays in and out of the kitchen cabinets every time I open one. And there is mildew creeping around the baseboards and window mullions in the bedroom teasing great wads of phlegm from

Jude

my throat. And the apartment above me's toilet is always overflowing staining my ceiling, seeping into my life. Who in clear conscience could collect rent on such a place? And this free pass I have? Well, it is destined to end. Then what?

Last March I was still working, playing some gigs here and there, even coffeehouses—and I thought coffeehouses went out with the Vietnam War but, no. Not down here in the backcountry South. Everything is fifty years behind the times down here. But not now. My gigs, such as they were, have all dried up, what with the pandemic closing everything down either by law or by fear. So I wasn't playing anymore and I quit my job as a cashier at the Super Shop. I'll be damned if I'll put my life on the line as an "essential" worker in a grocery store—what bullshit—so people can spit virus in my face in exchange for a quart of milk or a six-pack of beer? No paycheck is worth that. I just wish I had that check, free of the checkout line.

Oh, I can still pick up some change panhandling. When I need smokes or a can of tuna. A leftover from my brief California days, playing on the streets for quarters and dollars, when I still thought there was hope for you and me. No, not as man and woman. But as a duo. Like Ian and Sylvia. Remember how we loved them? Emulated them? Nobody knows who they are now. So I guess that would have been our fate too. A good run at fame then, erased by the music that came next. Somehow, that doesn't make me feel any better. Not now. Not tonight. Trying to find a match to light those candles.

Back then, I packed up my guitar and my suitcase and headed out to find you. To explain to you what I knew to be gospel, that you'd never find someone to get you like I do, be in such perfect sync. All the magic we shared making music, making time, making everything but love. But making a kind of love, yes, like a song of pure revival, a style that sanctified, like a touch of Muddy Waters' slide. But I couldn't reach you. It was like mistaking you for someone else, someone I thought I knew, but didn't. So I rose up and came back East understanding, finally, I could not work this life out the way I wanted it to, thought it would go. With you by my side.

Oh, but that is ancient history. Still, it's the hurt I sing every time I pick up my guitar, even now, panhandling, trying to sing my way into someone's wallet. In the Super Shop parking lot till they shooed me off premises. On the dusty, rundown, empty-store-fronted main street where I live. To buy a loaf of bread or some coffee. Buddy, will you spare me a dime. That old Depression tune sure does ring true in 2021. Now, little by little, I've run through my money like I've run through my time on this earth.

I don't feel scared. Only defiant. I'm seventy-one years old, I've never earned a regular paycheck, never had a social security handout, though I have had to make use of Medicaid, back when my pelvic floor collapsed, which seemed a kind of just reward after all the lovers I've had, and I landed in the hospital. I've gotten by. Not needed anything or anybody, that is, with one noteworthy exception, and that exception being dead of AIDS, as if he had to press home his point in no uncertain terms. People are kind, you know. Easy to tap if you're really hard-up. And, there's always a man to buy you a drink, well, not so much anymore, but I do keep a look out. Did. At the bars where I play. Played.

Before now, in my halcyon days rich men kept me in metaphorical mink. A string of them. I never thought of it as trading sex for hospitality or companionship for love. They thought of me as lovely, tall. Willowy was the term most often used to describe me. They believed I was talented as a musician and as a fine artist. They thought of me as good in bed. I thought of them as a meal ticket with benefits. Sometimes,

Jade

wonderful benefits. Like the guy who put up something like twenty grand to underwrite a solo art show for me at a gallery on Boston's tony Newbury Street. Or the man I was with longest, until his wife found out, who bought me an apartment on the Upper West Side that came with a parking place and a Mazda Miata, totally impractical for New York. But he liked to picture my hair swirling out behind me as I drove toward him in Hudson. It was a weird sex fantasy, I guess, because, in bed, he couldn't get enough of my hair. But finally, he, whichever he he was, would either get tired of me or his wife would find out, and I'd be footloose again.

As Tennessee Williams would say, "I've always depended on the kindness of strangers." Like those men. My family and friends? They do me no favors. Not so long ago, when I was really desperate, I called Mary Clay. I knew she had a big house on Cape Cod, because when we were teenagers, she and I spent a week visiting her grandmother there one June after school was out. That place must have seven or eight bedrooms, with a big old wrap around Victorian porch, a double living room and a killer view of the National Seashore. Mary Clay inherited that old place. I knew there was plenty of room. I was desperate enough to go to the library to look up her telephone number on the internet. The ultimate cold call. She was so surprised to hear from me, I almost talked her into renting me a room. Never mind that it had been decades since we'd seen each other. I figured that place was big enough for me to stake out an entire floor to myself if I wanted, or needed to. She was going to say yes, I could tell. I could hear it in the hesitation in her voice. I fed her loneliness with the promise of company and a walk-on from the good old days. Even when she asked if she could think about it for a few days, I thought I had her. But when I called back, her voice was hard. No, she told me. When I tried to argue, she just said

—Oh, Jude. No. Sorry. Really, I am. But I'm too set in my ways to live with anyone now.

I knew she was lying. All I can think is that she called Adie and Adie talked her out of it. She would. She thinks I'm a loser. Heh, there's always been a wall between us—the genius and the wanna-be. She was always envious of me. Adie, whose eyes are made of lasers, who never misses a thing, who could always ferret out a fraud, had no true gift to offer the world. As I do. Who was, still is, always trying to get between me and MC. Adie, who doesn't know the meaning of generosity, of friendship. She definitely would have told Mary Clay not to rent me a room.

My sisters were no better. The youngest one took me in for three years. I had the entire third floor of their house and tried to stay to myself. But my music bugged her husband and she ragged on me all the time about "not contributing." The other two took turns turning me away. "Come for the weekend." "Come for Christmas, stay through the New Year." They always set parameters on my welcome. I was not invited to linger.

But it's OK. First, it's my life. The one I chose, for better or worse. Ever since my father paid nightly visits to my bed when I was a kid, I have been able to take care of myself. Turns out, being used is a vivid lesson in the value of using in return. Hearts turns out to be just one suit in the deck. To be played or not.

I try not to think of my mother. She was weak. And common. I'll never understand why, to this day, Mary Clay made her a friend once we were all grown. She is a plain woman and mother to four girls and one boy. I am the middle child. The reed, my father called me. The brainy one. The one with a gift. That's what he would croon to me on those sultry summer nights when the windows were thrown open for the breeze and my mother's snores shutdown the treefrogs. I liked what he told me, liked

Jude

how he made me feel. I liked, mostly, what we did together. People say you're a child until you're eighteen. What kind of arbitrary nonsense is that? I was an adult the moment he came to me and I opened my arms. He didn't bamboozle me. I knew what I was doing then, what we were doing. I know incest is the big taboo. But not for me. Vice is nice but incest is best. I loved the man not the father and would romance him again now, but for the hag I've become.

Once, before he left on one of his business trips, he sat me down at the old upright piano we had in the front hall and showed me how each key sounded.

—I hear you singing.

I had a radio in my bedroom and was always singing along. I didn't think anyone could hear, so at first what he said embarrassed me.

—You've got a good voice, Judy. A good ear for music.

The fact that he noticed, the fact that he praised me, well, *that* was music to my ears. Then, a month or so later, when he came out of the den where he was writing some book or other and I was coming downstairs to set the table for dinner, he stopped me, put his arm around me and guided me back to that piano. This time he challenged me.

—I want you to play the Saints Go Marching In by the time I get back from this trip. One week. Hum it to yourself first, then find it here on these keys.

I did, and he told me I was Juilliard bound.

When he went away next time, he didn't come back. He didn't call or write or anything. Not my mother. Not me. My father was always telling us he was a famous author and that's why he was always going off on business trips like this, researching whatever book he was writing. Until this time, when he didn't come back. My brother wailed for him. My mother dusted the flour off her hands and told him to get a grip or pack his bags and go after the "old drunk." That's what she called him. That was news to us all. Then she cried. I didn't pity her, I pitied myself. They say as a child I was a little bit feral, with all the lunatic things I did. But I knew what was happening. I knew he never loved my mother, not like he loved me. But he still left. Left me.

That was the last time I played the piano. And the last time anyone called me Judy. I crushed the keys of that piano with a cement block. Some might say that was the devil's work but I'm here to say, it felt good, *really* good. I was grounded for a month because my mother had to pay to have that sorry thing carted away. And because I blamed her for pushing him out. And for naming me Judith, as pretentious a name as there is. In a class with Olivia or Clarissa or Octavia. Judy was just as bad, except when he said it. It was one of the most common names for girls of my generation. There were five Judys in my first grade at school. And more piled on as I got to middle and then high school. A million Judys. I refused then, as I refuse now, to be common. So, I refused to answer to Judy anymore, after my dad disappeared on me. Because to him I was special and Judy sat on his lips like a kiss. Remember, Sebastian? You were the first person I told, the first witness to the new declension of me—Judith. Judy. Jude. Judith. Judy. Jude.

Funny thing is, about my father? Now, in the age of the internet and Amazon, nothing shows up when I Google his name. He probably published under a pen name, so my mother couldn't find him, bleed him dry.

At my junior high school, in music class, when I said I could play the piano but didn't want to anymore, they handed me a violin. I've been a slave to stringed instruments ever since. Now, or in recent years, I play only the guitar. To make money. But by the time I graduated from high school, I could play violin, mandolin, bass, cello, even a sitar. We met in the school chorus, remember? I was part of a string trio, and you,

Jude

Sebastian, sang a solo. I wonder if you remember that? Or would, if you were still alive.

The guitar came naturally after that because it meant we could be a duo. You didn't play but I could. I could be the accompaniment, and that pleased you and I came every afternoon after school to sing with you at your house. We rehearsed and rehearsed. But for what? Dreamweaving, I guess. To play local gigs. That was enough for you but only a taste for me. I didn't mind the others because it gave us an audience but then, after high school, I began feeling you slip sliding away. First to State, then you came out to me and left for California. It was pride of course, but also a lot of hurt. Knew I had to make it without you, make the point, prove to you, OK, Sebastian, you bastard, I don't need you. I don't need anyone. Go solo, like Joan Baez, on the club circuit in New York or Cambridge, Massachusetts. The only thing missing in that plan was you. Because we were one, Sebastian, we were one. Even if you'd never admit it. And maybe luck was missing, too. I did get to the Newport Folk Festival in 1971 with a folk singing group. We didn't play the main stage because nobody'd ever heard of us. And it was raining. It was kind of a bust. And the others in our group said they were fed up with me bossing everybody around and fucking them in between. They said my poetry was lousy and my cunt lousier. So, that was it for me. I walked away from them and determined on a single act. Never looked back. Never played Newport again but Newport was never the same after '75 anyway.

My thoughts drift into the frozen night, numbly they ride on an icy wind that is you calling me, and the six candles beckoning. Snow is falling, covering up the ugliness all around outside. Covering some of the ugliness inside, too. Inside me. Beauty does that to me, even now. The trees break into shapes break into colors break into—I need wine, that vintage extraordinaire, Two Buck Chuck.

Ambient Light

I lift myself out of the old wingback that came with the apartment and scuff my way to the kitchen. Really just a half-fridge and a hot plate. I take out the bottle, another last. Find a glass on the counter, rinse it out, and then grab another, for you, and open the bottle of Chateau Le Screwtop. I think to pour myself a glass but defer. I have another idea for it, later. I take a long swig, a proper mouthful and fight to swallow. It tastes like a cross between battery acid and Nehi Grape soda.

I knew I'd know when the time was right for this. I've been planning for this day, saving up to make it possible, oh, probably since Mary Clay called me to tell me you were dead. Probably since then, all these long years with you not on this planet. How can that even be? When you went, I stepped into the echo chamber of your sweet voice. Can't numb you out of my mind. Try as I might, try as I have.

So we will share a glass of wine tonight, the dead you and the passing me, and some good weed I have put away for the occasion. Because some ceremony is called for, and that will help bring on the numbness I need. I scuff my slippered feet back into to the living room, with a glass for you and the bottle for me. I fortify myself with a little more fruit of the vine and pick up my guitar with my free hand.

—A toast to the passing horsemen!

I lift the half-gone bottle to the ceiling before pulling the ottoman up to the niche. Why, I've often wondered, is this niche here? In this little living room beside the bricked up fireplace. Who carved it into the wall, and why? For books? For flowers? For a statue of the Virgin Mary? I made of it the perfect use, as if this niche has been waiting in this wall, in this seedy apartment, for me to find it and dedicate it to you. Newspaper clippings, postcards postmarked San Francisco, three faded Polaroid photographs, tickets stubs from *Hair* and *Super Star* and the

Jude

Stones, notes passed at school and kept all these years. His handwriting, his face, his broken story. Now I light the six tiny candles.

I lay my guitar across my lap, and contemplate the past, those six years in his company. We were so different, Sebastian and me. He made friends easily, I did not. Thinking back on it now, he never judged. Anyone. Let It Be could have been his mantra. I, on the other hand, judge first, accept way later. If ever.

All my life since knowing you I have tried and failed to write you a song. I could never do you justice. I still believe you were my twin, that we were spiritually if not physically joined at the heart, no matter how often you turned away, no matter how you mocked me, no matter how exquisite our voices were together. How our harmony was the closest thing to God I've ever known. But you were a dream twister, Sebastian. Did you know? Did you know how much I needed you, how much, apart, our music was empty? I kept waiting for that half-cocked smile of yours to reveal that you were just pulling my chain, not wanting to be together, work together, sing together. To let the twinkle in your eye rest on me, by way of apology. By way of acknowledgement that we are one. A whole. Not a widening gyre but the great mandala, the two of us connected, our lives intertwined, no matter the separation of miles and time.

I wonder, do you ever think of me? Did you ever?

I imagine what kind of sanctuary we could have made together if you hadn't gone to California. If, when I came to you in San Francisco, you had welcomed me. Maybe you still won't admit it, but, the truth is, we always did feel the same. We just saw things from a different point of view. Right, Sebastian? You went on to live an honest short life. I went on to crawl through the years, heart-dead, seeking, always seeking. Why did I even bother? The days, weeks, months piling into decades of living, breathing emptiness. For the umpteenth time, I caress the neck of my trusty old instrument, my fingers feeling for the frets, and I think of making music one last time. Instead, I lean off my ottoman, stretching just far enough to pluck the old Polaroid of you and Mary Clay and Adie and me from its tab of sticky tape, so I can look closely at your face. But it is shaded by the position of the sun, and in three-quarter profile. And yet, there is just a hint of your smile in the turned-up fragment of lip I can just make out. Takes my breath away. If I close my eyes, I can still see you at fourteen, fifteen, at sixteen, at seventeen, at eighteen and nineteen, that quirky smile, that gap between your front teeth. I can smell your sweet breath as our faces nearly touch in front of a microphone.

Who took this picture? Who, among us, in those days had a camera? Maybe Breck. Or Grady. It doesn't matter. It only matters that I can almost hold you, holding this. This faded little square photograph with its scalloped edges. The only remaining testimony of your existence.

I find at the back of the niche my last joint, rolled this morning. I light it with the same book of matches that lit the six little candles, and suck the smoke deep deep into my lungs, and I hold it. Before the match burns down I light the corner of the photograph, blow out the match and let the image of you curl brown then black then grey until I have to drop it. I rub it, rub you, out on the stained rug with my worn out slipper.

The wine and the reefer are beginning to have the desired effect. Before I am too loopy to navigate, I go to the bathroom and find in the medicine cabinet the pills I have been saving for this night. I wash them down with the last of the wine. I expect to feel regret. Fear. To put my finger down my throat, but instead, I feel like Alice when logic and proportion have gone the way of all flesh. Pills, what power they have. However many I just swallowed, what I feel is serene.

Guitar in hand, I shuffle into my bedroom, and lie down. My instrument beside me, the only lover I've had that stayed, and I wait. I trace the

Jude

crack in the ceiling above me to the wall and the curling wallpaper and wait. Sleet wracks the window just as my stomach turns, vomit threatens. I choke it back. Release for this fieldstone heart is what I wish for, smooth passage on this cold, cold night.

Anthony

Why did I go? Why did I even go? I've followed all the stories in the news. What was I thinking? I didn't need the truth rubbed in my face. So why did I choose to go see that movie? Am I the king of ostriches? I believed Father Xavier when he told me I was special. All these years, I held on to that, even when story after story flashed into the headlines. It happened to them, not me. I have watched as the Catholic Church has imploded with accusations and I still didn't get it. Still wouldn't allow myself to see my face in that mirror. *You are special, Anthony. You're my special boy. I see great promise in you. I will guide you to a good Christian manhood. You are the best altar boy I've ever had.*

Now, I see my face in the mirror. No. I see my face in the Spotlight. The light shines on a boy deceived, a boy who was never special—to him; a boy who was no doubt just one in a long line of timid young boys, a boy too young to understand why one day Father Xavier was simply gone. Reassigned, we were told. Now, with the spotlight in my face, I see everything clearly. For the first time. I was never special to anyone, least of all Father Xavier. Why did I cling to that belief all these years? Why? Because I had no father? Because I needed to believe I mattered to someone, not counting my mother or my aunt? And what about them?

What about any of the people who ever claimed to love me? What is love, anyway? Emotional dependency? Shelter in the storm? A fantasy of Valentine's Days and New Year's Eves and mistletoe at Christmas? Jesus. No, wait. Not Jesus. Where has he ever been for me? Indeed, he fed me to all the sharks in my life—Mother, Auntie San, Father Xavier, Sandra. Because Jesus blesses and forgives all sinners.

I care not for his forgiveness. I do not seek, want or need it. Jesus and the Church and all its indoctrination can go fuck themselves. When I think Father Xavier told me I was the best altar boy he'd ever had, I know now, 'had' was the key word.

Now that the spotlight pans over my life, I just want to laugh. Except for one shadowy phase when I was a boy, those clueless years of growing up with Sebastian, every aspiration, every undertaking, every hope I have entertained has ended in disaster. I could just feel sorry for myself. Be honest, Tony. You do feel sorry for yourself. You should feel sorry for yourself. Look at you? A long and undistinguished career at the American Red Cross. A failed marriage. A lover murdered for loving you. A father who abandoned you. A mother, and maybe even an aunt, who packaged their resentment of me in smothering control. And a priest who deceived you with kindness, so he could mold you into a cocksucker. Or was I always one, just waiting to be revealed? What a life! It deserves a twenty-one-gun salute, a tickertape parade, a military flyover.

Instead, I will turn that spotlight off. Off me. That me. And become someone new. Why not? I will legally change my name, assume an entirely new identity. I certainly am not wedded to the being that is known as Anthony St. James. At sixty-six, I'm not too old to slough off this old skin and become a new creature, regenerating like a spring snake. Free to slither away.

Anthony

I will be the new disappeared. Not the kind in Argentina's dirty war. Not the kind you hear about in Mexico. Forty-three boys vanish into thin air. Thin graves. No, grave for me. No. Just a metamorphosis. One with no room for anything or anyone from the past.

Eliminating yourself without dying is an elaborate process, even more so than going trans, because at least then you can keep your name, or a form of it, and your family, if they are accepting. But with no family, no friends I wish to claim anymore, there is no emotional baggage holding me back. Tony is now Edward. I like the choice of the new name because it has no meaning, no associations, nothing, for me. But it is a strong name, Edward, not cluttered with soft sounds like Anthony.

All it took was a few strokes on my keyboard and the name change was done. So easy. It was the only easy part, though. I thought Ed would be jubilant but enough of the old Tony hung on, that instead of feeling released, my first reaction was to puke. I wept, in spite of myself. To be given a life, an identify, and fail both utterly is an unimaginable loss. But it's too late now. Tony is no more.

I got a letter from Adie awhile back. I don't know how she found me, but the internet is an insidious invader of privacy. That may have been the final nudge I needed to kill off the old me. When I checked my mailbox that day, there it was. Adie's letter. I recognized her handwriting, even though we have not been in touch for twenty or more years. I thought about tossing it out but I admit to curiosity. Instead, I cancelled my UPS box and subscribed to a virtual mailbox where at least I have the option to shred without reading. Not be tempted. By curiosity or anything else.

She wrote because she had lunch with Jude after not seeing each other in years.

Dear Tony,

Suffice it to say, if you are reading this, if I've actually found you, I hope you don't read it as an intrusion into your elusive presence on the planet. Read it instead as a quest accomplished on behalf of myself, Jude, Mary Clay, Breck and Grady. None of us understand why you vanished from our circle, but that is exclusively your business, and we all honor that. Just know you are missed and often the subject of the fondest recollections.

Jude and I had lunched the other day. It was kind of weird, pretty one-sided. She is looking for Sebastian memorabilia, and that got me to thinking about Fosterina and Donkey Heehaw. Do you still have the notebooks you and Sebastian made with all the characters you guys created? And didn't you make some cassette tapes, too? Not that I'm suggesting you send them to Jude or anything. I just got to thinking and smiling at all the mischief you two dreamed up. That got me thinking about you. Obviously. And wondering what's become of you. I hope you are well and happy and up to some other form of mischief these days. And if you ever want to get in touch, here's my —

I do not bite. I do not write her back. Not even an email. But I do, however much I am trying to erase my past, keep it. Don't ask me why.

Sebastian. I cannot picture the face of my mother or my aunt, the two people who raised me, but I can see Sebastian. My first friend, whom I loved beyond understanding, from the time we met at six or seven until he went away to college. To be reminded of him, those times, that hope, is beyond excruciating for me. I was sad to learn he died, what, twenty-two years ago now? Hard to believe because he haunts me still. But I was also glad. To have that awful force banished to the grave. Not as if we had seen each other for years, not since that last Christmas before he died, and he came back to see his mother. For years after he had confessed his troubling truth to me I did not want to be in touch with him. I was afraid, I think now, to learn of his friendships—and more—with other men. Perhaps be infected with my own sad truth. Mea culpa, Sebastian, mea maxima culpa.

So Adie's letter and the onrush, the assault of all those memories, a time when I was happy, truly happy and carefree and cushioned from the world by this powerful boy, shoved me toward the courthouse door, and the end of Tony.

There were other things to erase, not just a fantasy childhood. My marriage comes to mind. What a joke! Why did I cast my lot into the matrimonial ring in the first place, let alone with that virago? Sandra sold Cadillacs. That should have been my first clue, an aggressive sales person. That's the kind of personality you need to sell cars, especially cars that had one tire in the automotive grave at the time and catered to nouveau riche, middleclass, pot-bellied, cigar smoking retirees with bossy wives. It's the kind of personality that makes a meek man miserable. I am that meek man. But my aunt immediately loved her, because they shared the same given name, Sandra. And my mother, well, I guess the best word to describe my mother's reaction to our engagement was relief. And Sandra loved them. Or, probably more accurately, is she loved the way they lived. High style. If you just didn't get past the living and dining rooms.

My aunt and my mother lived by the Spanish proverb: living well is the best revenge. Once my father walked out, before I was born and just after he got wind of me, the sisters pooled their resources and moved in together. Sandra, or Auntie San, as I knew her, was a spinster with a lifelong blue rinse, who visited the beauty parlor every other week for a perm and a manicure. She worked in an insurance agency and retired as personal assistant to the president. It sounded prestigious, so she loved to tell people about her job whenever she had a chance. Her chance with Sandra came on our first dinner at our apartment.

All her life, I was my mother's sole crusade and she the keeper of the Big Secret. She would never tell me anything about my father, except, to use her term, he was 'scum.' The first time I asked her why she called him scum, she slapped my face, the one and only time she ever struck me. I never gave her cause again. She was, in every sense of the word, a fine Catholic martyr. She lived by the tenets of the Church. We went to mass, well, religiously every Sunday. We had no Christmas tree; we had a creche. No Santa, only Baby Jesus. Every Friday was fish sticks. I became an altar boy and Father X came to dinner once a month (but never on Fridays!). I remember once my mother saying to him as he was putting on his coat to leave after one of those dinners—

—We are so grateful to you, Father. You are so good to our boy. Thank you for taking him under your wing and being so very kind to him. You have become a second father to Tony.

I remember those words. I remember too the odd feeling it gave me, half pleasure, and something else. It was uneasiness, but I didn't recognize it then.

—Anthony is my star altar boy. He is a very bright, delightful boy. Father Xavier tousles my hair and I smile up at him.

—Please stay after services tomorrow, Anthony. I could very much use your assistance.

He winks at me, and still I blush.

In unison, my mother and my aunt chimed—

—Tony will be there, Father. He's looking forward to it, aren't you, dear? I smile. I do her bidding. I will do his.

In the same odd way that a hurricane in all its destructiveness can be a blessing, Sandra was for me, early on in our courtship, just that. Raised eyebrows in church, prying questions about my love life at work, faces turned away when I passed the gossips at church, even my oldest friends—Jude, Mary Clay, Breck, Adie—got their unexpected answer. I had a girl. She blew into my life at a Red Cross blood drive out in the field. She fainted when she stood up, a pint lower on O neg, and I was recruited to feed her orange juice and cookies once she came to, until her color was restored. I remember her eyes fluttering open and struggling for focus. She looked up at me as if I were her savior, big grateful adoring eyes. I fell hard.

At first the rising wind around her seemed refreshing, life-giving, exhilarating. We went to dances and concerts and parties. We worshipped together. I conducted myself like a gentleman, and she liked that. Thought it quaint that I kept my hands to myself, kissed her only lightly on the cheek or lips, did not try to sleep with her or even spend the night. She delighted in this old-fashioned respect for a woman. To her, it was cute. Our only point of discord arose around the subject of children. She desperately wanted them, and at thirty-six could see her opportunity slipping away. I, well, I played my cards close to my vest on that one. The idea of children scared me.

My mother, whom I called Mother, of course, welcomed Sandra into the fold but I've always suspected not liking her very much. But Sandra liked her, doted on her, wooed her, flattered her, talked to her about grandchildren, even before we were engaged—and my aunt as well. What Sandra saw was the fine Oriental rugs and the glistening mahogany sideboard in the dining room. The foot-high pair of sterling candelabra on our dining room table. The Royal Crown Derby tableware, the Tiffany flatware and the Chippendale chairs. Often she would lift her water glass and say how Lismore was her favorite Waterford pattern.

Once, when my mother and aunt were in the kitchen preparing to serve dinner, I saw her turn over a knife to authenticate it as Tiffany for herself.

Yes, Sandra loved status symbols. She loved the finest of everything, the more obvious the brand name the better. She loved that I wore Brooks Brothers shirts and khakis, even on Saturdays. Loved my Italian mocs. Loved that my scarves were cashmere and my sterling silver money clip monogrammed.

She loved that my winter coat was of classic camel hair and that I had a Barbour for rainy days. All these things that my mother sold her soul to make sure I had. "A good first impression is a lasting good impression," was her motto. Maybe this is why I have a weakness for ascots even now and have adopted a walking stick, not because I need one to walk but because I enjoy the look, like a good British gentleman of a certain age and class. Indoctrination, after all, dies hard, if it ever really dies away at all.

Sandra laughed when I told her my first life ambition was to drive a Greyhound Bus.

—That's so sweet, she cooed.

But when, embarrassed by this confession, I lied that my teenaged ambition was to become a scientist, wanting, stupidly, to impress her, because that's what you do when you're in love, right? Boast. Rewrite the resume for the job interview? What did she say?

—Gosh, Tony, and her eyes welled with admiration.

After we were married, Sandra quickly figured out that it was not only too late but that clothes may make the man but not necessarily the lover. The real me, under all the fancy trimmings, was an impotent lout. Lout. One of the kinder words she used to describe me. Not that I failed completely. Not as if she didn't practice emasculation as a contact sport. Oh, no. Sure, I knew the basics. I knew what was expected of me and I did it, what was expected of me. Sandra, on the other hand, made it known from the git-go that she was one very experienced lady and that I was one disappointingly inexperienced male. Lady. That's my word. Ugh. I need to expand my vocabulary!

As our sad marriage wore on, that's when the hurricane arrived in full force. Sandra lost whatever sense of social propriety she ever had. She regaled my friends with my sexual failings. She never missed an opportunity to humiliate me at work—at the time, I worked in the blood bank at the American Red Cross. She did not cross that threshold often because I wouldn't let her. But there were unavoidable times, like when there was a local disaster and the blood bank had to be kept open twenty-four-seven. She would swish in through the dock doors with a lunch box. "Here, Tony, something to keep you going. There's a ham sandwich and a pickle, in case you need one, wink, wink. And an orange juice. Hope you don't mind if I laced it with a little Viagra for later, ha ha. Just kidding. I mean, *that*'ll be the day!"

When she was around my friends, something unearthly and vicious found purchase in the slings and arrows she directed my way. Early on in our marriage, we made the mistake of inviting Sebastian, who was home visiting his mother, along with Breck, Adie and Mary Clay for dinner. All the old pack still in town. She'd met them all before, all except Sebastian, who was living in California. And everything had been hunky-dory. But once Sebastian was in the mix and we'd all had a couple of drinks, well, we reverted to idiot teenagers.

Three couples—Sandra loved couples—even though the other four were decidedly solo. Our apartment mirrored my mother's. Wingback Chippendale chairs in the living room, fine Persian rugs, Damask drapes, a tiger maple coffee table dating from the early 1800's, sterling ashtrays. We sat in the living room, in a circle reminiscent of what we as kids used to call Frank Sessions, laughing and joking the way we always did when we got together, talking old times, laced with inside jokes and allusions no one else on earth would get. We didn't mean to exclude her. We just fell into our old ways. Sandra resented it because it cut her out of the conversation. I wasn't smart enough, socially adept enough, nor did I really know her well enough then, to see her start to implode. So, when she came in with a silver salver of canapes—smoked salmon mousse, peach and prosciutto wraps, and something with watercress and cream cheese—the shit hit the fan.

—Canape, anyone? She offered cheerfully.

—Wow. Lawn clippings, Sebastian said, taking a watercress sandwich and examining it as if it would bite him back. Sandra scowled at that one, I remember. Hated being mocked, even though she was the queen of that form of torment. Adie, caught up in the spirit, and eyeing Sandra coyly, decided to twist the knife a little more.

—Be a sport, Sebastian, lawn clippings are full of nutrients. Like chlorophyll. You'd look good in green.

—It's not easy being green, Breck chimed in. And then we were all laughing. Laughing together, not laughing at Sandra. But that's not the way she heard it.

—Well, she said. I don't see what's funny. I spent hours making these canapes—

—Canapes? Mary Clay whispers to Adie. Where are the Fritos?

Adie, Sebastian, Breck and I choke back laughter. Fritos are an in joke with us. From when we were kids and stoked up on junk food.

But Sandra catches that. She thinks we are laughing at her, and I guess we are. Her pretentiousness. She puts the tray on the coffee table and standing very erect, shoulders back and bullet bra aimed at us like a double-barreled shotgun, she seems poised to make an announcement—or open fire.

Anthony

—Well, I just want to let you all know, Tony is a fairy. What he's got between his legs he couldn't make stand to attention for prize money. Not even a good hand job works. I've tried.

That shocked everyone into silence. It was Sandra's gotcha moment, not that I, we, didn't deserve it. And yet I could feel them all coming together for me without saying a word. A circling of the pack wagons.

—No one cares that my marriage to this milk toast is a disaster. I don't know why I invited any of you here this evening. It was just to—just to—please *him*. And yet you make fun of me and the effort I've made. Now get out of my house—

—Our house, I remind her. Which causes her to hiss—

—and take Tony with you!

Outside, we cluster together against the February chill and decide to go to Cunninghams, downtown, where we can get a proper dinner of ribs or steak and fries. By the time we get there, Sebastian has her pegged.

—Sandra, Sandra, the queen of apoplexy, give the girl a Pepsi to stuff inside her sexy, that ought to give Miss Sandra the thrill of Dostoyevsky.

Tears are running down my face, I'm laughing so hard. I love these guys so much. I hate Sandra more. We divorce. It is acrimonious because that is her given nature. She was born nasty. Indeed, once she had made two key discoveries about me, that I didn't want children and that there was no money, Sandra was done with me, the veil of civility tossed to the wind. Having a sperm donor was really the reason she pushed marriage in the first place, I finally figure out, what with her famous clock ticking toward spinsterhood and childlessness, both. And then that my mother and my aunt had poured their lifesavings into the front rooms of our little apartment and my private Catholic education, she wound herself up like a cobra and spat at my mother.

—He's nothing but a fag, your son.

I thought my mother was going to stroke out. I tried to intervene. Tried to get between those two women.

—Sandra, please!

—Don't you please Sandra me, you cocksucker.

And then my mother did faint and Auntie San, across the room, just stood aghast, her lower lip dangling. I wanted to kill Sandra. To grab her fat neck and break it. Instead, I shoved her, hard, toward the door, and in my sweetest voice said to her.

—Time to go back to the Caddy showroom, Sandra. To your real people. Where you belong.

I lost everything, needless to say. Sandra kept the apartment and everything in it, no matter where or how we acquired things, including gifts from my mother and my aunt. I lost, too, my mother's unquestioning regard; the door on the ugly truth had been cracked, giving life to her darkest fears for me. For her. Why she so wholeheartedly took Sandra at her word, I will never know. Not once, over the course of the rest of her life, did she ever ask me—me, her son—if Sandra was right about me.

Somehow Sebastian out in California got wind of the break up. Probably from Mary Clay, the Great Communicator. He sent me a postcard and all it said was NEVER DRIVE A CADILLAC in block letters.

Then there is Chad. Chad whom I loved and who I believe loved me. He came into my life in another kind of storm, a tornado, a real one that blew our town to smithereens. We both took refuge at the same bar—I, a creature void of form, Chad a proud gay man, wearing his most alluring skin. That's how I look back on that night now. We were together close to two years before—well, before that night. The night everything changed and Chad was gone.

I simply couldn't believe my good fortune, him finding me. He could be so kind. Such a wonderful sweet loving man. I thought we were

Anthony

building a life together. Looking back on that segment of my life, it was like playing house. Like Ozzie and Harriet. We used to joke about that, calling ourselves Ozzie and Ozzie. In our apartment, in our world, there were no bad guys, just the two of us bickering over which jam to spread on our toast and whose turn it was to make the bed or make a run to the deli or vacuum or take our shirts to the dry cleaners. Ordinary. Simple. Peaceful. Deluded. We pretended we were a married couple, exchanged gold bands, dreamt of a time when we might actually make it legal. Knowing full well that time would never come. But we fantasized about walking down the aisle all the time. After sex, sitting in bed smoking and drinking fine Scotch. We would both wear tuxes. That was a no-brainer. But where to have the ceremony—"No church!" said I—and the reception. Dreaming about the honeymoon was the best. We decided the only way to choose was to travel to every destination on our list, to sample the food and the romance. A villa in Italy, a castle in Ireland, the beaches of Costa Rica or Thailand, Richard Branson's Caribbean island, even if it were $40,000 a day. We were so happy, so naively happy in our dream world, that after we booked our tickets to Costa Rica, we went out to dinner to celebrate—to Cunningham's of course. Where we met and he seduced me. That was our mistake. Forgetting to hide our truth the moment we stepped out of our bubble, the moment we ventured into this hostile world wearing our happiness like a peacock its feathers. We were giddy with the excitement of our first "honeymoon" and so decided, a little drunk and a lot ecstatic, to take in the moonlit night with a walk in the park not two blocks from our apartment. I remember telling the police afterwards that I'd had a feeling we were being followed but whenever I snuck a glance behind us, there was no one there. We were walking arm in arm, Chad humming the Cole Porter tune, "Let's Do It," which got me laughing, all those double entendres combined with the prospect of our first trip together and how stinkingly, naively happy I was. He drew me down beside him on a park bench and we started to kiss, throwing all caution to the wind in the dark of night—

Everything after that is a blank. I know only what the police told me afterwards. Chad was killed instantly with what was a single blow to his head. A baseball bat or a tire iron or—or—what does it matter? I'm told I was dragged into the bushes. The doctor told me I must have protected my head with my arms because both were broken. They ruptured my spleen, tore up my liver and caused a lung to collapse. Presumably from being kicked. Something flammable was poured over my pants and set afire. All in all, I wish I'd suffered more. I wish I'd died with Chad, clinging to him, loving him.

Our friend Malcom came and sat with me in the hospital every day until I was released. He showed me the headline, buried in the second section of the newspaper. Man Killed, Lover Injured in Jefferson Park. Lover Injured. How did the reporter know we were gay?

I stayed in our apartment, even though our friends counseled me to leave those memories behind. But how could I? That was all I had left of Chad. He had been so kind to me the night of that tornado. He had always been so sweet. I didn't change the sheets on our bed for weeks, until the scent of him was really and truly gone.

Rewriting my destiny, assassinating that old self—and making way for a new one—to invite Edward to rise from the ashes of Tony's misery and reclaim life anew, is the stuff of hope. But even this simple desire comes at a price I didn't know and wasn't at all prepared to pay. Just the other day I, with my new name, finally managed to have my social security number changed, not just my new name with my old number. No, an altogether

Anthony

new number, the ultimate American identity switch. Another nuisance in the elaborate process. Uncle Sam frowns on changing your number. You have to go to the Social Security office, fill out a form and then convince them of potential bodily harm or harassment. It took me three tries to collect the medical records and police reports, enough to satisfy the bureaucrat sitting opposite me. Who never in her stunted little life had been anything other than delighted with her stunted little life. Had never asked herself the question, Is this all there is in this world for me?

I stood in a line forty minutes long just to get to her. So, yes, all was revealed to this weedy woman who took down my story, clipped the pages of the reports together in neat and unerring order, repeating out loud, in a room clamoring with other Social Security supplicants: hate crime, assault. I watched the heads spin to listen. I felt the people in line behind me and in lines on either side of me, leaning in to listen and judge. *Gay bashing*, I hear them thinking. Including her.

My heart thunders against my shattering rage, breaking through into another form of mortification. She has no right. No right to exhume the memory of Chad, the one good thing that ever happened to me, apart from Sebastian so long ago, to entertain this crowd of homophobes.

Quit it, Tony. You are Edward now.

I take my walking stick and stride out of the Social Security office, eyes shielded from all those prying eyes by the rim of my battered old fedora. My new number, matched to my new name, is processing. My head is high but I feel numb, dead, from my frozen expression down. Suddenly, I am struck with what I have done.

What if, when I get to heaven, Chad is there but he doesn't recognize this Edward fellow?

I stop in my tracks.

Don't be stupid, I tell myself. There is no heaven.

But what if there is? What. If. There. Is?

I head back to my apartment, with its doorman and double foyer, and pour myself a stiff bourbon. Standing on the balcony overlooking the city where I was born and raised. I toss back the Bulleit and pour myself another. And another.

There are just three things more I need to do to complete my disappearance: quit my job, find another place to live where no one knows me and walk the old neighborhood once last time.

For forty-five years, I have worked for the American Red Cross. I am head of statewide blood distribution now, but I started in our local blood bank when I was sixteen. It was a summer job, massaging plasma, dating blood donations, packaging up deliveries for hospitals. It was easy. It was comfortable. I felt important, that my job was a lifesaving one. Meanwhile, my mother pushed for college.

—Maybe a Jesuit one. Loyola or Fordham, my mother urges.

—Or Notre Dame, my aunt suggests.

—I'm done with priests and Catholic schools, I announce to their collective horror. Instead, I sign on permanently with the ARC, and it is the ARC I must now leave behind, with the rest of me.

Handing in my resignation is so painless I get the impression I've become redundant and they are merely kind in keeping me on. It is true, the computer will never replace pen and paper for me. No Excel spreadsheets. Give me my legal pad and a ruler. Of course, my pride is a bit nicked by the ease with which personnel shows me the door, in spite of a flurry of kind notes and well wishes from my co-workers. Beloved, some of them say. I smile, nod to them all a congenial farewell, and hold on to that as I walk to my car. Beloved? What a croc.

Anthony

    Instead of driving back to my apartment, which is all packing boxes and garbage bags, I drive to my old neighborhood. There's a service alley that used to run behind mansions that have all been torn down and replaced with fifties apartment complexes. Near the end of this alley, are eight parking slots that look down on an apartment quadrangle situated about forty feet below my car. I think, My God, Mother and Auntie San had to carry the groceries down these cement stairs, with its rickety, rusted, wrought-iron banister all those years. I must have seen them do it. I must have helped them do it. But I have no recollection of this labor, on their parts or mine. It is a sad omen, and I resist my first impulse, the reason I drove here in the first place, which was to visit where I once lived. Instead, I head across the alley to a tiny path that used to be there when I was a child, a shortcut through to the next street. Although overgrown, and the width of a child not an adult man, I crouch and push through musty leaves and grasping blackberry brambles, half kneeling. Making myself boy-sized again or trying to. Until a branch catches on my fedora and whips the hat off my head. Fumbling, going down on one knee, I retrieve it, dust it off, remembering, as I always do when I put it on, that it once belonged to Sebastian's father. This tattered, misshapen hat that is no compliment to my wardrobe.

    Once I emerge on the other side of the path, I drop down the street to Adie's house. Of course, it isn't Adie's anymore. But the memories fly back at me like old friends. Like the time Adie was home alone, when we were all about thirteen and her parents were away for the weekend. Sebastian and I shinnied up a drain pipe to the garage roof, and from there hopped onto the second-floor roof and, bent over like burglars, tiptoed up to her dormer window. It was nearly midnight; she was reading in bed. With our faces schmooshed against the window screen, flattening our noses to make us all the more hideous, we called out her name. She screamed so loudly it silenced the cicadas and porch lights popped on all around us. Sebastian and I laughed so hard we nearly rolled off the roof.

All that is reenacted in my mind's eye, just standing here on the sidewalk, looking up at that dormer.

I round the corner of Adie's house and head up the hill toward Sebastian's. It looks so small, like a scale model of the place that was such a sanctuary for me. Across the street, too, the steep hill we used to rush up playing Americans fighting the Germans and the Japanese, is hardly more than a rise above street level. Perspective. It's all perspective. When we are small the world around us looms large; when we are grown, we cannot imagine ever bending far enough down to drink from the water fountains in our first schools.

For maybe an hour, maybe more, maybe less, I lean against a sycamore tree on the edge of the sidewalk, staring at Sebastian's old house. If the opportunity to enter presented itself, I would refuse. I can see inside perfectly clearly, I can hear Sebastian's record player and his sweet tenor voice, a little like Pavarotti but without the range. I am inside with him, the others too—Adie, Breck, Jude, Mary Clay and Grady and whatever other hangers-on show up, and there were many. Just an ordinary summer afternoon.

Sebastian and I dream up spontaneous, irreverent—the more irreverent the better—pranks. We are the Prankensteins, Sebastian and me. Those days, his company, when he was my best friend and we spoke a language unto ourselves. It hurts me to be here this afternoon—the ordinariness of it then, the unattainability of it now. So much lived and lost and not even noticed until hindsight comes along and nips me in the butt. I really want to hate Sebastian. He may have had no idea, but he was a mean teaser. He teased me with his friendship. In sacred ritual, we became blood brothers at his suggestion, each of us cutting a forefinger with his Scout knife and pressing our fingers together. We had a secret handshake and a secret code.

I push off from the sycamore with a tip of my hat, pausing only a second to take one last look at the little arts and crafts bungalow, with its yellowed and peeling stucco, which had come, Sebastian's mother told us, straight out of the Sears Roebuck catalog. Even that is a fond memory, the idea of a house in a department store catalog. I cannot help but smile and head up the street, working my way back to my car. Past the field where we played pick-up football and baseball. Past the walnut tree we thought was as tall as the Eiffel Tower back in the days when we would climb up into its thinnest limbs. Or he would, and I would watch from safely below. Past the haunted house that wasn't haunted at all, just occupied by Miss Green, a spinster straight out of the nineteenth century, whom we decided, randomly, the way kids do, was a witch. She had an ice box and ice delivered every week from the back of a dripping cart. She never came outside except to get her knives sharpened by the traveling man or to buy strawberries from the hawker in summer. When she saw us, she would tilt her head down and curl her lip. No wonder we thought she was a witch. No wonder when we couldn't find Adie one day, Sebastian and I got it into our heads that she's been kidnapped by Miss Green and needed rescuing. From the sidewalk outside her house we yelled and yelled for Adie and talked ourselves into believing we could just hear her voice, coming from inside that house, begging for help. So, we broke Miss Green's picture window with bricks, to help Adie escape. Turns out, Adie wasn't there at all, and the old lady called the police. We took off and ran smack dab into Adie walking to Sebastian's house. She had been at her gymnastics class. Which we would have remembered, she told us, if we had half a brain between us.

Ambient Light

After that, we avoided walking anywhere near that rundown old dump. It was later that same summer that the old lady was found dead by a neighbor, partially eaten by her cat, rumor had it.

The house there now is not the same one. Hers was a teardown, of course, once her body was removed. The rumor was that she was a millionaire, with her mattress stuffed with dough. Sebastian and I thought about a midnight raid but chickened out.

Everything seems tinged with shenanigans as I walk back to my car. The apartment buildings we played hide and seek in as they were being built. The old chicken coup and the grapevines draped over it, vines we rode like Tarzans swinging among the apes. Great traps we dug and covered with twigs and leaves to capture some evil enemy or other. Streaking through the neighborhood on our bikes, standing up on the pedals, reaching for the sky. Those were the days, all right.

OK. Yes. I miss him. See how he prowls around in my head still?

When I get to my car, I know I have one more visit to pay, so I head down the old concrete staircase to our apartment quadrangle, gripping the railing for dear life, leaning on my walking stick just in case it gives out. I walk up and stop before the sorry excuse for our old front stoop. Five steps up to a concrete platform, two side-by-side doors, two identical black rubber doormats, two separate apartments. Ours was on the right. Until this second, a part of me, one given purchase only in my nighttime fantasies, wondered if I could move back in. If I could rent the apartment my mother and Auntie San and I had called home and live out my disappearance in plain sight, in splendid, ironic anonymity. Instead, I am overwhelmed with the sad truth. I grew up here but with few points of comparison. I knew only my own and Sebastian's home life, and in truth his was not so different from mine. His father was dead, mine had abandoned me. His mother worked, as did mine. He had a house but that's because his father lived long enough to buy it. These women who minded us, loved us but resented us too. So, our little apartment seemed vast and splendidly appointed to my child's eye. Not so now, on this March afternoon, with adult reality shining its cold light on my old life.

As a boy, I was not encouraged to dream. I was encouraged to be a "good" man and a "good" Catholic and to take care of them in their old age. Standing outside now brings tears to my eyes. The world my mother and aunt created for me was a lie, a big fat lie, all bells and whistles and no substance. I realize now, I have come back here not to actually consider repossessing this apartment and the past it represents. I have come to make myself see, so I can let go of this part of me too.

It was only after my mother died and my aunt was ailing too that Auntie San told me the truth about my father, that there never was a marriage, despite the gold band my mother wore on her ring finger.

—He was a soldier, just back from the war. He took advantage of your mother.

I knew it was uncommon for Catholic girls who got into trouble to keep their babies. But when I asked Auntie San about this, she waved me off.

—Aren't you glad she did? she said, smiling wanly. And that was all she would tell me.

Later, after they were both dead, I found three letters in a man's hand among my mother's papers. They were unopened. A note under the elastic said simply, 'Destroy.' I did not honor her wishes. They told me little, a name, Jerome, and three pleas to know if he had a son or a daughter. A son, a son, a son, I wanted to shout. Each letter had a different return address and the most recent was over sixty years old. When I was about six. He's long dead by now, if there had been any way to trace him. But with no last name and no fixed address, Jerome is as lost to me now as my mother wanted him to be back then. It is too late anyway for the questions knowing him might have answered.

Suddenly, looking up at our old apartment door, it all strikes me as hilarious. I strike me as hilarious. How preposterous I am. I am laughing now, bent double, hands on my knees gasping for breath between sobs of laughter. To think I gave enough thought to trying to re-enter this dingy little world to come here today. I sit down on the stoop step to collect myself, to blow my nose and catch my breath. An old man now. A silly old man. A door slams at another apartment in the complex and a child tears down the cement walk. Passing me, because there is no other way for him to go, he looks at me like what I am, a stranger. His eyes go big and he gives me a wide berth. Beware of strangers, his mother has wisely counseled him. A stranger! Exactly. Just what I wish to be. Thank God, I think. I can walk away. Chuckling to myself, I see the irony of it all. Priceless. As fine a place, no, the perfect place, to deposit the ghost of Tony for eternity. Edward won't be back.

The drive to the bridge and the next state takes no time. I am the disappeared.

Mary Clay

—Oof!

Pain, pain. I register pain and   and   something else. I open my eye to the blazing sun. Something pink gauzes over the other one. A petal? From my cherry tree? Oh, my God, what am I doing on the ground? My face pressed into the earth. I try to wink away the petal. I try to wink away the ruthless sun bearing down on me with its burning kiss. A lover turned rapist. I close my eyes again. The petal flutters off. What I see behind my lids is like a slo-mo video.

    I am
          dropping
                dropping to my knees.

Then I pitch forward onto my side. Silent, slow motion. Like a cowboy gunned down at the O.K. Corral. I try to take stock. So   so   so— I'm on my side, my left side. Yes. That eye gazes into a sea of pink petals. My nose presses into them. I smell the spring sweet grass beneath. The other eye combs the newly mowed lawn. Like a chipmunk might. Or a mole. For a moment I am suspended in surreal imagery.

Then

pain.

Oh, the jackhammer pounding in my head! Inside my chest, my heart stampedes. Why can't I move? Haul myself up? Call myself stupid for tripping over a tree root? Or turning my ankle in a mole hole? What is happening to me? What has happened? Was there even

ever

a tree root?

a hole?

HELP ME!   HELP ME! I scream. But the words don't form, only zing around in my skull. I try again HELP ME! What's happened to my voice? I hear myself screaming at the top of my lungs but no sound reaches the world. Like in nightmares when danger is bearing down and you cannot make a sound to save yourself.

HELP   HELP! I bellow silently.

WHAT HAS HAPPENED TO ME?

HELP ME!

I plead with the gods to answer. I plead.

I try to scream   but   nothing   nothing!   Just a gurgle. Maybe it's a nightmare and I need only to pull myself out of sleep's torture chamber—

My phone my phone my phone

In my hip pocket. But   but   but   I can't roll over.

Mary Clay

    Push

          push

                push up!

My body, my body, detached from my mind, like a yawl broken from its mooring, flounders. No   No   this is no nightmare—

    OK, Mary Clay,

            don't panic   don't panic

Methodical. Be methodical. Only way to save yourself. Take stock. Left hand accounted for. Under my body. Fingers working. But the right? I cannot feel my right arm. I try to push myself up on my left elbow

    but I can't

        I fall back

Still I have seen enough. My right arm limp on the ground behind me. O, God. SOMEONE HELP ME! PLEASE! the banshee screams in my head—

    Oh, the relentless, torturing sun! Burning   burning   down. This sun I have always revered as the engine of life in my garden and all the gardens I have tended since college. How I love to turn my face to it like a giant sunflower, feasting on its rays, lusting for it when stormy or dark skies rob me of my psychic fuel. Or did

    But not now

        Not today when I roast upon its spit.

I am breathing like a sprinter. As if all the air in the world has been sucked out and my lungs must claw their way to the finish line. Like I'm drowning in fresh air. OK, Mary Clay. Calm down. Calm down right now. Think. You have to think. It's the only way to save yourself.

    But I can't!   I can't!

WHAT HAS HAPPENED TO ME? My head   my head there is so much pain! I cannot think. As if a truck were rolling over it, splintering it into a million shards, and my brains are shot out like toothpaste.

HELP ME, I silently wail. SOMEBODY!

Suddenly I get it.

Suddenly I know: My grandmother, my mother and my mother's sister.

    No

        No

            Oh, no!

Panic bucks inside me. A bronco pitches me this way and that. Terror rising.

I could lie here for days   abed on these perfect pink petals   here under the gnarled old cherry tree I planted twenty-five years ago in my grandmother's garden after I inherited this place from her. Dahlia tubers strewn around everywhere too   I must have dropped them thrown them, falling. And the daffodils   mocking me   nodding their heads like a pitying Greek chorus, keening for me in brilliant yellow.

    no   No   NO!   Someone MUST come!

Mary Clay

Breathe, Mary Clay, breathe. In through the nose, out through the mouth. Like the comforting man on Headspace tells me to do. A meditation technique. One. Two. One, two. And another. You know the drill
use your Pilates training
                I squirm or try to
Please, somebody. Somebody come! Walk through the front gate and around the house beside the sun porch, under the canopy of arborvitae and down to the bottom of the garden where I lie.

       I

             Will

                    It

                          Now

                                Soon

Somebody?   Anybody?
But why would anyone do that? Not even the mail carrier would stray this far into my property without an invitation. Not even the neighbor's cat would venture here. Oh God, I must get to my phone. Try again, Mary Clay, try again to roll over. If you can just reach over to your right hip pocket free your left arm
But no, I can't do it—
Wait! Yes. Of course   they'll miss me when I don't turn up for my shift   at the restaurant this afternoon. I'm due in at five and
   it   must be
Look at the angle of the sun, Mary Clay. Think. What time is it now?

                            Nearly four?

—You can recruit a waiter off a sidewalk, but a bartender is an artist, Mackie always says whenever I ask for time off.

Do I have that long? Can I wait that long?

       YES

             Because what choice do I have?

                   None   None at all

Mackie. He will call yes, no. He will call and when I don't can't answer he will curse me like an Irish sailor. But he won't think I'm in trouble. Except with him. He's already giving me what-for for being late. I can hear him. And I want to shout,

       HELP ME
            COME LOOKING FOR ME
               MACKIE
                   PLEASE

My head, my head! I close my eyes against the terrible pounding provoked by the sun, as if it were a red-hot skewer thrust into my eyeball.

Think, Mary Clay.

    Stay awake.

                Do not fall asleep. Think—

Mary Clay

Yes   yes—   Maybe they'll miss me this afternoon at the garden center. When I haven't showed up to pick up that half ton of mulch. Or Fat Francis gets impatient   she is always impatient   even when I show up on time   so she'll call the garden center and say, Where is that lame excuse for a gardener, Mary Clay Lambert, with my mulch? And the garden center will call 911. Only they wouldn't do that, call 911. Why would they do that? Mary Clay, YOU need to call 911

Wait, girlfriend, there's Adie! Adie! Yes, you are supposed to talk to Adie this afternoon, remember? She's calling to talk you out of lending money to Jude. Not that I have loads of available cash. I don't. Never have. But Jude's my friend, so if I can help—

Always-down-on-her-luck Jude, Adie calls her.

Adie wants to talk me out of it, so she said she'd call. This afternoon. Now.

My phone! My phone. I just need to get to my phone. And then what, Mary Clay? You can't answer it. Oh, but I can grunt. Can I even do that?

—Uhuhuhuhuhuh!

Yes, I can!   She will know right away I'm in trouble and she will call 911! Yes. I just need to   to   get my phone   Oh, shit

    I just

        can't

            free my arm

Ambient Light

Wait. Count to ten. Think, Mary Clay, think.

She's in another state

does that matter when you dial 911?

I am so very tired. So very weak. My eyes, I cannot focus. I feel exhaustion sitting on my chest, Horton the Elephant, who cannot use a phone either. A tear escapes my skyward eye. It tickles across my cheek, catches in the fold of my nostril, runs down my lip and into my gaping mouth. I could lie here forever. In my garden. Lying on a blanket of cherry petals. And perish. It strikes me— such a strange and beautiful shroud, even now as the coastal breeze coaxes more loose petals to drift around me, onto me.

Just before I fight my way back into consciousness, the moment before I open my eyes, I feel the feather on my cheek, being so lightly drawn down my face like the breath of a lover. I know it is Sebastian. He is teasing me awake. All afternoon we have been playing by the river, stuffing ourselves with potato chips and Cokes, smoking Camels, watching the barges lumber past.

—Let's go skinny dipping, I say. I dare. I want to see him naked. I want him to see me naked. I want him to want me. We are fifteen and intoxicated with life.

—In that? Sebastian says, pointing to the filthy river. Over my dead body. It's full of floaters, MC. Turds. Tootsie Rolls.

And we both collapse in a hail of the giggles. The idea. It is the idea, the image of feces as perfectly formed as Tootsie Rolls in the water that is in itself the color of creamy chocolate milk, that sends us into a flood stage of stitch-in-the-side, tear-teasing, shove-festing belly laughing. We strip our clothes off and run for the water. I see Sebastian's perfect body. Perfect cock. He goes first and, ever the gentleman, does not look at me. We splash around in the gross water, Sebastian retrieving one stick after another that the current brings our way, waving each in the air and pronouncing them Goose Turd, Dog Turd, King Kong Turd, until I nearly drown from laughing, seeing his gap-toothed smile and water spiked hair, and wish only to be next to him, to hold him while the river and all life flow around us. Instead, he crawls up the bank, and ever the gentleman, keeps his back turned while he pulls on jeans and I slip back into my cutoffs and tee shirt, which sticks to my breasts, giving my nipples perfect definition. I see his eyes find them, then turn away, fumbling in his pocket for a smoke.

—You can touch them. If you want. I say, reaching for his hand. But he pulls away, his ears suddenly roseate.

—Aw, shucks, I'm not that sort of guy, he says mimicking Barney Fife, while the blush, careening down his face to his neck says something else. Something I don't understand. And when I begin to laugh, he laughs too. I roll over on my stomach and he crawls onto my butt. I hear the click of his Zippo, and drink in the sweetness of his first exhalation.

—Pinned you now! he says with exaltation.

—Pass the fag, I say. Sebastian rolls off my back. Hands me the Camel. Stretching out on the grassy bank now, we lie side by side, smoking. Trading intimacies.

—I saw you making out with Breck.

—It was nothing. I make out with everybody. Wanna try me?

Sebastian rolls onto his side, props himself up on one elbow, fag hanging from his lip James Dean style, and looks at me.

—Why do you do that?

—Do what?

—Suck face with everyone.

—Dunno. It's fun. Wanna try?

I lean toward his face but he shakes his head.

—These lips, these virgin kissers, are reserved for sacred duty, Sebastian says loftily, rolling onto his stomach and propping himself up on one elbow. Place this fag between your lips, he says placing it in my mouth. And now my lips and your lips will be joined in holy matrimony. He is bastardizing Shakespeare.

That stings. I turn my head, refuse the smoke. I change the subject.

— I think my mom and dad are going to get a divorce. I speak to the fair-weather clouds floating overhead, a blue river with fluffy white sails racing across it.

—Do you care?

—I don't know. No one does it. Gets divorced. I shrug away my worry, the sense of my world imploding.

—I found out my father has another kid. Sebastian speaks to the skylark flitting overhead. I have a brother, and no one told me.

—Wow. That's big, Sebastian. Like monumental.

He rolls onto his back beside me, our shoulders just touching. We are silent for a minute but curiosity gets the best of me. It usually does.

—How did you find out?

—My mother. Dropped it like a meteoroid in my lap a couple of nights ago at dinner. When she was pissed and pissed off at me. Because I said I wouldn't perform anymore illegal rescues.

—Illegal rescues?

—You know. Driving her car without a license to haul her off some park bench.

We are silent again. So silent we can hear the river washing up the banks, the hum of mosquito wings flying overhead, the sound of a leaf drifting down to earth.

—My father had a first wife, he says finally.

—What's his name, your new brother? Will you ever meet him?

—I hope not. She wouldn't tell me.

—Where is he now?

Sebastian shrugs. His hand finds mine and our fingers interlock. We do not look at each other but up at the sky. He puffs the Camel to a stub and flicks it expertly toward the river. Whose secret was worse, I wonder, his mother's, keeping that truth from him? Or his father's, not bringing that son along when he remarried? I have so many questions, but it is just too peaceful here on the river bank holding hands with Sebastian. I don't want to wreck this moment. I also know, somehow, instinctively, I guess, not to grill him. I drift to sleep warmed by the sun and the proximity of our bodies, feeling his hurt but not knowing what to say.

But it is not the feather Sebastian drew across my cheek to wake me that I'm feeling, to tell me it is time to head home. I open my eyes. He is not there. No. What I see is an ant engaged in lugging a piece of millet fallen from my birdfeeder just past my open eye, that one that is pressed against the ground. No. What I feel is a wisp of my own grey hair, come loose from the topknot I swirled at the top of my head this morning, with no care for style, only for containment, flitting across my cheek in the fitful April breeze.

I close my eyes again. My body, my mind wish only to recapture that moment by the river when Sebastian and I could hurt each other with a look, forgive each other with a bump of the shoulder, haul each other up when we were down with some hilarious insult, be sister to his brother, and brother to my sister. That pure, unsullied love that we never spoke of because how do you find adolescent words for something like that?

Sebastian is dead.

All those long years ago that was just yesterday.

And now so am I—

        I no longer feel the sun overhead.

Suddenly my phone vibrates in my pocket. My body vibrates with its urgency, my urgency. But I cannot reach it. I want to, in some distant, long, nearly forgotten way, but it is only in my tumbledown mind's eye, distorted now like a kaleidoscope breaking, breaking up into different fragments of unconnected color.

I see only Sebastian, his forgiving mocking welcoming ironic come-hither smile beaming down on me, a kiss of another sort.

        I exhale

Grady

thank you god for most this amazing day—my good day mantra sings in my head.

    I'm going for thirty-five miles today. Backroads. Two lanes only, no highways. Too dangerous getting mixed up with speeding cars. The traffic on these roads, lanes really, is sporadic. Farm equipment because it's sowing season and the occasional car. Especially this time of day, midday, there aren't many vehicles to contend with.

    Heading north toward Superior. Spring sun burning my back just as my calves begin to burn with the effort. Whoa. Spring is a long time coming up here but as I pedal past, there is wisteria draped from an arbor and I'm coming up on a wall of forsythia. Up the hill I'm climbing now, the country world goes by in slow mo. Suits me. My life is in slo mo these days, too. Double-wides and houses just one step up from shacks are circled in daffodils and window boxes with tulips, high enough off the ground the deer can't get them. Their winter wood piles down almost to scrap.

    On the downhill, I fly! Just let her rip. The wind whipping what's left of my hair back off my head. Beth wants me to wear a helmet. It's an ongoing fight. But, like when I was a kid, I want to feel every instant I'm riding a bike. I want to be exposed. I want the risk. Though when I was a squirt,

Ambient Light

I didn't know I was taking a risk riding like a madman, sometimes with no hands, zooming down a long long hill. Is risk greater once you know you're taking it? I wonder. Never mind. I don't think of these excursions in the country as any kind of risk. Maybe from a bee slapping you in the forehead if you happen to cruise into one. But that's all. I ride to ride. I ride to exercise, because that's what the doc wants me to do for my heart. I ride for goals to attain. Today is thirty-five miles, my longest since I started cycling seriously four months ago. So, this flashy enamel blue helmet Beth bought me last Christmas is in the garage gathering dust. Though I do wear it to please Beth when the two of us go for a ride together. Or did. Not anymore. Poor Beth. My poor poor Beth. Housebound now. Bad scare with breast cancer. She's on the mend after a double mastectomy, chemo, and radiation. Thank god. But she's become suddenly fearful of everything. *What if I fall off?* she worries when I suggest a bike ride. *What if I fall off, Grady?* Nothing like a taste of your own mortality to make you tread lightly. I mean, who can blame her? Not me.

So, now I ride alone. Just thinking that makes me feel like some kind of cowboy, the lone ranger with a receding hairline and progressive lenses. I'm smiling, laughing even, and that throws me into a teeter on this amazing downhill. A quick correction, restoration of concentration, zeal and I'm good as gold. Coming off the hill, I sit up straight and coast. See if I can coast for a couple hundred yards. Cornfields for as far as the eye can see to my west, soybeans, it looks like, on my left. A stand of aspen on either side of the road way up ahead looks to indicate a town. More like a village. I'd stop and poke around normally but I want to get my miles in and head back so I can be there for a five o'clock Face Time with Adie.

Adie. Wow. Found her on Facebook. There's much about that platform I don't care for, mostly all the political garbage and ads that pop up making me know—*know*—that Big Brother is alive and well and living at

Grady

their headquarters in Menlo Park. But Facebook is good for connecting. They even put potential "friends" on your feed, and one day, a couple of weeks ago, there was Adie. At least that's who I thought it had to be. I messaged her: Is this the Adie that had flower-lined brown denim bell bottoms? If it were Adie, the Adie I knew light-years ago when we were teenagers, she would get the reference. I noticed those flowers once when she was stripping off her jeans to go swimming. I never forgot them. It was the shock, of watching a girl peel out of her clothes, even if she had a bikini on underneath. It was also the shock of those flowers, that feminine touch hidden underneath her tomboy jeans like the ultimate tease.

It was that Adie. After fifty some years and very much alternate lives. She messaged me that she didn't remember the jeans but she recognized my name.

—Long time no hear from, she wrote.

So we agreed to FaceTime this afternoon. Couldn't be before today because of Beth's surgery and me having to clean up the loose ends of selling my business and really, finally, formally retiring, although Beth would argue we've been retired for about twenty years already because I made us wealthy with shoes.

I slow down to pass through the village, which actually turns out to be more like a small town, so I have to stop long enough to consult a map. The old-fashioned paper kind because I find them the most satisfying. Plus, the green dots of scenic routes are my go-to for itineraries. I have to weave my way through traffic and three stop lights before I get to the road I want to take from there north and can think about shoes again.

Thom McAn franchises made me a wealthy man. Who'd have ever thought that shoes could make you rich? But I am rich by anybody but Bill Gates' standards. And I got out before the internet began to wipe out retail in the 90s. Lemme think, lemme think. Yeah, total, I must have owned twelve or fifteen franchises located in malls all over the Midwest, from Nebraska to Cleveland. I'd have to go through my books to remember just how many because for a while there I bought and sold them like I was playing the market. I should do that, go through my books, just to see just how big my shoe empire was. It'd be interesting to know. Sort of. But really, my head is out here in the fresh air, riding my bike, where fresh air is stuffed up my nose. All that business stuff is ancient history. But I really should pay some kind of homage to old Thom McAn for what he did to turn my life around. On the path I was taking out of college—bass guitarist in a band—I was burning out by thirty and pretty disillusioned by just about everything. I had more drugs in my system than the local pharmacy—I was the poster child for STD, and I was broke.

Pumping now, pumping hard. This hill, this one is a bear. Man, maybe I'm too old for this after all. Maybe thirty-five miles of Wisconsin country roads is too much for this old man. Gotta keep in mind, gotta focus on the downhill to come. I tell myself I can get off and walk this two-wheeler up this goddamned endless hill if I have to. But that would be capitulating. And I'm not a quitter. Never have been, never will be.

                make this fucking hill—
           I will
     I will
I will
   Whoaaaaa!
     Down
        down
           down.

Like the first drop on a roller coaster. My speedometer says thirty miles an hour. I am flying! I can feel the adrenaline ripping through me.

Grady

Such a fine fine high. Like sex. Like ecstasy. Here I am, seventy-two years old and standing up on my pedals as the landscape blurs out beside me. Wow. I am a sucker for cheap thrills, that's for sure.

On the flats, I get reflective again, when the ride is just a sit-back coast. Guess I've reached that stage in life where I spend more time looking back than I do looking forward. Because the stop sign is just up ahead. The tarmac is narrowing toward an inevitable horizon. Which I try not to think about. So, like every old fisherman, I cast my line back for the bottom feeders not ahead for the jumping salmon. Somehow, I'm stuck on shoes this afternoon. Because I do owe Thom McAn our snowbird house in Vero Beach, our trips all over the world, even one around the world on a private jet. Oh, Beth loved that one. Such a soft touch for luxury.

Downsizing was a tough decision. I felt put out to pasture, so that's when I got into cycling. The club goes out every Sunday for ten or fifteen miles. These longer rides get the endorphins flowing and the blood pumping in a more intense way. All good, for an old man. Not that I'm old old. But I am reminded every day, just by where we're living now, that our futures are measured in weekly meds dispensers, not hopes, dreams, ambitions.

OK. Hold on. What's an eighteen-wheeler doing on this road? I'll just pedal up and see. Oh, well, OK. Farm equipment. Must be headed to the local feed store, wherever that is. I'm just going to cut off up here at the intersection and take the back, back route. Maybe even make it forty miles today. A personal best. But I'm not following those fumes for miles, no sirree.

Yeah, Adie. My first girlfriend. I can remember everything about her, down to her toenails. Seriously. She had a really big big-toe nail. I remember that. Used to tease her about her cookie sheet nails. Yeah.

She didn't like that much. What I remember first—there is a picture in my mind. I must have taken her in, observed her in this pose, absorbing every atom of her, so closely it's as imprinted in my memory as anything could be. Leaning against a radiator somewhere. Left foot crossed over right. One elbow on the wall, her other hand looped casually around her own front. Long brown hair down to below her shoulder blades, that glistened with gold threads when the light above caught it. And a come-hither look to her direct green eyes and unsmiling lips that was—what? Today, I'd say that look unnerved me then. Then? I think my response was pure lust. And when she spoke? Oh, I am eager to hear that voice again, experience that groin rush. Her voice was smoky, deep. Like Lauren Bacall. It was one of my great adolescent disappointments that I never got into her pants. I never figured out what she was waiting for. We did everything but. But she just wouldn't budge. I deluded myself that she was saving herself for marriage. Which I knew was a lie. Had to be a lie. She was too hot, too eager. She just said no to me. Many was the time she pronounced a no-marriage-under-any-circumstances philosophy of feminism. I remember coming home from college my freshman year, looking her up and announcing I'd finally gotten laid. If I could erase one single thing I've done in my life, that announcement would be it. Was I bragging? Punishing her? Trying to show her what she'd missed? God, being a teenager was excruciating.

    Now I'm pedaling alongside a beautiful tree-lined brook, swollen with winter melt-off, running fast and furious over rocks just poking through the water rushing over and around them. Northern white cedars, aromatic with spring sap, line its banks. I dismount and push my bike to lean it against a tree, then stumble down the bank to sit a minute and feel the spray. I am so damned lucky. In this moment, by this brook. In my life, so blessed with a wife I love who loves me back. Two grown boys, men, who are leading productive lives and raising young families Beth and I can spoil. Reasonable health. Still active. Hell, pedaling forty miles in one day! Couldn't have, wouldn't have done that when I was twenty! Nothing I want for. Nothing. Except maybe Beth's lemon bars. For Christmas, she gave me twenty tickets for twenty different baked treats. I can cash one in whenever I want and the next day, Voila! a sourdough loaf, beignets, Linzer torte, whatever. But I'm saving the lemon bars, because that is my all-time favorite thing she bakes. Maybe this afternoon, I will call in that chit after my talk with Adie.

But now, I lie back on the bank of the brook, its rocky nubs pushing into my shoulders, listening. Closing my eyes, the rush of water over and around rocks, forms a glissando in my mind's ear, from G sharp to E. I wonder, no I am convinced, there is no dissonance in nature. As with all forms of music, my spirit is stilled. All the pedaling adrenaline subsides. I am the water, I am its song. I am a simple vessel cast out onto the brook to be carried off by its burbling chorus. Carry me anywhere. To the sea, just so long as I don't have to open my eyes and spoil this perfect pleasure.

Oy. But I must go if I want to make it back in time for Adie. Eyes open now, I look back at the brook, just a teeming water course now, and scramble back up the bank. I refresh myself with a slug of water from my water bottle and mount up again. I can still make my outbound goal if I stop dilly-dallying around. Back in the saddle, I can feel the first signs of butt soreness, even though I'm wearing biking shorts with big foam crotch pads. A mile or so more on this detour and I reconnect with the main road. Main road being a relative term. Soon though I'm back on my appointed route, worked out this morning over coffee. Four more easy miles up the road and I reach Wausau and start the trek back. If there are no delays or detours, I should be home by four fifteen. My date with Adie is at five. Plenty of time to sit in the hot tub to ease these old muscles and my poor posterior and then grab a shower. For some obscure reason, I want to get cleaned up, look like a million bucks for Adie. What's that all about? It's not like she will be able to smell my aftershave—I wonder what she'll think when she sees me? All that curly black hair she used to love running her fingers through, gone. A wispy little comb-over, all that's left on this old pate.

Of course, the first, or nearly the first thing we will talk about is Sebastian. Dead now, oh, these thirty years. Really? Thirty? I start doing the math. No, not thirty but almost. Frankly, I don't want to talk about him. It's like he hacks my mind. The thought of Adie automatically frees him to plant cookies in my otherwise perfect day. Seriously, I am the only one who believes that Sebastian sold himself down the river, that he took his prodigious gifts and threw them overboard, that he traded music for sex. I know, I know he didn't want to compete with his famous brother. Telling me time and again, it was Carl, not him who was gifted, who was destined for the Rock & Roll Hall of Fame. I know that's what he said. But I know how gifted Sebastian was. I can hear that perfect tenor a cappella now, that perfect pitch. But he abdicated it all. He wanted to learn keyboard, so I taught him. He wanted to learn harmonica, so I taught him. Whatever musical instrument he touched he turned to gold. The Midas of music. While I, who had studied music since grade school, could not keep up. I would teach him and before I could blink, he would play better than I, better than I ever would or could. So naturally gifted, so disparaging of it. As if he were unworthy. Well, we all felt we were unworthy when we were kids. It was a tragedy, it was a torture. I, like Salieri, had to witness his Mozart, his genius swept away by his—his what?—his appetites? Or just debilitating timidity? Or his adoration for a reprobate brother who entered drug rehab so often we joked it was his personal resort spa. Oh, I remember that day, all right. When we all

Grady

met Carl, Sebastian's wastrel brother. There was so much hype. He was so famous. A real, card-carrying rock star. Oh how excited I was to meet him and then how I cringed to watch him mock Sebastian, like it was some hilarious joke. Which it wasn't. Not at all.

Why, why, why can I not get past Sebastian? Even now? Why, when I experience a moment of musical epiphany does he come barging back into my thoughts, to usurp it all again?

Anyway, before too very long I'll be shaking his hand at the Pearly Gates. That is soon enough for me. But Adie will want to reminisce, and I will not deny her. I just want to hear that voice. Close my eyes and see that lissome girl with the bedroom eyes and be carried into that bedroom of my adolescent dreams by the timbre of that voice that drips with oblivious sex. That's the reminiscing I want to do.

OK, then, Grady, get a move on. Pedal!

Boy, I am feeling the miles now. Only about ten or eleven miles to go. Every muscle in my body, even my ears, ache from the effort of pushing this bike over hill and dale this afternoon. I am looking forward to a hug from Beth, a New Glarus Belgian or three and stripping off these sweaty clothes. Pedal, man, pedal. I am on the outskirts of town now. Familiar ground. I can see the cheese factory up ahead and am tempted to stop and bring Beth some muenster, her favorite, but I've got to boogey. I'm not keeping up the outbound pace. Old legs pooping out, I guess. I start pedaling hard. Faster faster. So fast that the truck coming out of the factory, the one turning in front of me is barely a blur—

The Middle

The ghosts of cirrus clouds scud across the night sky. These ghosts are reflected in the still pool below, as black as the night itself. The man in the gibbous moon can also check his reflection below before, that is, the clouds obscure his oblong countenance as they pass by. As if in passing from view, vanishing behind a stand of darkened trees or an apartment building, they are gone forever. As if they are the ones moving, disappearing, and not us.

The water—lake or river or ocean—so long as it is still, is a perfect mirror of the heavenly bodies above. It is an optical illusion, bringing the celestial to earth, to glisten in the softly stirred water, as if a canoe could skim across and dart in and out of the Pleiades like so many islands. Or a child's finger points skyward to connect the dots of the lazy "w" that is Cassiopeia, before finding her five bright stars floating right before her eyes and knowing wonder for the first time.

All the stories of the heavens—and there are a multitude, enough to give rise to the zodiac, the constellations, the planets, even individual stars, like Sirius, the dog star and the brightest, and the navigator's friend, the North Star—all these tell stories that begin as simple tales until they are retold enough to become legends and then myths, finding their way into the night sky for safekeeping. In this way, the stories are passed on eternally, reflecting as they do both our feats as well as our fears.

On this summer night, when the clouds, illuminated by the moon's cold glow, appear and disappear, revealing the majesty of the universe to the water below, a boy can sweep up a star in a ladle or see the snake Hercules has slain come alive on a ripple. All fear of darkness is vanquished. For the black night and the black water sparkle with supernatural creatures and towering heroes, even children, like the Trojan boy Ganymede conveyed to Zeus by the celestial eagle Aquila.

At daybreak, all vanishes. And yet, does not. Another illusion, this time played out by the sun.

Mary Clay

There is something about California that is honey to a bear. Stan and I move to L.A. Venice Beach, actually. It is 1980. Why? Because we are just a couple of aging hippies—already —and California is *the* scene. So what if we're a decade late? California's reputation preceded itself to us Midwest kids. Haight-Ashbury. The Summer of Love. All that late 1960's stuff. Good dope, too, easily attained. Not the sweat it was to get weed in Kentucky, where it is, ironically, illegal, given that the state, at least every country county, is likely to have big time growers. Look at Johnny Boone. Always dodging the feds, his farm in Springfield produced the finest weed anywhere—Kentucky Bluegrass, it's called. Bluegrass, get it? The bluegrass state, ha!

    Anyway, Stan and I like California. It suits us and our restless spirits. We figure we can get jobs enough to pay the rent. Venice is cheap, filled with bums on the streets and musclemen pumping iron on the beach. Speaking of Venice Beach, it's the only beach in the world that has pigeons and not seagulls. No self-respecting sea gull would roost here. But pigeons, they're, well, less discriminating.

    I get a job at a florist. I know nothing about flowers, but they need someone to make deliveries and to help set up weddings and funerals.

About my speed. What I wasn't expecting was to actually care to know the difference between a calla lily and a day lily. Between a tea rose and a multiflora. Or that roses have medicinal purposes. I learn this later, when I stumble into a Venice health food store, looking for a multi-vitamin. Somehow the clerk, this anorexic chick with the body of a twelve-year-old and the face of a crone, gets off on talking medicinal remedies. She tells me, among many other forgettable facts, that indigenous Americans use wild rose flowers to treat colds and the seeds can be used for muscular pain. Rose oil, she tells me, helps with infections and urinary tract pain. This information changes my life. Vigorous sex with Stan, our daily sustenance, has led to a nearly chronic bladder infection.

—Oh, she says, and begins rummaging around on these chock-a-block shelves of little vials and boxes and jars that suggest no organizational methodology at all—how can she find anything in this mess? I end up going home with St. John's Wort, ginseng, feverfew, Echinacea and rose oil, of course, all these little samples, that only cost a few bucks each, so, she says, I can experiment with the benefits of holistic medicines, and do my body a favor.

—I just know you'll be back soon. Try the Echinacea the moment you feel a cold coming on, and she smiles a meek but confident smile.

Somehow, it hadn't occurred to me that I could get a cold in Southern California ... Oh, sure, I eventually had a chance to try that stuff out on a cold. Once we re-located to New England. In the meantime, the rose extracts work, and that makes me very very curious. About all those old native remedies—agave to treat sunburn and rashes, yeah, and to ferment into mescal and the yucca, for insect bites and constipation and fertility, just to mention two from around here.

I tell Stan I'm quitting my job at the florist. My sights are set higher now. I'm bored with cut flowers and temporary arrangements left behind at the reception or funeral home. I want to grow them, learn about the earth, get my hands dirty. So I sign on with a Beverly Hills landscaping crew. It's a schlepp to get there but I've found my calling, and so I don't mind the daisy chain of buses it takes me to get to the pick-up point. Now I am outside all day every day. Because as everybody knows, it never rains in Southern California. Haha. So, yeah, I am bronzing up nicely. Best of all, though? My hands are in soil all day, rich, warm, promising soil, and I am learning how to plant, maintain, prune, even weed gardens. My companions are not the Joes I work with but the Matilija poppies and Santa Barbara daisies, the California fuchsias and the desert mallows. In the evenings, I add rose water to my tea and rose oil to my bath.

    Meanwhile, I'm thinking we are running a hotel. No, a boarding house. No, a flop house. Grady is the first to show up, him and his girlfriend. They crash on our pullout couch, the one we just found at a thrift shop down on Ocean Boulevard, because we have only been in this apartment a month, sleeping on the floor ourselves, because the first and security all but clean us out. So, with my first check from the florist and Stan's restaurant tips, we buy a decent mattress, new, no importing bedbugs for me! No sirree. And then we luck into the Castro convertible, second hand, at that thrift shop, a couple of days before they are going to crash on our floor. In the meantime, by cruising the neighborhood on trash night, we pick up a beat-up old dropleaf table left on a street corner with the sign "Free" and two fraying ancient fake Oriental rugs left out for pickup. Same for two straight chairs for the table and a motheaten, seat-collapsed, arm-worn overstuffed chair left over from several previous Salvation Army salvages, no doubt. Now we are saving for a TV and some California Mary Jane. Fortunately, Grady, fresh from bluegrass-land, has some primo stuff with him, by way of a housewarming gift.

Stan's never met Grady but he's heard plenty about him. Grady wasn't one of the original members of the pack but he got to be a regular, singing like he did, and tutoring Sebastian on everything from the kazoo to a twelve-string acoustic. Those two made music together all right.

Grady and his girlfriend, a pale, emaciated thing who bears a striking resemblance to a praying mantis and is called BF, Grady's affectionate nickname meaning Best Fuck, though her real name is Francis Jean. BF, somehow, sticks. Mostly because BF herself prefers BF to Francis Jean. I'm not a fan of double-barreled names in girls, and I'm in a position to have an opinion, because it takes one to cringe at one. So, anyway, BF, the nickname, sticks just like gum to the underside of a school desk.

Whenever Grady gets a chance—helping me clean up after dinner or when BF is doing her hour-long morning ablutions or when she's still asleep and we're having coffee on the deck overlooking Beverly Hills—he's pumping me about Adie.

—You carrying a torch, Grady? I tease. I know I'm teasing because they broke up at the beginning of senior year in high school. Eons ago. When Adie kinda vanished on us.

—Nah. You just always wonder what happened to the people you connect with. I mean, don't you, MC?

—Weird thing is, I hear she went off the deep end. Took up scuba diving. Said it was her ticket to see the world.

—Really? Far out. But how does she make a living?

—All over the world. She's a dive master.

—A what?

—A paid hand-holder, only underwater. She leads recreational dives in beautiful places.

—What a trip. That's wild. That's just plain wild.

—She told me once it's like nursing. There's always a demand. Last

I heard she was working on a live-aboard dive boat in Indonesia. She sent me a picture of the boat. Looked like a souped up sampan with air tanks and wetsuits all over the place.

I can tell by the starry look in his eyes, he's still got the hots for her. That this information, about Adie's weird career, is titillating for him. Why, I cannot figure. She sure as hell dumped him without a word of explanation. I wonder how much he knows about that? Wonder if he knows who that mystery man was? She's sure-as-shootin' been tight-mouthed about it all with me, even after all these years. Anyway, Grady keeps coming back to her, to Adie, whenever BF's back is turned.

We don't get rid of Grady for a month. Not till after the Fourth of July when I get so sick. There's this giant Venice Beach block party to celebrate the holiday. It's a BYOE affair, bring your own everything. Beverage, eats, smokes. ABT brownies, shared bottles of tequila, mystery foods made from plant-based edibles that are indistinguishable from sawdust and not improved, in my judgment by hot sauce—are passed from hand to hand. We eat our eats, washing all down with a case of Corona, partake of the joints going around, and start several of our own in the debauched communal spirit of share and share alike, and snarf up the brownies. Stan, Grady and BF eat the sawdust but I spit it out and stick with the brownies, being something of a chocolate junkie. They are yummy. I am just about to learn they are also lethal.

What I remember is this: being collapsed on the bathroom floor, clinging to the toilet bowl like it was a life preserver thrown overboard to aid the drowning victim, me, and hallucinating. If I so much as move my head, a freight train blows through the bathroom wall at full speed, sending concrete everywhere, and coming straight for me. Stan told me later, after he and Grady rolled me into a sleeping bag, because even though it was 90 degrees outside, I was freezing. Teeth chattering so bad, my jaw bounced. Stan told me, too, that my temperature was like 102 degrees.

I remember coming to, broiling in the sleeping bag, throwing it off me like a curse.

—Thank God, Grady says. He helps me stand up and gets me some water. My shorts and tank top are soaked with sweat.

—What happened? What happened to me?

—Someone slipped you a mickey, MC. Stan thinks, and I agree, probably PCP. In the brownies. You had a really really scary trip. Stan and BF have gone back to the party, trying to find the joker who did this to you.

—PCP? I stagger to a chair, slump into it, my hand with the glass of water shaking so hard I have to put it down. My head too.

—Angel Dust. It's a horse tranquilizer.

Once everybody knew I was going to live, Grady and BF make plans to head north, to visit Sebastian. Sebastian is living in The Castro by now.

—Not that I'm gay, Grady anticipates. But it's a scene. Gotta see it. Sebastian too. Haven't seen him since we all spread out after high school.

They pack up and pack out, and none too soon. I remember Adie's mother, who was a crazy-mad needle-pointer, making a sofa cushion that read Don't Mistake Endurance for Hospitality. She'd quietly bring it out and put it on their sofa whenever houseguests overstayed their welcome. On more than one occasion, I had wished I'd had that pillow to drop like a subtle A-bomb on the never-made, never-put away pullout couch they slept on in our living room.

Jude is next to arrive, toting her guitar over one shoulder, its case plastered with peace signs, Chicago '68 stickers and an array of concert tickets glued in place. She tells us L.A. is the scene for someone like her, a great musician and gifted lyricist. Immediately, she is playing on Ocean Boulevard and somewhere along the main drag in Santa Monica, her case propped up against a parking meter or a palm tree, looking for handouts. She says this is only temporary, till she lands a proper gig. She brags that she made a fortune playing the subways in New York in between stints at bars. Whatever she makes in Venice or Santa Monica or wherever else she ventures, not once does she bring home a bottle of wine to share or offer to make dinner. She was, however, free with our dope. Until one day, Stan blows up and invites her out the door. Tomorrow.

—Fine, she huffs with studied haughtiness. Nothing's going on here anyway. The music scene here sucks. I'll head up to San Francisco. Sebastian'll put me up.

—Somebody warn the poor schlemiel, Stan says under his breath. Jude responds with an erect middle finger, but his back is already turned. He's fed up.

I give Jude a big hug the day she leaves. We've been close since junior high. But somehow she's changed. Harder. The humor gone. Adult life does not suit her.

But she makes me think of Sebastian, and my own desire to see him again. Funny, how that lurks just beneath the surface all the time. Sebastian. Having Jude around, we talk about him a lot. In fact, I don't think the two of us were alone for five minutes before his name came up. This kid we hung out with when we were fourteen and fifteen, till college sent us flying in different directions. I've kept up with him with letters. I've been writing to him, and him to me since the first time we were separated by spring break in our sophomore year in high school. Now that I think about it, now that Jude has strode away, her long brown hair wisping up behind her like smoke contrails—only in passing do any of the others in our group come up. Not Breck at all or Grady, beyond me mentioning that he was the first to flop. Not Adie or Tony. None of them. She only wants to talk about Sebastian, like he's some kind of god, or something. It is weird, and when I think about it, uncomfortable. And like Stan, I want to warn him. But it's not my business. They are friends too. She and Sebastian sang together all those years in junior and senior high—she, Joan Baez to his Bob Dylan. So, go in peace, I say to her back, old pal. But I'm also glad. Because Jude is high maintenance these days, and Stan's kvetching about her made for some tensions these last couple of weeks, like I was salt water taffy being pulled between them.

A couple of months pass, and I get this letter from Sebastian. He's had this god-awful experience. He and his lover had a bad fight. When Sebastian orders him out of their apartment and threatens to call the cops if he doesn't get out, the guy jumps from the second-floor window. Sebastian describes the horror, leaning out afterwards and seeing the body bent up funny on the stairs up to the front porch, stilled, a rivulet of blood trickling down a step. He is shaken beyond belief, even though the guy survives.

He wanted to own me, MC, he writes. He found out I had lovers. Well, of course I do. This is The Castro, for god's sake. Marathon promiscuity is a way of life here, one I wholeheartedly welcome. So many years of pretending I was some other kind of man. When I got out of the closet, I felt like Sisyphus casting off that boulder. The straight world. So, I told him he was free to do the same. And he freaked. He came at me with a kitchen knife, screaming I'd betrayed him. And what kind of reward for his loyalty, his fidelity, his LOVE was I showing him? he yelled. And I yelled back that I never promised him a rose garden. I'M A GAY MAN LIVING A GAY LIFE, I shouted back, finally. And nobody—nobody—is going to take that away from me ever again. So, all the while I am dodging this crazy man and his knife, so I start throwing his shit out the window. And he gets more enraged and lunges. So I grab the phone and call the cops. He just looks at me, crying now. He drops the knife, turns and dives out the goddamn window. Everything went into slow motion, MC. It was the weirdest thing. Like he was hanging in the air there for solid minutes. The police came. And an ambulance. I watched them take him away. I thought he was dead, MC. I thought I'd killed Craig.

The day after I get this letter, Stan and I get bus tickets to San Francisco. I just know I need to get to him ASAP. Needless to say, I call Sebastian before, just to make sure he knows we're coming, and I know we are not walking into some scene that will embarrass the hell out of both of us. But I have to go to him. He sounds really grateful, and it is some kind of wonderful to hear his voice. As soon as I do, I can see him. Not The Castro Sebastian, but the teenaged one. White button-down oxford shirt, pressed jeans, close cropped light brown hair with a cowlick at his brow like a question mark, playing air guitar and tilting his singing face toward the skies, eyes closed, like he was praying or something.

The Sebastian we find at the bus station in Frisco is not that boy. He is heavily bearded and wild-haired. Over his bare chest, covered in weedy hair, he's got this serape-like number draped over his shoulders. It's heavily embroidered, maybe from Guatemala or Mexico. Maybe Mexico because he used to idolize Wolfman Jack and his radio show that broadcast from there. In fact, above his trademark Levi 501's, he kinda looks like a wolf. In a funky Red Riding Hood's cape. Oh, and his super-trademark high-top Keds, also probably dating back to high school, judging by the worn bunion and big-toe holes. I hardly recognize him, having not seen him since college. Until he smiles. The notch between his two front teeth, combined with the grey-green eyes that crinkle mischievously at the corners. Those identify him to me so clearly that I run up, jump into his arms, so that he staggers back. I wrap my legs around him and he holds me like a child. The crowd of travelers and bums and junkies burst into a cheer.

—How the hell are you? Damn, I'm bummed about Craig freaking you out, I say as I slide free of him and hold him at arm's length, just drinking him in.

—God, it's been so long. Let's get out of here. Oh, Sebastian, hold on a sec, I say stepping back, this is Stan.

The two men look each other over. For a second I think there's going to be a cock fight. It's one of the things I've never been able to get across to Stan. That another man can be just a friend. You'd think a gay guy would be a no-brainer but Stan has strong hetero reflexes. Sebastian chips the ice free, and says, Cool. And we head out to a bar in The Castro, his turf, his community, and order some beers and light up a joint. No problem here, he tells us. The place he takes us is called the Elephant Walk. Sebastian tells us it was one of the first gay bars in the neighborhood.

—Harvey Milk used to come here a lot, he tells us.

And, of course, I look around for him, forgetting that he's dead. Which is why all I see are a couple of guys dressed like women drinking at the bar. It's hard not to stare. To wonder.

Sebastian raises an eyebrow, and I haul in my curiosity. He keeps saying how glad he is to see me and then apologizes over and over to Stan, until the two of them, highly stoned by now, are laughing and hugging and making fun of me. They are good. I can tell it. Stan has always been a great judge of character, and getting tight with Sebastian, with whom I have such a long history and Stan has heard so much about, well, that's just the best.

We get a little short of funds and longer and longer on rowdy behavior, so we leave the bar and start walking to Sebastian's place. The first thing he points out is Harvey Milk's Camera Shop, just around the corner from the Elephant Walk.

—There was more processed in that shop than just film, he says. But now, well, now there's talk of putting up a plaque.

I take in everything I see. First off, the camera shop looks deserted. Then I start taking in all the people on the streets. It's like one big block party, it being Friday night. Gorgeous men everywhere, leaning against cars or lampposts or headed into bars, and not a one for Mary Clay. I give Stan a sidelong glance and silently apologize for this collective lusting I'm entertaining. Studley Dudleys coming home from work in straight world San Francisco, parading their Gucci suits and Italian shoes as they head home or out for a drink. Others, though, are dressed like farmers or construction workers or cowboys. In their super-tight jeans and plaid shirts, open to the waist. Or in T-shirts that might as well be painted on, every washboard muscle exaggerated. And then there are these guys who resemble the bear on the California State Flag, big, burly, huge beards, and uncombed, wild hair.

—It's a look, Sebastian tells me as he catches me gawking.

Suddenly, a wave of I-don't-belong-here uneasiness threatens to knock my socks off. What helps me chill is all the hippies. The bell-bottoms and hip-huggers. Like some kind of time warp but since I warp in the same old hipster way, these guys look like me. I mean not really, they're guys. And they're all probably gay. What a scene, groovy but alien too. Not that I have my head in the sand. I've been to P-town. Many times. When I was a kid visiting my grandmother on the Cape, we'd drive out there for the views, and it wasn't the ocean we had in mind. But The Castro makes Provincetown look like the closet. All-in-all, Sebastian's adopted hometown is an eye-poppin' place.

So, if Venice Beach is a cross between hippietown and a dumpsite, The Castro is a cross between a hometown and a meat market.

As we walk up Castro Street, Sebastian—he's like a proud father—is pointing everything out. He calls it the Main Street of Gay America, and then he starts waxing poetic. It's the weed and the beer talking, but also something much more.

—You have to understand, I never thought I'd live in a place where I actually belong. Where there are other people just like me, and it's not illegal to be like me. Back when we were kids, MC, not in my wildest prayers did I ever believe I could come out, stay out, live out and be proud out.

It makes me think of when he came out to me. I was home for spring break. We were sitting across from each other on the top step of his mother's Sears Roebuck house, each of us with our back against the cold yellow stucco, smoking cigarettes. We were talking about what a mess college was. I was going on about hating school in the Midwest and wondering how I ever ended up there, when he sat forward, held my eyes and said, I've got something I need to tell you.

I remember not knowing what to say. Part of me, I guess, had known for years. But part of me was crushed too. Not only was he my best friend ever but I had harbored feelings for him since we were fourteen. He told me back then he wanted to move to California, though that would not happen for another five or six years. And I thought, California? I'll never see him again.

What did I say to his announcement?

—It doesn't matter. I'll always love you. And he said he loved me, back. We hugged and I fought back tears.

I look at him now, a sidelong sly observing. He is smiling that mesmerizing smile and pulling us along up Castro Street, passing Castro Theatre, which he duly points out as the neighborhood's most enduring landmark, like it's the Statue of Liberty or something. Come to think of it, maybe it is. To him.

We deviate —ha, great choice of terms!— over to 18th and Market. For a sec, Sebastian just stands on the corner like a stand-in for a lamp-post. Then, he's off again, telling us how this intersection is the crossroads of the gay world. Not just America. The globe. And that's why, he says, all four crosswalks are painted the pastel colors of the gay rights flag. Then we're backtracking, and pretty soon we're outside Sebastian's house. A tall white, paint-peeling three-story Victorian that still looks a lot like some elongated Greek temple rising from a mini-acropolis. So, no, it's not his house. He has the second-floor apartment. In San Francisco, everything is uphill and involves a climb, even his digs. There's a set of concrete stairs, then another set of wooden ones set at a right angle, just to get up to the front porch. Tight and tired as I am, I long for our ground floor Ocean Boulevard apartment. Stan and I haul ourselves up, heaving. Only Sebastian is used to the mountain climb to get to the front door. I bend over, hands on knees and suck in air. Stan has a coughing fit. Sebastian laughs.

—Come on. Still one more flight to go, you couple'a lightweights. He's torturing us now, while fumbling to extract his keys from his jeans' pockets.

His apartment is huge but grungy. Walls haven't seen a coat of fresh paint since the last war. No wait. That was Vietnam, not so very long ago at all. What saves this place from hovel status, are the high ceilings and the tall floor-to-ceiling windows, one in the living room where we are and another, I will discover, in his bedroom while I prowl around. I take all this in while Stan and Sebastian head to the kitchen to get some

Ambient Light

wine, talking about Harvey Milk. But I can see for myself, just looking around Sebastian's place, that Milk was some kind of hero. Harvey Milk campaign posters, right up to those for the race he won to become the first openly gay city supervisor, and newspaper clippings, cheaply framed but no less revered, cover one entire wall in the hallway to his bedroom. I'm staring at the Chronicle coverage of the candlelight vigil the night Milk was shot. Thousands upon thousands of people crowding up to City Hall. I zero in, certain Sebastian is among them.

When Stan and Sebastian reappear, one is carrying three glasses and the other an open bottle of chardonnay. I hear the tinkle of glass on glass and turn to join them. The three of us sit Indian style on the floor which has a million faux Navajo pillows by way of furniture. Sebastian is talking about taking part in Milk's human billboard political campaigning—gays and lesbians, arms linked, stretching for blocks, spelling out VOTE FOR MILK. Then he's telling Stan —and me—how he met Milk in his camera shop slash campaign headquarters when he first got to town. He tells us about Milk's mongrel dog who came right up to him and offered him a paw, the beat-up old couch just inside the storefront window where camera supplies ought to have been displayed, and that if you were looking for that stuff, it was tough to see any, even though that—and Milk's reputation—was why he'd walked in the door in the first place. To get some film processed. Everybody knew about Milk, he tells us, as if we didn't already know that. By now, the man is a legend, and not just in the gay world. He, Sebastian tells us, helped lots of guys get a foothold in The Castro, and so the word spread. Milk looked at all the gay kids flocking to the neighborhood and called them refugees from disgrace.

—He thought of himself as the Mayor of Castro Street, Sebastian says while pouring out the wine in equal measures, but he really was more like a prophet. Touched in the head. Part man-ho, part saint.

—Man-ho?

—He had a live-in lover, but he slept around too.

—Huh, I say. That sounds familiar. Sebastian laughs at the insinuation, and polishes off his glass of wine.

—I'm telling you, he goes on, rolling another joint now, crazy as Harvey was, and he was, I looked up to that guy. He put gay rights on the map. He gave us a sense of purpose and dignity. The day he got shot, I thought the world would end. We all did. We all expected the cops to sweep in and sweep us back into the closet. You know—and for a moment Sebastian is somewhere else. His eyes look past Stan, and so I know he is watching some interior movie.

—You know, don't you, he always knew he would die young?

—I didn't, Stan says. You've told me more about him in the last three minutes than I ever knew. I just know he's a martyr, in the gay world.

Sebastian is nodding and lighting up, all at the same time. It is one fat joint he starts passing around.

—Been saving this for a special occasion. Guess you two are it. He takes a long, deep drag.

Coils of smoke escape from the corners of his mouth. Then he goes on.

—I'm kinda on the same page. It's something Harvey and I had in common. The dying young thing.

—Yeah, Stan says. I get that.

This is definitely TMI from both of them. He is so strange to me and so familiar. He's reminiscing now to Stan about moving from Kentucky to Haight-Ashbury in 1974 and finding it not a haven of peace and love but instead a hardcore drug scene—smack, crack, acid, meth, any cocktail you wanted, he says—and murders, with chalk body outlines on every street corner.

—Fucked with my head. I got outta there, pronto. He's musing now, he inhales deeply and lets a curl of pot-fragrant smoke trickle past his lips. If you're from Kentucky, you're always late to the party. So I jumped over the hill to The Castro, drawn by Milk, and the rumor of a promised land. Thank ya, Jesus.

He is lying back grinning now, and Stan has the joint, and stretches out too. Examining the ceiling for incoming aliens. I take a hit but am too restless. I definitely am not digging this. I hold it in till my lungs are on fire and stand up. Taking up my wine, I begin my prowl around Sebastian's pad. I wonder about remnants of Craig but it looks to me as if he's been completely obliterated like a carpet stain covered over with a throw rug. This is Sebastian's world and Sebastian's world only. The men are silly now, so I keep poking, studying everything down to the rolls of loose dust in the corners. I am drawn to the wide-open window first. The one his friend Craig flew out of, the one that, from up here, overlooks Castro Street a block away and, beyond, the last glow of a setting sun. I just have to see. If there's blood. A brown stain. On the steps below. I am creeping myself out, but I put my hands on the sill and lean as far out as I dare. No. Nothing. Nothing there. Am I relieved? Or disappointed? I toss the question aside and hope Sebastian didn't notice what I was doing. Fresh air, I am about to proclaim, in the event I need to save myself from his disappointment or condemnation or whatever he would be feeling seeing me gawk out the window for traces of his lover's blood.

But I am safe. His eyes are closed. But Stan is up on one elbow, watching me. I let him. I feel no need to explain myself to him, and he does not ask. That will come later when we are alone on the bus gliding through the night toward L.A.

Then something tucked in the little hallway between the kitchen and the living room catches my eye. A closet with the doors off. I can see the marks where hinges once were but now, the doors are gone and Sebastian has converted it into—what?—Oh My God, I think. Sebastian has filled the cavity with shelves that are lined with his old LP and 45s collections. The old portable record player he had when we were kids — vintage, a genuine antique now—is enshrined on a table in the middle of this sacred cubby hole. Its top is propped open, the turntable just waiting. Beneath it, on the floor, are a scattering of 45s as if Sebastian has just been interrupted while playing them. As I come closer, I feel my childhood flood back to me in bars of music, lines of old songs. They're all here. All the old chestnuts we so loved as kids. He has kept them all. The "Duke of Earl" pops into my head—the refraining Duke echoing in my head. I run my fingers over that old turntable, as gently as a lover, for the wellspring of memories this ancient stereo conjures is formidable, all the music he deeded to us, back then.

Suddenly Sebastian is beside me, looking over my shoulder and offering me another hit. I always knew music meant everything to him but here, here is the sanctuary he has built to that other, older, golden time, when we were young together and the biggest thing in our lives was mowing enough lawns or babysitting enough rug-rats to buy the latest record. Now vinyl is mostly a thing of the past. Cassette tapes, they're just not the same, even though I see he has a goodly number of those too now. I take an LP out of its sleeve with the same delicacy a librarian might touch a rare book, and just admire it, remembering too.

Sebastian puts his hand on my shoulder. He doesn't need to say anything. He is feeling just the same.

—Put one on. Go ahead.

And for the next hour, while the boys go out for more wine and some munchies, I take one 45 after another out of its thin paper sleeve —"Walk On By," "Steal Away," "Pretty Woman," "Pain in My Heart,"

"Shop Around," "Ain't Too Proud to Beg," "Uptight" and on and on—and just in reading the titles I am in his old living room again, with him and all the others. Adie, Breck, Grady, Tony, Mary Clay, Jude. Adie, Jude and I are the Supremes. We know all their moves. Grady, Tony, Breck and Sebastian become the Four Tops or the Miracles—Sebastian is Smokey Robinson, of course—or the Temptations, their moves perfect, the choreography down pat, the records blaring in the background and his mother retiring upstairs with a cocktail to escape the din.

Only when Sebastian and Stan get back, and Sebastian nudges me aside and puts on a tune, do I re-enter the now. Very very unwillingly. Because life has never seemed so sweet since.

Later, we go out for burgers and head for the bus stop. We are stoned and we are happy, especially me, just to draft behind him again after so long. Sebastian sees us onto the overnight Greyhound, but not before saying.

—Heh, MC, remember, Tony wanted to grow up to be a Greyhound bus driver? I always think of him when I see one. Or was that before you knew him?

—Before.

Sebastian's eyes are alive now, and again he is watching an interior movie, not playing on Stan's or my mind screen.

—Haven't heard from him. You?

—No, I say, not since I wrote him after his divorce. The letter was returned.

—Me either. I always wondered—

—What? Wondered what?

—If Tony. Oh, never mind. No way to answer my own question.

So, we haul our asses up into the bus, Stan relieved and me so sorry to go, to say goodbye. I nab the window seat and press my hand to the glass but Sebastian has already turned, already headed out.

Fast Forward. It is unusual for Sebastian to phone. No one calls long distance, unless they're on a company line. Too expensive. My dad still shouts on long distance calls as if he must make his voice carry to Baltimore or Chicago. To say nothing of Paris, France. I'm not interested in picking up the phone because I am in the middle of powwowing with my sister over my grandmother's estate. She has died and the two of us have inherited the house on Cape Cod, and the nightmare that entails. Her illness was the reason Stan and I move back to the East Coast, to protect my interests but also because we were just done with California. Stan is thinking of going back to school to get some kind of advanced degree and then get the proverbial, "real job." The idea of a decent paying job and benefits has slowly grown on him, if not on me. If he gets into some graduate program, that will make me the breadwinner. And the only bread I know how to make is in landscaping, not exactly a year-round job in New England. So, we'll see. In the meantime, the phone is ringing and I wave to Stan to make himself useful and answer the damned thing, while my sister and I plow through the old lady's papers.

—Hullo?

Suddenly Stan is clicking his fingers madly and waving me over. I can tell by his expression that it is bad. Very very bad.

And that is how I learn Sebastian has AIDS. He tells me he skipped the HIV part and just went into full-blown AIDS. He is forty-two. It is 1991. His voice is the same old Sebastian voice, not a grim, terrified, resigned version of it, making it hard for me to process what I'm hearing. I don't know much about AIDS, except that it's the gay plague. He is joking about getting caught with his pants down. He is laughing about not being able to keep his zipper zipped. I can see his wide smile, almost a grin, telling me everything will be fine. They've got him on AZT.

For a year and a half, life goes on for everyone, even Sebastian, as it was foretold to be. Stan knocks off a master's degree in social work and goes to work for Action for Boston Community Development. I gather up my courage and start my own landscaping business. My grandmother knew just about everyone who is anyone within a fifteen-mile radius from her house in Eastham, and certainly plenty of people who are too rich to bother with garden care for themselves. Enter me. Cha-ching, cha-ching.

The correspondence between me and Sebastian continues. I know he isn't telling me everything, whether because he thinks it would upset me or because he's in denial himself. I know that he is leaning more on holistic remedies than medical ones. After all, he's been working in a health food store for fourteen years. That worries me. Especially when he tells me he's quit the AZT. It wasn't working he says. It was making him sick. *I don't want to slide through my days like a zombie, MC. I want to go skinny dipping at Kirby Cove Beach. I want to walk the headlands north of the Bay. I want to feel the sun on my back and howl at the moon.*

I want to howl with him. I want to be with him. To float in his presence again. And again. But that's not what he wants, or he would say so and I'd be there on the next plane. He lives in a different world from me and is kind enough not to be blunt about it. He is surrounded by men who love him. Their North Star now, not mine.

Occasionally I call him. Just to hear his voice, hear his smile, hear his mind. One time, he does not pick up. Someone else does. A woman. This takes me aback. I ask for him and identify myself. Suddenly she is laughing.

—Oh Mary Clay! You won't remember me but I remember you, and all the kids in Sebastian's cabal. That's what Carl and I called you guys. It's Irene, remember me? I was married to Sebastian's bro—

—Yes, yes, of course. I do remember you. But what are you doing—

Mary Clay

I have only met Irene once. When Sebastian's drummer brother brought her home to meet his mother. She was strikingly beautiful. Very Joni Mitchell. And kind. Not like his brother. He was an abusive bastard, so it came as no surprise when I heard they split. But that was eons ago. Sebastian never told me he kept up with Irene, so her voice on his phone comes as a shock. And now here she is. Recruited? Or volunteered? A part of me is stung by this. Why didn't he call me? Of course, the answer is Stan. Irene is unencumbered.

—Mary Clay, she says. The news is not good. Sebastian's in the hospital. He stopped taking the AZT, you know, because he thought it was poisoning him. Maybe it was, I don't know. He doesn't know. From what I've been told, he went downhill pretty quickly. I've been looking after him here, in his apartment, for the last couple of months. Then it got real bad and the visiting nurse said we had to get him to a hospital.

—Why? Why did he have to go to the hospital, Irene? Why?

—He had uncontrollable diarrhea. And was so weak, Mary Clay. So weak and losing weight, a lot of weight. His doc thinks he may have some opportunistic cancer. He's talking non-Hodgkin's lymphoma. Which is bad. Very bad, if true.

There is no processing any of this shit. My stomach is in my mouth. I dry heave, my hand over the receiver so Irene can't hear.

—We're not sure he'll be coming home, sorrow chokes her voice. A kind of resignation. I came out here as soon as his ex-lover told me the situation. They still share an apartment but haven't been together, not in that way, since before Sebastian got sick. And he couldn't cope. Too personal. Too scary. Too who knows? The guy's a wimp, what can I say?

—I would have come, I say weakly, pathetically, feeling myself one foot in quicksand. I may even have said this to myself because what I hear myself say is this:

—Soon as I can get organized here, I'm coming out there. Maybe a week, longest.

—We're doing okay here. The visiting nurses are terrific—

—I'm coming out.

It takes four days to re-schedule all my clients. I tell them my return is indefinite. Even though I know it is not. But I will stay as long as he'll let me. If he'll even see me.

Stan, taking a week off work, and I arrive in San Francisco and go directly to the three-story beat-up old Victorian Greek temple he still lives in, where we find Irene looking haggard, a broom in her hand. The sweetest, saddest smile crosses her face when she sees me. We hug for a long time.

Stan and I hole up in a bed & breakfast a few blocks away, run by a couple of guys, who we learn later have a fetish for dress-up, but in the moment they are open-armed, like two hairy mothers welcoming home their lost lambs.

—We have a vacancy, if it will suit you. It's our smallest room, on the top floor but it is very *cute!*

—How many nights will you be joining us? says the other proprietor.

—Just one. Maybe a couple, maybe more.

It is up four flights of stairs and is made big enough to accommodate the smallest of double beds only by a dormer extension. But it is cute. In fact, it is adorable. Not overdone at all. Not drag-queen cute but cute of an exceptional nature. A kind of garret embrace. The curtains hang from gold rings covering the solitary window and pull open with gold tasseled tie-backs. They and the bed skirt are Jacobean in inspiration, with swirling green vines and salmon trumpet flowers. A miniature antique dresser, a well-stamped steamer trunk and an oval rope rug that compliments the curtains make up for the fact that the bathroom is down the hall.

—Look at all those pillows, I gush, hardly able to restrain myself from taking a dive onto the bed.

When they worm out of us why we want a place to crash in The Castro, the hospitality overflows and the outpouring of support is like a drowning in crinoline.

Next day, we see Sebastian. He's just been released from the hospital "to go home." His big grin, though oddly lopsided, is the first thing I see. Then his belly. Distended like a kid with malnutrition. He, Stan and I go out to lunch at a place he likes called Island Restaurant. It is, he tells us, a Castro institution. Sebastian hardly eats. We hardly eat either. It is impossible not to notice the lesions on the back of his hands and crawling up his neck around his right ear. That is all of him that is visible to us. I see too the dark circles under his eyes and his grey, pallid complexion. So we throw a Hail Mary and fall back on reminiscences to change the subject, even though no words have been spoken about his AIDS. Sebastian regales Stan with tales of our misspent past, the car-to-car egg fight that destroyed the paint jobs of five of our parents' cars; of him, Tony and Breck kidnapping Adie the night before her sixteenth birthday and driving her over the Indiana state line, in order to rape her, statutorily speaking that is; of starting a bonfire of Latin books on the steps of our junior high on the last day of ninth grade. We are all reduced to coughs of laughter, only Sebastian's coughs take an ugly turn. Stan pays the bill while I shepherd Sebastian, one arm firmly around his waist, the other cradling his arm, out of the restaurant. We get him home, Stan and me. Then we use an old scouting trick to get him up all those stairs, crisscrossing arms to make a seat for Sebastian, and in this way we carry him up to his apartment. Irene has seen us coming and is half way down the stairs before she realizes there isn't room for a fourth person in this transfer and backs back up the stairs to the apartment, holding the door open. The look on her face is that of grief anticipated.

It is the first time I've been in Sebastian's apartment since the time Stan and I rushed up to support him after his then-lover's suicide attempt. I hope against hope that the shock does not show on my face. There are pill bottles and herbal remedies all over the place. Like a rogue pharmacy. An IV pole, with bags of saline and meds hanging off it, and other medical and homeopathic devices surround his bed like a devil's halo. Whatever I think I've grasped about his situation before, I now know has been delusion. We get Sebastian to bed and he immediately, without embarrassment or second thought given the company he has, asks Irene for the bedpan. Irene finds it for him and ushers us into the living room. A god-awful smell follows us out.

—He'll need to sleep now.

—I'd like to stay and help, Irene.

But she slowly shakes her head.

—I know you would. But it's probably not a good idea, friend. Having you here will only prolong things. It's time for him to let go.

—I—I— swore to protect him.

She reaches for me and enfolds me in a long hug. Tears spring to my eyes.

—OK if I say goodbye, Irene? I'm trying to stay casual but I know my face is screaming.

—Sure. Just give me a moment in there first. You know, she says turning back to me, try to forget what you've seen here. Hold that happy-go-lucky boy in your heart, and not this scene.

Instantly, I see him, that boy. I time-tumble back to childhood. To the time Sebastian suggests we swear our friendship for life. We are sitting side-by-side on his front porch swing, each of us pushing it with a toe. I had just run away from home to his house, our hangout, after my mother grounded me for six weeks. He had just put his mother to bed after a drinking binge. He offers me his pinky finger to hook with mine. They interlock as do our eyes.

—I swear if by my life or death I can protect you, I will, he says. Now you. As I repeat the words I feel something rise in me that I've never known before. It will be years before I can identify it, but when I do, I know what he gave me that day was my first real taste of safety.

We end with a pinky tug and smiles.

—We'll always be in this together, MC, trying to survive our for-shit parents, he says. He fishes around in his jeans' pocket, until he wrestles out a Boy Scout pen knife. He makes a small cut on the inside of his left wrist. Blood bubbles up along the tiny incision. He hands me the knife, and I do the same. We press our wrists together and he solemnly says to me

—Forever.

It's a couple of years later before I learn he and Tony were blood brothers first. That doesn't bother me because Tony was his first friend. Even though I wish it had been something just between the two of us.

Stan I and wait for what seems like forever. Then there he is, leaning against Irene at the door to his bedroom. He is fighting to smile. Fighting to stand. He is fighting but the fight is all but gone.

—Oh, Sebastian—my voice catches in my throat. Then I say, Keep your powder dry, my voice an octave higher with the strain of trying to get the words out, to sound hopeful. I reach for him, throw my arms around his neck, while Irene and the door frame bolster him up. We part, and Stan extends his hand. Sebastian takes it and holds on. They speak silently to each other with their eyes. Look after her, Sebastian's seem to say.

Down on the sidewalk, Stan and I turn to each other. We know. We both know. I grab Stan's shoulders with both hands so hard, my nails dig in. But he does not flinch. Our eyes lock with the certainty of what we know to be true, what I've lost. We are weeping for the world to see, for the world to share.

Jude

When Abe comes home and tells me he has a surprise for me, I think, God, no, please don't let him say he's divorcing his wife! I like my life just the way it is, thank you very much. But he really does have a surprise. In fact, it was a gobsmacking one. Abe, dear wan, sparsely bearded, mostly bald, investment banker Jewish lover, Abe, has arranged a one-woman show of my art at this swish gallery on Newbury Street in Boston. He fancies himself a connoisseur of art and something of a collector, but his pocketbook runs to prints and forgotten Old Masters, like his Federico Barocci, purchased from an estate sale before anyone had ever heard of him. That's my opinion, of course. I've seen his collection. Once. When Gloria, his wife, was out of town at her mother's for Seder—Abe couldn't go because he was working on an imminent IPO, whatever that is. He took me to his apartment and was very proud. I smiled my way around his penthouse, nodding and looking as appreciative as I could muster. But really I was taking in Gloria, her choices in furniture, drapes and wallpaper which all veered toward the gaudy. I observe her reading runs to tacky romances. Danielle Steel, Nora Roberts, Nicholas Sparks. While the piano was covered in a slew of family photos, mostly of their four kids when they were little. Alongside a tired little brass menorah.

Picturing her made me smile. Abe thought I was approving of his art. Oh, well.

Boston is his town, not mine. He jumped at the chance when Fidelity wanted to transfer him up here from New York. Why? a thoughtful person might ask. Good question. Boston over New York? But it's his hometown and he's a sentimental Jew. His penthouse is near his Fidelity office in the financial district and I live in the apartment he bought me in Belmont. Close enough for him to commute to see me when he's "out of town" on business or "at the office" on a Saturday afternoon. Which is frequently. But not so frequently that I have to change the sheets more than once a week. I think he really believes he loves me. I harbor no such illusion.

But the news about the solo show almost—almost—makes me throw my arms around him and declare my undying love. I stop at declaring my love even if it is beyond nice of him to have thought up this gift all by himself, Abe not being prone to imagination. Rewarding him with a hug, a kiss and a meandering hand that finds his tool is the least I can do. He peels himself out of his three-piece suit and I lie back for him.

My paintings have been categorized as abstract expressionism in the small group shows I've been in over the years but I, like Picasso, bristle at the hubris of being pigeon-holed by morons. It reminds me of that old saw, "if you can't write, teach English, and if you can't teach English teach gym." The genius of my art is the reflection of my mind, in all its complications, contradictions, and misplaced metaphors, on canvas. So, if those who claim to "understand" my work can't see inside my head, then it ought to be off to the gymnasium for them. And of course, they can't. See inside the intricate and innovative workings of my phantasmagoric mind. Abe doesn't get my work, doesn't even pretend to. I don't expect him to. He is my lover, not my biographer. Simply put, it takes

Jude

genius to appreciate genius, and I've never met anyone—yet—who gets my art, who sees the profundity of what I'm doing, who can discard the human need for association for the pure aesthetics I put before their eyes. The "yet" is for Boston. This show, my first very solo show, where I can showcase my best work before informed critics and art appreciators gives me hope. Abe says the gallery owner will make sure the most discriminating buyers of contemporary art in the greater Boston areas will be invited to the opening. From the Museum of Fine Arts too. Because he has business associates who are on the board. And there should be reviews, in the Phoenix, maybe even the Globe. I can feel it. Really feel it, in my gut. This is going to be my breakout moment, and about time too. Abe has arranged it so that the show opens on my fiftieth birthday, not that anyone will know that, except the two of us. It's really rather sweet. Abe has a sweet side. A generous side, too, dear man.

Get going, Jude! Have you got work to do! The gallery wants me to write all my own labels. But that should be easy: Untitled 1, Untitled 2, Untitled 3. Never will I use descriptive words unless I want to lead the witness, tell the viewer what they are seeing. No. What I want is for people to be carried into my paintings by their own mishegoss, the madness of their own minds, and *feel* a violent rupture from the norm, the everyday, and *see something unknowable*. But in the meantime, I've got to paint. Oh, the ideas are avalanching, blowing my head apart, demanding birthing like some kind of monster child. Abe says the gallery wants at least twenty paintings, because my canvases run large, six-to-ten feet square, on average. I have to get to work. Pull together some old ones, finish others. But finished? How do you know when a painting is finished? Like Valery's poetry, I've merely abandoned them. Leonardo da Vinci's *Adoration of the Magi* comes to mind. As do Picasso's *Carafe and Candlestick* and Klimt's *The Bride*. Are they lesser for being unfinished?

Or far far more interesting, a real glimpse into the mysterious minds of these masters? Like standing beside them at the easel and watching them step back from their painting to consider, and perhaps to complete. But perhaps not.

Oh, Jude, what does it matter? You must have paintings ready to be hung on Newbury Street in less than six months, some just conceptual messes zinging around in your head like splatter paint.

Abe found me the perfect set up. My apartment has extraordinary light for painting because of its high ceilings. There're the large balcony sliders that face north and a skylight above what a normal person would use as a living room. I use it as my studio. The northern exposure lends a quality of light you don't get from south facing windows, where the light can be blinding. Or from east or west facing windows where you only get good light half the day. Maybe. This is, after all, Massachusetts, not Taos, where good light can be at a premium.

The first thing is to get stuff brought up here from my little sister's basement, where most of my early canvases have been stored for years. My sister is elated.

—Oh, Jude, that's wonderful news. I get my basement back. Just in time. I was going to phone you about all that crap of yours. Jim and I want to finish the basement as a rec room now that our boys are teenagers.

Crap? Crap? Really. I've always known she was a philistine. But I just say

—Great. I'll arrange everything.

Actually, Abe will. My sister doesn't even ask me where I am, if I have milk on the table, anything. She clearly doesn't want to know. I remember when we were all kids and my brother would have a go at her because she was the smallest, and I'd get in the middle. Fend him off. Beat him off if I had to. I was taller, and he was a wimpy, pimply-faced bully.

Jude

And this is the thanks I get from her? Oh well. If she thinks the ice in her blood chills me at all, she's got another thing coming.

The paintings come, and it's a little like Christmas unpacking them. I am amazed at how good some of the early ones are. Of course, how dreadful most are. These, from the years when I was in my apprenticeship to serious art, conceived and executed while I was still singing with the band. That's the problem with being gifted in vastly different directions: it's hard to know which path to follow, so you just chase your passions in and out and up and down and around and around until, miraculously, or by dint of diminishing alternatives, one pops to the surface. You think, I thought, forever. But that's the problem with being good in more than one genre, you can't help but ask yourself, maybe I should stick to music (last month) or go full steam ahead with my painting (this month), or vice versa? Should I really be pursuing X because maybe my genius really lies in Y. It's a form of self-torture, wondering if you have sacrificed the wrong twin. If you've left your life playbook behind in the terminal. At first I thought it was music that called me. All the years, all those hours, practicing my violin! From junior high until Juilliard fucked with me. I could have made first violin, I could have. So I was five minutes late. A measly five minutes. All the auditions were running late, but I lost my place all the same. I walked out onto Lincoln Center Plaza and stuffed my violin down a trash bin, and never looked back.

Next was my band. My guitar, this guitar, the same one I've always played is like a third arm. I was serious about the violin but it was the guitar that walked the walk with me, from the days of Sebastian on. Folk music. I went from there. Started my own group. We even got invited to the Newport Folk Festival. Once. We even cut three albums in a back-alley Nashville sound studio. But nothing ever connected. Never saw the ass end of the pop charts. Couldn't even get along well enough together to call it quits as friends.

But by then, seeing the handwriting on the wall, I hooked up with a community studio space and earned money modeling for drawing classes. There was an older guy in one of those classes who took me out for a beer and bent my ear about his midlife crisis. Couple of months later we were living together on his salary as an engineering consultant for the City, and I turned his Hackensack garage into a painting studio. Thought about wrapping my guitar around the tree out front of his place but just couldn't bring myself to do that. Playing the guitar is still, just as it was then, the only thing that's kept me close to sane in this warped world.

I'd been in Belmont several months when Mary Clay tracked me down. Mary Clay, the thread that runs so true since we were just kids. How, or better question, why is it she has so diligently kept up with all six, no five, of us, I'll never understand. She got wind of my show on a postcard the gallery sent out by way of advertisement, I learn. Not to her, but to my mother. That's how she found me this time, through my mother, who ratted me out, told MC I was just up the road in the Boston area. My mother lives on Cape Cod. Retired there. Mary Clay is down there too, holding the fort in her grandmother's mansion. My mother hadn't been any closer to the ocean than Kansas her entire life before she got it in her head to visit Cape Cod, and stayed. Well, not exactly stayed. Once she'd done her time as an eighth grade science teacher and could get out with a pension, she up and bought a cottage in Dennis. On a whim. Which is so like her. And wouldn't you know, Mary Clay and my mom ran into each other at a discount wine depot and the rest is unfortunate history. They had lots of old stories to share. Mary Clay reports my mom was dying to know about our teenaged escapades, ones

Jude

she only had fringe knowledge of, like the truth behind the dents she found all over her car one September Sunday morning. That began, again according to MC—I don't communicate with my mother—a nostalgia frenzy that became a habit of shared wine and old times. MC says it is great fun to shock my mom with our youthful antics—our parents knew nothing about what we were getting into back then. There were plenty of things we did not want them to know about, and my mother's awareness of any of them falls into the less than one percentile range. I was grounded often enough, like half my life from twelve to twenty when I split. Still. It appalls me. My mother and my friend. Though neither has been either recently.

—Call Adie up, Mary Clay says. If you're in Boston. Where she teaches is pretty close to there. Maybe she'd come in, since you've got this big show. I'm sure she'd love to see you—how long has it been — well, never mind. Maybe she'll buy one of your paintings. I mean, she's a college professor, so she's bound to have some interest in art.

—But probably no money.

Mary Clay is laughing now, on the other end of the phone. At herself. At the idea of setting up Adie this way.

—Oh, well, Jude, you two could have lunch. Maybe I'll drive up from the Cape and join you. It'll be like old times, Jude. The three of us together again.

The three of us together is a nightmare, I think in response. There's something about adolescent girls that only works in twos. Whether it's with a girlfriend or a boyfriend. Add a third person, and it's a recipe for blood-letting. What I remember from those days when we were growing up in Sebastian's living room is that one of us was often on the outs. And it was usually Adie. She drove me crazy with her insecurities. Still, the idea of getting in touch with her takes hold in my mind, like an invasive species. I keep denying it, but it keeps crawling back into my thoughts, growing larger, more demanding, sucking the air out of my days. Why? Why obsess over seeing someone from my distant past? Except. Except this: we shared Sebastian.

One Sunday evening, after Abe had headed home, I phone her and we make a lunch date at a favorite restaurant of his in Copley Square, Abe & Louie's. The name strikes me as ironic. Though the restaurant Abe bears no resemblance, other than ethnicity, to my Abe. An old-world steakhouse. Classy. Expensive. Too fancy for lunch but the location is good. Not too far from the gallery. The show closes in two weeks. Only one red dot. So far. But one is better than none, I guess. It's one of the smaller ones. Tossed bedsheets, the curve of one buttock. That was the inspiration for the piece but it is all suggestion, all bold line and geometric shadow and the curve. It could be a melon or a country road or some psychic phantasmagoria. Only one red dot. Abe assures me there will be others. Of course.

Adie agrees to train in from her little college town in Nowhere, New England. Still. It all has to be arranged around her schedule.

—I'd love to see you, Jude, but I teach Monday, Wednesday, Friday and have committee meetings on Thursdays. So, could we do it either Tuesday or Saturday?

It ends up being Saturday. The last day of the show.

Somehow, this strikes me as typical too. Adie calling the shots. But what choice do I have? Now that the prospect of seeing her again after all these years has me by the jugular, I, of course, agree. I get that she has a fixed schedule and I do not. But I always bristled at her bossy nature, and still do. That know-it-all kid who would correct my grammar and then pee her pants if one of us dared to correct her. Oh, but come on, Jude. That was a long time ago. You've come a long way. She probably has too.

Jude

Look, a solo gallery show. What could Adie possibly have to show for herself that's equal to that? A book. Of course, she has a book. She's an academic. So she may have written a book to buy her tenure, but nobody reads those except other academics. Art lovers, sophisticated people, are coming to my show. Just one red dot. I know, I know. But that'll change. People have their eye on a piece and flock in to buy just before the show ends. Playing the game: if it's still there, the piece they lust after, damn the price, it's destiny to buy!

We meet on a sunny mid-April day, with ornamental pear trees dusting the sidewalks on either side of the square with their snowy petals. I get there first and snare a window table right by the door. I see her slide into view, coming around the corner on Dartmouth onto Boylston from the Copley T station, get her bearings and head my way. She's a strider, long-legged like a crane. Her head is down, lost in thought probably or girding her loins. Anyway, she doesn't see me until she practically runs me over.

—Jude! She looks up and I am met with a delighted grin. Wow, it's been so long. It's good to see you.

After a perfunctory hug, we look each other over. It's uncanny, we could have just walked out of the twelfth grade. And that's what we say to each other as if it had been scripted.

—God, you haven't changed a bit!

So banal. But harrowingly true. Adie's hair is going white like her mother's, that's the only solid change in her appearance. But the easy athleticism that defines her walk, the limber body language, the clear green eyes that want to look over my shoulder and not into mine, that's the Adie I knew back then, in high school.

—Mary Clay's not coming?

—Three's a crowd. It's you I really wanted to see, Adie.

We order wine to go with her chicken Caesar salad and my filet mignon BLT. Adie has already offered to pick up the tab, so I think, Eat up, kiddo!

—Mary Clay told me all about your solo show up on Newbury Street, Jude. That's so amazing.

—Amazing? Really? How?

—Oh, I don't mean it that way, critically. I mean amazing in that I'm surprised its art, not music, the path you ended up following. I always imagined you on the folk-singing circuit.

For once, she looks me directly in the eye. So I laugh. I throw back my head and laugh. She's so sincere. It strikes me as laughingly ridiculous.

—Did I miss something?

I want to say, of course, you clueless bitch. But instead, I buckle to propriety. No, I buckle to my ulterior motive. I need Adie to be my friend in this moment. I need to woo her, not insult her.

—Not at all. I'm laughing because seeing you brings back so many memories, our escapades, you, me, Mary Clay. Sebastian.

Now, she's breaking into a grin. I watch as her cheeks fold up into a grin, her eyes narrow and the folds around her nose deepen. It's not a face I would want to paint but there is something about the lines, her face broken into pieces, that briefly captures my artist's eye. Just as quickly, I am over it, and over her.

—So, Jude. I thought you were still somewhere in the Midwest. Indiana? Or someplace?

—Yeah, well. That was before. This will probably shock you, Adie. You always were such a straight arrow. But I'm a kept woman now. All right, all right, don't laugh. I'm serious. And I'm here because Abe got transferred from the New York office up to Boston. He doesn't have a clue what my art is about but he believes in me. He arranged the whole thing.

Jude

—Wow.

—Wow, what?

—Wow, you're right up front about being a kept woman. Wow, I knew you could draw—remember that great graffiti you did in the girl's bathroom at school that almost got you expelled? Wow, this guy Abe gets you a gallery show on Newbury Street. That's all pretty crazy.

—Crazy? I try to keep the edge out of my voice but just what is she insinuating?

—Crazy, cool.

—You're not shocked? About the married lover part?

I just cannot help myself. It was always fun to play with Adie's morals.

—Jude, you may find this hard to believe, since you seem to have an idee fixe about me. But I grew up too.

—Touché. Well, after lunch I hope you'll go see my show. I mean, you shouldn't miss it. Not just that it closes today but, heh, I'm your friend, and maybe I'm on my way to being famous with this show. Want me to autograph your napkin?

—I did see the review. In the *Phoenix*.

—Yeah, well. The reviewer was a schmuck. Abe says he's the fill-in critic for the regular guy. You can't go by reviews, anyway.

Adie smiles at this and takes the last remaining sip of her wine. That smile, its inscrutable. Is she laughing at me?

—Maybe you'll see something you can't live without and take home a piece of your old friend Jude for your office, I say, trying hard to stay on course. The students will think you're hip collecting modern art.

She looks at me now like I'm pressing, begging, making her uncomfortable. Because she probably doesn't have the means to buy one of my pieces, anyway. They all run into five figures. I need to back off. Get down to business.

—Terrible about Sebastian, I say. And I mean it.

It's an unfathomable consequence of love. The love he had for whatever lowlife got him sick. The love I carry like a talisman. But I must not let myself lose focus here.

—Six years, Jude. Can you believe it?

—No. No, I can't.

Triumph. She reaches her hand across the table and takes mine.

—It was hard. For all of us. Especially for you, Jude, I'd think. Remember when we tried to steal his diary to find out which of us he liked best? I knew it had to be you. Because you could read each other's minds.

—That's nice of you to say.

Oh, the platitude! When what I want to do is wring the life out of her fake sympathy. Instead, I stay on point.

—So, Adie, when did you learn he died? I ask, trying to sound casual, conversational. I want, no need, to know I was not the last to hear about it.

—I was the last to find out, she says as if she just read my mind. As if she feels compelled to treat me like an injured bird, needing her support to fly.

—I've always been the last to know anything about Sebastian, she goes on. The last to learn he was gay, the last to learn about AIDS, the last. I was never a confidante of his, like Mary Clay. Or you.

Now she's fishing for my sympathy? Well, she's thrown her line into the wrong stream.

—When did you hear about it? About Sebastian?

—Mary Clay told me he died.

—Naturally, I say, thinking who else but MC?

—I heard from Grady early on that he had some weird disease, pneumocystis, or something like that. I put two and two together later.

Jude

It was a shock, I'll tell you. When I realized.
—They both stayed in touch with him. Till the end.
—I know.
—I wrote him, Adie says. When Mary Clay told me he was sick. I was too broke to fly to California, and don't know that I would have if I could have afforded it. I'd just lost my husband too. Did you know about that? Oh, God, Jude. Those are just excuses. Sad, miserable excuses.

Adie pauses to touch a napkin to the corner of her eye and takes a long draw on her water glass before she goes on.

—I was afraid I wouldn't recognize the California Sebastian. I was afraid, you know? I wasn't sure he'd remember who I was by then. I was scared to see him. See him sick. So, I wrote him this lame letter. I should have gone to see him. I should have robbed a goddamn bank and gone out there.

Now she really is fishing for my sympathy. Fish, away, Adie. Fish away. But there is something about her words, the anguish that I unavoidably share with her, however much I wish it were not so.

—I didn't see him when he was sick, either. And for pretty much the same reason. No money. I did go out to San Francisco, oh, it must have been in the early 80's sometime. I was hoping he might, we might sing together again. But he was way into his gay modus. There was no place for me. He was the same funny, crazy-wise, beautiful man. But not the same either. The Sebastian I knew was gone—

—Gone?

—Yeah. The old Sebastian. The kid. What we had, well, whatever that was, back when we were teenagers, was long gone. A case of mistaken identity.

I could tell Adie didn't know what to say after that. She swished the water around in her glass, staring intently at it, not looking at me. It was awkward, and I thought I'd better get to the point. Because there was a point. I did not invite her to lunch to make small talk about old times.

—Let's get another, and I wave my wine glass in the direction of the waiter. He nods back, and when the glasses are set down before us and before she can even reach for hers.

—Adie, I was wondering. Do you have anything of Sebastian's?

—What do you mean, anything of Sebastian's?

—I mean, like old photos, letters, any of the poems he wrote, any of his old stuff?

—Well, I didn't keep any of his old socks, if that's what you mean. This incenses me.

—Nooo, I say slowly, modulating my rage into a silent accusation of stupidity. No. I just wondered if you kept anything from those years. Of his. Pictures. Old letters. His poetry. Anything.

—Gosh, Jude. There wasn't much. I think maybe Breck was the only one who had a camera. Didn't he show up at Sebastian's once or twice with his dad's Polaroid? You might try him. I think all I have are copies of the high school literary magazine. When I had stuff in them, usually he did too. I didn't keep a scrapbook or anything like that from those years, if that's what you mean. Even my so-called journals are embarrassing. *Got my period. Breck touched my boobs but he doesn't really like me like me.* Stuff like that.

—Oh. I see. OK, then. I was just curious. Breck's still at the same restaurant?

—Yes. He is. Some things never change.

—Thanks. I'll try and track him down.

I do not want Adie to see my disappointment, to understand, but

Jude

she probably already has figured out that the reason I wanted to have lunch with her had nothing to do with her at all.

—I wish I did, Jude. Some photograph of him. Of all of us. If I had anything, you could have it. If it would mean something to you. But I just don't. Sorry.

If it would mean something to me? If it would mean something to me!

—I think about him all the time, I say out loud.

Oooh, I didn't mean for that to come out, not one little bit but there it hangs over the table, a soul confession.

—Me too, Jude. Me too.

And that was our lunch. The last time I will see Adie, I figure. But that's OK. We really only have Sebastian in common and that's, obviously, a pretty threadbare connection these days. Only six years. But it feels like yesterday-forever. Maybe he died the first time for me when he blew me off in California. But Adie? She couldn't—or wouldn't—help me collect stuff of his, memorabilia, things that couldn't mean as much to her as they would to me. I know she has stuff. She must. She has to be lying. I remember the journals she kept, part adolescent pissing and moaning about boys she had crushes on, including Sebastian, and part ticket stubs and pressed flowers. I know because I read them. Basically, she's right. They were full of adolescent garbage. She was full of adolescent garbage. Still is, garbage, that is.

We faux hug and I watch her go. An insignificant part of my past. I notice too, as we part company, that Adie walks back toward the Copley T stop, not down Exeter. She's heading home, not to Newbury Street. Damned Phoenix review, I curse silently.

As if to make up for her not bothering, I head over to the gallery one last time. There are two or three people looking around. I try to listen in on their comments, their critiques, if that's what they are. But they are

Ambient Light

whispering. I continue my victory lap, taking in the gallery, my work on these walls, the tiny young woman in stiletto heels minding the desk, greeting anyone who comes in, handing out a flyer about me and my work. I continue and find only one red dot—still.

I walk to the bus stop. In my mind's eye, my head is in Sebastian's lap. He is alive beside me. His laughter curls through my mind. I can conjure time with him even now just like this. When the bus comes, we climb aboard, me and a seventeen-year-old Sebastian. I pick a seat at the back for the two of us. My eyes are focused on Sebastian, looking up at the stubble on his chin. The interior me is singing an old Ike and Tina Turner duet with him. "River Deep Mountain High." His voice flows through my being. My longing is river deep.

Oh, but this for-shit day isn't over yet. Tonight, there's a party for select friends of Abe's after the show closes. When I get back to my place to clean up and put on my party face, there's a message on my machine from Abe.

Uh, um ... Look, Jude ... something bad has happened ... You and me. It's over. ... I'm so sorry, Jude, but ... but ... oh, shit, Jude. My wife found out. .. yeah. So this isn't easy . . isn't want I want ... but ... but ... See? The gallery called our apartment this afternoon. ... and asked for.... for you, Jude. When Gloria didn't know who Jude was, the woman at the gallery told her she was looking for Abe Cohen's wife. ... oh, God, Jude. It was awful ... when I got home ... Gloria ... demanded to know who this Jude person was ... Oh, Jude, oh babe. It's over, Jude ... Please stay in the apartment ... till you can make other arrangements. Jude, Jude Jude ... I loved our time together. I love you. But ... you know, you know ... I can't leave her ... I told you that, honey? Right? ... Oh, Jude ... Thank God I'll have a painting of yours to—

I push the delete button to shut him up, the wimp. I step back from

Jude

the phone. Take one deep breath, then another. Then I throw the phone across the room. Then a lamp. Then I slash my paintings lying against one wall with a kitchen knife.

    The prick.

    His red dot.

Adie

When the phone rings in my office, I jump. My head has been buried in grading blue book exams. More than anything, I want to get these essays read and graded and be done. Semester over. Summer on the horizon, and a dive trip to the Galapagos in late June to look forward to. A couple of old dive pals cooked up a plan to do Machu Picchu, then rent a fourteen-passenger dive boat and stuff it full of our scuba friends, with the clear intent of diving the northern islands, Wolf and Darwin, where novice divers aren't allowed to venture. I am as excited as an astronaut striding across the launch pad.

For now, the only water I can get to quickly is a fast-running river about a dozen miles from campus. I strapped my kayak to the top of my Jeep before coming to class this morning. I'm ready to go. Can't think of a better way to clear my head of Diane di Parma. I added her to my feminist literature studies seminar only two years ago and am already exhausted by her. The Beat poets know how to beat a dead horse. The Beat poets, ironically, lack rhythm, beat. Deadbeats. Now I am amusing myself with silly punning, a clear sign I need a break. When the damned phone refuses to stop ringing, I concede the point and take the call.

—Yes? Mary Clay? My gosh!

We exchange life highlights experienced since the last time we saw each other, also the last time we spoke, years ago now. Of course, I would know her voice anywhere, any time. She tells me that her partner, Stan, is dying of some rare cancer found only in Central Africa and never in white men. She asks about Michael and I must say the god-forsaken word: dead.

—Oh, no, Adie, I'm so sorry. Was he ill?

—No. Diving accident.

—What? But you were both professionals.

—There are those who would say that makes us most vulnerable. Anyway, long story short, we couldn't get him to a hyperbaric chamber fast enough to save him.

—Would you mind? Do you mind me asking—

—Oh, Mary Clay. I sigh. Deeply because I do not want to say the words again. Not one more time, ever.

—Never mind, she says, hearing that sigh, knowing what it means. But I know she wants to know what happened, in detail, and in some ways, I'm glad for her comfortable curiosity. Unlike just about everyone else I know, she is not shying away from her questions, her desire to understand.

—It's okay. He chased a diver, a photographer, who had lost track of her depth. Too busy getting close ups of nudibranchs on the wall, probably. She was like that. Self-absorbed behind her camera. Anyway, she got swept in a down current to about two hundred feet, we think, when he caught up to her.

I pause. Hold back. I don't want my fury to overtake me yet again. But I say what I'm thinking anyway. Because MC of all people will get it. Because her Stan is cruising toward that detestable maw as we speak.

—She should have been the one to get the bends, not Michael. He inflated her buoyancy vest so she would shoot up to the surface, while he followed. We think she dropped her camera and Michael went back to try to retrieve it. That was our best guess. Anyway, he got bent. Badly. Nitrogen bubbles blew up in his lungs and his brain.

—God, Adie. I don't know what to say. Geez. How long ago was that? she finally asks.

—Say nothing. Now you know and we never have to talk about it again. It's been almost eleven years, in Indonesia. And I flash to our wedding on the beach. How beautiful it was, he was.

—Never. No. Except. I wish you'd told me. I could have been there for you.

—Oh, MC, nobody could be there for me.

So, I go on to tell her our kids are thriving, by way of not quite changing the subject exactly, telling her both Michael Junior and Elise's husband, his best friend, are budding Wall Street tycoons.

—Making a fortune, I say, quoting my son to MC. Can you imagine?

—And Elise?

—Think I told you. She got herself preggers. Twins, no less. Runs in the family, given that she's a twin. She wanted a career but made the choice to be a stay-at-home mom.

We commiserate, while all the time I am staring at the pictures of Michael on my desk, the aching leitmotiv of my life since his death comes looping again into my thoughts—who was the bigger fool, that photographer? Or Michael? Michael, Michael, Michael, how could you?

Gently now, she pushes on.

—Is that why you gave up diving?

—No. Just got antsy. It was time for me to grow up and own my life. Put all this education to work.

—Anybody—anybody—now?

—No. I answer a bit too sharply. And then I think, Really, MC? Really? Then I haul in my tone.

—Not any good at relationships. Not in that way, anyway, I lie.

—Always was, she says, then adds, but that doesn't keep them from slipping away.

I know she is referring to Stan, maybe others. MC always was the romantic among us. But she has also lifted the burden of bad fortune with men from my back and assumed its weight herself. Her way of lightening my load. I am grateful but also fear the conversation, with its maudlin nature, has gone on too long. I have said too much. Peeled back the shroud.

—So, MC, why the sudden, if welcome, call?

—It's Jude.

I could have guessed.

—Has something happened to her?

—No. It may be what's about to happen to me.

Even though we are spread all over the country, even though our noble leader is dead of AIDS, the fibers that run between us run strong. It's as if the members of our old teenaged pack are all strung out on elastic bands that retract with a snap every so often, whipping us back into each other's lives again. In this rebound way, we have kept up with each other. I could probably drive to Mary Clay's place on Cape Cod in three, four hours. But I never have. Nor has she sought me out, not in person. That close in miles and we only connect by keeping our distance. By phone in the old days, now by email mostly. As if those fibers that held us together once would not survive the test of propinquity now. Our friendship is of another time and another place and yet, from time to time, we need a shot of each other. To hear each other's voices. As if our shared past is the wellspring of our lives and occasionally, we need to bring up the bucket for a refresher.

—So. Jude, she says, by way of bringing the conversation back to her reason for calling.

Adie

I sit back in my chair, its creaking mimicking my own instinctive sense of caution. All too often when Mary Clay and I communicate, it has to do with Jude. Or Sebastian. But since Sebastian's death, it's always about Jude.

—She phoned me up, Mary Clay says. Asked me if I would rent her a room. She knows this place. She knows there's space. Lots of it.

And we both know Jude who, such a pistol when we were kids, is a loose cannon now. Broke. Desperate. Always amoral. Worst of all, a user. I know the stories. She's always looking for a free ride. From men. From her sisters. From friends who don't know better. And now, she's hitting up Mary Clay.

—Oh, Mary Clay. Be careful. Don't let your old friendship delude you. If you let her in, you will never get her out.

—I know, I know. But—

—No buts.

—But she says she has nowhere else to go.

—Tell her about Stan. Tell her he's too ill—

—She knows he's in hospice. I let that drop when she called yesterday. Before I knew what she was on about.

I want to shake her. Wake her up. But she's already wide awake. She knows all about Jude's neediness and her life mantra—unrecognized, unappreciated genius artist, deserving of riches and fame, but denied. But back when we were kids, they were best friends and that's the Jude she remembers. That's the Jude I can recall too—funny, bitchy, wild, but demanding too. Even then, even of us, her friends. Especially with Sebastian, whom we all idolized, who she wanted for herself.

—I think it's a bad idea, MC.

—I know. I do too. Still, what if she's as broke and homeless as she says she is?

—Too bad her mother isn't still alive. She could have gone there.
—Never. Not in a million years. Jude? Live with her mother?
I'm smiling now, remembering that noxious relationship.
—I miss her, MC allows.
—Jude?
—Well, yes. Sort of. But I meant her mother. You know I bumped into her down here not long after I moved into Gran's house, right? We were almost neighbors. I ended up doing some gardening for her and, all the time, she was having Stan and me over for wine and revelation. She loved hearing about our adventures, even though she could still get mad about the things that happened—
—To her Rambler?
—For starters. Turns out she loved that car. She wept, too, when I told her about Sebastian. All she could say was That boy, that boy.

This amazes me. The mother among all our mothers that we made an art of tormenting takes her daughter's place in MC's life. And loved Sebastian too. Funny, funny, funny, the way the world turns, and turns in on itself.

—I gotta go, MC. Stay cool. Oh, and let me know what you decide to do.

I swivel in my old office chair to look out the window. But I'm really looking back in time. To the last time I saw Jude, for lunch in Boston. When not once did she ask me a single thing about my life but talked only, obsessively about Sebastian. Was she even my friend? Ever? I know she made me feel insignificant but almost everybody did in those days. I know that Mary Clay and I were friends first, and then Jude moved in down the block from her when we were in the seventh grade, the start of the Sebastian years, and we became a threesome. If I were honest, I would have to admit that she lorded it over me, and I accepted that.

Adie

Because the force of her self-assurance overwhelmed the teenaged me, who always doubted my dreams. Jude never did. She never doubted herself, ever. I wasn't, aren't like that. Doubt was my teenaged stock-in-trade. Odd how things turn out. I sit in a cubbyhole office, embraced by the books that line the walls, a tenured professor of twentieth-century women's literature. And Jude, a miserable sexagenarian still-wanna-be. The moral? Your gift lies not where you will it to be but where your life, propelled by unanticipated influences, takes you instead. We, none of us, led the lives we thought we were destined for.

A breeze pops up and suddenly the view outside my office window is full of maple seeds. A blizzard of twirling yellow helicopters. It must be a masting year for maples, I deduce. I love it when this happens. How a species of trees will conspire through root communication to over-seed for best repopulation results. The forest floor can be so covered in acorns, during an oak masting, that it's like trying to walk on a blanket of marbles.

I am too old, gone fifty for heaven's sake, and must keep to certain levels of decorum on campus, but I long to go outside and dance, twirl like a human maple seed. Be among and apart of this spectacle of life renewing. I long to be eighteen again. Given the chance, I would live my teen years again, even with all the misery and angst that came along with them, just to be as free as a maple seed spinning new in the world with my cohort spinning free beside me—Breck and Grady, Mary Clay and Jude, Tony and Sebastian—unaware of the hard landings ahead, oblivious to the scramble for survival we would all face, one way or the other.

Ah, but time is the masked marauder, dangling carrots before us fool asses to make us rush all the faster toward the precipice it knows is there, but we do not. Pushing us to hurry up and hurl ourselves forward. Drivers' license. Draft card. Legal drinking. College education. Job, marriage, mortgage, children. Remember, Adie, when you used to say you took your retirement in your twenties? With not a little pride and of course a complement of hubris? Because you dodged employment, marriage and mortgages? And you did it in a wetsuit? Yes, well. But I paid an awful price, didn't I? When Michael died on my watch. It should have been the photographer who died, not you, and me pregnant with twins. You should have let her drown.

I pick up the photo of us, taken on that last dive trip, decked out in full scuba regalia, smiling idiotically. We did not know, when that shot was taken, that we were pregnant but we knew Indonesia would be our final live-aboard.

Hanging up our fins, you said. Heading back to the real world, you said. Just how real, I soon learned. It was no picnic having those babies with you gone, your brain burst with nitrogen bubbles and me with no fixed place to live, a new job, and children I no longer wanted, not without you to share them with, crowding my belly like gas.

I run a finger over your lovely photographed body, and that godforsaken loneliness grabs me by the lungs and stops my breathing. Yet again. As if your blue-lipped, glazed but terrified eyes, were staring back at me from the boat's dive platform all over again.

Putting our portrait down, I pick up the picture of our two grown children, a boy and a girl, just as we were when we set off to explore the oceans' blue. I can't see you in either of them, as I so hoped I would. So counted on you being a living, visible presence in one or both of them, so that you would still be with me in that tangible way. But these two are a stew of us, a ragout. Your nose and chin, my eyes and hairline, and vice versa.

Oh, Mike. What would we have become together? Would our love have survived dry land? I've always wondered that. And doubted it.

Adie

It's like going to Disney World and thinking you cannot live without a Mickey Mouse sweatshirt only to get it home and, out of context of time and place, look at that garment with a clear eye, flush red, laugh at yourself and toss it into the pile for Goodwill. I wish, though, you had known Mike Junior and Elise. I wish they had known you. But what are wishes but hope misplaced?

Shit, Adie. Pity party over. I need to knuckle down. Get back to grading these essays on di Parma's Revolutionary Letters and the relevancy of her poetry in today's world. I need to get to the river. I must clear my head of my dead husband's dead body and get back to work. Excise the life of the heart for the more comforting, insensate world of the head. Concentrating on the impassioned prose of impressionable youth trying to understand an age of hatred from their age of innocence handily walls off that old life, that old love. Like Poe's *Cask of the Amontillado*.

I turn my attention to di Parma. There is a lot of Trump bashing in my students' efforts, and doesn't di Parma just invite that with her *now we must organize, obey the rules, so that later/we can be free*? Organize, work the system, get out the vote to get out the president. As trite as many of these essays are, I celebrate my students' conviction. They so remind me of my eager recreational divers. However alien the underwater world, they couldn't get enough of it, borne along on the twin currents of exploration and understanding. Just like my students trying to parse out di Parma.

Then, it dawns on me, like a cannon going off right next to my ear: Sebastian probably knew of di Parma if he didn't actually know her himself. She was in San Francisco, writing, teaching at the Art Institute and co-founding the San Francisco Institute of Magical and Healing Arts at the same time as he was living there, a poet himself. Maybe she frequented the health food store where he worked. Wasn't he himself the kind of bird who flew backwards? Who threw off convention to live a life in the face of discrimination and marginalization, just as di Parma did, in the all-male, testosterone-charged world of Kerouac, Ginsberg and Burroughs?

Was it possible that this connection, subconsciously, led me to di Parma in the first place? The thought crowds out the falling maple seeds, the essays, the call from MC, even Michael. Didn't di Parma write *learn the magic, learn to believe?* Wasn't Sebastian, even as a boy, the king of magical thinking? A seeker longing to believe? Remember, Adie that poem he wrote when he was seventeen, the one about God? Think, think! How did it go? Yes.

> What is this?
> Where is God?
> How do I get in touch with Him?
> > I haven't met Him yet
> > But
> > He sounds
> > Like
> > A great Guy
> > Secluded and shy
> > Slightly deaf.
> > Maybe we have a bad
> > Connection —
> > Maybe a line's down up the road.

It was published in the school literary magazine. One of the ones I kept because a piece of my own was included too. He called it "The Relationship Between Him and Me." I've never forgotten it because he

Adie

was looking for a God everyone in our pack vigorously denied. Sebastian though, he *wanted* to believe. A secret, one of many, I guess, he kept very much to himself. I wonder now, when MC, Jude, and I tried to steal his diary that time, what truths he could not speak aloud then we would have found revealed there. A private petri dish of pain behind the public façade of that joy-mongering boy.

I still have that magazine. Not just it but all the magazines in which our juvenilia made print. I could have told Jude about them when we had lunch. I could have. But didn't. I could have told her I own, somewhere, in some cigar box, one or two old Polaroid photos of Sebastian. She would have keeled over in her BLT if I'd let on I know where Sebastian's old guitar is. That Grady has it. I might have told her, I might have even given all my stuff of his to her, if she'd just once stopped talking about herself.

Darn it, I will have to finish grading these exams over the weekend. I will have to re-read this one I started when MC's phone call interrupted me. And Michael's ghost reappeared. Along with Sebastian's. That mind-stealing switchback to the boy we thought we knew so well but didn't know at all. I wonder how, and when, he found the courage to step out of his diary and into the world.

What I need is the river, with its still pools and gamboling runs over rocky patches of white water, to free my head not of my work but of loves lost.

Breck

The last patrons of the restaurant are clearing out, but those at the bar will have to be invited to leave when we close at one a.m. This is my life six days a week. I never had much ambition, sort of like Tony, although we all thought he was destined for the priesthood. No one thought I was destined for anything, including myself. So, when an old high school classmate started this restaurant after college and asked me to manage it, I jumped at the chance. That was over twenty years ago now. The rhythm, the routine, the smells, the camaraderie—I know just about everyone who comes in here—this is more home to me than home. Since my wife left me and my daughter to fend for ourselves.

So, tonight I'm surprised by the knock on the door I've already locked. It's just gone one and the bartender has called last round.

—A little leeway, Breck, a little leeway, he sings to me every night. That last, forbidden cocktail, because it is now after hours, he tells me, is worth a hundred dollars more to him in tips. People, I've noticed, love to get away with things. Like kids when told no who get off on saying Oh, yes I will. These delinquent adults, drinking their illicit shots or final beers, are prepared to pay for the privilege of being privileged enough to be allowed just one more. I can't argue with that.

But I can argue with whoever it is who is trying to get in when the door is locked. Locked door—isn't that signal enough that we're closed? The knock is now a fist-pounding. So I slide off my stool at the end of the bar and go see who's trying to break in. It's Rae. My daughter. She's a mess. Hair all over the place, mascara running, and the look in her eye, well, it reminds me of a trapped animal. It also reminds me of the look she gave me the morning she woke up to no mother. Just gone. No explanation. I take all this in in a split second while I fumble with the dead bolt and the secondary lock.

—Rae. Rae honey. I'm speaking to her through the glass while I fumble. Maybe I'm shouting, because Paulie, the bartender comes up behind me.

—Heh, what's going—Breck, that's your kid—

When I get the door open, she falls into my arms, then pushes past me, pushes past Paulie, and heads straight to the bar.

—Paulie, can I get a double vodka with lime.

—Rae, honey, I start to say, as I sidle up to sit beside her. One of the regulars, seeing a family drama unfold, gets up, moves down a couple of places, making room for me. He tosses back the remainder of his drink, leaves some folded bills on the bar and heads out.

It's a while and two double vodkas, before I dare to ask her any questions. Her hair, that gorgeous gold-streaked chestnut mane, falls around her face like a privacy veil, so I wait. There for her. Always there for her.

—We broke up, she says finally. Danny and me.

—Oh, honey—I start, feeling pathetic, feeling helpless, wanting to kill the guy who is breaking my daughter's heart. Never mind that I can barely remember a time without Danny. She and Danny have been an item since, for how long? I have to think back to a time pre-Dan. I don't even know. High school some time. Maybe even middle school.

Breck

—You want to tell me about it? Or do you just want me to take you home? I mean back to home home. Not your apartment.

Rae looks at me. The vodka has done its work. Calmed her, brought her back to fuzzy earth. Slump shouldered, she sighs. A long heart-wrenching sigh.

I hear this sorrow and my anger switch flips on. How could he do this to her? After all these years? So I wasn't prepared for what she said next.

—I broke up with him, Pop. There's something I need to tell you. But not here, not in the restaurant.

So Paulie and I shoo out the last remaining patrons, do some quick clean-up. I check the kitchen for burners left on and lights. Paulie's out the door first and makes a beeline for his car. He's visibly tired, but he also wants to leave Rae and me to ourselves. He's a thoughtful guy and a good friend, Paulie is. Whatever this drama is that is unfolding, he's giving us space.

—'night, Rae. Breck. Sorry about Danny.

Of course, Paulie has overheard. He also thinks of Danny as an appendage of Rae's. We've all come to think of him that way. A fixture. For so many years, their names have been glued together as if one: Raeanddanny.

I check all the doors, set the alarm and then we are out in the wee hours of an October night, moonless and clear. The slightest chill in the air reminds me that Indian summer is over and I need to meet with the chef to think about our Thanksgiving menu. I put an arm around Rae, hug her to me just a little and am surprised when she loops her arm around my waist and hooks a thumb in my beltloop.

Years ago, I bought a modest little house within walking distance of work. The restaurant is located on a main thoroughfare, on the edge of the city, near some pretty upscale neighborhoods, from whom we draw most of our clientele. My place used to be a carriage house for one of those houses owned by some wealthy magnate of this or that. I like it. Like its ivy-covered brick walls. I like it's two up, two down coziness. A kitchen, a living room and two bedrooms. I'll have to clear off the second bed for Rae tonight. No one's slept in that room since she left for college five years ago.

She asks if I have anything to drink, before she's even shed her coat or dumped her backpack on the floor.

—Oh, that's right. I forgot. You're a teetotaler now.

—I have a bottle of cooking sherry—

—I'll take it.

—Or I could make some coffee?

—Cooking sherry, Pop. Just hand me the bottle. Make yourself coffee and then come sit with me.

She pats the seat beside her on the couch when I come in from the kitchen, a mug of coffee in one hand, sherry bottle in the other.

—What happened with Danny, Rae? I want to say, that boy was like a part of the family. Who'll clean out my gutters now? But of course I don't say that. I don't say anything about missing him. But I will. It's a shock to realize it, in this moment when my one and only daughter is suffering and chugging cooking sherry, that I loved that boy, who as suddenly as a sinkhole has been sucked from our lives.

—Pop. Oh, Pop. I don't know how to tell you. Except to tell you. And I don't want to tell you because I don't want to break your heart.

—My heart? I thought it was your heart that was broken?

—No. My heart is just confused, really really confused. But my head isn't. I love Danny, I always will. But I can't be with him anymore. Because— because —oh, Pop, he caught me with someone else.

Breck

—Is this new boy someone you care about? I mean, more than Danny.

—Differently. Differently, Pop. Oh, Pop, oh Pop. The new boy is—well, he's a she. I'm so sorry, Pop. I'm so very sorry. But I think I may be gay. I don't expect you to understand, I don't expect Danny to. I'm not sure I do. It just happened—

And then she spewed out the whole story. About her feelings toward certain girlfriends when she was as young as a kindergartener. About her certainty that that's why her mother left us, that she too is gay, and that she, Rae, inherited it from her.

—Or Mom suspected it in me and was disgusted.

—That's nonsense, Rae. Your mother walked out when you were barely four.

Then, this insane fear. Had I done something wrong in raising her? Had I caused this? But then I snap myself into line. You don't cause homosexuality, any more than you can cause cancer in another. I know this. But there must just be some kneejerk parental hiccup that jumps to the mind of even the most well informed of us. Shame blushes my cheeks and I am glad the room is too dark for Rae to see.

—Danny. Danny. He's just always been there. Would do anything for me. I can hardly remember a time when he wasn't part of my life.

Our lives, I think.

—I think I was hiding behind him, Pop. I'm so sorry. I know this is a shock. And you will tell me you support me in anything I do, any choice I make, you always have. But what about now, Pop? What about this?

I want to say, Are you sure? But know it's not for me to ask. Experience, Sebastian, taught me otherwise.

Then she is crying, and I am crying and we both are a couple of slobbering fools huddled together against the onslaught of this emotional storm. She half drunk, me half shattered. Not knowing how to support her, what to say except the obvious platitudes—*I love you, honey. I'll support you always, and honor your choices. Whatever makes you happy, Rae.* But I don't say any of that shit. Because even she doesn't know, or isn't sure what happiness looks like, any more than I do. Then, hugging her there, I thought about no children. The thought came like a lightning bolt. *But, honey, you've always wanted children*—This brings more tears to my eyes and I clutch my baby girl harder than ever.

Eventually I realize she has fallen asleep in my arms, the sherry bottle not quite dry. I stretch her out full on the couch, retrieve a pillow and a blanket from my bed, take her shoes off and cover her. Tucking the blanket up under her chin, as I did every night she was motherless, I listen to her even breathing, a little husky, a little ripe from all the alcohol, and am reminded, like it or not, she is not a child anymore. Her life is hers.

There is no sleep for me this night. I sit back in the recliner across the room from Rae and pull an old afghan over my legs. My coffee is still warm. I sip it, with the mug on my chest, and my eyes closed. In the morning I will ask her if this woman she has been with was a necessary experiment or a new, and right, lover. I relax a little, now that she is asleep and I know the source of her upset, that abandoned look at the restaurant door earlier, when she knew she had to tell me. Because it was the right thing to do. Because she couldn't let the news come to me from Danny.

I drift a little. But not very far. Because what Rae can't know is that I have been down this road before with my old friend Sebastian. There is so much past Rae's news has dredged up. I drift back to Sebastian's living room, where I hung out all my high school years. I am there again. Seven of us, the pack, are all there. Adie, Jude, Grady, Sebastian, Mary Clay, and Tony. We are sitting around the coffee table, Sebastian popping up from time to time to stack up another round of 45s on the record player, while we smoke and eat Twinkies and Ding Dongs. Grady somehow has purloined a case of beer, and we begin daring each other to torpedo them. Adie, Sebastian and Grady scored on their first attempts, popping the top and slugging the whole can down in one go. So did I. Mary Clay and Jude took the high road, and chickened out by saying the beer was too precious to waste that way. But when Tony tried, he hurled the whole can back up at us, drenching the table, wrecking our cigarettes, getting Jude wet and some of Sebastian's record sleeves.

—Look what you did, you queer, Jude says.

—Hermaphrodite, Adie adds. I like this word better.

—You would, MC says, you are the 'queen' of big words.

And then we were off on a pun-fest. We are calling each homo names, creating on the spot, and laughing till we are choking on our spit and smoke. The famous circus act, the flamer-throwers. Tinker Bell's Peter. The tight-ass, Mr. I. M. Fudgepacker. The comedy act, Abutt and Cosfellow. Pouf the dandy dragon, who frolics in his light-ish loafers, someone sings. Fish Hand Luke, as limp-wristed as a dead carp. But who's carping? Dead-Eye Dick. And on and on.

All of us. Even Sebastian. I believe even Sebastian was playing, and certainly Tony, the best of our punsters. We were shouting these at each other and laughing and throwing cigarette butts at each other—butts, get it?—until Mrs. T stomped down the stairs—I'll never forget it—and called us foul-mouthed adolescents and sent us home. From then on, we were always calling each other fairies or queers or faggots. It was a joke. We meant it as a joke.

Sitting here, across the room from a lightly snoring Rae, I ache at the memory.

Once, when Sebastian was at State and I was going to DePauw, he asked me down for a weekend. It was our senior year, only months before we were supposed to take responsibility for ourselves as men of the world, as productive members of society. Something that terrified me for sure. I drove up there and he met me in the parking lot.

—We're going to a party.

—We are?

—You can dump your stuff in my room first, and then we'll go over to the auditorium.

Even now, I can picture how happy he was. While I was freaking out about my directionless life on the eve of graduation, Sebastian was just in the moment, relishing every second, as if he knew he was on the cusp of big change, and it had nothing to do with a career or even being grown up. That Friday night he took me to this big dance and set me up with a friend of his, a pretty little thing named Barbara, and then he was off. He was working that night, DJ-ing the dance, and it was clear right off the bat that he was in his element, that he had fans, kids who came to the dance just because he was spinning the vinyl. As soon as he stepped up behind the soundboard, the place erupts in cheers.

—Sebastian the Assassin of Sound! They chanted, stomping their feet, screaming it. It was amazing.

From the first record on the turntable to the last, Sebastian was on in a way I'd never seen before. Not like when we were kids in his living room when he would dance and sing along with the music he collected and loved like Midas. This was different. He acted out each song. He became whatever artist he was playing, a super smooth Marvin Gaye, a manic Little Richard, a caped James Brown. He knew all the choreography of any Black group you could name. He knew them all by heart. The Temptations, The Miracles, the Four Tops, the Impressions, the Drifters, all of them, while miming the words. The crowd went wild. Of course, he knew all the words, had since high school and our karaoke sessions in his living room, but he did not sing while DJ'ing.

—You can sing with the best of them, Sebastian, I said to him during a break. Why don't you?

—Oh, he said, grinning like the cat who ate the canary. I wouldn't want to upstage the masters.

I will never forget that weekend. I will never forget watching Sebastian live his dream, DJ-ing for a big crowd, and living the music at the same time. He was transported. I mean, watching him, he simply was not of this world. He was happy, on a plane ordinary mortals like me can barely imagine.

On Sunday, when he was driving me back to town to catch the bus back to DePauw, he made a detour to a place we called The Great Paved Area. It was this huge four-lane road out in the middle of nowhere that didn't go anywhere and never had a car on it. As kids, we speculated that it was built by the government for planes to land when the Russians invaded. Of course, once we were older and that road was surrounded by cookie cutter mansions, we knew better. But as teenagers, we used it to lay rubber, taking our parents' cars out there, putting the pedal to the metal, then throwing on the brakes to fishtail all over the place, the girls screaming in the backseat.

To go there, just us two guys, was weird, but I could tell Sebastian had some big thing on his mind. We sat on the shoulder of the Great Paved Area, windows down, smoking a reefer he rolled in his lap, looking for comets and not talking, except when we spotted one flashing across the sky.

—What are we doing here. Sebastian, I finally ask.

—Breck, you remember Barbara?

—Course. Why?

—I slept with her a couple of weeks ago.

—Goddamn it, Sebastian! That's great, man. You scored. Wow. Was that your first time?

For a very long minute he doesn't say anything. Just sucks in the smoke and then lets it float out of the sides of his mouth, looking like some kind of hippie vampire. I get this uneasy feeling. Especially since he just looks straight ahead. As if he were reading cue cards through the windshield that are plastered on the trees ahead. Then, he nods sort of slowly.

—Yup. First time. And. Last.

—Last? I remember asking that stupid question. But I didn't get it, of course. I made him spell it out to me because I just couldn't dig what he meant.

—Yeah. I gave it a try. I wanted to make sure.

—What do you mean? Make sure? What did you try?

—Sex with a woman, Breck. Sex with Barbara. She volunteered. A kind of test run, you know? It didn't work. So now I know, and so do you. And don't worry, I'm not coming on to you. I just wanted to be the one to tell you.

I remember staring at him, not saying anything. Because what was running through my mind like a B movie, were all the times I'd called him a fag or a fairy. All the things we said that must have insulted him, hurt him, coming as they did from his so-called friends. We were just messing around. Just in fun. If I'd known, if any of us had realized—

I open my eyes. Rae is sitting up on the couch, looking at me.

—Pop, you OK? I think you were having a nightmare. Please tell me it wasn't about me—

There is a moment of re-entry. When Sebastian sitting in that car, smoking and confessing, fades into Rae, disheveled, dear, half-sober Rae.

Breck

Something about both their expressions merge into one. Expectation. Of my reaction to their revelations, overlapping in time now, with Rae sitting opposite me and Sebastian dead of AIDS.

I wish I had the right words for both of them. It's times like this when you know love is not enough.

Grady

The red and blue runway lights glow up against the jet black December sky, moonless, starless mostly too, because of all the houses around. I remember this as a little airport, way out of town, serving a tiny city in a not vastly populated state, where you could see the planets and the constellations from the observation deck. Clearly, those days are gone. How long has it been since I've been out to this airport, anyway? Twenty years or something? The approach to this airport used to be a two-lane road that split just before the terminal, sending one lane to departures and the other to arrivals, both on the ground floor. Now there is signage and four lanes and two stories, and acres of additional terminal. Like some kind of ugly cancer that just keeps replicating and absorbing the natural landscape, eating the earth alive. Driving in, not expecting all this change, though I probably could have guessed it if I'd thought about it, I have to really slow down. Read the signs. Make sure I can find parking—we used to just pull up in front and leave the car at the curb—and from there the TWA terminal.

Just the finest, lightest inconsequential snow peppers the windshield. God's dandruff after a good scratch. It is December twenty-third, so maybe a dusting for Christmas. That would be unusual but also a little celebratory. It never snows in this part of the country. Ice, yes. Whoa can they get ice storms here! Snow, no. A white Christmas, almost unheard of. Already, it is petering out. Just a tiny squall, just a little itch. I look at my watch. I am here in plenty of time to meet Sebastian's flight. He's on the red eye from San Francisco, which ought to be landing in about an hour. I made better time driving down from Wisconsin than I expected. Which leaves me shivering in my car now, waiting.

 I have to wonder if I'll recognize him. He's sick, I know. We all know about his AIDS. So, what will he look like? Heh, come on, Grady. You'd recognize those mischievous hazel eyes, that crooked, waggish smile. Anywhere. The disease can't rob him of those. I hope. Oh, boy, I am not looking forward to this. I am definitely not looking forward to this. I don't know why I said I'd meet him. Except he wrote me a letter, a hilarious letter full of scatological innuendo and nonsense fantasy, just like he used to when we corresponded for a while in college, and after. The letters died out after he'd been in San Francisco a while, I've always thought because he was a new, very different Sebastian out there. What we had had in common, music mostly, almost entirely, had somehow fallen by the wayside. I was still committed; he was not. So, when I got this last letter, telling me he was sick, which I already knew—Mary Clay had put it out on the jungle drums—and that he was coming home for Christmas to see his mother, I read between the lines, for the last time. I said, of course, I'd be there. Even though I live three states away now. It was a summons. A strange one, to be sure. I mean, why not ask Breck, who still lives in town? But he didn't. He asked me. He wanted to see me, and that was all the incentive I needed, I guess.

 Beth was not happy about it, leaving her with the two boys already bouncing around the house, jacked up on pre-Christmas excitement, and driving seven hours overnight all the way down here. To pick up someone I hadn't seen in fourteen years. She was broiling. It just seemed nuts to her. It is nuts. Doubly so because I'll likely be too late for our big family Christmas dinner, always on Christmas Eve, and not early enough to get the maniacs manacled to their bunk beds before Beth and I commit infanticide. My parents, her parents, a stuffed goose and all the trimmings, sitting around the fire afterwards caroling. The boys, pumped on holiday adrenaline, having a squabble-fest, trying to sneak peeks under the tree until we finally "give in"—this is a time-honored part of the tradition—and let them open one gift. Always selected by me and always teasingly nondescript. Batteries or a section of track—but it is for a train or a car?—something like that.

—But what's it *for*, Dad? they wail in unison. To which Beth traditionally answers

—Wait and see pudding. A family joke. This is the same line she uses when the boys demand to know what's for dinner.

We wrestle them into bed with a special treat under each pillow and a pledge that Santa will not stop here if they so much as set a foot out of bed before six in the morning.

With my luck, I'll run into a lake effect blizzard, and not make it home until after Christmas.

But I explained I just had to go and when she asked why it was so important to see Sebastian again, I just shook my head.

—Because it is. I don't know, honey. I just have to go. He asked me. I have to. He's coming home to say goodbye to his mother, Beth. That's hard.

Still, the *why me* lingered, not convincingly answered for either of us.

—And you need to say goodbye to him too, is that it, Grady?

It's why I married her. She can read my mind and forgive me for what she finds there. On my way to the car, she handed me a couple of ham sandwiches and a thermos of coffee.

—Drive safe.

Sebastian, coming off the plane, appears like something a Mexican cat has dragged in. He is wrapped in an ancient serape that looks as if he has rolled around on a dusty roadside in it for the last year. I searched for those eyes, that smile. But his pale face, what isn't lost to a wildly thick beard, is so chalklike, so ghostly, so other-worldly white that I have to stop myself from backing away from him. When he spots me, he breaks out into that intoxicating grin of his and I rush forward to greet him. But he holds up a hand, holds it out actually. So we shake on it, and hold on, both of us, for a beat too long. The old Sebastian is under there, all right. In that handshake, the old unspoken connection and in those eyes, lit up like sparklers, friendship is restored as if it were just yesterday and I teaching him finger picking.

At baggage claim, I am surprised to see he has brought a guitar. I recognize the battered old case, covered in peace symbols and a McCarthy for President bumper sticker along with newer stickers, reflecting newer allegiances—an ACT UP emblem, a pastel rainbow, a Harvey Milk for Supervisor bumper sticker. This is the same guitar I gave him way back when, when we must have been sophomores in high school, and I was his tutor. I am heartened to think he wants to jam, sick as he is, and sorry, even blushing inwardly, that I didn't think to bring my own instrument down from Wisconsin. I am busy beating myself up on that score when we walk into the concourse and Sebastian stops cold.

—Let's go up on the observation deck, Grady, the way we used to. Look at the stars, watch some planes come in. Mine's got to be about to turn around and head back to San Francisco. Come on, let's—

Grady

—We can't, Sebastian. The observation deck has been closed for years. Tony sent me a clipping when they sealed it off. New security precautions, the article said. Now it's a restaurant, probably added when they expanded the terminal.

—Oh.

We walk toward the parking garage in heavy silence. I can feel his disappointment. All the summer nights we had driven out here to watch planes land and take off when we were in high school. As soon as he had wheels, Sebastian would drive us out to the airport. He and Tony were like aviation experts. Adie, Mary Clay, Breck, and I just came along for the ride, to hang over the railing and belt out "Leaving On a Jet Plane." As if we could. As if our dreams could have wings and fly us away from all our earthbound problems—parents, grades, unrequited love, a sexless existence, candy-ass futures living our father's sorry lives.

Just then, we heard the jet engines roar.

—There, Sebastian, there! Just taking off. Look!

The two of us stand there in the middle of the road, half way between the terminal and the garage, the first grey touch of dawn just beginning to line the horizon, starring up at the jet just lifting off. We don't speak because our heads are twenty-five years in the past. Two boys alive with the wonder of flight. When all that is left of the jet is its blinking red tail light, we walk on in silence.

—I'll drop you off at your mother's, right? It's kinda early though.

—Oh, she'll be up. She'll be waiting.

—Tonight, later on. Breck wants us to come by the restaurant. You up for that?

—Sure. Who all will be there?

—Just the guys. Mary Clay is living on Cape Cod now. Jude is somewhere, god knows where.

—Last time I heard from her, she was playing the club scene in Cambridge.

—Yeah? She making a living doing that?

—Not everything's about money, Grady. She hasn't sold out. I admire that.

I get the reference. I get the dig. I've known for some time that Sebastian thinks I'm the one who sold out. Bought a shoe franchise and kissed my music goodbye. I know that's what he thinks. But not everyone can feed themselves on wishful thinking, no matter how hard they're willing to try, no matter the sacrifices. Genius is just a word unless it builds into something tangible. A record contract. Concerts. Critical recognition. None of that ever came my way. But an inheritance did, when my dad died. So, I bought my first Thom McAn franchise and plunked it down in the closest mall I could find, one with a substantial anchor business, in my case, a sprawling Macy's department store. I figured then, before I really did burn out, that the store would underwrite my band. What I never expected was getting into bed with mediocrity. I believed that my love of music and practicing my guts out all the time would pay off. But desire isn't success, passion doesn't cash at the bank, talent, even big talent, needs friends in high places. It was Sebastian who taught me that in no uncertain terms, without his ever even perceiving he did, just by being Sebastian. A talent like his wouldn't have been pestered with such problems. He even had a profligate brother who was famous on the hard rock scene.

—I admire that too, I say. About Jude. I wish her well.

But I am thinking, I just couldn't pull it off. Didn't have the gift. Didn't have the guts. Neither does she. But I keep my mouth shut and redirect the conversation back to the evening plan.

—I tried to get hold of Adie, but that's a no-go. She's teaching at some little college in New England.

Grady

—Remember what she said she wanted to do when she grew up? At that Frank Session just before we all left for college? Sebastian's eyes sparkle at this story. When I shake my head, so does he, but his is a knowing shake. Or more like a disbelieving one. His eyes dance at the memory but he changes the subject.

—So, what time are we meeting up? I'd like to stay with Mom till she goes to bed.

—Later is better, Breck says. When the restaurant quiets down after the dinner rush. Wanna say eleven?

When we meet at the restaurant, we are four old friends getting drunk on wine and nostalgia. No intoxicants can rival it for highs. Breck has arranged a private room, which is too big for our foursome but not for the expanse of our memories. The table soon is covered in dead soldiers, wine bottles, beer bottles, seltzer bottles, since Sebastian isn't drinking. Says it messes with his medication. The stolen cars. The egg fight. Setting off smoke bombs on his porch, then ringing the doorbell, only to have his mother, not Sebastian, open the door, pulling the smoke into the living room. The long drives to other cities with bigger concert venues, bigger names and singing our way home in the middle of the night, drunk on music. Me driving, Sebastian being the radio, his voice peeling out the open window like a meadowlark on speed.

—Gawd, Sebastian says, in that old familiar drawl of his, those were the days. His thin face splinters into lines when he smiles at the memories.

—Like that bonfire? Remember that? Breck holds up a nearly empty bottle of bourbon by way of punctuation. Chuckles all around, even Tony, whom as I recall it, was a little freaked out.

—When you could be outrageous and not be pilloried by society. Sebastian leans back in his chair and shakes his head. Like, no one knows more about that than he does.

—Yeah, Tony says. Think of all the characters we created back then that today would be absolute no-nos. Suddenly, he's standing, his hip thrust out, his hand, fingers backward resting on it, and the other hand is shaking an ominous finger at us. He is Fosterina, and she is giving us what for. Sebastian picks it right up.

—Fosterina! Fosterina! Don't whup us!

Then he was Sebastian again, finishing his more philosophical thought—

—When play was play. We were so naive.

His face clouds over.

—Innocence is really just a trap, he says. A great big Venus fly trap. Eat you alive.

That shuts us up. Shuts down the laughter. We reel in our raucousness like caught delinquents and all of us take sudden measure of our youthful transgressions, those now fabled times made legendary in the lexicon of our teenaged pack. We exchange glances, take stock, take in the situation. Sebastian dying. The myth of him vanquished by this dreadful reality. An impossibility, only not. Although his beard hides them well, as does his long hair, creepy blotches crawl out from behind this cover like snakes seeking sunshine. It is hard not to notice, though we all pretend not to. I watch the eyes of the others zero in, then look away. The tone of the evening has gone somber. Everyone feels it.

—I should go, Tony says, picking up an old fedora, one that had belonged to Sebastian's father, who died when he was three. Sebastian and Tony found it and other treasures during an attic raid of a mothballed chest of the old man's belongings, carefully stowed away by Sebastian's mother. He wears it tonight as a tribute, one not lost on any of us because we all know the hat's history, and its theft. Before Tony pops it on his head, he tips it toward Sebastian. No words said, just this

Grady

one last small gesture that says everything that was in Tony's grieving heart for his oldest, dearest, most beloved friend. Sebastian watches him go, tears in his eyes, and so, then, naturally in all of ours.

—So long, Saint Anthony. Friend.

Breck breaks the awful spell by pushing back his chair. He leaves us because it is time to close down the restaurant, nudge the last late-stayers out the door, get the bartender to make his last call really the last, and check that the kitchen is properly put to bed, as he says. No gas burners left on, the freezer doors shut, the floor properly mopped clean.

—Be about twenty minutes, he tells us.

I pour myself my umpteenth glass of wine, emptying out bottles into one glass, all my standards shot to the wind.

—How was seeing your mom, I ask. Genuinely gentle. Knowing, feeling it could not have been easy.

Sebastian shrugs, coughs, coughs some more, a kind of chest-crushing cough. I slide him some seltzer and he takes a tentative sip.

—Good. She's the same old battle-axe with a bourbon in her hand. Yeah. It was good.

Sebastian sighs. It was probably hard for him to get that much out, rein in the weight of all the emotion churning up a dust storm in his heart.

—You'll go by and see her from time to time, won't you, Grady?

—Whenever I'm in town. You can count on it.

—Yeah, Adie and Mary Clay wrote me the same thing.

—We're all good for it. You can count on us.

—I know. I know I can depend on you. Finally, my payback. And he cocks his head at me, and there is that little pulling-one-over-on-you smile that is so Sebastian. He rests a minute, tugs at his eyebrow. Sips the water. As if he's gathering his courage.

—You all wanted so much of me, he says finally, eyes looking off into the distance.

—What?

—All of you, seemed to want a part of me. Of my soul. Of my being. I was just a kid, you know. You know what I'm saying, Grady? I was just a kid too.

—Not me—

—Yes, you too. Maybe most of all. You wanted me to validate your music. You wanted me to *be* your music.

—I, I—Sebastian, you were the one with the gift. Not me. I never wanted anything from you. I just wanted you to *use* what God gave you. To seize those gifts and milk them and be them. OK, OK, you had what I wanted, the gift. But I shared everything with you, everything. I taught you everything about music that I knew. Harmonica, guitar, keyboard. Remember that huge keyboard I dragged over to your house? Remember how pissed your mother was to have that gigantic thing take up her dining room?

But I am losing my momentum. I am losing my anger. In an instant though I reclaim it.

—You think I sold out, Sebastian? Quit the band, bought into the little wife and the white picket fence in the suburbs, the financial security? That's what you think? OK, then. Yes, I did. But you sold out your genius, you pissed away your music. What's being a DJ that is so different from being a shoe salesman, man? Nothing. If I sold out, so did you.

Sebastian looks at me like I'm the sorriest excuse for a man he's ever seen, and then he starts laughing. Throws his head back and guffaws until he is choked into a coughing fit. And still he laughs. Uproarious infectious catastrophic laughter. His coughing fit lasts for ten minutes

Grady

or more. His cheeks burn with blood, colored by the superhuman effort it takes to breathe, to get his coughing under control.

—You win, you win, he wheezes. We both sold out. Difference is, Grady, I never wanted to buy in. If you believe anything about me, believe that. I never wanted to buy in. I just wanted to live an honest life surrounded by good people. And I think I have. I think I have. Can you dig that? Can you?

I nod. It doesn't matter whether I do or not. Nothing can change the fact, certainly not a stupid argument, that this man I so admired once is on borrowed time.

Breck comes back in the room. Looks from one to the other of us. Can feel something, something bad, has gone down between us. But he is the knife that cuts the tension. Now, we are no longer facing off, me and Sebastian. We are the old triumvirate.

I say goodbye to him that night, when I drop him off at his mother's. To look in a man's eyes and know you will never see him again because the blood running in his veins is as contaminated as the Cuyahoga River, humbles me. If only he hadn't been so cavalier, if only he had had my ambition, if only his gift had been mine. But all these if onlys only make me feel small. Needy. Jealous. Angry. At this ghost with a beard. Seeing Sebastian for the first time, perhaps, as who he really is, a man flailed by fate, disembodied by bad goddamn luck. I think of my shoe store franchises and my need to martyr myself before him, and I am filled with self-loathing. Think how simple his wish for his life, to live honestly among friends. And how bereft mine, my longing for a talent I don't have, for fame I would never acquire, for a mark made and left upon this world that would be indelible. Sebastian could have had all that, and he wanted none of it.

Outside his mother's house, we end as we began, with a handshake. No words. There are no words. There is just death in a dirty serape.

—Wait! he cries suddenly. Wait. I almost forgot. He shuffles up to his mother's door and comes back with that old guitar.

—I almost forgot, Grady. I want you to have this back. You keep playing for both of us, so I can live on in the chords, ya hear?

I drive straight through. Home is like a beacon on a headland in a crazy wild storm. One where the rain blows sideways and flags are shredded in a night. Beside me, in the passenger seat, is Sebastian's guitar. Strapped in. So nothing will happen to it if I crash. Like a person. A body. I try to keep my eyes and my head on the road but neither effort is very successful. I am forever looking over at that guitar. What it symbolizes. What it now manifests in responsibility. Will I ever be able to touch it? Play it? Won't that erase the oil of his own fingers that must still linger on those six strings?

Tears tickle my cheeks and I do not bother to wipe them away. I want to feel them. I need them to ameliorate this profound sorrow, this aching loss, this fury that a man so talented, my friend, must die such an unnecessary death. Why didn't he use condoms? Why did he have to be a gay man during a plague? Why was he dealt this hand? And I? Why was I dealt this ordinary life, with all the ordinary trappings, where my only misstep, my only disappointment, was my inability to be the brilliant musician I so strove to be? And now, this guitar, like an accusation. Like a celestial harp, too.

I push the remote to open the garage door. All the lights in the house are off, except the Christmas tree lights blinking behind the living room curtains, one lamp in the hall to light my path and one in the bedroom that Beth has left on in hopeful welcome. It is Christmas morning. I did not make it home in time for our big family Christmas

Eve dinner but I did make it home in time, if I only kiss Beth awake, to set up the air hockey table we bought for the boys. She is on her side, away from the table lamp, snoring lightly. I turn out the light, brush her ear with my lips.

—I'm home, love. Don't stir. I'll be down in the rec room setting up the hockey game.

—Come to bed.

—Soon.

It's not as arduous as I thought it would be to unbox and set up the table. Instead of going to bed, I slip out to the garage and retrieve Sebastian's guitar. Undoing its seatbelt, I bring it into the living room, where the fire in the fireplace is reduced to nothing but embers. There, like this, without Sebastian's eyes locked with mine and the guitar exchanging hands, it is just an instrument. An old Martin Dreadnought that dates to the early 50s probably. The one I bought at a pawn shop when I was eleven, the one I gave to Sebastian when we were sixteen and he was my protégé. That thought brings a wistful half-smile to my face. I can feel it tug at my cheeks where the tears dried and tightened my skin. I know, if I'm ever going to play it, it must be tonight, before it becomes so supercharged with association, I will never be able to pick it up again. And it will have to be sold or given away or ceremoniously burned in the backyard.

Using the fire poker, I stir the near-dead embers back to glowing. Beth, in the tradition of our family Christmas dinner, didn't forget this detail. A fire in the fireplace to ward off the frigid Wisconsin night. A little warmth stirs up. I throw on some kindling to give it a boost, then some seasoned oak I cut and split two autumns ago.

I take the guitar by its neck and lift it like a relic from its decrepit old case. I put my right knee up on a chair on which to prop the instrument

Ambient Light

while I tune it. The strings are lax but respond immediately to my fingers; their sound, as they individually come into tune, golden. I know Sebastian is asleep at his mother's. Not dead. Not yet. Still, the tune that comes to mind is an old Black spiritual. Though he lives, he is lost to me. And only music will sooth my ache away. Pushing the ottoman in front of the now crackling fire, I sit down with the guitar and caress it, taking in the mother-of-pearl inlay, its tortoise shell strike guard, its pudgy body. Kind of like mine. Seen some use. Seen some love.

    I strum some nonsense, just getting the feel of my old friend again, before I am ready to sing for him. Humming first, while I get the tune and the tune carries the refrain back to me, solid and strong.

> I am bound
> I am bound
> I am bound for the promised land.
> No chilling winds nor poisonous breath
> Can reach that healthful shore;
> Sickness, sorrow, pain and death,
> Are felt and feared no more.

Rest, Sebastian. Rest. We will take it from here.

Tony

I sit in my tiny windowless office at the Red Cross scheduling blood bank dates around the city when my supervisor rushes in and tells me a tornado has been spotted heading our way. Our building is a cement block fortress. Where I am in it, buried close to the center of the structure, I am as safe as anyone can be. As is anyone in the building who is not glued to some window watching, waiting and watching. Alas, curiosity is a powerful motivator, so I push back, my metal chair scraping mercilessly against the linoleum floor. I walk to the main lobby. People, my colleagues, have already begun to gather there. Even the Disaster Team is in limbo. This thing has got to blow over, we all have to survive it, before they can get down to business.

There is a feeling in the air when a tornado approaches. Of course, there is the stillness, oppressive, seriously ominous, like a coffin lid closing in on the living. But just as common is this odd greenish hue to the sky, and beyond, clouds blacker than Satan's gullet. I push past the gawkers, a gawker myself now, and out the door. I long to feel doom approaching. I long to hear it.

—Tony! No! Come back, someone yells after me.

I stand outside and listen. The roar of a tornado is often compared to a rushing locomotive. But it's really nothing like that. It is as if the world has been uprooted and is hurtling at you. God in his black wrath is taking a scythe to man's earthly impertinences, his monuments to himself, great and small, built upon his creation. Houses, hospitals, office buildings, gas stations dissolve into piles of rubble, but also playgrounds and schools, fast food dives, revival tents, even ornamental trees. The sound is of things being wrenched from their superficial perches by the swing of that great blade, of gigantic necks cracking as they are wrung lifeless.

There is debris in the air around me already, some whirring by—lawn chairs, twisted strands of gutter, leaves by the billions and dust, black dust swirling with unidentifiable matter. Some come crashing by—a stop sign torn loose tripping up the street in a metallic clattering dance. Standing under the portico to the Red Cross, I nurse feelings of both false security and desire. Desire to run toward the blackened sky.

—Come back inside, Tony. We're all headed for the basement.

A hand takes my bicep and I am tugged back into the building by Willis, our daytime security guard. I like Willis. I nod, comply.

—I didn't take you for a dumb cracker, Willis laughs.

—That I am, Willis. That I am.

—Come on, son. Let's take the stairs to the basement. Safe down there.

But I pull myself free of his good-natured aid.

—You go on ahead, Willis. I need to dash into my office for something.

—OK, son. OK. But you hurry on down with us, you hear?

The storm comes and goes while I am in my office. I hear nothing. I see nothing. Only when the town all-clear siren blows and I can hear the

Tony

scurrying of the people in Disaster Services running, shouting orders, streaming toward the back of the building to the blood bank and the fleet of RC cars, do I know the worst of the storm is over.

Later we all learn, it was a Force Four tornado and that our town is torn to shreds, a three-mile swathe of what we knew to be there is obliterated. Trees turned to matchsticks, built and natural landmarks rearranged to be unrecognizable. But that was later.

Right now, while the storm apparently is raging all around us, I want to finish the month's blood drive schedule. I also have to attend to my divorce papers. That is a storm of another nature, and one no more avoidable than the one outside. These papers have been on my desk for weeks. This is my only pitiful revenge, dragging it out. Actually, no. My real revenge is refusing to have our marriage annulled. That is the path Sandra wanted to take, so she could marry again in the Catholic Church. I have no intention of remarrying, so I held out for divorce, even after a visit from our priest—I say "our," he is Mother and Auntie San's priest, the one who married us and the last time I set foot in a church except to marry or bury someone else. Sandra is furious. Annulment would have been her version of public shaming. She would have blabbed all over town that our marriage was never consummated, that I was incapable of consummating it. Which of course is a lie. It's the lie that empowers her and reduces me to an empty rag of a man. So, I smiled reverently at the priest, let him have his say, nodded in all the appropriate places, gave him the impression of compliance, but as soon as he walked out the door, blessing me, of course, with a nod and a tone that was laced with pity, I turned back to a temporarily triumphant wife.

—No way.

—But I want to remarry. A real man, a man with a functional dick.

—You'll just have to live in sin.

Ambient Light

—I can always file on my own, you know. She is defiant but unconvincing.

—Good luck with that. Good luck.

So, the divorce papers sit here, under a pile of other business papers, growing mold. Despite calls from her lawyer and mine. Thanks to Mother and Auntie San, I am not out of pocket for any of the legal expenses associated with ridding myself of this piranha. Ever since Sandra accused me of being a homosexual to my mother's face, ever since they got a firsthand taste of Sandra's crude, rude underbelly, they have defended me better than the walls of Jericho were defended by the Canaanites, with their joint checkbook open.

I had thought to go down to my lawyer's office this afternoon after work and drop them off. Finally. Be done with it all. I'm tired of holding Sandra at bay, tired of her repeated telephone tirades. They clog up my answering machine with verbal bile. But now I can't. A tornado has come to assist me in my delay. I am ready to be done with the legalities, put her in the rearview mirror and speed on to—what? What indeed. Another day at the ARC, another month, another year? That's not so bad, really. It is peaceful, quiet, and not too demanding. In all ways, the opposite of my four years of marital torment. Plus, it's a worthy organization in which to make a career, however modest, one I can feel proud to be part of.

I retrieve a large manila envelope from the bookcase of office supplies behind my desk, put all the signed legal papers in it, address it to my lawyer and put it in my Out mailbox. It will get to him eventually, since it is likely, given what I believe to be the path of the tornado, his office was demolished, or close to it. And thus, I lick the envelope on my married life, sealing it into my past, to be, if not forgotten, placed in the garbage bin of my life experiences.

Tony

Outside, feeling lighthearted and uncharacteristically reckless, I all but bound to my car. That's when another reality sets in. Sirens scream near and far. The world around me is a disaster area. The fencing around the parking lot is crumpled, the electric gate has been ripped off and is gone. I can see live power lines crackling and jigging like Mexican jumping beans just up the boulevard. Trees, sturdy great sycamores planted in the late 1800s along both sides of the road to lend it shade and elegance, are broken off at the waist, one after another. God's scythe at work. I'm sure there's much more damage all around me that I cannot see, on other streets and God knows how far in each direction. I long for a bird's eye view and consider going back into the building and up to the roof, just to take it all in. My new apartment is in the old part of town, one rehabbed during Urban Renewal, and I hope just far enough south of the tornado's path to be OK. If it is in ruins, it will be the Wrath of Sandra, visited upon me. I wouldn't put it past her to have stirred up this storm from her own store of fury, aiming it at my lovely new home, full of antiques she would love to get her hands on.

It is not hard to find my car, but it is a pain in the ass to extricate it. Truly, I'm one of the lucky ones, car-wise. Mine is scraped up by, I assume, flying branches and it is covered in leaves, as if God tried to camouflage it and did a lousy job, and other bits, I can only think, of curb garbage—a tampon is plastered against my windshield. But my car is drivable. Some of my colleagues will need to wait—and probably a very long time, since demand will be high—for a tow truck. Light poles, bent fencing, thrown paving stones from a neighboring construction site have clobbered many of them, squashing roofs, flattening tires, blocking paths.

My Camry is drivable, all right, but I can't say as much for the streets. I head away from the downed power lines, maneuvering this way and that around the most amazing stuff. It's as if Dorothy's house blew in from Kansas and exploded upon landing. Some stuff requires me to straddle the curb in order to get around it; other things I can manually move—a charcoal grill lies on its side like a huge, decapitated ant in the middle of the road. Several television antennae litter the road, no doubt blown off the sides and roofs of apartment buildings. Sofa cushions, bed pillows, a mattress are strewn all around me. A doll lies face down in the gutter like a premonition.

As I proceed, I can see into those apartment buildings. As if their facades had melted to the street. A heap of bricks and debris from people's lives chucked out on the street. I even see people inside, all stunned, some bloodied, some not, one sitting at a kitchen table, one clinging to a bedpost. As if to breath would be a dangerous act, might cause another wall to shift and come crashing down on them. It is surreal.

It takes me close to two hours to negotiate my way out of the tornado's wasteland. Even here, the sirens scream on and off, back and forth, fire trucks, ambulances, police cars, more ambulances. I feel like a voyeur. Here in my car, smoking a cigarette, unharmed, driving through the late afternoon sunshine, is equally surreal. Since my window is down, I can smell the tornado's aftermath—the steaming asphalt; something sweet, too, maybe sap from all the downed trees; something acrid, almost surely blown electrical transformers. I am suddenly reminded of a time Sebastian and I were walking back to his house and a car out on the four-lane road that skirted our neighborhood, missed a curve and plowed into and snapped a telephone pole. At its top was a transformer that exploded in a white burst of light and then there was that smell, of fried electrical wiring. It's a smell you don't forget. We stayed to watch the police come and the ambulance, and to take the stilled and blood-covered driver away, that odor clinging to our clothes and our imaginations.

Tony

I need gas by the time I'm really clear of the mess downtown and I find a station unharmed and open. It's the first time since I left work that I can breathe easily, the first time I release my mind from emergency duty. And that feeling of recklessness rises again. I do something I never do. I buy a two-dollar scratch ticket as I'm handing over the cash for my fill-up. When it pays one hundred dollars, I know my luck has changed. Sandra used to love scratch tickets, but she never won a dime. I laugh out loud. I am still chortling to myself, humming now, happy, even happy-go-lucky, when it occurs to me not to go straight home, where most likely the electricity is out, if not worse. Instead, I head to Cunningham's, this classy old-world restaurant with servers in crisp white jackets, black bow ties and a linen towel draped over one arm, because I love the food, but I love the bar even more. Gleaming mahogany a mile long, with a brass footrail and high-back, raised cane chairs, not bar stools, maybe twenty of them, situated in a tidy row facing a beveled mirror etched in cursive with the name and date of the place, Cunninghams, est. 1921. I have been coming here since before I could legally drink. The management was lax about those kinds of rules, as long as we conducted ourselves like gentlemen. Cunningham's has ambience, class and a hint of something under-the-table. Prohibition in the old days, no doubt. The lights are so low in the place, when you have a meal at one of the tables, you have to tip your menu up near the candle to read it. Unless, like me, and most of the patrons, you know the menu by heart. That low light and the musky smell of alcohol-infused wood, at the bar and at the dining tables as well, is what gives Cunningham's its atmosphere of secrecy, and who isn't intrigued by other people's secrets?

It was my intent, coming here, to spend my hundred-dollar windfall on shots of Johnny Walker Black, and then have a bite to eat. My way of celebrating.

—I'm a free man, Marcus, I say when he places the first shot before me.
—S'that so?

I toss the Johnny Walker back and let it roll like lightning down my throat.

—Yes sir. Mailed off my divorce papers this afternoon.

—You 'spect them to go anywhere what with the 'nader today, and all?

—Outta sight, outta mind. Pour me another, would you? In fact, a round for everyone at the bar this evening.

I do not know what came over me to do that, but I like this moment of living large, the taste of largesse as fine on my palate as the rarest of Scotch. To my surprise, this brings several men who had been clustered at the end of the bar down to where I sit, about in the middle, to thank me and return the favor. They are, I'm guessing, younger than I am by a decade but very well turned out, all of them. Crisp three-piece suits, maybe tailored in Hong Kong or on Jermyn Street. I have an eye for these things. Before long, we are old friends and I am very drunk. I am laughing too loud, I know. So, I suggest we get a booth and eat something before we all fall off our chairs.

—Let's get one of the private rooms. Heh, Marcus, can we get a table for six in the back? one of them says. A bottle of champagne, no two, for the table to celebrate our friend Tony's release from matrimonial imprisonment.

The private rooms are tiny and fit a table just big enough to accommodate parties of four, six or eight. Louvred saloon doors close out the rest of the restaurant and create a sense of intimacy, that is the only word for it, that can be suitable for discrete business transactions or for lovers. We are well past our steaks, and I am on a first name basis with them all—Chad, Jeff, Arthur, Malcolm and Jon—before I know I'm in for more than I bargained for. As we wait for dessert, and several of

Tony

us light up, I feel a hand on my knee. Chad gently squeezes it and then trails his fingers higher. I sit frozen. The look on my face must give me away because their sense of propriety drops away in winks and nudges and teasing. Each other, as well as me. Then Jeff leans over and kisses Malcolm on the lips. A long deep kiss. It is very upsetting to watch. But also thrilling. My crotch throbs. Chad brushes his fingers against my erection. I squirm, embarrassed, confused beyond reckoning, blushing to my hair follicles. He pulls his hand away.

—Just a friendly hello, Tony, nothing serious.

—I think I need to go home now.

—Nonsense, Malcolm says. Let's keep the party going. Let's go to my place. I've got lots of booze and some good dope. The world is shut because of the tornado. No work for any of us tomorrow.

Two of them usher me into Malcolm's car like a perp, surrounding me with their bodies, their laughter, their aftershave. The other two, Arthur and Jon, are in a car behind us. I think I'm going to be sick. I am sick. Chad only just gets my head out the window in time to save himself from the spew, while Malcolm jerks his car to the curb.

—Please. I can just walk from here. My car—

—Don't be a party pooper, Tony, Jeff says. Don't worry about your car. We'll give you a lift back in the morning. Come on, now. You know you want to come—

That sends Chad and Jeff into paroxysms of laughter. I get it. But I am sick with fear. Sick with longing. Sick, sick, sick. Chad puts an arm around me, half embracing me, half holding me still. He pulls me into him and unzips my pants. My head lolls back. I can hear myself moaning but I am no longer in that car. I am with Sebastian in his mother's Biscayne when he tells me he is gay, and I can't think of anything to say. I don't know what to say. I know he is waiting for me to say something, to react. I look over at him and repeat some lame joke of ours about pickled peters. We were always making fun of fags and homo and poufs. And now he tells me he's one of them, smiling at me and is that pitying in his eyes?

Chad starts to go down on me but it is Sebastian's face I see, and his eyes are saying, it's OK, Tony, it's OK. OK about what? That I failed him. That it is Sebastian I want. That Chad has touched the tip of my cock with his tongue. That I come before Chad's lips take my dick. I come all over his face. Sitting in the Biscayne with Sebastian, I see the tears running down my face and Chad wiping his face on a monogrammed handkerchief.

Memories pummel me now. Of not finding words to answer Sebastian's confession. Wondering if in telling me, he was coming on to me. Tears stream down my face. Because I failed him. Who knows if I failed myself that night too but I failed him, all right. Because I was afraid, so afraid. I threw out his letters, didn't return his calls. Whenever Sebastian came back into town from San Francisco, I would make excuses when the group all got together, only saw him twice between high school and his funeral, at a disastrous dinner my ex arranged for us old friends and that last visit when we met at Breck's bar. I let him suffer and die, my blood brother, without reaching out, because I am a coward. Yet he is here tonight in this car with Chad and Jeff and Malcolm, my new friends, my new destiny. He has found his way to me through the false strata of the physical world. He may have departed this earth but he lives on in me. I see it now. I can hear his voice, hear it rise with the timber of pleasure as he whispers in my ear, *Better late than never, brother.*

—I'm sorry, I'm so sorry! I wail. To the memory of Sebastian. To Chad as he wipes cum from his cheek. Malcolm is checking on us both in the rearview mirror.

Tony

—Everything OK, Chad? Tony? Should I pullover?

—We're good, aren't we, Tony? Chad says, and he kisses me on the cheek.

—It's OK, it's OK. Right, Tony? Chad croons in my ear. Was this your first time, man? I think it was your first time. God, Tony's a virgin. Aren't you? Wow. You've lived a chaste life all these years? But wait? Marriage? Is that why you're getting divorce. I bet it is. It's OK, really. We'll do a better job of it when we get to Malcolm's place. Ok? Tony? OK? Don't be afraid.

And I'm not. I'm not afraid. Not anymore. Chad is so kind. I want to know all that he knows and know it first in his arms. I look straight ahead. Beyond the back of Malcolm's head, who is whistling now, at the dark night that blankets all signs of the tornado, and I know everything will be OK. Because Sebastian is riding shotgun. Malcolm's headlights range over the road before us, stretching out into whatever comes next. I feel like I am shedding some skin, some medieval armor that has protected me from everyone's expectations for me, my mother's and aunt's, the priest's who pushed my head down time and time again into the folds of his cassock; and the horrifying, damaging hypocrisy of the Church, to say nothing of the society that condemns what I see I am and strong-armed me into marriage to Sandra. I relax. Maybe for the first time in my life.

—I'm good. Never better. I put a tentative hand on Chad's thigh, and he covers my hand with his. Chad, then Jeff, then I pick up the tune Malcolm is whistling, and pretty soon we are all belting out "Dancing Queen."

The Beginning

It is a time of no ambient light. The city, which would come to prosper and burn with lights around the clock, sleeps like its occupants. There is a stillness, disturbed only now and again by a puff of breeze, warmed by summer, that silences the peepers for a second. Then their cacophony erupts again, for nothing can still them for long. They are night's choristers.

Overhead, the star-dense Milky Way paves a white blaze across the sky, so dense it is hard to perceive it is comprised of individual stars, the kind wishes are made on. Now though with the dwellings dark and the moon, days before Amavasya, unseen, its bold bright band sweeps across the night sky, a celestial tiara crowning the earth with its majesty.

In truth, the Milky Way does not crown Earth, though this is the way humans perceive it, arcing from night horizon to night horizon. In truth, it encircles us. This blue planet does not stand apart from it but is giftwrapped by it. The Milky Way was venerated by the Ancient Egyptians, who sent their dead pharaohs by star ship up to be transported along the celestial river—a reflection of the Nile in the heavens—to the afterlife. Just as it was revered by the ancient Maya, a world away, a time away, who believed the same thing. Cast their dead nobles on the star river so that they might be carried on to eternal life.

Tony

—Good evening, my name is Professor Jackoff, president of Cream Top Dairy and your masterdebater extraordinaire for this evening's entertainment.

My bully pulpit is the landing on the stairs leading up to the second story of Sebastian's house and his mother's lair. I have everyone on their knees with laugher and expectation. Just the way I like them. When I grow up maybe I'll be a stand-up comic like Red Skelton. Mary Clay's blush reaches down to her ankles. If there's one thing I love, it's shock value. Breck is staring at me, wide-eyed, mouth open and pointing madly with his hand at the ceiling. I know he means that Mrs. T might hear and stomp downstairs and send us all home. So I ignore him. It's easy to ignore Breck because he can never seem to get words out. Drool yes—this is his weird adolescent trademark, drooling. Adie, sitting cross-legged in her cutoff jeans on the floor manages to fold herself into a pretzel, forehead to the carpet to muffle her guffaws. And Jude, her head cocked to one side, half smiling her Won't You Grow Up smile of the chronically critical. But I love Sebastian's reaction best of all, maybe because we are on the same wavelength, maybe because he is the ultimate showman and doesn't want to be outdone by a Catholic schoolboy. He jumps up beside me and snatches my phantom mic.

—Professor Jackoff, I just want to start by welcoming you and introducing myself. You may have used my services in the past? I am Manuel Dick, proprietor of The Dick X-Ray Company—

Now I am laughing. Because along with his verbal introduction, he seems to suffer from some kind of palsy because his left hand is flailing—like he's giving himself a hand—

—Don't be a jerk, Dick.

Now Adie and Breck and Mary Clay are up and throwing popcorn at us. Jude, aloof, watches us all and clips her nails with her teeth.

—Don't be a dick, Dick.

—But I am a Dick, Jackoff. Now, about that masterdebating you promised us—

From upstairs comes a stentorian SEBASTIAN! And a chorus of shushing comes from our little audience, and we tumble out of the living room pushing and shoving each other into the kitchen where the door swings closed after us. In case she actually comes downstairs. But she never does. She never intervenes. That's why Sebastian can smoke, why we all can smoke at his house, even though most of our parents would kill us if they found out. Hypocrites that they are, because they all smoke. We are, after all, only fourteen and fifteen years old.

When silence prevails from on high, we trip our way back into the living room and fall onto the couch, the floor or Sebastian's dead father's memorial chair, Coke bottles in hand and devour a bag of Fritos and the rest of the popcorn, before lighting up and settling into a spontaneous Frank Session. We are laughed out, so the serious questions begin. Sometimes, like today, they follow on whatever foolishness we've been up to. Today it was Professor Jackoff and Manuel Dick, but it may be other

Tony

characters Sebastian and I have created and inhabit willfully depending on our mood—Donkey HeeHaw, a takeoff on a neighbor of Adie's who has this bulbous, W.C. Fields nose and laughs with a snort. Or, there is Sir Basil Wrench of Trash-Upon-Dump, Surrey, who is rumored to have been eaten alive by a gigantic killer bee, so maybe a call to Pest Control would be in order? Or Dr. Su Su Foo, head of the Ancient Stuff Department at the local university, a take-off on a colleague of Mary Clay's father, who is a professor of geology. Dr. Su Su Foo is, we have decided, in charge of carbon paper dating of, well, ancient stuff. Or Fosterina, maybe our favorite of all. She's a big bossy Black woman who knows all and tells. Everyone is afraid of Fosterina, including us, who created her, because there is no messing with her. She's always whipping us in shape. Or just whipping us. She has no tolerance for white folk. Especially snot-nosed white boys. But we love bringing her out of our bag of tricks because—why do we love Fosterina best? I think it's because Sebastian wishes she were his mother.

We, Sebastian and I, are always making people and stuff up. Especially, we love playing on the phone. Making crank calls. Calling up Sam Swope Pontiac and insisting that an eagle swooped down on our Bonneville while we were crossing the desert in Arizona and snatched off our convertible top, and how is Sam Swope planning to make our loss right? Or calling up the local crematorium and trying to make an appointment, pretending to be the little old lady who, though not dead yet, is planning on it soon. Or calling up the local TV station and saying we are Billy and Sammy Paul Tingley and we have an exclusive news story for them. And when they bite, we tell them if they look up in the sky, as we, Billy and Sammy Paul, are doing right this minute, they'll see what we see—the profile of Jesus in clouds. A sign! we scream into the telephone. Thank ya, Jesus! A sign!

Everybody hangs up on us but that doesn't stop us the next time we're together. Sam Swope can practically count on that eagle once a week.

Sitting around the coffee table is like sitting around a corporate conference table. With a Frank Session the rules are simple. You can ask anything; if asked, you must answer the truth and if the truth is too hard to say out loud, you're allowed to go into the kitchen and write the answer on a piece of paper, then pass it around for everyone to read. Today's topic, probably suggested by my master status, is masturbation. Adie wants to know if we, Breck, Sebastian and I, do it. Breck answers Hell, yes, and the girls' faces' turn a stunning array of grey. I'm a poet and I know it and my feet are Longfellows. Ha ha.

—Don't know what you find funny about that, Breck says with mock defensiveness. It's almost as good as the real thing.

—As if you know anything about the real thing, Adie counters.

—Wellllll, Mary Clay says, and rolls her eyes behind her bottle-glass spectacles. Now all eyes ping pong between the two of them. Spotlight on Breck, now, who drools. Then on Mary Clay, who smiles a little girl coy smile. Adie groans at this. Jude loses all patience.

—Seriously? I mean, come on. All of you. Breck, you're disgusting. You're all disgusting. And with that, Jude tosses her mane of hair over her shoulder and fishes in her pocket for a crushed pack of smokes.

—Sebastian, if we're not going to rehearse, I'm going home. Besides, she goes on, lighting up, there's no way Breck slept with Mary Clay. That's just impossible.

—Wellll, Mary Clay says again. I wouldn't be so sure about that. And she winks at Breck.

—Deny it, Breck.

—My lips are sealed. They almost are, except for a streamer of drool that sets Adie and Mary Clay to eye-rolling laughter. Adie fishes

Tony

a wadded up, fraying tissue from her pockets and wipes his mouth.

—Ick. You guys diverted our inquiry, Adie says, pulling herself together. Tony? Sebastian? What about you guys? Do you—you know—do it?

Sebastian and I exchange glances. We head to the kitchen. Sebastian hands us each a piece of scrap paper. He writes yes on his in his distinctive angular handwriting. I sit down and look at the blank piece of paper. It stares back at me like an accusation. I sigh and look up to Sebastian.

—Never? he asks.

—Once I woke up to something sticky on my bedsheets. But, jerk off? No. Never. Mother says it is a sin. She says she will take me to mass with my hands wrapped in gauze bandages so everyone will know what I've done, if I ever touch myself. That way.

—God, Tony. Sebastian pulls at his eyebrow, a tic he has whenever he doesn't know how to get out of something.

—OK, look, it's the rule. We don't lie in Frank Sessions. So, go ahead. Write No on your piece of paper. In block letters.

—But Sebastian, they'll laugh me out of the room.

—No, they won't.

He wadded up his first answer, took another piece of paper and in block letters wrote YES. We'll hand them in together and not claim either.

—No fair, Adie says. Who said yes? Who said no?

—That's for us to know and you to find out.

—Gross, says Mary Clay, I don't want to find out!

—You all are so juvenile. I'm going home. Jude collects her satchel and her guitar and bangs out through the screen door.

—Wait, Jude, Mary Clay calls after her. I'll walk home with you. And she too is out the door.

—Come on, damn it, Breck yells after them. It was the boys' turn to ask a question. He jumps up and runs out onto the porch and at the top of his lungs screams after them

—I want to know if girls masturbate!

Breck, out in the June air, windows open up and down the street, freezes.

—SEBASTIAN! another stentorian bellow comes from above. Mrs. T's bedroom is right above his head and Breck turns to see her scowling out the window.

—Time for you to go home, young man, she calls down.

Sebastian and I, without saying a word to each other, which is how we often communicate, go out on the porch to stand with Breck. Solidarity. Poor Breck, he is dying of embarrassment. And probably curiosity. Now, we'll all have to wait for the next Frank Session to get the answer to his, well, pressing question.

That evening, Sebastian holds a backyard campout for us guys, with a bonfire and hot dogs and s'mores and a thousand bags of chips and Ding Dongs for the morning. There's a cooler full of soft drinks and ice. When Sebastian produces a bottle of bourbon, one he pinched from his mother's basement stockpile, we are set for the evening. Or at least for a while.

I've never been to a campout before. I've never stayed up all night. I've never slept under the stars. And I'm worried about ants in my sleeping bag. Or rats in the alley behind Sebastian's house. Or rain, even though you can see the moon. I want to feel like Lewis or Clark eating buffalo on the plains with wolves calling off in the distance. Or like Gene Autry singing on his horse as he rides across the prairie. I want to believe sleeping on the ground is a groovy thing to do. But as I toss out my borrowed (from Sebastian) sleeping bag, that smells like mildew,

Tony

onto a thin grassy patch of yard, I know it will be as uncomfortable as lying on my back doing calisthenics in gym class. And I want my pillow.

At first my mother wouldn't let me come and not just because it was fish sticks night at home. She didn't believe me when I said it was just guys.

—Four boys, Mother. That's all. Nobody else is coming.

—Anthony—she calls me that when I'm in trouble—Anthony, boys of fifteen don't have parties without girls. What in the world will you do outside all night, anyway? I'm sure you will get up to no good.

—Mother, I promise!

So, Sebastian has his mother call my mother to extend the invitation personally and to say she will be on hand as chaperone. Mother begrudgingly agrees, especially after I plead with her.

So, the first thing we do, the four of us, is build this humongous bonfire that crackles and sends sparks flying high over the stockade fence that goes around Sebastian's yard. Sebastian and Breck have assembled a huge pile of firewood. At first we pretend we're burning effigies of all the teachers we hate. Sebastian's Latin teacher. Grady's "dumb shit" football coach history teacher. Breck's sixth grade teacher who gave him detention for two weeks for trying to save the life of a crawdad he found baking on the playground.

—That was years ago, Breck, I say.

—Well, she's the only teacher I've ever hated.

When it comes to me, I lie. I say it's my Latin teacher too. All Catholic kids take Latin. Only I'm not thinking of him when I stoke the fire, I'm thinking of the priest at our church.

The fire gets so hot we strip off our shirts. Our sweat glistens like sequins on our chests. I cannot remember ever being happier than I am in this moment. Even the threat of rodents vanishes as we half dance, half prance, half cavort around the fire. Breck does a series of three back flips, without hands. His glasses skitter off his face and land somewhere in the grass. Grady pulls his guitar from its case and he and Sebastian fall into a spontaneous hootenanny, singing old blues and country tunes we've known since forever. I pull up a metal yard chair and just watch, not wanting this moment to ever end. Grady has one foot up on the kindling box so he can prop his guitar on his knee. Sebastian leans into him till their shoulders about touch and together they fill the night with soul.

Sebastian and Jude sing together all the time, too, have been for all the years we've been hanging out together, two at least, fancying themselves versions of Bob Dylan and Joan Baez. Jude is in love with Sebastian but not in the ordinary sense. Not boy-girl so much as teen idol. Though she would hate me to say that about her, that she is star struck. But with Grady, it's different. He isn't competing with Sebastian when they make music together, the way Jude often seems to be doing. Listening now, I think of the Righteous Brothers, of Peter and Gordon.

They met, him and Sebastian, at a funky coffeehouse called Open Dialogue earlier this summer. It was down near the stockyards, with the smell of blood and manure side by side with the cloud of cigarette smoke hanging overhead. It was kind of an open mic night. Sebastian wanted to go, and he dragged me along.

—Gotta have one friendly face in the audience, he said.

It was kind of like a lottery. You put your name in a jar and when you get called, you're on. When it was Sebastian's turn, he went out on stage without an instrument, because he didn't know how to play one, to do an a cappella version of Dylan's "If Not for You," turning his sweet face up to the ceiling, and his voice to God. He was coming up on the last verse when Grady sidled out onto the stage, already strumming his

Tony

guitar in sync with the words Sebastian was singing and melted in right beside him. Sebastian opened one eye, grinning, and finished the song. Didn't even know the guy. Didn't miss a beat.

By the time Grady went on that night, they were like best friends. Couldn't stop talking about music, in song-speak. I had nothing to add and might have slipped out and walked home, but I wanted to see what this cat Grady could do. First thing he did when he got on stage was to light up the place with a Pete Townsend riff on bass guitar. Like Jude, like Sebastian, you could see right away that Grady had clefs running in his veins. Sebastian was so excited, I thought he would pee his pants. He was standing up, clapping, pounding the meat off his paws and at the same time, his Ked-covered toes slapped the floor, keeping time like he was possessed, or going that way.

Ever since, Grady's been hanging out with us, a guitar always strapped to his back, like Johnny Cash, singing with Sebastian and sometimes Jude too, and trying to get Sebastian to take a lesson or two.

—Maybe. Someday.

Out under the stars, Breck is mixing bourbon and coke for everybody, while I try to keep this feeble old chair from collapsing under me. Grady and Sebastian stop singing only long enough to chug their drinks and work out another set, testing each other's range and knowledge. Grady's voice is nice with Sebastian's but Sebastian's is, in my opinion, kinda heavenly, like there are angels singing through him. We've kind of settled down now, listening to the radio, feeling a buzz—this is the first time I've ever had anything other than communion wine to drink, and there was plenty of that in the sacristy—throwing more wood on the fire when it starts to burn down too much. Mellowing out, Breck calls it.

When the neighbors start calling over the fence for us to pipe down, I look at my watch. It's after midnight, so we know without saying that it's fair for them to ask us to quit. Sebastian and Grady plop down on the ground in front of the fire and Breck hands them the bourbon. We pass the bottle now, taking long sharp swigs, sitting on our sleeping bags, four spokes around the fire's hub. Lots of room in between them. Nobody wants to go to sleep. We plan to stay up all night, messing around, getting drunk, gorging on hot dogs and getting all sticky-handed with charred marshmallows.

Then somebody, Breck probably, has the idea to have a pissing contest. That gets us all laughing till our bellies ache. We've been drinking enough to have a goodly supply of firepower, Grady remarks, and then goes out into the alley behind Sebastian's house and drags a garbage can into the yard.

—Target, he announces.

Breck takes a piece of kindling and draws a starting line.

We line up, pricks in hand, and, one by one, see if we can piss in the can. It's dark enough that you can't really see each other's wiener, so it's kinda private. I don't feel too exposed. Instead I feel like a kid who cut school. That garbage can turns out to be farther than we think and only Grady, who has thought to whiz a great arcing trajectory, manages to get anything inside it. Mostly, we are wetting the sides of it like dogs at a hydrant. We're gut-laughing again now. All except Sebastian, who is looking away, like he's ducking something. I try to catch his eye. Another dodge. I'm getting a weird vibe.

A second later, though, he slips inside the kitchen and down into the basement. We see the light in the window well come on. Then he's back with not one but two more bottles of JW Dant. Rot gut, Sebastian says of his mother's favorite tipple. We're on the second bottle like flies

Tony

on honey. Getting drunker, wilder, rowdier by the minute. That's when Grady gets his big idea.

—Come on, you guys, let's have a bone ranger contest. Breck stands stock still, his hand pausing in zipping up his fly.

—A what? Breck says.

—A shoot out.

—A shoot out? I ask. We don't have any cap guns.

—Seriously, Tony? Cap guns? Grady makes a face at Sebastian that asks in a not polite manner at all, Who is this guy?

—Grady's talking about another kind of shooting match, Sebastian says, avoiding my eyes. I get that weird feeling again but brush it off.

—A circle jerk, Grady adds.

At first I don't get it. When I do, I can't help pushing back in my rickety lawn chair, like I'm trying to seem extra cool—so I cross my foot onto my knee—or sick at the thought. Prickles of fear course up my spine, just as the chair collapses under me. I roll off onto the ground while Sebastian, Grady and Breck bust out laughing. I roll into the darkness, tears jettisoning from my eyes, but in the dark, they just look like drops of sweat. I hope. That is if anyone can see them. It doesn't matter. It feels like they can see everything. I feel so exposed. Like my dick is already hanging out. Erect. And they are laughing.

—Whoa, what a boner of an idea, Breck giggles when he finally gets a hold of himself and comes to help me up.

I wipe the tears away with the back of my arm, pretending it is sweat in my eyes. I can hardly stand. It isn't the booze. My head is violently clear. What they want to do, what they expect me to do with them, now violently clear. I try to look at Sebastian, but he's across the bonfire from me, and he's eye-dueling with Grady.

—Not my scene, Sebastian says.

—Chicken?

—Nope. Mr. D, here, isn't scared. He doesn't go in for group activities.

You call your dick Mr. D? Breck slaps his forehead in wonder.

—Mr. D. Yes. For Ding-dong dickie ding-dong.

This makes me smile. Cracks the crushing cone of anxiety I'm feeling. But he's not looking my way.

—Chicken. You're chicken, Grady accuses.

—See it anyway you like. Sebastian says ultra-casually.

—You just did participate in a group activity, Breck observes.

—Yup. I did.

—Hypocrite. Grady turns his head and spits into the grass.

—Heh, I jump in. If you want a real adventure, let's jump a boxcar. All eyes swivel around to me.

—Do what? Grady's attention is now squarely on me. I take a deep breath.

—Jump a boxcar? Breck says, giving me a look that's asking if I'm insane.

—You're just saving your friend's meat. Grady points at me.

—I thought you were my friend, too. The edge in Sebastian's voice is razor sharp.

—What's the matter, Grady? *You* chicken?

I gather up my wobbly legs and stride around the fire to Sebastian's side.

—We can take Mrs. T's Biscayne down to the tracks and hop a boxcar. Ride to the next stop.

—That could be St. Louis, you moron.

—No, I fire back. We jump the *local*, you asshole.

Now Grady is steaming, and heading my way in a real aggressive, drunk manner.

Tony

—I am your fucking friend, Grady says to Sebastian. But I don't appreciate a hypocrite. And who are you, Mr. Jackoff, to call me an asshole?

—Calls 'em the way he sees 'em, Breck says.

Just as suddenly as it looked like I was going to humiliate myself, it now looks like I'm about to get beat up.

—Watch it, Grady says to Breck.

—Seriously, way more fun to jump a boxcar. I am dancing in the firelight now, spinning. Come on, you guys, jumping a boxcar is radical.

—You don't know what you're talking about, you little faggot.

—Hell I don't, Mr. Shit For Brains.

Sebastian steps in front of Grady. Everybody's drunk and everything's gotten out of control.

—Yes, he does, Sebastian says.

—He's a savant, Breck adds.

—Knows every train schedule going in and out of the yard.

—Yeah? Don't believe it. Grady has his hand out to Sebastian's chest, about to push him out of the way. Sebastian is the only thing between him and my ass on the ground with a broken nose.

—My school is on the other side of the yard, I say. Lots of kids cut across the tracks to get to school. It's a shortcut. Way longer to go to the crossing. I know every fence hole. I know where every freight train is going, and when. I memorized it.

—Why would you do that, punk? I can feel the threat coming off Grady.

—He loves schedules. Trains and buses. He knows every schedule in town, Sebastian, my defender, my blood brother, tells him.

—Whoa. You're a freak.

I smile. Trying to turn the tense, threatening look on his face into one that isn't threatening and tense.

—That's me, Grady. Let's drink to that. I scoop up the almost empty bottle of bourbon that is at my feet.

Grady takes the bottle, downs the rest of the brown stuff. And eases back. Steps back from Sebastian, who I can feel relax, see him breathing again now. Like me. Now I think I'm going to faint. But Breck is there beside me with another bottle.

—Here, Tony. You look like you could use a little fortification, as my dad likes to say.

I do take a swig. A long, scalding one, feeling my throat and stomach burning up. And a shot of speed ricochets around my brain.

—OK, far out weird, Tony. Let's go jump that boxcar! Grady pushes back.

I check my watch in the light of the waning bonfire.

—We can catch the 3:06, then the 5:17 back.

—Maybe there'll even be some real hobos on board, Grady challenges again, goading.

—Nah. Not on the local. Those boys only ride the long-haul routes.

And we're back to square one. Making bad puns, joking around, laughing the night away. But the terrible threat, because that's what it felt like, has passed. I won't have to jerk off. I won't have to confess what a prude I am. My so-called masculinity is still intact. Because, heh, I did do the pissing contest.

All comrades again. All in it together. We're going to go jump a boxcar. I've always wanted to jump a boxcar. But I never had the courage. Now these guys, my friends, will be my courage. All I have to do is pretend I know what I'm doing and let them lead the way.

—We gotta douse this fire, first, Sebastian says.

But before we can even get started with that a car engine dies in the alley out back.

Tony

—Cops? Breck whispers, hopping around from one foot to the other while tugging at the shirt caught in his zipper. We are all scrambling now to hide the booze, to drag the garbage can, reeking of piss, over to a corner of the yard, straightening our clothes as we do.

Adie, Jude and Mary Clay burst in upon us, the fence door banging open with the force of their combined energy.

—We've come to crash your party, Jude exclaims breathlessly, her long brown hair swirling behind her like a horse's mane. Adie sidesteps around Jude, her face underlit by the bonfire, distorting it into a Halloween mask.

—What's going on here?

—We're going to go jump a boxcar, Grady announces, like it was his idea in the first place.

—Oh. It's only the girls, Breck says, relief on his face.

—What do you mean "only the girls?" Adie wants to know, hands on hips, head cocked to one side.

—We stole Jude's mother's car! And she's only got her learners' permit. We are going to be in sooooo much trouble! Mary Clay barks with a kind of crazy pride, pulling the gate closed again. Because they *are* going to be in trouble. Big time.

—Heh, we can take Jude's car to the railyard. That way Mrs. T won't report hers missing—

—You mean, while my mother does?

—Soooo? There's something funny in the air here, Adie says, poking her blue tennis shoe in and around the food wrappers and soda cans, like a detective on the prowl.

—I smell pee, Mary Clay says.

Sebastian? I swear he winks at her, that twinkle in his eye flickering in the firelight.

—Come off it. You guys aren't sitting out here just having some kind of kumbaya moment, are you? Jude looks at Grady, then picks up his guitar to inspect it. Heh, what's this? Bourbon bottles? Three of them?

—Yeah. A kumbaya moment, and both Grady and Sebastian pick up the tune. But that's a minute before Adie, eagle-eyed Adie, uncovers evidence of a degenerate mind. Grady's.

—Heh, what are these?

Adie finds a couple of Playboy centerfolds tucked into Grady's guitar case. Guess he had intent all the while. But I keep my trap shut. I try to look busy cleaning up some of our mess.

Waving them over her head, she dances around us, around the fire.

—It's a bachelor party, Grady says. Girls not invited.

—I really do smell pee, Mary Clay insists.

We try to avoid each other's eyes. But Jude picks up on it.

—Me too. God, it's coming from over here. Jude follows her nose to the garbage can. What? You used this as a toilet?

—When a guy's gotta go, he's gotta go, Sebastian says, with what I observe is studied nonchalance.

—Gross. This is Jude and Mary Clay in unison. Boys are gross.

—I wish I could pee like that. Instead of the rigamarole girls have to go through, Adie says.

—Guys, if we're going to jump the 3:06, we kinda have to leave now, I urge.

But Adie is stuck on the centerfolds.

—Well, well, well, Adie interrupts. She stops her dance and snaps one of the centerfolds wide open. Exhibit A. Looks like you've had girls on your mind, after all. So, heh, here we are. Let's play strip poker.

But that idea isn't even addressed. When we've played this before, the girls always win. Because they have shoelaces and bobby pins and rings to take off.

Tony

Jude finds the bottle of bourbon. She tips it back and takes a cowboy's swig, wiping her mouth on the arm of her tee shirt. Then she passes it around and everyone—everyone except me—does the same. My head is already over submerged.

Mary Clay breaks out some weed she got off her sister, and the party suddenly becomes a party again, only this time with girls. My mother's worst fear and my first co-ed shindig.

I'm glad they've come. With the girls here, nobody pays any attention to me and my inhibitions. That part's a relief. Still, I'm beating myself up for being such a wuss. Then I see the pun I've just made, and I burst out laughing. Laughing, laughing, laughing. Bent over double. Coughing and wheezing and about to pee my pants. Everybody is staring at me. Of course. And I won't explain. Of course. So I just saunter over to my sleeping bag and wiggle down inside. Then Sebastian is beside me, crouched down by my head. The fingers of his left hand splayed across the ground to keep him propped up.

—Thanks, Tony.

—For what?

—You know. And he's up and gone to help Breck and Grady stoke up the fire.

I don't. And then I do. He thinks the boxcar idea was to save his ass. Oh well. Two asses saved, I guess.

It's a hot night but the heat that fire throws my way makes me sleepy. That and the booze. And the weed. And the near miss. And the girls. And the starry night overhead. When I've never been up this late, outside, at a co-ed sleepover. My mother would crap. That thought brings me up on one elbow. Yup, my mother would crap. That may be the best part of this entire night.

—Heh, Breck says, like he's had some kind of hallelujah moment.

We can pick up where we left off, this afternoon, when you girls cut out. Just as it was our turn to ask a question. The topic was masturbation—

All the guys start guffawing. Breck, Grady and Sebastian double over, laughing. And me? In the sleeping bag? I smile too. Because at least I came to the campout. At least the girls will think I'm one of the guys. When they find out what we've been up to. And they will. Breck is already whispering in Mary Clay's ear. Even behind her glasses, her eyes glow huge in the firelight.

—What's so funny? Adie asks.

Sebastian draws Grady and Breck into a kind of conga line. They snake around the backyard, around the fire, singing "Do the Jerk," at the top of their lungs.

Mary Clay

I dibs Mary Wilson. Adie takes Flo Ballard. We both know Jude is Diana Ross. Because Jude actually has a voice and because. Well, just because Jude is Jude. Sebastian takes the arm of the record player and carefully puts it on the spinning 45. Then, he turns and, mimicking Ed Sullivan, announces us. "Stop in the Name of Love" by the Supremes! The three of us know the dance steps by heart. On stop, we thrust out our right arms, palm and fingers erect to make a stop sign. On "in the name of love," we float our arms back to our sides, with three synced finger snaps and a final tap of the hip. Jude steps forward, pretend mic in her left hand and belts out the lyrics while Adie and I do back-up, woo-a-wooing and swaying our hips.

It was only a couple of weeks ago we saw the Supremes at the State Fair. They were wearing these slinky red sequined gowns and looked both elegant and skinny-sick. Even in our seats, we were aping their moves with cotton candy microphones. I don't want to be labeled a fan of anything, but I can't help myself. They are gorgeous, even with the scent of cow manure floating over from the live farm animal displays and the comings and goings of acts from the midway. There is the boy from one of the shooting galleries and the fat lady, slinking behind the stage to take their breaks.

Ambient Light

I don't mind not being Diana Ross when we're at Sebastian's, and we're always at Sebastian's on summer days because his mother is at work and because we can smoke and, well, because. Just because. When it's the boys' turn, Sebastian becomes Smokey Robinson and Tony and Breck his back-up singers in the Miracles. Breck gets into it too but Tony only mouths the words, interrupted all the time by chuckling. It's kind of like a tic, the pursed-lipped way he laughs that suggests bottled up mirth with a little bit of cynicism mixed in. Basically, he's just too shy. Maybe timid is a better word. But Sebastian? He is, really is, Smokey Robinson now, mimicking that falsetto and getting all Smokey's dance moves down perfectly. Sebastian stands before us in jeans and a white button-down shirt with the sleeves rolled to the elbows, but the moment he begins to sing I see him in Smokey's tuxedo and white silk shirt with red tie and red pocket triangle. Even his chalk white skin seems to darken into delicious milk chocolate as he gives himself over completely to this Black dude he likes so much. I can feel that Adie and Jude, sitting on the couch with me now, watch with the same fascination. I wonder, can you become who you idolize? All I know is, if Smokey walked in the door right now, he would see his double in a white boy.

We play this game all afternoon, every afternoon, acting out all the hit songs on WBLK, the Negro station. It is the only radio station Sebastian will listen to, unless one of us, usually Grady or Jude, insists on a pop chart station, one that plays the folk music Jude loves or the rock-and-roll Grady prefers. I don't much care, one way or the other. The three of them are the music nuts, so they have all the authority in station choice. But just the other day, as we all sat around his living room smoking and drinking Cokes and bingeing on Fritos, Sebastian jumped up out of his father's old chair and spun around and pointed a finger at me.

Mary Clay

—We need an emcee and Mary Clay is it! Get it? Her initials? Come on, you morons. The others groan and roll their eyes, while Sebastian rifles through his stacks of 45 and puts about twenty on the spindle.

—Me? Really, Sebastian? Me? OK then. Far out. Wow. Not quite believing it's me he's chosen. I know it's a joke, really, just a play on my initials. He loves puns and word play. Like, he reads phone numbers as words. And rhymes stuff all the time. He's like a genius with words. Only Adie can beat him at it. Some of the time.

From the first bars, I know it is the Four Tops. I make a pathetic stab at introducing the first song because, inside, I am burning up with flattery. I know my face shows it, and my stammering. I cannot believe Sebastian picked me. I've always been the ugly duckling, the girl too awkward and weighed down by supposed judgment, the one my father mocks and my mother loses patience with, to ever be special. I am weak with gratitude. I feel him next to me, coaching me, cheering me on, and my confidence grows. Just as Jude chimes in—

—That's not "Sugar Pie, Honey Bunch." That's "I Can't Help Myself." If you're going to be Emcee, MC, at least get it right.

She is jealous, I know. That Sebastian picked me, not her. And then I remind myself, it's not an honor. It's just my initials. I start away from the record player, shamed by my short-lived ego blast. Prickly sense rises behind my eyes. I go to sit down next to Adie, but Sebastian stops me. He puts his arm around me and now my emotions are zinging around like a dancing firecracker.

—She'll get the hang of it, won't you, MC?

—Suck up, Jude whispers to Adie.

She thinks I don't hear. But I do. So now I'm pissed off. I turn back to the turntable and really get into it. I'm dancing now.

—Little Anthony, I call out. Then Gladys Knight and the Pips,

Wilson Picket, the Marvelettes, Ike and Tina, The Drifters, Little Stevie Wonder.

Adie, Jude and Breck are clapping and laughing and dancin' to the music. Tony watches, smiling, chuckling, his eyes bright as bulbs on a Christmas tree. Sebastian is in croon mode. Another Miracles tune drops onto the turntable. Sebastian becomes Levi Stubbs, baritone and all.

When Sebastian's mother comes home from work, the singing and the dancing and record playing at full blast all quit. We have kind of wrecked her living room, as we do almost every day we hang out here. Which is every summer day, every school weekend, every Friday and Saturday night till she throws us out. She is very tolerant. We are all fonder of her than Sebastian is. But that's always the way with parents.

The silence crashes around us like storm waves. We all fall onto the couch or the floor or Sebastian's father's old chair. He is dead, so we cannot offend him. His mother has "retired"—that's what she says—upstairs, with a tall bourbon and water, so we can't offend her either. So long as we keep our voices down. Keeping our voices down plunges us into the void. It is real easy to be depressed. We talk about this all the time, whenever we have Frank Sessions, which is pretty often, because the music always stops. And there we are, looking at each other, wondering what do we do now? None of us wants to go home. That's the last thing we want to do, except Adie who actually likes her parents. Breck lives downtown in a hotel. He met Sebastian at a YMCA summer camp when they were junior counsellors. Jude and I live a couple of miles away, on the same block, that's how we know each other. That's how we got to be friends. Adie and I have been friends since sixth grade and were such snots to our teachers that when we went to middle school, we were not allowed to have any classes together. She lives down the street from

Sebastian. Tony lives over a couple of blocks and has known Sebastian since grade school. We hear stories all the time about how they played war across the street on a neighbor's front yard when they were kids.

—Killing Japs.

Those two are always making up stories. They're like Abbott and Costello, except when they talk about playing war when they were kids. Then they are General Patton and General Eisenhower, and the enemy is a character they call the Green Jap. Sebastian's father fought in the battle of the Green Islands in World War II, so that's how they invented Green Jap. As Tony tells it, they would run up their neighbor's front yard like it was Iwo Jima, get to the top, have a gun battle using arm rifles with the Green Jap. They would both get shot and roll down the hill. Then do it all over again. They laugh about it now, whenever it comes up. Green Jap though, lives on. We know all about him by now, so whenever we decide we hate somebody, that person automatically is known as the Green Jap. It's like code. We can call somebody who bums us out Green Jap, and we all know what that means. And they don't.

Basically, we're all a bunch of misfits. Jude says the reason is we're artists. But I'm not. And Breck is not. And Tony definitely isn't. Jury's out on Adie. Who is smart. But when has smart ever been an art?

So, when the music stops, we either drift outside and go play basketball in Sebastian's neighbor's driveway. Her son has gone to college and doesn't use the hoop himself anymore, so it's OK. She doesn't mind, just so long as it's not at night, when we can wake her up. Or, we sit around Sebastian's coffee table, smoking, and get down to some serious talking. Frank Sessions.

Tonight though is different. Tonight everyone is coming to my house. Plus, my sister's friends. Plus, anyone else who gets wind of the party.

—Come on, Jude. Let's go, I say.

It's a two-mile walk to our street. And I need to get going 'cause I've got to be home for dinner soon. Can't give my parents any excuse to get mad at me and decide not to go to the Cape. I have to be on perfect behavior. This once. So does my sister, only they are never on her case. She is the *preferred* daughter. Ha, ha.

Afterwards, after dinner, our parents are going to my grandmother's house for the weekend. They think my sister will supervise me and our little sister. Ha, ha again. That's she old enough and mature enough to stay home alone and look after us runts.

—What time can we come over tonight? Sebastian asks, draped on the couch like Cleopatra.

—Any time after seven should be OK. I'll phone and let it ring two times and hang up if they decide not to go.

—OK. I'll pick you and Adie up, Tony. Breck if you don't want to take the bus downtown and then back again, you can hang out here. There's bound to be something to eat. Spaghetti-O's or something.

—Can't come, Tony says, looking hangdog disappointed. It's Friday.

—Oh, right. Fish sticks, Adie says.

And there is the kind of silence that could be church-y, if it weren't for the fact that church was the problem.

—Might as well head home myself, Tony says, picking up his pack of Lucky Strikes from the table. See you guys tomorrow. And he is gone, screen door banging shut behind him.

We all feel bad for Tony, that he has to eat fish sticks every Friday, that he lives with his mother and his aunt, that his father walked out on them, that he is the funniest one among us and goes home sad.

—OK, Mary Clay. Let's go too.

Jude tries to haul herself out of Sebastian's dad's overstuffed chair. She reminds me of a spider, those long long legs and long long arms, fighting to free her butt from the springless chair. Sebastian rescues her, pulling her to her feet. They stand face to face, not a foot apart, Jude holding his hands. I think she's going to kiss him, and my stomach somersaults. But Sebastian twirls away and whatever was going on between them in that second is over.

The talk between us as we walk home is one of our favorite conversations: which of us does Sebastian like best? We never say it but we each want to be the one. So instead we worry over Adie. Maybe she's the one he likes. I mean, he's gone out on dates with me. I think. I think they were dates but we've never been out on a date, just the two of us. It's always all of us, with so-called couples happening along the way. Adie and Breck. Breck and Jude. Sebastian and Adie. Or Jude. Or me. It's confusing and that's why we can't stop talking about it. To be special for Sebastian is kind of like the holy grail. He is, after all, a boy and we are girls. So it must be one of us.

By eight o'clock that night there are thirty or more teenagers crushing into my parents' living room and kitchen. There is more beer than I've ever seen in one place. The boys start a beer can pyramid beside the staircase to the second floor. Pretty soon everyone gets into building it, adding more cans across the bottom to support more cans on top as it grows and grows.

Sebastian is DJ'ing at the record player, so happy his grin is non-stop. And he's dancing. Dancing in place or with whoever walks by and wants to dance the Twist or the Mashed Potato or the Watusi, or whatever he's playing. Slow songs don't interest him much. Someone of my sister's friends or I bump him out of the way, so we can slow dance. To Sam Cooke or Elvis or Frankie Valli.

—Go ahead, he says. I'm going to get a beer. Or some air. I'll sit this one out.

Breck and I really get into it, our bodies melting into each other. Except for what rises between us. He knows I can feel it. He wants me to and pushes himself tighter to me. I have my head on his shoulder, breathing into his neck, smelling his sweat and maybe shampoo or deodorant. The music wraps around us like mummy tape. Every nerve in my body is on high sizzle. I want to reach down and touch him. I want to faint. I want whatever comes next to come right now.

—I'll give you a dollar each if you two make out for five minutes, Adie dares, both inserting reality—my parent's house, my sister watching and laughing, Sebastian with his head in his hands—and encouragement. Breck and I earn our dollars. And I earn a reputation as a flirt and a make-out queen. That night. Even though I don't neck with anyone else at the party, and there were some pretty cute boys in my sister's class. Breck just walks away like a conqueror, but one with swollen lips, to get another beer. Some things just aren't fair.

By midnight the party is a brawl. Someone starts a baloney fight and soon there are grease rings everywhere in the living room, on a portrait of my great-grandfather hanging over the fireplace, on the ceiling and the walls. Because we don't have a bathroom on the first floor, the boys start filling Coke bottles with pee and weeing in my mother's potted plants, while the girls watch. It is the first time I see a boy's thing. I stare at first. But they are so small, not at all what I've read about in those paperbacks Adie and I found under a bush after school one day.

My sister is nowhere to be seen. Neither is her brand new boyfriend. Someone she just met tonight who doesn't go to our school, I know, because I've never seen him before this evening. When I ask her girlfriend, she shrugs and her eyes go to the ceiling. At first I don't get it. Then I do. They've gone upstairs. My sister is a virgin. Or she was till now. We talk about it all the time. What it will be like? Will it hurt?

What if he doesn't use a condom? I can't decide if I feel sick because I've had too much beer or because of what she might be doing upstairs with this boy she's just met. Me? I want romance. I want love. I'm not going to waste my first time on some stranger.

That's when I notice that Breck and Sebastian are missing. It's just after one in the morning, so at first I think he's just gone home and given Breck a ride. I'm disappointed because that only leaves Adie and Jude, and Adie is asleep on the couch in the den and Jude is in the kitchen deep in a debate about civil rights. But before I feel abandoned, back comes Sebastian. With Breck and three other boys from my sister's class. Only he doesn't walk into the house because all five of them are carrying, dragging something ginormous in with them. They are drunk and laughing so hard they cannot speak. Then this thing is sitting there in the foyer of my parent's house. A traffic light. A real traffic light. It must be four feet tall. Red, yellow and green lights dimmed. One kid comes up and sticks his head into the visor surrounding the red light. Everyone still at the party has gathered round. Everyone is amazed. At the sight. At the chutzpah it took to bring off this theft. Only I am wondering, how am I going to get that thing out of here? Then Sebastian, hands on his knees, trying to catch his breath, from the effort of getting that bulky thing up into the house, from the laughter, explains.

—We just went out to get more beer. And we were waiting at this light. Waiting for it to turn green. And it just wouldn't. There was no one coming, no one around, so I said, why don't we just take it down? So we did. Drove the Biscayne under it, got on the roof, three of us, and got it down.

—But, but—you can't just leave it here, I whine, wishing my sister were here to back me up, that it didn't fall to me to be the spoil sport.

—We'll get rid of it. Somehow, Breck says.

—Yeah. 'Course. It's groovy, don't worry, Sebastian backpedals.

A couple of beers later the clowns come up with a plan. They will leave it on the steps of our high school.

—A token of our esteem, Sebastian says grandly.

—Cut the gravitas, Adie says, coming to my rescue. And get that thing out of MC's house.

As the five guys are maneuvering the traffic light back out the door, the beer can pyramid, all two-and-a-half stories of it, crashes to the floor. The walls seemed to quake from the vibration, and the boys hugging the traffic light start accusing each other of causing it.

—Look what you did! Breck says to no one in particular.

—Look what you did?

—Did not.

—Did too. They are all lip-locked drunk and laughing.

The crashing beer cans have shaken my sister back downstairs. She and the boy stumble down the stairs, hair and clothes a mess, dodging cans that fell all over the risers. She rushes the boy out the back door to the alley. I hear his motorcycle roar off and wince. Then she comes stampeding back, scanning the mess and zeroing in on the light.

—What the hell is *that?*

The party stops cold.

—I don't know where, or how, you got that. But get it out of here now. Somebody's bound to call the cops.

Her eyes go from the light to the beer cans and back. Then to me to Sebastian.

—Now!

Everyone begins to scatter, some trying to push past the guys blocking the front door with that insane light; others scrambling for the back door. Like rats when the manhole cover is lifted. My sister, hands on hips, and I, eyes downcast, as if proven guilty when I had nothing to do with either fiasco, we just stand there in the front hall, knee deep in beer cans, some still rolling back and forth. Are we waiting for the doorbell and the cops? Or have we just been cast in stone by the wreckage before us? Am I guilty by default because my friends—along with three of hers, I might add, stole a real, honest-to-god traffic light and brought it here? Or does losing your virginity make you speechless? I'll have to ask my sister about that sometime. Sometime other. Right now, we just stand there.

By the time Sebastian gets back an hour later, we are working like a couple of serfs to clean up the house. The boys, he tells me, dumped the traffic light at the school. Then he ran Breck home. Leaning against the door frame into the living room, he surveys the mess and starts to laugh.

—Not funny, my sister scowls at him and hands him a broom.

—Make yourself useful, buster, she commands.

Sebastian looks at me. I shrug. We both stifle laughs and get to work helping.

Stale beer soaks the air. So does the smell of pee. Beer cans have rolled all over the place, besides making a big pile by the stairs.

—Where is everybody? he asks, and I point. The beer cans really do speak for themselves.

—Adie's in the den, passed out. Jude left, saying we are all delinquents.

—Um, I just came back to see if you were mad at me. You seemed mad. About the traffic light. I wanted to make sure—

I shake my head. Am I saying, no, I'm not mad? Or shut up, you turd? I'm too tired to know, and frozen in place, too, by the task ahead of us. We will be up all night, my sister with a tale to tell, me with nothing except a reputation. So, I guess I am mad. At the universe. And at the traffic light and beer cans for breaking up the best party of my life.

—OK. Put me to work, Sebastian says, taking the broom. But first, I'll get Adie's ass out here to help. The four of us, we can get things spick and span in a jiffy.

For the next couple of hours, Adie, me, my sister, and Sebastian, wash glasses and pick up trash and empty ashtrays and try to get the baloney stains off the walls. He climbs up a stepladder with a sponge and tries to get them off the ceiling and off my great-grandfather. We carry Coke bottles filled with pee up the stairs to empty in the toilet. Sebastian has the bright idea to get my father's wheelbarrow out of the shed and roll it to the kitchen steps. We fill grocery bags with beer cans and slog them over and over and over down the stairs, filling the wheelbarrow six or seven times. Each time Sebastian pushes the barrow out to the back alley and spreads the evidence out among our neighbors' garbage cans. It is three-thirty in the morning before we finish vacuuming and mopping and emptying and straightening and hiding the places we cannot clean—turning cushions over, dragging the coffee table over some stain that won't budge, moving a big ficus plant a little to the left to cover the burn in the wall where some toad crushed out his cigarette.

Adie finds the den couch again, and crashes. I give her a pillow from my room. Her mother knows she's spending the night. That's how she got permission to come over to my house in the first place. My sister has gone upstairs to take a shower and go to bed. Sebastian puts a Sam Cooke record on to play, the volume way down low. Then he collapses onto the living room sofa next to me. We are too wound up to sleep, too exhausted not to. He gives me a Camel. I stretch out with my head in his lap. He blows perfect smoke rings over me. I try but choke instead. "You Send Me" drifts over us. My eyes begin to close in spite of myself when "A Change is Gonna Come" starts to play. I feel his chest rise and fall as he breathes, and I wonder if a change is about to come for me.

—You can stay the night. If you want. What's left of it, I mean.

He twists around in his seat and looks down at me.

—You wouldn't mind?

Words I have dreamt of hearing. I try to act nonchalant.

—Come on. I stand up and take his hand, pulling him to his feet. We stub out our cigarettes and head upstairs. My heart is doing back flips.

We lie on top of the sheets, smoking. The fan turns so fast, its casing rattles. I have an ashtray on my chest. Our Camels burn in unison. Side by side, we stare up at the glow-in-the-dark stars that have been up there since I was a kid. It is hot in my bedroom. But the heat cannot match my steamy hopes.

—If you could be a constellation, he asks, which one would you be?

This question makes me smile. It is so Sebastian. I look up at the ones on my ceiling. I've never ever thought about this before, so I just say the first one that comes to me.

—Scorpio. That's my sign.

—Good one.

—What would you be, Sebastian?

—Oh, he says, taking a thoughtful drag on his cigarette. No question about it. The Big Dipper.

Between a yawn and a beer-giggle, I nudge him with my elbow. He wiggles away a little, then settles back, our shoulders just touching.

—That's dumb.

—No, it's not.

—Then, why? Why the Big Dipper?

—Because I want to be able to scoop up as much life as I can. And drink it down.

I don't know what to say to that, but I know we are both looking up at the dipper's fuzzy twin. I wish we were outside in the dark looking up at the real one, the summer crickets and peepers singing in the trees, the leaves wagging. And that he would kiss me. Instead, here we are on my bed, in our clothes, even though it's hot enough up here to strip off everything, and nothing is happening. I wonder for the first time if he likes someone at school, someone none of us knows anything about. I want to ask him, make him say he likes me best or find out who his secret gjrl is. But before I can—

—If you could go anywhere in the world, he asks, where would you go?

—You mean, leavin' on a jet plane?

—Or, like a rolling stone? Sebastian rises to the bait. I can feel him smiling, and I'm about as happy as I can be, having him here in the dark, his voice like a blanket tucked up under my chin.

—Are you ready to go? Bags packed?

There is something now about his tone, distant, as if he's already out the door.

—I'm homeward bound.

As suddenly as it began, the game is over. Sebastian shifts to one side and puts his ashtray on the nightstand. Then he rolls to his other side, facing me in the dark. He is propped up on one elbow. I can smell his smoky breath and just make out the glistening whites of his eyes. He is so near to me, his face just above mine, heat throbs between my legs.

—If I tell you something, will you swear not to say anything to the others? Or anyone else? The rustle of my head on the pillow he hears as my yes.

—As soon as high school is over, I'm getting as far away from here as I can. Maybe Europe or Alaska or Mexico City.

This news is like a slap across the face. I thought he was going to tell me he loved me and wanted to make love. Instead, he wants to get as far away from me as he can. Across the planet where his Big Dipper will shine more brightly for him. I fight them back but one tear rolls across my check and wets the pillowcase.

—Why? Why, Sebastian? I thought we were tight. All of us.

—Aw, MC, gee. That's not what I meant. You can come too. Or we can meet up or—I arch up and kiss him.

—I love you, Sebastian.

I can feel his shock. It's bouncing off the walls, making the windows rattle and the fan cough. He rolls back onto his back and catches his breath. Regret bursts like a fireball in my head.

—I'm sorry! I'm sorry, Sebastian. Only it's the truth.

—Don't be sorry, please don't be. It's not you, it's me. And I do love you too, Mary Clay—but—

—But like a friend?

—Yes.

There is nothing more to say but he laces his fingers with mine and squeezes gently. I look up at the glowing Big Dipper, with its seven stars. I think, one for each of us. I know then that I will never look at that constellation ever again without thinking of Sebastian. His friendship is better than nothing, I guess. We are still holding hands when we fall asleep.

We don't wake up until eleven the next morning, cotton-mouthed and hair a fright, both of us. The bedding is a mess, so it looks like something happened but, really, it was just us thrashing in the heat. We look at each other and giggle.

—What will your sister say?

—Oooo! I shrug and smile. So does he. We both know what she will think and we both want her to think it.

Jude

The wind blows in through Sebastian's open car windows like a cleanser. My eyes are closed and my nostrils are as flared as I can make them, trying to flush the smell of permanent solution out of my being. Adie and Breck are sitting beside me in the backseat bantering away like a couple of crows about the hospital, trying to top each other with horror stories. Oh God, that it could only be one day in that hell hole! I don't need to look to know Sebastian is driving with one elbow propped out the window and the other hand wheeling the power steering with a couple of fingers. This is the way he drives everywhere, at least when it isn't freezing. Mary Clay is beside him up front because she dibbed it first. Everyone is smoking. When MC flicks her ashes out the window, some fly back at me, brushing my cheek. I don't care. I just want to get as far away from this place as I can, as fast as I can and try to forget everything I've seen, smelled, even tasted today—after a while, you can taste those chemicals. Why do women do it? Have their hair permed? How can they stand to do that every couple'a months? The chemicals are so harsh, they would burn our hands if we hadn't worn rubber gloves all afternoon. God. Shit. Awful. And those women? Oh my God. Hair as brittle as uncooked spaghetti. And the scabs. And the keening, even in the chair but always as they wait their turn, restrained—that's the word our supervisor user—in the hallway.

—Tell me why, Sebastian. Tell me why we're doing this? Why your mother volunteered us to work in a mental hospital all summer? I think to myself. Then I open my eyes and say it out loud.

—Because we're too old for summer camp, Adie says. To 'occupy' us, my mother says.

—Wasn't talking to you.

Sebastian's eyes smile at me from the rearview mirror.

—Gawd! He says. Wasn't it a scene?

—I didn't know there were people like that, MC observes in her obscure way.

I mean, where has she been, that she hasn't seen retards before?

—That's no hospital, Breck announces. It's a looney bin. Those people aren't sick, they're doomed. You know, that dump is where the state sends the sick-o's who can't pay. The rich whack-o's go to the Country Club where they get really fancy treatment and private rooms.

—The Country Club? Sebastian asks, searching for Breck in the mirror.

—Yeah, Breck tells us. That's what they call Our Lady of Grace, the Country Club. I know, because my cousin got sent there when he went catatonic over some girl. At State Hospital, they get handcuffed to their beds and are given lobotomies and shock treatment, where they attach little electrodes to your head and try to fry your brain. At the Country Club, the worst you get is insulin shock therapy, but mostly high-class drugs.

Wow, I think, this is the most talking I've ever heard Breck do in his life. I also think he's seen too many horror movies. How could he possibly know that stuff? All we saw, in the women's ward, were people lining the halls in these chairs that sort of held them in place.

Jude

—At least you guys had each other, Adie says. I was on my own with kids. Kids! Little kids, some with heads the size of watermelons, some twisted up like licorice sticks. Then there was one—

—Not interested, I say.

—I don't care if you're interested, Jude. You and MC had each other. And you were with adults. There was one kid who was perfectly normal and had just been dropped off there because his parents didn't want him—

—You don't know that, MC chimes in, taking the words right out of my mouth.

—That's what I was told. Little kids. I mean, little deformed kids. Ones who could only grunt. Kids rolled up into balls on the floor. Wetting their pants all the time.

—You think giving permanents to toothless women who pick at themselves all day is some kind of picnic? Who scream just to scream. Who spit at you if you smile at them? And all those chemicals. They eat skin—

—They do not, Adie butts in.

—Do too, MC says, again voicing my exact sentiments but not my rage. I don't know why I'm so pissed off. But I'm plenty pissed off.

—This was your fault, Sebastian. I'm not going back. I'm not breathing those fumes one more day. Or risking my hands.

—It's one day a week, Adie says but I cut her off.

—One day too many.

—Yeah, Adie, MC says. Jude's future is in her hands. Think about it. If she burns the skin off her fingertips giving those nut cases a perm, because there's a hole in one of those gloves or something, she might never be able to play the violin again.

—Girls, girls, girls. This is from Sebastian, playing our

sixteen-year-old father figure. It wasn't so bad. Goes to show, the freaks in the movies are based on fact.

I ponder this. All art draws from life, right? So, once again Sebastian has a point, however perverted.

—It wasn't so groovy in the men's barbershop either, Breck says. His voice is so quiet, I look over at him and see he's kind of shell-shocked. Like all of us, I guess. He seems so wounded, it calms me down for some weird reason.

—There were men in strait jackets getting their hair cut, Sebastian says into the rearview mirror.

—See! Breck says. I mean, how crazy is that, he goes on, then catches himself. Oops! Sorry.

Now we are all guffawing. How crazy is right.

—Let's get something to eat, Sebastian says, and puts on his blinker, sort of at the last minute, turns, bumps the curb, the car swerves a little and the three of us in the backseat bounce off each other, and we head back into town. Then we're at Hap's Big Boy, and life is looking up. The afternoon and its horrors are behind us. Sort of. Burgers and fries all around. Hamburger juice runs down my fingers. I lick them and then tuck my hair behind my ear to keep it out of my burger. We're all face down in our food, or that's what I think until I see Sebastian, his burger with one bite out of it, staring out the window. Somewhere else.

—Sebastian?

—What? Oh.

And he is back. Back with us.

—Sorry, I was just thinking. About the hospital—

—Ugh. The hospital? MC and I react in unison.

—Not about the freakshow out there. No. I was just wondering, where was God for those people?

Jude

We all stop stuffing our mouths. MC has a French fry that freezes half way there. I, all of us, stare at Sebastian. I want to say something profound, join him in his quest for understanding. Be as wise as he is. But I am not. I'm just an ego twerp, compared to him. We all are. Sebastian thinks about the universe. The rest of us, me at least, can't get beyond the next pop quiz, the next cool concert, the next fight with my mother. I hate feeling this small, courtesy of his totally unconscious gift for somehow rising above us all.

—Wow, Adie finally says, breaking the awe wall Sebastian has created, and not for the first time, not by a long shot.

—That's deep, MC says, looking adoringly at him. I want to wash her mouth out with soap. Throw lye in those eyes. I mean, what a suck-up she can be. Never mind, that it *was* deep.

—No wonder you love soul music, Breck says. Just like him, I think, another weird connection. Sebastian has soul just like the Black musicians he idolizes. I wish I'd thought of that, said that.

—It's the luck of the draw, isn't it? he goes on. Maybe we weren't born with silver spoons in our mouths, but we get to grow up and live productive lives. That's all.

Then he takes a big bite out of his burger while the rest of us wait for him to release us from this whopping big thought of his.

—What? I got ketchup on my nose?

But we all just duck our heads and dig into our fries. Meanwhile, I'm thinking, maybe he'll write a poem about how he feels and I'll set it to music. Once he's got the words, they can be lyrics. We can work on it together. Sebastian and Jude. Just the two of us.

When it's time to head out and we've paid up, MC, Adie, and I decide to walk home. Sebastian needs to drive Breck way downtown to where he lives in that residential hotel, and we're aimed in the opposite direction. Besides, I still need the fresh air to flush out those chemical smells clinging to the hairs in my nose, the grey cells of my brain, and to wipe out this feeling of inadequacy. Adie and MC are good for that because it's real easy for me to feel superior to them.

—You know the annoying thing about Sebastian? MC says as we walk. He can make me feel the world-is-my-oyster great one minute and a hamster in a wheel the next.

—Yeah. But he doesn't mean to. He's just a thinker, Adie says. He thinks. About stuff. All the time.

—And what are we? I want to know. Dopes?

—If the shoe fits, and Adie flashes me one of her rare Conquistador smiles.

—He asked me to the Joni Mitchell concert next weekend. MC says, out of the blue, and it throws me, damn her.

—Sebastian asked you, Mary Clay? I thought we were all going as a group. Like always.

—Breck asked me, Adie says. I guess it's a date thing.

—Breck asked you? It's a date thing? Well, what about me?

—You can go with Grady, Jude. Or Tony. We'll triple date.

—Grady didn't exactly ask me. And Tony can't go out this Saturday. There's a mass or something, remember?

—Well, Grady will. Because he has to. No, wait. I didn't mean it like that—

—Thanks a bunch, Adie.

—Not cool, Adie. Not cool at all. MC, my protector, at work.

—What I mean is, it's really just like always. The whole pack. You want to go, Grady wants to go. We all want to go. It's really just a seating arrangement.

My instinct is to wring Adie's neck. Seating arrangement my ass.

Jude

—You know, don't you—

It's out of my mouth before I can reel it back in.

—You know, don't you, that Sebastian and I have a thing going on.

Don't I love the look of utter shock on their faces.

—Then why did he ask me?

—Pity.

—God, Jude. Don't be a bitch. This is Adie. I ignore her of course.

—He didn't ask me out of pity, MC snarls back at me. Maybe it's news to you, but he likes me best. That's why he asked me, Jude.

—I know you two are close, Adie says. Friends. But Grady told me yesterday that Sebastian likes me. More than a friend. He was kinda jealous, Grady. Which was kinda sweet. Anyway, that's what he told me.

—Oh, come on, you two. What does Grady know, Adie? It's what you want to believe, I know. But you don't do music with him. Neither of you sings. You're just groupies.

The three of us stand in a nasty little triangle in the middle of the sidewalk as traffic whizzes past. I hold my ground because as harsh as it is, I speak the truth. I don't know why other than pity he would actually ask MC to the Joni Mitchell concert. But I do know, he is nice to her. Why? Who knows? Except pity. How could he like a girl whose eyes are crossed behind her glasses and whose mother puts a bowl over her head to cut her hair? I also know Adie is too damned stand-offish for Sebastian. Too know-it-all. He has the hots for her. Why would Grady tell her that? It doesn't make any sense.

—There's only one way to find out, MC finally says, breaking the ice wad stacked up between us.

—One way, what?

—To find out which one of us Sebastian likes best. You know, *likes*. Suddenly MC looks cunning. I can tell she has a diabolical idea.

—Yeah? So? I urge.

—Yeah, tell us, Adie says.

—Steal his diary.

—Whoa! I don't know. Steal Sebastian's diary?

—Well, we all know he keeps one. He talks about it all the time. It's where he keeps his poetry, right?

God, almighty, I think. Why not?

—Why not?

It takes some plotting, and we work on it all the way back to Adie's house, where MC and I will split off home ourselves. We settle on the following Monday. His mother will be at work and Sebastian has his part-time job at the car wash. His house will be empty all morning. We wrestle with how to get in and Adie nails it.

—The bulkhead. To the basement. The padlock is rusty, so it only looks locked. Remember?

We do remember. Because at the bonfire Sebastian got into his mom's bourbon stash. Remember? In the basement? He brought it out to us through that bulkhead.

—Bingo!

On Monday, we meet at Adie's because it's closest to Sebastian's. Adie tells her mom we're going to the park to play tennis. Which is partially true because that's what we plan on doing after we read the diary. That is, if we're still speaking.

We walk up the alley that runs behind Sebastian's house. The only living thing we see is a stray dog with a knocked over garbage can, going to town. Inside the fence to his backyard, we tap Adie to sneak up and make sure the car is gone from out front. It is. So, we peel back the bulkhead door, creaky on its hinges but who cares? There's no one to hear us.

—Let's go!

Jude

I'm first in. It's wicked stinky down here but with the bulkhead door open I can see the stairs and make a run for them. We tiptoe-tumble up the stairs, open the door very carefully, just in case. Nobody. Not a sound. Until MC gets a case of the giggles, then Adie catches them, so I push them through the swinging door into the kitchen, and we are all bent over double trying not to make a sound, which makes no sense to me because there's no one home. But the whole breaking-and-entering thing we've just done requires stealth, not giggles, as I see it. Funny how weird it feels to be in somebody else's house when you're not supposed to be there. Especially Sebastian's. Because we practically live here anyway. Like thieves. But we are thieves, or hope to be, soon. I guess.

—What are we going to do when we find it? I ask, the reality striking me cold that we have not discussed this part.

—We can just read it up there and put it back where we find it, MC whispers.

—No way, Adie whispers back. That could take forever. Let's take it and bring it back when we finish.

—You mean, and break in again? What, are you kidding? God, Adie, sometimes you can be so dense. OK, I decide. We read it and leave it where we found it. Agreed? They agree. Which is a good thing because already this is beginning to creep me out. And I'm not sure anymore that I want to know what's in his diary. Because what if—

MC leads the way out of the kitchen. We tiptoe over to the bottom of the stairs and start up. I can hear them breathing. A step squeaks as I start up. We are up on the landing when a vacuum cleaner roars to life overhead.

—Shit!
—Shit!
—Shit!

And we are falling, tripping, pushing down the stairs, across the room, down the basement steps, where we are safe enough to stop and listen. The open bulkhead door calls out to me but none of us dares to move. My heart is going bananas in my chest. But then, there it is, upstairs, the distant hum of the vacuum. We look at each other and know how dumb we are, how close a call this was, because what if Sebastian were to find out? Who would have figured on a cleaning lady? We bolt up the bulkhead steps, across the yard, out the fence and are half way down the alley when it hits me.

—Adie, MC. Crap, we left the bulkhead door open.

A round of blame game follows, each of us accusing the other of being stupid and arguing about if someone needs to go back and shut it and who that someone should be. In the end, Adie volunteers. As soon as she heads off, MC and I take off. If she gets caught, neither one of us wants to be anywhere around. Sebastian and I have a rehearsal later. I can't get caught. Plus, I think MC is thinking what I'm thinking: if Adie gets caught and Sebastian finds out, that'll be one fewer of us wondering who he likes best. We need to know, the three of us. Really need to know. Because maybe he's too shy to take the next step, but we're not. I know I'm not because I know what his diary says. I know. It's me. Gotta be.

Later, Mary Clay and Adie ask if they can come to the rehearsal.

—No, dumb shits. No, you can't, I say, speaking the obvious. We're working. We've got some tough harmonies to figure out before the talent contest at the Open Dialogue.

But that's not the real reason. Because we're a shoo-in to win. That is, if Sebastian actually gets his act together. I don't know why he drags his feet about us doing actual performances. Like Ian and Sylvia.

Jude

We could be famous. Cut records. Do USA concert tours. Be on Ed Sullivan. Problem is, Sebastian doesn't want to be famous. It's like he doesn't want to draw attention to himself or something, but he will do those stupid coffeehouse gigs, like where he met and acquired Grady. Another unfortunate thing. Grady. That boy has more ambition in his little finger than Sebastian has, total. And he's talented. If I liked him as much, I could shift my allegiance to Grady because he would have no objections to fame. None at all. But I'm not leaving Sebastian's side because I am the melody and he is the harmony. We are two halves of the same person. Yin and yang, whatever they are. So the real reason why I don't want Mary Clay and Adie coming tonight is because time alone with him is precious, singing shoulder to shoulder, his sweet tenor and my alto melding, like gold and diamonds into a ring. Like a marriage of true minds. So I tell Adie and MC, emphatically, not to barge in on us.

When I get to Sebastian's, he's gobbling down a can of Spaghetti-O's because his mother is already non-compos upstairs. He looks at me as he shovels in the last spoonful of that orange goo, and I have a real pang of pity. I think I've got a shitty home life but maybe his tops mine. So, I sit down at the kitchen table, first propping my guitar against the sink, and wait for him to say something.

—Hi.

Finally.

—Can you digest that rubber shit and still sing?

I get a grin out of him with that one, scrunching up those gorgeous eyes.

—We'll see, and he polishes off a glass of milk. When I move out of here, I'm going to open up a restaurant and eat really fancy food. Like foie gras. Or Duck a l'Orange.

Ambient Light

—Have you even tasted those things? I want to mention his milk moustache because it makes him look eight-years-old. But I don't. He's being too serious.

—No. But even brussel sprouts sound good to me after this—what did you call it?—rubber shit?

He gets up, rinses his bowl, puts the sauce pan to soak, taps a Camel out of the pack he carries in his shirt pocket and lights up.

—Come on. I'm ready, he says, taking a long draw on the cigarette so that the tip burns red.

First, we talk about our set list. All covers, of course. I want to add in a poem he wrote and I set to music. But he nixes that.

—Why did you waste your time putting that piece of shit to music, Jude?

It's not shit and I say so, but I'm stung all the same. I worked extra hard on that tune. I wish he'd at least listen to it because it is so smooth and his message—about longing to wander—so great … but I give up before I even try with him. One thing I've learned from Sebastian—I can't twist his arm, ever.

For an hour or more, we sing Simon and Garfunkel, Pete Seeger, Joni Mitchell and a little Dylan, like "The Times They Are A'Changin,'" because our times are a'changin'. I know Sebastian is worried about Vietnam, worried the draft will be re-instated. If it is, he says he knows a way out of it. But he's all hush-hush about what he means. Much as I like Dylan, I'd like to chop off his balls for writing songs that just scare the crap out of guys our age. Finally, a blessing to have been born a girl.

We include Ian and Sylvia, too, because we both think they're tops, especially tunes like "Four Strong Winds" and "Southern Comfort." I remind Sebastian that Ian and Sylvia wrote those too.

—You know, singer-songwriters like—

Jude

—Yeah, yeah, yeah. I know, I know. Like Peaches and Herb.

—They didn't write their own stuff, I argue uselessly.

He's mocking me. Mocking my ambitions for the two of us. He's mocking us. But I let it go, at least on the surface, because I'm afraid he'll throw me out. Refuse to sing with me. At least I talked him into this community talent contest. Which is something. It is a reason for me to be here three nights a week, just the two of us, making music which is a kind of making love. At least for a couple more weeks.

—What if we win? I ask, during a break in our session.

—Win what?

—The contest, dumbbell.

He shrugs.

—What if we do?

—Well, you know. Can we take our show on the road? We can take out a reel-to-reel recorder from the library, make a tape and, you know, send it to Nashville or someplace. What do you say?

Sabastian sighs. Looks at me, shaking his head.

—No? My disappointment not only blares out in that single word but I want to get on my knees and beg.

—I didn't say no. I just think you're like crazy beautiful when you don't get your way. You go all pouty mouthed and your cheeks go all taut. Like a kid whose mother tosses out her favorite toy.

—So are you saying yes?

I can't believe he may have changed his mind. I can't believe we might go on singing together for the rest of our lives. It's in his eyes. I can see the yes, even though he won't say it, and then I know—I know—we are good, we are one.

—I'm saying, let's see if we win, and then maybe I'll give you your toy back.

It was about now that I hear a sneeze. Adie and MC. They're on the porch. Listening, for I don't know how long. Probably since the Spaghetti-O's. Eavesdropping. Never mind. There is yes in his eyes. I'm the one.

Breck

I wish I weren't so shy around girls. I wish the girls that I like would like me back. But it never goes that way. This is my sixteenth birthday, and I wanted to have a proper date. Like Sebastian does. Not that it's easy from here. I mean, in the past when I've wanted to take a girl out, I have to take the bus. Then take her by bus to the movies or concert or coffeehouse, wherever we're going by bus. Then take her home by bus. Then take myself home by bus. The bus takes the romance out of it, for sure. Oh, yeah, that time with Adie's friend Ruth? I wanted to die on the spot. Yeah. Sad. There I am, trying to make it, or at least something, with her, putting my arm around her and getting close and stuff, and those three hoods in the back of the bus? They start hooting and hollering and start singing, Tightass skinny boy, tightass blonde girl, sittin' on a bus, K-I-S-S-I-N-G, First comes condom, then comes cum—I thought Ruth would die of embarrassment. Me too. She moved up a whole row on the bus, and when we got to her stop, she said—
—Don't bother.
And those hoods in the back? They cracked up. She never would speak to me again. I liked her. A lot. She was cute. But that was that. The bus is no place to get it on with a girl.

But today, I turn sixteen and get my driver's license. Whoo-hoo. All I need now is a car to drive. Sebastian, I know he will let me drive his mother's bomb. All the rest have driven it, everyone who's got a license, that is. But he's got his own date tonight, and I'm stuck with Adie. Again. She can't mind if I take the bus to pick her up, because she knows we'll get Sebastian's backseat to the concert. It's like a birthday present from everyone, my Temptations' ticket. My parents' birthday present is letting me have everyone over for dinner first. Which means they all have to drive downtown, to where I live, a residential hotel. In my life, I've never had friends over. Part embarrassment that I don't have a house like the rest of them, that my parents have dumped us here in this building, miles from everything. And everybody. It's not my fault my father got fired from his last pharmacy job. Something about bad pill counts, or something, and we ended up here. The management gave us an apartment, rent free, in exchange for Dad running the in-house drugstore and soda fountain.

The other reason I've never had anybody over is because our apartment is too small, and my mother is sickly. Not really, but she plays at it. But because this is a *big* birthday, as my mom says, and a milestone, as my dad says, they got the bright idea to have the party for me at the soda fountain. Just my friends. No family. Meanwhile, I'm thinking: right? Dad lets seven teenagers loose in his drugstore? Where's the camera? That's what I want to know. He's got to have some way of spying. Maybe the mirror in the pharmacy door is two-way? Nah. I'd have figured that out.

Dad closes the shop early. Puts a sign on the door: Closed for Coming-of-Age Party. I mean, really? I'm only sixteen. But he gets off on it, and my mom and sister get off on making this creepy party table for dinner. With paper hats and crepe-paper garlands and a crown for me with a big sixteen coming out of the top, and one wrapped package at my place, about the size of a deck of cards. From my dad. When they all get here, they are like freaked-out silent. No one knows how to act. It's such a weird place for a birthday party. My mom greets everyone, kids I hang out with all the time who she's never met before, like it is old home week. Like they are her long lost best friends. Even though she really doesn't know who is who. Not until the formalities are over and my mom announces the menu—hot dogs, baked beans, chips, milk, and later, all the ice cream we can eat from the soda fountain. A real feast. Only when she and my sister leave, do we all begin to relax. Mostly they just stroll around, opening drawers full of first aid stuff and cosmetics and men's grooming tools and all sorts of pharmaceutical junk. Tony finds a toothbrush, then a mustache comb. He holds the toothbrush under his lip and begins stroking it with the comb. We fall all over each other laughing. I look over my shoulder—I can't help it—thinking my dad will burst in, on the war path, but he doesn't. No dictator dad, so I start to relax a little more. Then Sebastian opens a drawer and finds a rubber thumb sleeve, the kind you use to protect yourself from paper cuts and such. But that's not how Sebastian sees it.

—Look, you guys! It's a thumb condom!

Then everybody is rooting around in that drawer and grabbing one, sometimes two. Me too. I've seen these things all my life and never thought of them as thumb condoms. Now they are forever that. Pretty soon Sebastian and Tony start a thumb condom puppet show from the back of the soda fountain counter. Four thumbs fighting each other is all we can see.

—My thumb is bigger than your thumb!

—Well, suck my ... thumb!

Now we are howling. I think: is sex all we ever think about, a glob of drool poised in the corner of my mouth? Yes, yes, yes! I answer myself.

Ambient Light

The sound of the elevator coming down the shaft, and we all freeze. It's like a Laurel and Hardy show, us trying to get those things off our thumbs and back in the drawer or into our pockets or stuffed behind the hosiery display. Then, like musical chairs, we all try to grab a seat at the table and try to look as if we've always been there, as if we are conducting ourselves like young ladies and gentlemen, politely, quietly waiting for a hot dog—a weiner! I have to look away. Both Tony and Sebastian are choking back laughter. As soon as my mom and sister have served us and left, Sebastian ceremoniously places a thumb condom on the end of his dog and wiggles it from the other end. It is the best birthday of my life, and I'll never be able to tell my family anything about any of it. No loss. I don't share much with them on the best of days. Hope my dad doesn't get fired because there's a shortage of thumb sleeves!

Tonight, after my birthday party we, most of us anyway, are heading to the Temptations' gig. And I get to drive my dad's Lincoln Continental! My own set of keys was in the wrapped package. My own set! When he shows up again, I give him a big hug. Can't remember the last time I hugged my dad. If ever. But tonight was the night for it. Car keys and a date and a concert! Best best birthday ever!

Sebastian is taking Brenda, the girl he's been hanging with for the last month. She never comes over to his house in the afternoons. It's like he's hoarding her or something. Or maybe he doesn't want to pollute her by exposing her to us. Or maybe it's because of Jude. We all know Jude is madly in love with Sebastian. All the girls are. That's what I don't get. Sebastian, most of the time, acts like he's not interested in anybody. But maybe it's because to get it on with Jude or Adie or Mary Clay would just be pack-weird. That's what we call it when any one of us gets the hots for one or the other of us. Which is all the time. It's like a round robin. Good thing is, nothing ever can come of it because of the audience. That especially applies to outsiders. Like Brenda. Which is why I shouldn't worry about Adie, but I do. Because I wish it were some hottie who thinks I hung the moon coming with me tonight. Like Brenda. With Sebastian.

Fact is, Sebastian is taking Brenda and Adie is telling everyone that she is my date. Which is awkward. Because that's not the way I see it. I mean, she so seriously weirded me out at that Joni Mitchell concert. She's got this wild crush on me, I guess. She put her head on my shoulder and then—*then*—she said I could put my arm around her if I wanted. I did not want. So, here I am stuck with her again, because this time, she asked me. I didn't want to be a prick. So I said yes. God. I wish it were Brenda. Or that girl Ruth.

Six of us are going to the concert—Sebastian and Brenda, me and Adie, Mary Clay and Grady. Tony doesn't want to come because he says he's a bigot. He really isn't but he'd rather be taken for one than for a mama's boy. Which is closer to the truth. Jude can't come on account of the fact she's grounded. Her mother let her come to my party because it was a special occasion, but she had to go straight home afterward. Stole her mother's car again last weekend. She and Mary Clay didn't quite get the car in park—at least this is what they told us—and since Jude's driveway is uphill, it rolled back down, crossed the street and knocked over a mailbox. Jude is grounded, she says for the rest of her natural life, but she's only saying that because she hates her mother and thinks the rest of her natural life will last to eternity. Truth is, we all get to *ditch the bitch* in seven months when we graduate from *life at home*. Besides, Jude's mom will need to re-enslave her to chauffeuring and other domestic duties requiring a car.

Never mind about Jude. I'm obsessing over Sebastian and Brenda. Because I'm jealous? Am I jealous? No. Not really. Besides, no one knows what's going on between them. I don't know. There's something about them, together, that just feels off. She's cute, all right, with her long blonde ponytail, teensy frame and big blue eyes. But she never says a thing. Smiles a lot, hangs on Sebastian's every word. Which so annoys all three of the girls that it's funny. Tony and I started teasing them about being jealous. Maybe it's true about a woman scorned, but three jealous girls in the same room makes hell look like a pretty tame place to chill out. Haha. I just made a joke—

Maybe Adie's right about one thing. She says Brenda's intimidated by all of us, that when wolves run in packs, it's hard for anyone new to break in. Adie also says Brenda is brain dead. But then Adie is the worst intellectual snob who thinks she's stupid, in the world. Maybe in the universe.

—Grady didn't have any problem, Adie says.

—No. But Grady's a guy, and a musician, and Sebastian asked him over. Which is like asking somebody *in*. Brenda's just a date. An outside matter.

—You know, don't you, Breck, Adie says, whenever they're out together, nothing happens. I've seen Sebastian hold her hand but in two months or however long it's been, no goodnight kiss, no making out, no feeling up. That's it. Ask Mary Clay or Jude. We've all noticed it.

—More like, you've been spying.

—Well—Adie shrugs, throws me a crooked grin. Maybe so.

—You're all just jealous.

That shuts Adie up. She knows truth when she hears it. One thing I know about those three, they all like to cozy up to Sebastian, like he was some idol, some rock star. Something I don't get at all. Except I do. 'Cause I ask myself all the time, what am I doing hanging out with this crowd? The girls all gravitate to Sebastian, not counting some minor flirting with Grady and me. Like the time Adie bet us a dollar each that I wouldn't make out with Mary Clay. I did and MC and I shared a banana split to celebrate our winnings. Anyway, I'm kind of on the outside too. I live downtown, not in this neighborhood. I don't go to their school. I'm not talented like the others. I confessed this to Jude the other day, why I don't know, and she didn't even have to think—

—Oh, that's because you're a dead ringer for Buddy Holly. You fit right in with us misfits because you are dead.

That was a kick in the nuts, all right. I took that home with me and looked in the mirror. Don't see it now, never would have made the connection. But after this, Jude starts calling me Buddy and Adie and MC call me The Ghost. So where am I? I know I'm not really dead to them because Adie wants to get in my pants and MC creamed when we made out. That's what she told me, and I still can't believe she said it. I'm just a prude, I guess. Or maybe I really am dead.

The girls flirting with Grady doesn't really count *because* he's new too. He's only been hanging with us since the summer. New blood for the bloodsucking females to go after while they're fighting for Sebastian's favor. By now, Grady's part of the pack because Sebastian wants him around to make music with. The guy is really talented, like Jude. I don't think he has much of a voice but it's pretty amazing what he can do with a guitar and a harmonica. Put him on the radio, and his sound is as good as Dylan's, any day. Just not the voice.

One thing I do know, though it's not something I'd say to anybody. The reason, the real reason, why I hang out with them, is because there is just something about Sebastian. I don't know the word for it. Maybe passion, but not *that* kind of passion. I don't know. He's feels stuff. Deep stuff. The way he feels his music, the way, when he's singing, he looks up, like he's asking God for something. Something from another planet or another universe or another astral plane. I'm such an earthling compared to him. He doesn't seem to have time for the things we all care so much about—pairing up, sex—not that we aren't all virgins, or at least I think we all still are. Maybe not MC. Don't know about Grady. Sebastian though, well, I wish I knew what was going on in that head. None of us, not just Brenda, ever really seem to reach him. It's like when he's singing, he is out of this world, looking down on us, his friends, yes. But also somewhere else, where none of us exist, and oh so happy. But I don't think he's happy at all. I think he's singing to escape and wherever that takes him—he is happier and freer. I wish I knew. 'Cause I'd like to go on that magic carpet ride too.

Tonight, tonight, if Adie starts all that clingy stuff again, I'm going to have to say something. To thine own self be true, John Breckinridge Taylor. To thine own self. Right on.

But I'm not and she does, and I'm a wimp. At least it was the Temptations and not some folksinger, some touchy-feely moment. No, the Temptations get us all dancing—in place, in the aisles, and Adie, on one of the railings. Balancing up there like the gymnast she is, she knows all the Temptations' moves. She is dancing and people around her begin applauding—for her—because she's really good and because it's an incredible balancing act. You have to be impressed. Adie is lost in the dance, completely. Until David Ruffin calls her out from onstage.

—Young lady! Young lady!

When Adie hears that the spell is broken, her arms start pinwheeling trying to keep from falling. Sebastian and I catch her, help her down, and before any of us know it, our Adie is heading for the stage. The Temptations invite her onstage, and she goes!

—Come on up here, young lady. What is your name?

—Adeline, she says, mouse-like, and using her given name. What's that all about, I want to know?

—Girl, you sure do seem to know our moves. Why don't you stay up here and show everybody what you can do? OK, boys—

The intro to "The Way You Do the Things You Do" strikes up.

—Good Gawd, Sebastian whispers next to my ear. That's David Ruffin with her. Oh my God, oh my God, oh my God, is he going to hand her the mic?

David Ruffin does not hand her the mic. He's the show. But as soon as the five men are moving to the music and singing, so is Adie. Up there on stage, our Adie is dancing with the Temptations, and her moves are good. Real good. Sexy even. She is not embarrassing herself. She is not.

—Adie just met David Ruffin and Paul and Otis Williams. Sebastian, who can't take his eyes off what's happening on stage—none of us can—whispers this in my ear. Ruffin, I know, is a personal idol of his. I can hear the awe. I can feel it. All I think is: this is crazy. Adie is crazy.

The song ends. Adie is elated. I've never seen her so wired, so on, so ecstatic. When David Ruffin thanks her and kisses her on the cheek, both Adie and Sebastian swoon. I swear it. Adie on stage, Sebastian shoulder to shoulder with me.

The rest of the concert is a blur. We are all over Adie. Sebastian even kisses the cheek David Ruffin had kissed. Laughing and hugging her and people all around us, people we don't even know, are patting her on the back and laughing with us and asking for her autograph. Adie is high, truly high. They say, Get High on Life, Not Drugs. And for the first time in my life I see what this looks like. We all do. We are all infected by it, by Adie, pulling off something so outrageous, so wild and so out of character. I put my arm around her and mean it this time.

After the concert, we are still all fired up by Adie's stunt. Besides it's Saturday night and only 10:20 when the encores finally end. So we start piling into the cars, me and Adie in my dad's Lincoln. Sebastian and Brenda are alone in his mother's Biscayne. Grady gives MC a ride home on his Honda 250 bike. Except that instead of going home, we agree to meet at White Castle for some sliders and Cokes. On the way there, Grady stops to get some gas and I follow him in. So does Sebastian. While he's gassing up his bike, MC goes into the convenience store because, we learn later, Grady's mother needs eggs and asked him to pick some up on his way home. She comes out with a dozen.

—Here, MC, give those to me, Adie says. I'll take them in the car where they'll be safe. You don't want to ride on the back of that bike holding a bunch of eggs. That makes some sense, since we're meeting up again to get sliders, and off we go, our little caravan, with us in the lead and a dozen eggs between us on the front seat.

Maybe it is because Adie was already on fire or maybe it is because I was really enjoying her company and wanted to keep things riding high. But when we are all stacked up at a red light, I look at Adie. I look at the eggs. She seems to know exactly what I am thinking. She takes out two eggs and I take out one.

—On the count of three—

We throw open the Continental's doors, step out and fire off three eggs at Sebastian's windshield. Two splat on the glass and one sails over his car and catches the front bumper of Grady's shiny new motorcycle. Oops. We jump back in the car, the light turns green and we take off at a ridiculously high rate of speed. The chase is on. They're on us, until they both disappear in different directions. We know what's what. They've peeled off to load up on ammunition themselves, so I put the pedal to the metal. Adie suggests I drop her off at her house after we stock up on more eggs so we can change cars.

—Hide your car in the alley behind my house and we'll take Daddy's car to find them. They won't be looking for a Ford station wagon. They'll be looking for your father's Lincoln.

For the next two hours, we play car-to-car dodge 'em all over town. Sneak attacks are countered with bumper-to-bumper skirmishes. Somehow more cars get involved. Suddenly Jude is with MC and Grady in Jude's mother's Rambler—stolen again—and they are loaded up with eggs and now tomatoes. Sebastian engages sort-of-complete strangers, kids he recognizes from his school. We careen in and out of one fast food hangout after another—a McDonalds, a Kentucky Fried Chicken, and a Big Boy—terrifying the lovely Brenda. Either they play the game or get covered in eggs. Sometimes both. Sebastian even drives to Tony's house, throws pebbles at this window and gets him to sneak out, so now it's Tony and Brenda in the car, it's hood and windshield covered in direct hits. Adie and me in her father's car, also a casualty by now. MC, Jude, and Grady in the Rambler, reeking now of egg. My dad's car hidden—or so I gleefully believe.

It's about two in the morning when we run out of money for more eggs. All we have are the leftover tomatoes, which just sit there in a store bag looking left out. A life lesson, as they say, is before us: a ripe tomato, the kind sold in stores, doesn't splat, it bounces.

In a truce that comes after a near collision just down from Sebastian's house, we all jump out of our cars, armed with our last eggs, and fire them off at each other in fierce hand-to-egg combat. When two zing past Jude's open car door and fly inside, to explode all over the interior, that stops us in our tracks. First, the car is stolen (yada yada). Second, it's not going to be easy cleaning the egg off the upholstery.

—Shit, Jude says.

She knows, we all know, this spells real trouble. All we have to do for the rest of the cars involved is wash them. Then, good as new!

Or, so we think. There are a lot of "so we thinks" this evening. We agree to meet at Grady's to wash off the cars because his house has a hose long enough to reach the street. On our way there, Adie and I go back to her house to fetch my father's car. The next *so we think* is that in hiding my dad's car, it would remain hidden. But it is clear it has been found because it looks like an omelet. Someone has fired off at least a dozen eggs at point blank range. Uh oh. I can't help thinking, this is the first time my dad let me use his car, and what if—

But I couldn't go there. So I climb in, rev her up and follow Adie to Grady's house, where car-washing is well under way. We line up behind the others to have time with the hose. But Sebastian and Tony are already out inspecting the damage. The real damage. I only have to look into their faces to know something is very very wrong. Sebastian can't even speak. He just points. At his mother's car. When I don't react, he drags me by the collar for a closer look. Then he points again. It's a pock mark. Then I notice his mother's car is dotted with pock marks. ALL our cars are dotted with them. One pock mark for every egg landed.

We can wash off the egg—which is a good thing because some seem to be cooking on the hot hoods, with an unseasonably warm September night not helping matters. Can't get the hose on those cars fast enough. But those pock marks, they aren't going anywhere. I run back to my father's Lincoln, hit by a barrage of eggs from a distance of no more than three feet. What I see is terrifying. My mouth fills with saliva and I hurl. Right there on the street, along with the eggshells and pooling hose water.

—Breck, what is it? Adie asks. In the dark she can't see that the same thing has happened to her father's Ford.

—Oh, no. Oh, God, I moan. But it could just as well have been Adie. Or Sebastian. Or Jude. Or even Grady, whose bike didn't exactly escape unmolested. He has a cracked front headlight.

Breck

—We are up shit creek. Possibly one of us actually said this out loud but we are all thinking it. We are all trying to grapple with doom.

In the end, we have ruined the paint jobs on five cars. That we know of. I mean, there are the others at the fast food joints.

As we scrub the egg off all those cars, we hold a silent-ish vigil for our respective lives. There are a whole lot of supplications to God to save us. Even though none of us, except Tony, is on an intimate basis with Him. Finally, the egg and eggshell fragments are washed off and the hose is recoiled and returned to its place so Grady's parents won't be suspicious. Then, we head home. Each of us praying our parents won't notice the dents in their car's paint job. As if.

Next morning, being Sunday, everybody in my apartment is sleeping in. Not me. I get the bus—two transfers—over to Sebastian's. I don't want to be around when my dad gets up and starts to grill me about the concert. And the date. And getting the car for the first time. This spares me from lying to his face. It also spares me the rod. Because he is going to see. He is going to find out. He is going to kill me.

Everybody else is already there. Except Tony, who is making his obligatory genuflection at St. Benedict's. Adie, Mary Clay, Sebastian, and I all pile into the Biscayne and head over to the scene of the crime. Crooks always do that, right? Return to the scene of the crime? So, Grady. Grady is on his porch waiting for us with one more *so we think*. We don't get the go-away signal he's making. Only later do we figure out he was trying to deflect us from his mother's inquiries. But too late. She spots us and corners Sebastian.

—Sebastian, Grady's mom half growls at him, pinning him against the porch railing. Are you the ringleader for whatever went on here last night?

—No, m'am. He smiles. Can't think what you mean, m'am.

I can see her melting. Then, just when I think we're going to get away with it, she points out to the street, and her face goes taut like a drum head.

—Look out there, Sebastian. What do you see?

—Um, nothing, m'am.

—Best you level with me, if you want to spare your friend Grady a month of being grounded. False loyalty, boys, false loyalty makes you complicit through silence. Sebastian, before I call your mother and get you grounded too, be a good boy, and tell me why it is that every dog in the neighborhood was out licking the pavement in front of our house this morning?

—No idea, ma'am. Dogs'll be dog's is all.

Adie looks at Grady, Grady looks at MC, who looks at Jude, who looks at me. We all want to just bust out laughing but we know to hold it in. Instead, what goes around among us is a domino effect solemn face. Pack solidarity Exhibit I.

No one is in a hurry to head home that day, so of course, once we could gracefully take our leave of Grady's house—that is, as soon as his mother shakes her head solemnly at solemn Sebastian and disappears into the house—we pile into Sebastian's mother's Biscayne and head for his house, with a detour to White Castle. We only just make the turn onto Frankfurt before we explode with laughter, the car sways as both Adie, from the backseat and MC from the front, grab Sebastian, who is driving, or trying to, and start kissing him all over his neck and face.

At Sebastian's, with one-hundred-and-forty-four White Castle boxes strewn all over the coffee table and spilling on to the floor, we clutch our extra-large Cokes and fall into a spontaneous Frank Session.

—Now what are we going to do? I say.

—Dogs licking the sidewalk, Adie says. That's too funny. The dogs ratted us out.

Between stuffing our mouths and chugging Cokes, we get the giggles. But only for a sec before reality smacks us in the face.

—Yeah, but, MC chimes in. They're going to notice. Our parents are going to kill us.

—Not yours, MC.

—My dad will see right off, I say. He loves that car. As soon as he pulls out of the garage, he's going to see all the pock marks on the hood. If he doesn't notice them first on the driver's door. Oh God. I don't think I can ever go home again.

—We need a story. We need to stick together. We need—

—No, we don't, Adie. We need a plan but we don't want to stick together on this. I'm going to blame it on the hickory tree. I'm going to tell Mom I forgot it was hickory nut season and parked underneath it by accident. Then, when she threatens to ground me—again—I'm going to say she can't blame me for an act of God.

—But we stole the Rambler—

—Oh, yeah. Right.

—You're already grounded.

—For life. Right. Well then, Jude ponders, I don't need you losers at all. I'm already toast.

—Jude's got a point, though. The rest of us need a plan, Sebastian says. I'm OK. My mother won't notice. She wouldn't notice if I had that car repainted in neon pink.

—What about you then, Adie? Grady asks.

—My father will notice. He definitely will notice. And he will go ballistic. But—and we all hold our breathes as she thinks it through—but. Oh, crap, I'll just have to tell him what happened.

—Oh, no you don't! we all roar together.

—No, no, no. You do that, Jude the schemester chimes in, and your parents will be on to MC's parents who will be on to my mother, who will phone Grady's mother, who will then, for real and true, call Sebastian's mother. And we all be grounded for life.

—How much does it cost to get a car repainted? Mary Clay asks, and that question is so dumb, so hopeless that we start crushing slider boxes and throwing them at her.

—This is why we need a plan. Each one of us. And not a story we all tell. So, Adie, think of something else, Jude insists. You've got to. Otherwise, we all fall like dominos.

I know Jude is right. It's every kid for himself, getting out of this mess.

Adie looks like she's going to cry. I put my arm around her.

—It's OK, Adie. Your dad's car barely got hit. Plus, it's dark blue. Some of those pock marks will be hard to see. Just plead ignorance. Or, the two of us can pack up our bandanas, put our thumbs out. Hitchhike to the moon and back.

Adie smiles and hugs me back.

—Thanks, Breck. I'd hitch with you any day.

—Jude's got a point. So does Breck. All you have to do is plead ignorance, Adie. Blame it on your brother. Breck's the one in trouble. Of all of us.

—Yeah.

—This calls for reefer all around, Sebastian says, and the next thing we know he is rolling a joint the thickness of a thumb. Before long, we are stretched out across his living room floor, all touching somehow, legs entwined, heads on stomachs, hands finding hands, passing it around. Because we are in this together, this moment, this life, this spinning world. I take a deep drag and fight the urge to cough it right out. Hold it until

Breck

I feel it. I can't help smiling. Just this big stupid grin that takes over my face. I have this crazy thought. My dad will have to come through them to get to me, and they won't let that happen. They have my back. These guys are the only family I need. And, it's a feeling like church. Until—

Heavy boots bang up the wooden porch steps to Sebastian's front door. We all sit up. Very still. Mary Clay fans away the pot smoke. Then—

The screen door bangs open and a heavy voice cries out from somewhere out there

—We've got 'em! They're in there, Officer. Send in the dogs! Sick 'em, Rex!!

—The cops! Jude coughs out. Run!

As one, we all levitate to standing, frozen, dumb, panicked. We start falling over each other trying to bolt.

Jude pushes out of the knot of us and heads for the kitchen and the backdoor. The other five of us can't move, we're so terrified. But nothing else happens. A second passes, then more. Nothing happens. No cops. No dogs. Nothing.

—Pranked! Sebastian says, when it dawns on him. Tony!

Then we are all running, out the door, down the porch steps, out to the sidewalk. Tony is laughing so hard he gets a stitch in his side, which bends him over. There's no getting away from us now. In a minute we all are on him, tackling him in a giant flesh pile. Under us, he struggles to catch his breath. Somewhere in the middle, my arm entwined with Grady's, my legs with Mary Clay and somebody else's, I see my father's face. Set, clenching his teeth so hard his mustache twitches. Arms crossed over his chest. Heavy-set legs splayed. I am doomed. But right now, right now, I am laughing, laughing hard. My fate so sealed I might as well.

Grady

—You nearly broke my arm.

—I saved your life.

—Shots weren't anywhere near us.

—Yes, they were, Sebastian. Just behind us. Didn't you hear that woman scream?

We are sitting on the floor of his living room, encircled by dozens of 45s, talking about the James Brown concert the night before, where gunfire had broken out. And for reasons unclear, I threw my body on Sebastian's, forcing him to the auditorium floor. Why save him? And not myself? I barely know the guy. Why dive on top of him and not Adie, my date?

—Did she get hit, that woman, he asks, picking out a 45 and putting it on the spindle. "Lonely Teardrops" begins to play. Sebastian croons along with it, low, eyes closed, just this side of ecstasy looks like to me.

—How should I know? We didn't stick around to find out, you may recall. I dragged your sorry ass out of there—

—And squeezed Adie's pretty one. Sebastian interrupts his singing to get in this jab. He smiles. That smile could melt a drill sergeant's heart. Then he is singing again, lost in the words, the melody, crooning the refrain.

While Sebastian remains submerged in his Jackie Wilson trance, I sift through all these records. Sebastian must own hundreds. Some from singers I've never heard of before—like this cat Robert Johnson or Charley Patton or Muddy Waters—great name though. And on labels I've never heard of. Regal, Okeh, Victor Talking Machine. I mean, strange. I'm familiar with Columbia and Atlantic and even Motown.

—Who are these guys, Sebastian? I'm holding up a Willie McTell single. "Stomp Down Rider," and when I flip it, "Scary Day Blues" on the B side.

—Him? Blind Willie McTell? He's an old-timer. Black blues singer. Outta the Piedmont. Played blues, ragtime, hokum. He could play slide guitar to make you weep. Played twelve-string, too, like you do, Grady. That was rare in those days. Twenties, thirties. A Negro.

—Is most of your collection that kind of music? I ask, cautiously.

—Mostly. Truth is, Grady, I wish I'd been born a Negro. You should have seen the look on my mother's face when I dropped that one on her!

The memory pleases him. You can see it in his eyes. Reaching into his shirt pocket, he pulls out a pack of Camels and offers me one. I shake my head. He shrugs and lights up.

—"Over my dead cracker body," she said. He's laughing now. So am I. But I'm also shaking my head to myself. I can't imagine saying something like that to my mother. And my father? He'd have thrown me out on my ear.

Don't you disrespect your own good mother, my father would have said, seconds before the belt came out and his shoe print marked my backside as he kicked me out the door.

—Why would you say that, Sebastian? You don't mean it—

—Oh, but I do, man. I do mean it. They don't call rhythm and blues soul music for nothing. They got something here – and he taps

Grady

his chest—something in here that white singers just don't have. You go to church, right? Most Sundays?

—Not so much these days. But I sure did when I was a kid. Why? Why do you ask? Do you?

—Wouldn't be caught dead in a white church. Haven't you ever noticed? All they talk about is sin and damnation. All their hymns are these dirges. But Negro music, no matter if it's church or speakeasy, it's all over about joy. Hell, they make parties out of funerals, with all respect intended. They get up in church and sing along with the choir. They sway and clap their hands and sing out Hallelujahs. They're moved, Grady, moved by the spirit. Sing and sway and belt out thank you, Jesuses. White church is tightass puritanical. Negro? It's about celebration. Their funerals, man? They're happy affairs. Celebrations of life, Grady, not loss. As a white man, I just can't get there. It's not in me. White soul? What is that? It's nothing. Like white bread. So. Yeah. If I'd been born a Negro I would be born to that joy. It would come right out of my pores and put soul in my song.

—Wow.

What else was I supposed to say? Where was this boy I'd only just met this summer from, anyway? Not from any planet I am familiar with. I feel like I'm talking to a cross between a saint and the worst damned heretic in the world.

—Do you think she got hit, that woman?

He is back to the shots fired at the concert.

—If she did, it'll be in the paper this morning.

Sebastian shakes his head.

—Nah. He continues shaking his head. No, it won't. Negro crime never gets reported in the papers. Oh, it makes the police blotter all right, but not the white written, published and owned newspaper of record. No indeed, not.

—Huh. Again, I cannot think what to say to this new friend of mine, this boy who is barely sixteen and is talking like some kind of alien.

—Here. Listen to this.

He rustles around in all the records that surround us on the floor—the idea had been, when I got here this morning, to go through them all and make an inventory. He finds what he is looking for. Taking it gingerly out of its sleeve as if it were gold or maybe gossamer, he takes the arm off the McTell and puts this new record on the spindle.

—This is Robert Johnson. They say he sold his soul to the devil. Devil, he said, make me a great blues player, and I'm all yours. He only played for about three years before he died. Died young. Cursed, some said. He's one of the greats, Grady. If you like Dylan or Keith Richards, you're listening to the legacy of Robert Johnson, who died thirty years ago. One of the greatest blues guitarists of all time. You should listen to him, learn his tricks. He plays like a magician.

Sebastian lets the record drop, and I instantly understand what he means. It is scratchy and the sound distant, like it was recorded through gauze, but the guitar playing is incredible. I feel it in my bones and begin faux fingering the guitar I am not holding, just to see if I can keep up with this Black guy I've never heard of.

All morning long, my education in Negro music, from Delta to Piedmont blues, up to our own times and the Motown Sound, continues. Sebastian talks non-stop, except when he falls to singing a few bars, letting the music carry him somewhere other, miles out of his living room, maybe to the moon, his hazel eyes half closed, his head twisting on his neck as if he's listening to some celestial accompaniment. I am blown away, watching this guy. I get this outta sight idea: I'll teach him to play.

He doesn't play a single instrument. I learn this at the Open Dialogue coffeehouse where we met earlier this summer. Right after

Grady

school was out. It was a kind of open mic night advertised on telephone poles all over town and pinned up on the bulletin boards of our separate schools. Me to riff on my twelve-string acoustic, Sebastian to test the waters. All he had was a tambourine. When I heard him sing, this smooth but powerful tenor coming from that slight boy's body, I knew I had to know him. So, I just went out there on stage with my guitar, like he was the north pole to my south. We were good together. We hit it off too. I thought I'd found a Simon to my Garfunkel, though at the time, before I knew any better, I'd have reversed those two names.

Anyway, that's how I got invited "inside," as I like to think of it now. Because breaking into their pack is like a kind of induction, with hazing and all. Their group is almost a cult, with a distinct inner sanctum, namely Sebastian's living room. There are seven of us, counting Sebastian, but really there are six satellites, counting me now. Almost from the start, I got that I needed to somehow prove myself to them, earn their trust, earn their acceptance. Only I had no idea where to start. Except with my guitar, that being my connection to Sebastian.

It didn't take me long to figure out that the girl named Mary Clay but mostly called MC, with her roving eye and bowl haircut, is close to Sebastian like best friends. That Tony, the spindly Catholic kid with the huge laugh and outrageous sense of humor is close to Sebastian like allies. That Jude—oh, I got off on the wrong foot with her when I called her Judy by mistake and she all but cut my throat with a verbal straight razor—that she is close to Sebastian like twins, not always seeing eye-to-eye but connected in some unseeable way. That the boy Breck, who looks just like Buddy Holly, is close to Sebastian like rivals, they being the two boys they all lust after. That Adie is close to Sebastian like foils, the banter never stopping. They all make me feel definitely on my guard, so I try to maneuver times like this morning, when it's just

Sebastian and me talking or making music. Or I use Adie as my shield. She is this stalky branch of a girl with bedroom eyes who sees more than she says and is somehow on the outside too. Like me. Even though she's been hanging with them since she was thirteen or something like that. I don't quite get it but she tells me all the time that the others don't really like her much. Though you'd never know it from the way they goof off together and hang out *all* the time. I figure, it's just what she's telling me, so I'll pay extra attention to her. Which is easy. Because she is hot. I want to be with her all the time, though I try to ration myself. If I come on too strong, she'll bolt. Like an unbroken filly with a saddle heading her way. But, boy, do my lips hurt after an evening with her in the back of Sebastian's mother's car.

—You know, I say to Sebastian after the ancient Johnson recording stops, I could teach you how to play. Any instrument you want. Name it. I know you'd pick it up in no time. Harmonica? Guitar? Keyboard?

—Really?

—Really.

That afternoon we have our first guitar session on an old six-string Martin acoustic of mine. It was my first guitar. Got it at a pawn shop when I was eleven for forty hard earned, paper-route dollars. By the end of the first lesson, he's got the basic idea for C Major, D Major, E Major and G Major. The next time we meet, four days later, he's worked out a rough but passable "Love Me Do," and, well, the only word that comes to mind, is he's glowing. That big grin that pushes his eyes into his forehead. Like he's having the time of his life. He *is* having the time of his life.

—Making music! Grady. I'm *making* music.

—You do that all the time with your voice, Sebastian.

—But this—and he holds the guitar up like a trophy—is an instrument!

Grady

    This is around the Fourth of July. By the end of the month he is mastering fingerpicking, his long facile fingers on his left hand finding the frets with his eyes closed. I teach him the basics of the harmonica, and he picks that up right up away, too. He gets his mother to buy him a rack to hold it around his neck, so he can free up his hands for the guitar. He works on Peter, Paul and Mary tunes until he masters them. And I mean masters them. Eyes closed, I'm not sure I could tell the difference between the guitar work of this prodigy of mine and Paul Stookey.

    What slowly dawns on me is that he picks up an instrument, gets to playing it passably, so quickly I know, I mean I *know*, he's got this innate genius for it, then he puts it aside. He just drops it. It's crazy. I am like this volcano of musical ambition. I practice every free second. I'm working out chord progressions in my head all the time. Doing my best to really master the twelve-bar blues progression, because, just as he knew I would be, I am inspired by the old-timers he's introduced me to. Music is my life. And I can't understand why it isn't his. It just kills me. When I try to talk to him about it, encourage him, try to make him understand that I, I would kill to be as talented as he is, that he should take his music seriously, he just sloughs me off. Like a gnat. Some bug in his face.

    —Not my scene, is all he says about it.

    I hear this and I want to pick him up and throw him off the L&N Bridge. Not his scene? Give me a break.

    Adie tells me all about Sebastian's famous rock star brother. A drummer in the band Roswell, named for the place aliens come from in New Mexico. They've played on Ed Sullivan. The Hollywood Bowl, too, and with Jefferson Airplane and the Grateful Dead. They are huge. I know who his brother is. Yes, I do. He's always got a fifth of Wild Turkey on stage with him. He's famous for taking swigs with one hand

and working his snares with the other in the middle of a concert. Adie says that Breck told her that Sebastian went out to Colorado to visit him last summer and came home a week early. Sebastian's no stranger to weed but he told Breck all the heroin, coke and meth freaked him out. Guns, too. Adie says this wild man brother of his has a death wish and is always waving some gun around.

—So, what's this got to do with Sebastian not doing music? I want to know.

—Fame hasn't done much to elevate his brother's moral compass, Adie says. But he idolizes him all the same. That's the Sebastian dichotomy.

I have to think about this. Really hard. I take that information and roll it into a joint and smoke it. Let it seep deep into my lungs, my blood, until it reaches my brain and makes me dizzy.

Our inventory of his record collection is a joke. We start off trying to alphabetize them but right off the bat we can't decide to do it by artist or song title. And what about the B sides? What are they, chopped liver? We are laughing now, hard enough to start winging singles at each other. Basically, give up, we give up. The best filing system we can come up with is to make piles on the floor by vague categories devised by Sebastian: soul, gospel, blues, rhythm and blues, Motown, folk, and finally a category he dubs *everything else*. This category still leaves dozens of homeless 45s strew all over the living room floor. A few neat stacks, and a sea of undeclared discs. We fill a couple of peach boxes with the ones he's labeled, and because the sleeves stick out of the top, it's easy to rifle through them to find one you want. That is, if the one you want belongs in one of his very subjective groupings. Because, as he says and I agree, all this music is interconnected. Any style or elements of many styles of music influencing upstart newbies, like folk rock and punk, even

Grady

good old-fashioned rock and roll. If Keith Richards learned something from Robert Johnson, well, hell—anyway, it's a joke, a real rip-snorter, our trying to make sense of Mr. Eclectic's record collection.

So we decide to walk up to Karma Records and buy some more. It's a funky place we both love because of the listening booths and the concert posters that cover the walls and the autographed LP sleeves on the ceiling, so no one can steal them. But most of all because Karma has the largest collection of records for sale in the state. It's like a used bookstore. Both smell like decaying paper, in the case of Karma, all those ancient record sleeves, so you know you're in the presence of very vulnerable history. Blink and it may be gone. Like music never recorded. Like art painted with disappearing ink.

Sebastian flags me over. He's pulled an album, an LP, called *An Evening with Andres Segovia*.

—Ever heard of this dude? When I shake my head, he says, I thought not. I'm buying it for you, Grady. You, you of all people, need to hear this.

—Wait. What? Why?

But he is gone. Zippity-do-dah and he's at the cashier buying this record for me. Then, the door to Karma opens and in pours the pack. Breck and Tony, Mary Clay, Adie and Jude. All of them. They scuffle and sidestep inside the shop.

—Told'ja, Jude says. I said you'd be at Karma, Sebastian.

—Oh, hi, Grady, Mary Clay says, like the afterthought I am. Adie slips over and puts her hand down my back pocket and squeezes. I immediately start to go hard and have to silently talk my dick back into submission.

—What'd you buy? Jude wants to know. She snatches the album off the cashier's counter and rolls her eyes.

—Segovia? Really?

—For Grady. Who's never heard of him.

—Just the greatest guitarist ever. She looks at me with what, contempt? Hatred? What's she got against me, anyway? But I know. I do know. I take her envy—an entire morning alone with Sebastian, talking music, buying *me* music — roll it up like a locker room towel and snap it back at her.

Casually, as casually as I can make myself, I take the album away from her. I look at the plump, balding man on the album cover and wonder exactly what's in store for me. In the meantime, I look Jude in the eye. Then I drape an arm around Sebastian.

—Far out, Sebastian. Thanks.

Adie

We are sitting on the porch in the early afternoon, waiting for the Saint to arrive, Sebastian's brother Carl, the drummer with Roswell, his band almost as famous as Led Zeppelin or The Dead. Sebastian is so crazy with excitement to show off his big brother that he can't sit still. Keeps bouncing up and pacing. And it's contagious. Tony and MC are on the porch swing, making that thing fly back and forth. Grady sits on the porch railing, kicking his feet against its shingles and slapping his knees to some foreign wacky rhythm of his own making. Jude sits on the top step, her eyes fixed down the street, wanting to be the first to spot him driving up on his Harley. Breck paces in and out of Sebastian, like the two of them are doing some weird mating dance. I just watch. I watch them all. Already jaded. Being contrary I guess. They're prepared to fawn all over the guy. They're already fawning, and he's not even here yet. But I just watch.

When he and Irene finally varoom up to the curb on his mammoth Harley, the first thing I notice, after the engine noise dies away with a final rev, is the outfit. Brown leather biker's jacket, black leather pants spray painted on, big honkin' boots with fake spurs on the heels. One arm is draped like ownership around Irene's shoulders, the other one wrapped around the neck of a bottle of Wild Turkey. A perfect parody of himself, I think ruefully. He strides on up to us as if we were the Red Sea and he's about to part us. Sebastian rushes up, grinning like he just won the lottery, and moves as if he's going to hug him. Instead, Carl swings Irene into Sebastian's unexpecting arms.

—Whoa!

—Sebastian, Irene. Irene, this is my baby brother.

Irene lingers in the hug because she's a hugger but Sebastian reels away, his eyes both confused and wary.

—Hi, Little Brother, Irene says, and sidesteps to free Sebastian from the awkward embrace. She smiles at Sebastian. A coy little girl smile. Like she knows something he doesn't. But it's Carl who breaks the spell.

—How ya doing, Sebastian? Still playing with yourself in the dark? Carl says. Then he punches Sebastian so hard on the arm it sends him reeling into Tony, who has just gotten up off the porch swing. Tony's eyes cool. The grin on Sebastian's face is now fixed, phony, shocked, hurt. All those things. It's like a tsunami of feelings rippling across his face, while the rest of us—except Tony and me, our eyes meeting—are all tumbling after The Drummer into Sebastian's living room.

—Hullo, Mother. This is Irene.

He pushes past her as if she were an offense. Mrs. T takes a step back, the widest smile I'd ever seen on her face falls to the floor the minute he speaks. We hear the water running in the kitchen sink and then he comes back in with two glasses full of ice balanced on the palm of one hand and the whiskey bottle in the other. He pours out two tumbler loads of the stuff while we all reverently watch, one for Irene, the other for himself. He downs it in a second, then swigs from the bottle.

—Help yourself, Mommy. Oh—and he winks at the glass she already has in hand—I see you have your own stash. In your bedside

Adie

bar, as usual? Mrs. T pulls herself up straight, looks him dead in the eye, and lifts her half-filled glass to her lips.

—The acorn doesn't fall far from the tree, she says.

—Clever, Mommy. Did you think that line up all by yourself?

Mrs. T refills her glass from the bottle of Wild Turkey he wields like a matador's estoque, which causes him to turn icy eyes on her. But he doesn't stop her. Instead he shifts his attention to his audience. Us. He takes a long swig from the bottle by way of a prelude, then starts sparring with his mother. As if it's payback for her taking his juice. That's when I notice she is three sheets to the wind too. They're arguing and swearing at each other is like some kind of sporting event. Like verbal World Wrestling—both fake and scary. Sebastian told me she could be like this but it is crazy seeing her spitting venom at a man a foot and a half taller than she is. Even crazier watching him. Maybe it's me. Just a big baby. Brought up to "respect my elders" and all. And here he is this rock star behaving like a stereotype of himself. Holy crap.

But almost as quickly, Carl fixes on the lineup of us schmucks, piled onto the couch gawking at him like starving sparrows. So he starts regaling us with his band's exploits. They've just finished a concert tour called ET, after their latest album, he says. Now he's dissing on the fans like they were bobbleheaded dopes.

—Some of the girls stripped off their shirts, everybody was stoned! They were climbing all over the stage. I could have slept with any of them. But I could only manage so many before we hit the road.

I try to picture this. I try to picture Sebastian's brother, Mrs. T's son bedding the bobble-heads. I sneak a glance at Irene. I can't help myself. Does she dig Carl saying this stuff? But she, just like his mother, bathes him with adoring eyes. What's going on in her head is too obtuse for me to figure out.

Carl's laughing, a huge raucous laugh now that comes in hiccups like a Gatling gun, like he is describing a magic show in little flaming bursts—full of feints of hand and mind—waving the bottle in the air like a conductor's baton.

—The babes. Not even hard candies. Soft. Melt in your mouth.

I groan. To myself, of course.

On and on he goes. I can't take my eyes off him. So supercharged with testosterone is he that I suddenly understand. Why the "babes" he's talking about threw off their clothes. Why Irene, tiny, fragile, beautiful Irene, can't take her eyes off him. She's the one. She's the one he's chosen. For her, that must be enough.

I watch him, yes. But mostly I watch the others. Awe like a virus. Mary Clay is bug-eyed and slack-jawed, the very picture of starstruck groupie. His lips suddenly glistening, I can tell Breck is working up a good drool. *Please don't humiliate yourself, Breck* I want to shout at him. Irene sits on the edge of the couch, her knees clamped shut, rolling the ice cubes in her glass with one hand and twisting her hair around a finger with the other. Grady, oh man, Grady is like the guy in the desert who sees the ground shimmering and thinks it's an oasis. He so wants to be a rock star himself. While everyone else is piled on the couch, Jude has claimed the dead father's chair. One daddy long leg is twined around the other. She is lying back, blowing smoke rings to the ceiling, her eyes averted. As if she doesn't care. As if she isn't listening to him. But I know that look, that pretend indifference of hers. I can tell his pull is powerful in her direction. She is hot for him. Tony, though, Tony is genuinely aloof. Sitting on the steps up to the landing, away from all the rest of us. He is watching too because he's looking at the devil in leather, and for him the devil is cause, not for veneration, but deep respectful fear.

At just this moment, Carl sees Sebastian's record player. More

Adie

accurately, he lands on it like a cat pouncing on a mouse and begins shuffling the LPs and 45s strewn around the floor with his toe.

—Ooo, what have we here little brother? Nothing by Roswell? Not one of our albums? Just this baby stuff?

—I ... I have some of your albums, Carl. Look here.

Sebastian heads for a bookcase filled with LPs. But Carl has turned away. He is not interested. Instead, he makes for the radio by their dead father's chair and spins the dial until he finds a rock station. Then he sweeps Irene, tumbler in hand, long blond hair flying out behind her, into his arms for a crazy kind of dance. It's like they're copulating with their clothes on. I see Mrs.T look away. I watch MC stare from the couch likes she's watching a peep show and catch Breck and Grady with their mouths hanging open. Jude, Jude her eyes are fixed on the show as she rifles through her pocketbook. For what? A dog-eared notebook. What? She's angling for an autograph? All this is happening. I see it all. I feel like a shotgun of disgust has just peppered my body.

The song ends and he spins Irene away, who reels into the couch, landing next to a gape-mouthed MC. The next song, amazingly, is a Roswell platinum number called "Where the Sun Don't Shine." Then, Carl's on her. On Mary Clay. He swoops down, brings her to her feet and pulls her into him. I see Mary Clay swoon. That's exactly what it is, a swoon. Like in the old movies when the girl faints with longing. In seconds he is grinding away at her. She is both a little shocked and a lot thrilled, letting him grasp her butt cheeks like handles, turning her mouth up to his. I know what she's thinking—*I'm dancing with the drummer from Roswell*. But Sebastian flinches. I see this too. It's one thing for him to dance with Irene that way, his eyes seem to say, quite another to grope Mary Clay in front of us, his mother. Sebastian does the only thing he can do to stop it. He cuts in.

—My turn.

But he lacks resolve and Carl plays it.

—Your turn? Your turn, little brother? She doesn't want to dance with a wimp like you—

But MC surprises him, surprises us all, so visibly lost in the trance of his magnetism has she been. She pushes Mr. Roswell away.

—Oh, yes, I do. I'll never say no to a dance with Sebastian.

She's smiling now, triumphant.

—Thanks for the dance. She spins away from him and into Sebastian's chest. He gropes clumsily for her, not expecting it, as if someone has just tossed him a greased balloon. Then he's smiling too. I see Mrs. T. relax a little. Meanwhile, Breck and Grady are starting to act like the biggest suck-ups in the world, especially Grady. They're all over Carl, trying to talk music, while Jude is angling for her and Sebastian to play with his band. Tony sits it all out, sizing up Carl, like Joe Friday, squinting through the smoke from his cigarette, sizing up a perp.

I would have seen more if Grady hadn't pulled me out into the middle of the room to dance too, to throw covert fencing around Sebastian and MC. I didn't think Grady was all that astute, all that tuned in. But he is defending his friend. I can see that too, and this makes me bold.

When the radio DJ goes to an ad, I whisper to Grady that I'm going home. Meeting Carl is a gigantic letdown. I expected—What? What did I expect? Who knows what it would be like meeting John Lennon? Or Elvis Presley? Or even David Ruffin, off stage? Maybe just as much of a comeuppance. Maybe fame, this kind of fame anyway, makes you into a dick. Maybe it's not Carl's fault that he is a dick with a capital D.

—You can't leave now, Grady whispers back. He just got here! We may never get this chance again, Adie—

Adie

I know where he's going. Grady may choose to sacrifice himself on the altar of Roswell ululation. But not me. Not I.

I am sick, too, for Sebastian, caught in a tug-'o'-war between blind loyalty and a huge reality check. This scene, this whole scene, is whopperjawed, backwards, insane. And Sebastian's brother. He's a drummer with one of the biggest bands playing. He's a real rock star. It isn't supposed to go like this. Being ugly to his mother and mean to his brother. Dry fucking Irene and, for heaven's sake, MC in his mother's living room, with us all watching. Sixteen-year-old MC. He's supposed to be a hero. He's supposed to be a god. I don't know how Sebastian stands it. But I know I feel betrayed. We're supposed to be sitting around listening to his stories, what it's like to top the charts all the time, to play with all the greatest bands of our time, to have met Lennon and Marley and Jerry Garcia. We all were half psyched out of our minds to meet him, hear all about his famous life, slip, if only for an afternoon, into that sacred inner sanctum of platinum records and recording studios. Our backstage pass into a world of our deepest imaginings. Especially Grady and Jude who want Carl to *notice* them, take them seriously as musicians. Maybe even extend an invitation. Maybe even free Roswell tickets. Sebastian too.

I am halfway down the porch steps when I hear the screen door bang shut behind me.

—Wait up, Adie.

It's Sebastian. Why is he coming after me?

—Don't go. Not yet. Somebody sane has to keep me company. Come on. Sit.

I smile. We both sit down on the cement step, shoulder to shoulder. Unless, you know, you *have* to go?

He's fishing. Why else, he figures, would I just walk out? He's also giving me the perfect excuse to bail: my mystery man. But, no. I won't lie to Sebastian.

—Nah. This—and I point with my shoulder to the screen door—I don't know, isn't for me. I think I should say something about what a cool brother he has, but I can't. He reads my mind, not for the first time.

—He's OK, one on one. But he puts on his Dr. Hyde act when he has an audience. He likes to shock, I guess.

I know what I saw and I know what I cannot say in response. So I don't. I just know how I feel, sick to my stomach. Then I think, am I a square or something? Am I so uncool that *this* melee really is a party, and I'm missing the point? Probably. Or I'm a lousy voyeur. That too. Oh, well. Cool has never been my strongest suit.

—I wouldn't want to be Irene, I finally say.

—She's wonderful, she really is.

—I believe that, OK. But how does she stand him?

I shouldn't have blurted this out. But I did because we, the pack, make such a big deal of being honest all the time. Plus, I'm not saying half of what I want to say. I want to pillory his brother with my prissy indignation. I want to castrate him with the shears of my moral outrage.

Sebastian looks away. He pulls at his eyebrow, that tic of his, when he's flustered or doesn't know what to say.

I take a look at my watch, get up and take a step down to the front walkway.

—Adie! Come on. Stay.

—No. Thanks. Enjoy the party. I gotta go.

—Besides—

—Heh, wait! Besides, what?

I turn to look at him. I have to be somewhere, I could say. But of course I cannot tell him that. He is leaning back on the step with his

Adie

elbows resting on the porch floor, his legs splayed. His hair is tousled and he's wearing his Cheshire Cat face. I can see something is coming.

—Heh. It was cool what you did yesterday. The walkout your organized, getting all the lifeguards at the pool to walk off the job. What did that guy in the woods call it?

—Civil disobedience. Thanks.

I half-smile. Protests, walk-outs, sit-ins, demonstrations, against the war or Nixon or for better wages, work conditions or women's rights, or Black rights or anybody's rights—it's the in thing. He's trying to reel me back with a compliment.

Sebastian stands and turns to go back inside. Someone turns up the volume inside. Now it's Procol Harum. Just as he's about to go back inside, he calls out over his shoulder.

—See you tomorrow? Afternoon? Sebastian cocks his head toward the party inside. He'll be gone by then.

I nod and wave. Besides. The screen bangs shut behind him. The strains of "Whiter Shade of Pale" shadow me past the parked Harley, down the street, to nearly the corner where I have to turn to go home. Once around the corner, I can no longer make out the chords but the words reverberate in my head ... cartwheels ... seasick ... the crowd, the pack wanting more more more of Carl.

On the walk home, I feel like I'm breaking apart, breaking away from them, my best friends. I have this other life now. But it's more than that. So much more. We don't seem to be on the same wavelength anymore. There's this kind of wall. As if they're on one side of the glass and I'm on the other, looking in. I watch them fawn over Carl and am disgusted. My world is roiling under my feet.

Ambient Light

The next afternoon the motorcycle is gone when I get there. I walk into that living room and something has changed, only nothing has. Everything is in exactly the same place as it always is, but it's like the walls have been painted with a thin coat of invisible vibrating material. They seem to shiver like walls can during an earthquake. Sebastian is going through his records, gathering the first set he's going to play for us. Jude is sitting on the bottom step of the staircase, hunched over her guitar, tuning it, her long brown hair obliterating her face, her long fingers, like spindly tentacles, keep caressing the strings, playing at tuning some more. Tony is thumbing through the phonebook, no doubt looking for the next victim of the Prankensteins. Mary Clay, Breck, and Grady are playing poker on the coffee table using Cheetos as chips. I sit down next to them. Everything is the same, but I feel one step away from them all. Because I did not fawn, because I did not stay?

—Deal me in, I say, very much wanting to feel reinstated.

Very seriously Breck counts out twenty Cheetos from the bag and passes them over to me, while stuffing another few in his mouth. All of them, me too now, have orange flecks on our lips to go with the orange on our fingers that finds its way onto the cards. Evidence. If we all died right this second, the coroner would find the cards tainted orange, nod his head and solemnly pronounce: Mass suicide. Death by Cheetos overdose.

I begin to relax a little, smiling between bites. That way, we'd always be together, me included.

Grady throws his cards down, stands up, and stretches, revealing the fine black hair above his belt and below his belly button.

—I can't eat another one of those orange death bombs. Heh, I've got an idea. Now that Adie's here, let's up the ante and play strip poker. How about it?

Adie

—Get a room, Sebastian calls from over by the record player. The stack of 45s drops the first record on the turntable. Junior Walker & the All Stars begins to play "Shotgun." Sebastian springs up, all the way up on to tiptoes, air guitar in hand and he becomes the song, turning his right arm into a shotgun in time to the lyrics.

He belts out the refrain, as he sprays the air with his rapid arm rifle.

We're all up dancing to his karaoke number, shooting each other to the music, and falling dead on the floor. Everyone except Jude and of course Sebastian. I'm feeling better already. Back in sync.

—Shoot 'em! We shout, firing our own pretend rifles at each other.

When the song ends and we are, four of us, piled on the floor, not Jude—too immature, not Tony—too much trouble—but the rest of us, we let the 45s just keep dropping, while we listen, sing along, move in place rather than get up and dance. When the last record finishes, Sebastian leads the way into the kitchen. We raid the fridge, then the pantry. Breck and Sebastian cradle armloads of Cokes and Grape Nehi's out to the coffee table. Jude, MC, and I make light work of Mrs. T's stash of snacks, dumping a half dozen bags next to the drinks.

We dig in. Sebastian and I are on the couch, his arm draped over my shoulder, my hand boldly on his thigh. He doesn't flinch, so I think I'm good. But then he does. Gets up and ejects Tony from his dead father's chair and takes the throne. Everybody is gabbing on about school and rules until Jude stands on the landing so she can make an announcement over the din.

—I want to come live with one of you. Either that or I'm going to run away. Or kill my mother.

—Or both, MC and I chime in together.

—I'm not joking. And it's clear she's not. She looks like somebody facing the gallows.

The room went from summer to winter, from hot and sweaty and carefree to Nordic. All eyes on Jude. Who looks uncharacteristically humble, maybe even beaten.

—I'm serious, you guys. I'm either going to hit the road, Kerouac-style, or hang myself. If I can't get out of that dump.

—You wouldn't want to live in my house. Although it was Grady who said it, it was a six-way mantra that opened up another Frank Session.

—Would you want to live with a drunk who leaves work, passes out in a public park and you get the call to come and get her. Even before you can drive? So you have to get a taxi you know you can't pay for, and can only hope there's enough money to cover it in her pocketbook, if it hasn't already been snatched. And the cabbie has to help you haul your mother into the backseat?

Sebastian points a finger to the ceiling.

—You want to live with that, Jude?

—Mine offers a life of Saturday fish sticks, Sunday mass and no friends over. You're welcome to my life, Jude, Tony offers crossing himself.

—Oh, well, you don't want to live my life. Not after the egg fight. Since, technically, I'm grounded for the rest of my life. My father has sworn never to let me drive again, Breck says.

—Then how are you here? If you're grounded for life? I ask.

—God, Adie. You're such a literalist, Jude moans, ripping at her cuticles with her teeth.

—Work detail. Tony called my dad, throwing his voice and pretending to be your father, Adie.

—Sorry, Breck offers sheepishly, seeing the horror on my face.

—My father? You pretended to be my father?

—Yeah, OK, yes. Anyway, Tony, pretending to be your dad, convinced my dad that he needed some yard work help—

Adie

—My father? Why my father?

—You sound like a stuck record, Adie. Because you live a block away from here, that's why.

We are all so dumbfounded by this deception we knew nothing about that a Cheeto-throwing war breaks out in celebration. It's a wonderful war when you get to eat the ammo.

—You knew, Sebastian? I ask, hearing the tinge of anger flicker in my voice.

Sebastian shrugs, his expression glowing with mischief. He cannot hold back a crooked smile.

—Well, not at first. I knew when he showed up here like a thief on the lam.

—How could you not tell us, Sebastian? Jude asks. There's an edge to her voice, of disappointment. I know that feeling of being left out. Mary Clay and Jude routinely do it to me.

—Couldn't risk you guys ratting us out accidentally. 'Specially Adie.

—You can move in with me, Jude. We have an extra room, Grady says, more or less changing the subject. Only thing is, being a girl, you'd have a curfew like my sisters.

—No thanks.

—There's always the YWCA, I suggest.

Then all eyes swing to me.

—What about you, Adie.

—What about me?

Sebastian gets up, empties a bag of chips on the table, and places it on my head.

—We now crown you Child of The Best Parents. A dubious distinction because now we are all moving into your house.

I don't know how to take this. Are they mocking me? But when they have me dancing in a shower of Coke shaken out of bottles, I accept the honor. Because maybe that's just what it is. I know for sure, I would not trade my hardly perfect parents for any of their trainwreck birthers.

—This is a sticky situation, I laugh, dripping Coke.

But before I can even head for the bathroom to clean up, everyone is pushing and shoving me out onto the porch, a crazy conga line because Coke was dripping from my hair, dripping from my clothes, running down my arms in rivulets of brown sugar, and then onto their hands, their clothes, we have to get outside quick, like right away, to staunch the damage to Sebastian's living room. He double-steps down the porch steps, unravels a garden hose and fires. Pretty soon we are all soaked and dancing under the shower in his front yard. Right about then, the poor halfwit mailman comes by, doesn't duck in time, and gets sprayed.

—Uh, I'll just leave ... your ... mail ... out here.

Sebastian, relentless in his mischief, shoots a water jet at his departing back.

—Heh! Cut that out!

As he turns to shout, Sebastian, whether on purpose or not, I'll never know, gets the mailman right in the mouth. He scrambles up the street spitting and cursing, and we collapse into a muddy, wet pile, laughing so hard we can't catch our breaths, until we each sit up, completely soaked. Like three-year-olds playing in a mud puddle.

—Now what? Grady asks.

—Ugh. I need to go home and take a shower, Jude says.

—Didn't you just have one? I tease.

—Haha. If you could see your hair, Adie, you wouldn't be making jokes.

I touch my hair. It lies in stiff, sticky clumps on my shoulders.

—Your clothes are kind of a wreck too.

Sebastian is up like a flash.

—I got an idea.

Back he comes with his transistor radio under one arm. Placing it on the porch railing, turning it on, and up, we hear the WBLK DJ smooth talking his next spin. Then he loops the garden hose up and through a disused planter hook on the porch ceiling. Sebastian is very very busy cooking something up, all right. He pops up and down the steps, makes sure the radio is far enough away not to get wet. Like a mad scientist, he twists the dials till he's got them just right. I can just make out the strains of "Mustang Sally," until he turns the volume up loud. Then he bounces down the stairs and twists the nozzle on the hose to spray. He offers me his hand and pulls me to my feet.

—Come on, Adie. Let's dance in the rain. I'll be Gene Kelly and you can be Debbie Reynolds.

—To Wilson Pickett? I try to complain. But we're already dancing up and down the stairs. He's very agile, being a basketball player, and I'm a gymnast, so we make a pretty decent Gene and Debbie. At the bottom he twirls me around. We dance back up and he holds me under the makeshift shower. I toss my head back and let the water rinse the Coke out of my hair. Then we're both trying to get Sally to reign in that horse. Down in the yard, the rest of the pack is air-drying and applauding. Sebastian and I, drenched now, collapse on the bottom step, the hose still pumping a river of water under and around us. Happy doesn't begin to cover how I feel, being goofy with him.

When the radio switches to the news, everyone begins thinking again about heading home. Grady, Breck and Tony are chattering away about some baseball game, Jude has popped back inside to get her guitar, Mary Clay and I are talking about playing tennis on Saturday, our last full day of summer vacation. We are all heading out for home when we hear Sebastian say

—Hold on a minute! Hold on. Did you hear that? Did you hear what the announcer just said? Listen up, you all. This is important.

But we've all missed it. All we can do is exchange what-the-fuck looks.

Sebastian stares at us as if he's been hit with a stun gun, legs splayed, wet hair plastered against his head, arms dangling at his side, his mouth open, ready to catch flies. He stands in place and makes three complete turns as if he doesn't know which direction to take.

—Holy Moly. Oh my God. Did you hear that?

And he's looking at us like we are a bunch of class-act losers because of our blank stares.

—What? Jude insists.

—Earth to zombie, earth to zombie. Comeback to earth, zombie man, Tony says.

—This is big. This is so big. Come on, your numbnuts. Saturday night. This Saturday night. Martin Luther King is going to be leading a civil rights march downtown. Oh, man, I have got to be there!

I don't know when, if ever, I've seen Sebastian like this, stopped in his tracks by news he heard on the radio. At least not since Kennedy was shot.

—Do you guys have any idea? Do you even know what this means? Sebastian is dancing in his high-top Keds, doing a little soft shoe in the mud puddle that his yard has become.

We don't know what it means. We don't have any idea. Except that the Black leader of the Civil Rights Movement is going to be marching in our town. It's not like he is anything other than a kind of Huntley or Brinkley, a guy we see on the evening news all the time. Yes, yes, of course,

Adie

we know he's a big whoop-de-do. But he apparently means a whole shitload more to Sebastian, so we just haul ourselves up to attention, and wait for him to tell us.

—So? Grady demands.

—It means, Mr. Toejam. We can go down there. We can see the man. Maybe even shake his hand.

—Martin Luther King ain't shakin' no honkey hand.

—He will too, Tony. He will too. Because we're all in this together.

—In what? I ask, feeling incredibly stupid for having to ask.

—The struggle for acceptance, Adie.

In one leap, he jumps up on the third porch step and whirls around, arms spread upward, facing us.

—Whose coming with me?

We still have our dumb looks on, all the rest of us.

—Don't you get it, King's fighting for all of us, too. All us strangers in a strange land. We just want a way to be included too, right?

—Who you calling strange? Tony says in his Cagney voice.

—This is serious, Tony. Who wants to come? Come on, you guys!

In the end, only Grady and I go with him. We're the only ones whose parents think it's a good thing to participate in the democratic process, as my mother puts it. She's big on world politics and equality for all—except when it comes to her children or she wouldn't give me the same allowance she gave my brother, who is a decade older than me. Needless to say, I lost the argument about inflation striking children too. The others? They hem and haw, but each finds a reason not to come.

Sebastian drives his mother's old junker downtown, early enough to park right on the parade route. The sun hasn't gone down yet. Grady makes a run to the KFC down the block and comes back with a bucket of chicken. We sit crossed-legged on the Biscayne's hood, me and Sebastian leaning against the windshield, Grady beside us handing out drumsticks and wings. Sebastian is on some other plane of being. Sucking on bones, eyes on the sunset.

—Penny? I ask.

Sebastian hauls himself in from wherever he's been. Looks at me, blinks, like he's trying to remember who I am. Which doesn't make me feel so great.

—Oh, I was just thinking. If I were a Black dude, I could be right down there with him. With Mr. King. Working for equality. Holding the Declaration of Independence to its word—all men are created equal.

I want to snipe: well, what about women, Sebastian? What about us? But instead, I just feel out of it. I don't know about Grady but, boy, do I feel like an interloper. Wearing my ignorance like too much lipstick. I don't know a thing about Dr. King, except the speech he gave in Washington, but I hardly paid any attention to it because who likes speeches and besides, I was waiting to hear Bob Dylan and Joan Baez, and to see Peter, Paul and Mary. Up until this night, I never even knew he was a hero of Sebastian's, since Dr. King doesn't sing or make music. His love of this Black man stumps me. Yeah, I know he wishes he'd been born Black. But why Dr. King so much? Sometimes I just don't get him at all. Sometimes I think Sebastian has more secrets than 45s. Every time I think I know him, he springs something like this on me.

About an hour after the streetlights come on and almost as long since the parade was supposed to start, we begin to hear a crowd shouting far off in the distance. Not long after, the shouting has moved right in front of us. The sidewalks are crowded with people, a lot of them hecklers. There are people hanging out of hotel and apartment building windows, watching, taking picture. Black kids have shinnied up lampposts and are standing on mailboxes just to get a glimpse.

Adie

A group of Black men, maybe twenty strong, all dressed in suits, ties, and hats, despite the humid September evening, are moving down the street, a man at either end holding a banner that reads WE ALL BLEED THE SAME COLOR, One Nation One People. The marchers are chanting "We Shall Overcome" as they pass the hecklers. There, in the middle of them is Dr. Martin Luther King, holding himself just as if he were one, a king. He is regal and serene.

—Go back to Africa! We hear someone shout.

Some whites follow the marchers, jeering and cursing, some throwing stones and beer cans. There's the pop-pop-pop of firecrackers dropped from a fire escape that cause us and lots of other people to duck, thinking gunfire.

But the block of Black men and white civil rights demonstrators walk tall, maintaining their dignity despite the taunts and the shouting. I am struck by the force of their confidence striding on either side and behind Dr. King.

—There's John Lewis, Sebastian whispers to us, his voice raw with awe. Next to King. And Hosea Williams.

Sebastian now is standing on top of the car belting out "We Shall Overcome," with his hand on his heart. I stand up beside him and belt it out too. He looks over at me, his eyes smiling his love for me, and I feel so empowered. By him. By Dr. King. True enough, I soon can see that there are other white people elbow to elbow with the hecklers singing along too. I see scuffles breakout among them but the parade keeps coming, keeps singing, keeps getting bigger and bigger with more and more people pushing through the sidewalk crowds to walk behind Dr. King. When the parade reaches us, comes even with Mrs. T's old Biscayne, I swear Dr. King looks up at us, at Sebastian and nods. Just the slightest little tip of his head. I hug Sebastian and we are holding on to each other bouncing up and down on the hood of the car, holding his arms wide in case we need catching. Until the song is dim in our ears, parade long gone, Dr. King disappeared in the midst of it, and the hecklers dispersed.

That night in bed, I lie in the dark and ask myself, what just happened?

I am dying to ask Sebastian that question next time I see him. But the time and the timing aren't right. He and Jude are deep in a rehearsal, trying to get down a tricky harmony. The rest of the pack is lounging around his living room, like always, smoking, talking, complaining about parents, and school looming in a few days. I fall in with them, and it's as if nothing's happened. Grady looks at me and I return the unspoken message. Something happened, all right. When he and Jude join us, it is clear Sebastian is disengaged and Jude is pissed off at him because of it. A bad rehearsal, I say to myself, betting that Sebastian's head is still downtown under the street lights. Mine still is, I know for sure.

A yawn and a stretch later, Sebastian, his voice distant, dreamy even, opens up a Frank Session. The rules are always the same. You have to tell the absolute truth, no matter the question.

—If you could be or do anything in the world when you grow up, what would it be?

We go around the table. Tony first. He shrugs.

—I think I'm doomed to the priesthood.

—If you could be anything? Sebastian insists.

—Anything? If I could be anything? Tony is gazing into space as if rifling through a mental filing cabinet. Then he pops it on us.

—I would be an astrophysicist.

—A what? Breck asks, starting to giggle.

—An astrophysicist. So I could learn about the universe. I want to know the truth. About God. Not just the Biblical malarkey I've been force-fed my entire life.

Grady rolls his eyes.

We are all blown away by this. Somehow, it's weirdly unsettling for Tony to go all serious. And about something so big. I mean, the universe?

Sebastian clears his throat. I want to fidget but exercise supreme self-control. There's an awkward silence. None of us knows what to say to this, say to Tony. An astrophysicist? Tony?

—First Catholic to discover heaven, Grady pipes up, breaking the awkward silence.

All eyes swing to Tony.

—No, second, I chime in. Wouldn't that be St. Peter? Doesn't he guard the gates of heaven?

—The universe, you apes. The universe! Tony explodes with laughter. You guys are such Cretans. Don't you know the difference between heaven and the universe?

—One requires Sunday school, the other a telescope? Breck offers, a streamer of drool punctuating his earnestness.

We, the Cretans, pour our relief into a spontaneous food fight, until Tony becomes Fosterina and scolds us all for making a pig sty of Mrs. T's living room. Fosterina, if not Tony, settles us down and back to our Frank Session.

—Can you even name the planets? Jude goads. Before Tony can answer, Jude butts in. OK. Can we just talk reality for a sec? Like she can't wait another nanosecond to swing the Frank Session her way.

—First violin in a symphony orchestra, Jude announces. Any good symphony orchestra.

This is not news to any of us. Her guitar is her inamorato but the violin is the man she wants to marry. Ever since the seventh grade, when she first picked one up. Mary Clay and I yawn in unison. So, Sebastian takes charge and points to Grady.

—Wait. You mean no one is going to say anything?

—But everyone knows what you want to be, Jude, Breck says.

Jude winds herself into Sebastian's dead father's chair, pouting. Sebastian turns to Grady.

—You?

—Anything? If I could be anything? Gee. Easy.

Grady picks up his guitar and strums a little blues riff.

—I would be the best blues guitarist of the late 20th century with a hundred platinum albums and a handful of Grammys.

—No surprise there either, Jude says huffily. MC and I reprise our yawn, but make it louder.

—OK. Breck, what about you? Surprise us. Please.

—I am ambitionless. I'd like to grow up to be alive and well.

—Come on. In your wildest dreams.

—In my wildest dreams? Well, OK. If I could be anything, I'd play third base for the Reds and I'd knock in nine home runs—

—to win the '66 World Series, Sebastian jumps in. You'd be Tommy Helms —

—Right! Breck leaps across the room to trade fist bumps with Sebastian.

—Wrong. Jude says while idly playing with a streamer of hair. You can't be the ghost of Tommy whoever when we all know you are the ghost of Buddy Holly.

—Two ghosts do not make a man, I add.

Everyone groans.

—So, Adie? What about you? he asks, deflecting the attention from himself.

Adie

I wonder if the others think what I think—Breck never really gives us an answer. I look from one to the other of my friends but see only their expectation aimed in my direction.

I shrug and wiggle a little. I know the answer but I don't want to say, don't want them mocking me. I sigh and scan the group. *These are my friends*, I think. So, I take a deep breath and dive in.

—I want to see the world and write the Great American Novel.

—Something modest, I see, Grady says.

Their hoots of laughter cause me to fold in on myself and color fireball red.

—Well, you asked. You said, anything.

—That was a planned speech. This is Jude. Of course.

—Well, I say, timid now, I've thought a lot about what I want to do. It's like the Schlitz beer ad, You only go around once in this life, so grab for all the gusto.

—Only you, Adie, would glue together a beer ad and the Great American Novel.

Even I have to laugh at that. Jude at her best, with her nose for irony.

—Mary Clay, you're turn, Sebastian says, getting us back on track, to my great relief.

—Me? What I'd really like to do? Really? You'll laugh.

—Promise we won't, Sebastian says.

—But I *know* you will!

We submit to a respectful silence. We wait for MC.

—If I could be anything? *Anything?* If the talent and money and connections didn't stand in the way? Anything? No. I can't Sebastian.

—Go in the kitchen then. Write it down. Then pass it around. You know how we do it.

Mary Clay isn't gone three minutes. Which means to me, she's dying to tell us. And isn't. All at the same time. She hands the note to Sebastian.

—Far out, Mary Clay, he says after reading it.

—SHARE! the rest of us scream in unison.

Sebastian clears his throat, preparatory to reading, and to making it ceremonial.

—Mary Clay wants to be a fashion designer. And not just any fashion designer. She wants to be famous from Hollywood to Paris. Design for the stars.

—You? Jude says. Fashion? And bursts out laughing.

I too am struck dumb with disbelief. Can't help myself either. I run my eyes over MC's old cutoff jeans and stretched out striped T-shirt. Her glasses don't help either.

—Shut your lip, Jude. We promised.

—I never knew you were interested in fashion, I say, trying to not judge but judging all the same.

—You didn't ask. None of you did. You all judged this book by her bad haircut and awful glasses. But when I can make up my own mind about that stuff, I'll surprise the hell out of all of you.

—I think you just did, Sebastian says, lighting up. He blows a string of smoke rings into the air. Buying time, it looks like to me.

But now Mary Clay is crying.

—You said *anything*. And now you're all making fun of me.

—No, we're not, Tony shrugs. We're processing.

—I am a can of Spam! This from Breck, making no sense but trying to restore the mood.

—Yes, you are. None of you believe me. You think I'm nuts. But you said *anything* and I can dream, can't I? Can't I? Wanting to be a fashion designer isn't any stranger than Tony wanting to be an astrophysicist to look for God or Adie thinking she can be a great writer. I really hate you all.

Adie

Tears are streaming down her puckered face now.

No one moves. Mary Clay has made hypocrites of us all. I go to her. Put my arm around her.

—You don't mean that, MC, but you're right. We're all jerks. We did agree. No real dream was off the table. We're not laughing. Are we? The others, made uncomfortable now, shake their heads but do not look at her.

She shrugs me off.

—Platitudes—

—No. They're not.

—You all promised! You look at me, this ugly duckling, and can't believe I could ever possibly have a sense of style. Well, have any of you ever seen a picture of Edith Head as a teenager? Well, have you?

Sebastian moves between us. He takes MC in his arms. Her head drops to his chest while her back heaves with sobs.

—Dreams freed for the world to see for the first time can be punishing, he says.

This is so Sebastian, we all look away, ashamed of ourselves. But he goes on—

—We just needed a sec to see you as that MC Get it? I can see it now. Promise. I can see you now in a gown of your own design, dazzling us in gold lame, receiving an Oscar for best costume design. Your hair swept up in a French twist. And no glasses. The glasses are gone. We all can see it now. Right?

Mary Clay finds her t-shirt sleeve and stretches it up to mop her face and nose.

Then Jude takes up the baton.

—There's an elite school in New York, MC. Parsons School of Design. You could go there, and I'll be at Juilliard. We could get an apartment together—

—Cool, MC says guardedly. That would be cool. A smile begins to break over MC's face.

We're all okay again.

—Oh, brother, Tony laughs. Look out New York.

Why not? I think. Why shouldn't Mary Clay be a fashion designer? Just because it's the best kept secret among us, or maybe it isn't—I throw a look Sebastian's way. We can be our dreams. Why not? We may be loners but that doesn't mean we won't take the world by storm. I mean, giving myself a pep talk of one, why the hell shouldn't we?

It's coming up to dinner time, when we all need to be accounted for by our respective jailers. Breck, who has the furthest to travel, tips me off when he looks at his watch. As one, we start to gather up our things to head home. But Mary Clay stops us.

—Wait. Hold on a sec. What about you, Sebastian?

—Oh, Easy. I want to be Wolfman Jack and DJ at WERF.

—You've always wanted to do that, Tony moans.

—What's wrong with knowing your own mind? Look, there are three of us in this room who know, and have known for a long time, exactly what we want to do with our lives. That's kind of crazy wonderful, right? Believe me, I'd welcome not being me anymore. But instead a wild man. Like Wolfman Jack.

—That'll never happen. I mean, the persona part, definitely. You've already got that part down. But not WERF, Grady says. Besides, you'd have to move to Mexico.

—Maybe I will, maybe I will.

We all fall still. Only the rustle of a cigarette pack, the snap of the match, breaks the silence. Not counting how loud we all are thinking. We're kids, just kids. Does that mean we can't dream big? And mean it? Who's to stop us? But we're not kids either. We are on the

Adie

cusp of adulthood and in our newly shared ambitions, we have each put ourselves on the line. These open declarations are at once the stuff of magical thinking and an invitation to implode. Are we ready to step out? Out into the world? And be these things?

On the walk home, I can't get all that out of my head. Not just the Frank Session and the odd things it revealed about kids I thought I knew inside and out. Ambitions we don't even talk about among ourselves, for fear. Of what? Making a fool of ourselves. Put down by parents, put down by teachers. Even our friends are not above poking fun at each other's dreams, poking a big hole in a balloon stretched thin with idealism. But last night, when Martin Luther King went from two- to three-dimensional right before my eyes, something happened. We can rise up. We can overcome. And be. A physicist. A symphony violinist. A world-renowned fashion designer. A writer. Yes, a writer.

Before I turn the key in the lock of our front door and face the evening parental inquisition—where have you been, what have you been doing, and with whom?—I step back into the front yard and maybe because of Tony's wild ambition, I don't know, up I look. The sky in twilight is ribboned with variegated blues. I am strangely moved. Is this the first time I've realized that I am part of the universe and the universe is part of me? And I can't help thinking, we were born to do these things. We are the future. Maybe we will be famous. Or rich. But mostly, taken seriously. This is the beginning.

Time passes. It is the now. The Milky Way is unchanged. For as long as Earth has orbited the sun, for as long as our solar system has existed, the Milky Way has held us in the cradle of its starburst hand and made dreamers of us all. But it also reminds man of his insignificance, for how can any man, who is just a pinpoint, not even that, in this celestial realm, matter?

Clothed in darkness, the city lies dormant beneath the swath of stars that fills the night sky from south to north. On a rooftop, a boy sits and stares upward. From below, his milky white face glows in the dark like a tiny tiny moon just rising over the roofline. The blazing firmament above him makes him feel small and trivial but also large with possibility. It puts wings on the feet of his imagination and carries him heavenward.

Acknowledgments

Ambient Light was a long time coming, and a short time coming. It began its life in play form in the 1990s and was called, in that iteration, *Shadows of Love*. As theatre, it failed to evolve. Then the pandemic hit, erasing my calendar, giving me plenty of time to devote to it and the story's novel form, *Ambient Light*, erupted as a first draft like a fissure on Etna—hot and flowing and taking with it anything in its path, from my ideas to my intentions, and parking them in unanticipated places.

First, I am indebted to Motown and WLOU in Louisville, Kentucky in the 1960s. Without those songs in my ear, without the cadence of those Black DJs, *Ambient Light* would have no soul. Secondarily, I owe a similar debt of gratitude to the folksingers who, simultaneously, introduced my generation to the workings of social consciousness and political action. Those two musical genres were the backdrop of my life and so, inevitably perhaps, provide the backdrop to this novel, and in part why it ends at the beginning—when all that music was playing.

As *Ambient Light* was in development, I recruited several thoughtful readers, some I knew, some I did not. I especially thank those I did not know because that was the best way for me to receive unencumbered reactions. Rick Hoyt-McDaniels and Nick Giedris read thoughtfully and deeply and provided me with not just an overview but also more specific suggestions that helped my novel be both more accurate and more sensitive. Of course, I prevailed upon several close friends to read and comment, and we all know that when a friend says, Will you read my novel? you can be laying your friendship on the line by agreeing. So, indeed, loving thanks to Pete Funkhouser, Peter Bergquist, Toni Courtin, Nancy Guilliom, Vicki Johnson, and Rupert Macnee, who read and commented and helped *Ambient Light* grow, and our friendships survived!

I am deeply indebted to my friend and guru Vicki Johnson who, in addition to reading an early draft, welcomed the task of designing the cover. She instinctively understood what I wanted and delivered it with incomparable sensitivity and beauty. She got it. She got the book. She gets me.

This novel would never have seen the light of day without the patience and encouragement of Amanda Miller at My Word Publishing. If you are reading this and thinking of self-publishing, search no further. For me, a literary traditionalist, self-publishing sat at the back of the bus when it came to my idea of how I wanted my work to make its way to you, Dear Reader. Apparently, I have traveled too many times around the sun to attract a "real" agent or a "real" publisher. After a year and a half of diligently courting them, Excel spreadsheet as my witness, I rarely received the courtesy of any reply at all. That was just plain rude and got my back up. Enter Amanda and My Word Publishing. No second thoughts here.

Then there were those people who helped with research, who were there as kids and served me as memory springboards—Nancy Guilliom, Pete Peters, Lou Warren and Alanna Nash. A special nod, as well, to Dennis Gibbon whose input and guidance were essential.

Most of all, though, there were two men who believed in me, believed I could do it and, finally, believed, unequivocally, that I *had*

Acknowledgments

done it. My friend and playwright, Bob Barnett, whom I met on a bus going down into the heart of Rome when we were nineteen. He came out to me that night — in 1969 — setting the stage both for his continued guidance on all matters gay as they arise in *Ambient Light* and for a shared lifetime commitment to the written word, a commitment he has never for a second compromised or considered abandoning. He has my undying respect, love, and gratitude.

But there would be no *Ambient Light* had it not been for my husband, Pete Funkhouser, a writer himself. Yes, he provided me with a dandy room of my own. Yes, he knew not to interrupt me if my hands were flying over the keyboard. Yes, he cooked for me every evening. Yes, he cheered me on, and read many drafts, and kept the encouragement coming. Yes, there was all this love he showered on me. Yes.

About the Author

Kate Stout is a jane-of-all-genres. A graduate of the Columbia School of Journalism, she started, edited, and published a newspaper on Nantucket Island, The Nantucket Map & Legend. She has written for the Washington Post and The New York Times as well as magazines as varied as MS. Magazine and Bride, People and Saturday Review. By her own account she has written every composition there is to write except a PhD thesis. This includes: a children's book, *Adventures of a Nantucket Dog;* two compilations from The Map & Legend, *The Best of Blanche Lyon on Nantucket* and *The Best for Kids;* and Nantucket's Historic District's design guideline manual, *Building With Nantucket in Mind.* Her plays have been produced in New York City, Chicago, and Nantucket. *Ambient Light,* her first novel, will not be her last. One great gift of the pandemic was the erasure of her type A+ calendar, giving her time to spend in a room of her own where she produced *Ambient Light* and the forthcoming *Something Deeply Hidden.* For more information, please visit her website: kate-stout.com

Made in the USA
Middletown, DE
12 January 2024